BROOKLYN BRIDGE

ം‍ര

By

Lynne McLean

To Rebecca, Best Wishes, Lynne McLean.

Published in 2010 by New Generation Publishing

Copyright © Lynne McLean

First Edition

The author asserts the moral right under the Copyright, Designs and Patents Act 1988 to be identified as the author of this work.

All Rights reserved. No part of this publication may be reproduced, stored in a retrieval system or transmitted, in any form or by any means without the prior consent of the author, nor be otherwise circulated in any form of binding or cover other than that which it is published and without a similar condition being imposed on the subsequent purchaser.

This book is dedicated to the memory of my parents, Vera and Walter McLean, whose devotion to each other was living testimony that true love can survive the test of time, including separation by war. They were married for over forty years. They are now together for eternity.

Cover designed by Bradley Wind

ACKNOWLEDGEMENTS

I would like to thank my dear Auntie Hilda for her encouragement and Jacky Bradbury for giving me the confidence to "do it." They gave me the nudge I needed to carry on with the story.

Thanks to all my good friends for their encouragement and support, particularly Irene Wilson, my prime reader and critic; the first person to shed a tear over Brooklyn Bridge and the second, after me, to love my characters.

I also want to thank all the wonderful people on the Authonomy web site for their great reviews, and especially Bev Dulson, who has given me so much feed-back and who delighted me with her reaction to the book.

Last, but by no means least, a special thank you to my dear friend, Claudene Murray of Wisconsin, USA, for co-editing Brooklyn Bridge. Without her, this book would never have been completed. She picked me up when I was down and about to give up, and her unwavering belief in me has been an inspiration. Thank you "Ems".

BROOKLYN BRIDGE

CONTENTS

7	PROLOGUE : 1978
9	PART I : THE EARLY YEARS : 1988
85	PART II : LONELINESS : 1998
165	NEW BEGINNINGS : 2003
305	PART IV : LOVE UNLIMITED : 2006
431	EPILOGUE : 2008

✖ *PROLOGUE 1978* ✖

The tall black man walked up the steps of the Boys' State Orphanage, clutching the hand of the little boy by his side. They crossed the great hall together and the child was told to sit on a wooden bench. Sitting next to him was a small white boy looking equally terrified and uncomfortable. The man disappeared into an office for a brief time and then reappeared, his handsome face a picture of sorrow.

"I'm real sorry 'bout this son, but now your Momma's died, I just can't keep you with me. I'll come back for you when I can."

Then he was gone.

A harsh-looking, unsmiling woman came out of the office and addressed the black child in a surprisingly kindly tone of voice.

"Stand up, Maples. Your father has informed me that your mother died. I'm very sorry to hear that, but the sooner you accept the fact that this is your home now, the sooner you will settle into your new life."

"Simmonds," she said, turning to the white boy. "This is Robert Maples. You are to show him to the dormitory. Help him unpack and settle in."

Simmonds turned to the frightened child and held out his hand. "Jeff," he said with a grin. "My name's Jeff and I'm gonna call you Bob. I think we're gonna be friends."

PART ONE

☙❧

1988 - 1997

THE EARLY YEARS

Chapter one

Carolyn Davidson looked out of the window of the plane, seeing only the white, fluffy clouds floating in the azure sky below. In the far distance another plane, travelling in the opposite direction, appeared so still it could have been glued to the horizon, like a cut-out on a child's picture. The condensation on the bottom of the window reminded her of frost on a winter morning and she shivered, despite the warmth of the cabin. She turned to smile up at her brother; her wonderful, strong big-brother. Only ten years older than her, at twenty four, he had the demeanour and self-confidence of a more mature man.

"I'm so flippin' excited. This is like a wonderful adventure, isn't it? I've only ever dreamed of going to America and now it's really happening. Nothing can stop us now, can it? I somehow never thought I would live anywhere else but Birkenhead."

John shook his head and smiled back at her. "No Caro, this is it. We're on our way at last. After everything that's happened, I can hardly believe it myself."

She let her small hand rest in his and looked at him with adoration. What I can't believe is that this time last week I was as miserable as sin, thinking I was going to live in foster homes for the rest of my life." A shadow fell over her face as she said "When Mum and Dad died and I was put into care, I never thought I'd be happy again but I knew you'd find a way somehow."

He squeezed her hand affectionately, biting his bottom lip and smiling to himself.

"What are you thinking?" Carolyn asked, watching his face express his emotions.

"I was thinking how lucky it was that this temporary exchange in Brooklyn should come up, just when I needed it. The gang at the bank couldn't understand why I was so eager. I nearly hugged Mr. Masters when he said I'd been chosen. I wonder how the American chap will cope with my job."

Now a new life beckoned. She glanced again at John. What a lovely brother he was. Tall and lean with thick, silky fair hair; Carolyn had always thought she would have liked to have hair like John's, instead of her own dark brown curls. Although chestnut highlights made her look far from ordinary, she thought her brother's hair was wasted on a boy. She smiled as a lock fell over his eyes as he bent forward. He brushed it back in a gesture she recognised so well. They both shared their mother's green eyes and had the same charming smile, but there the similarity ended. John was gentle and kind; an intelligent, quiet, serious young man; whereas Carolyn, in happier times had always been joking and laughing. Her brother had lots of friends because his personality always drew people to him. Their

Dad used to say John was a born leader and would have made a good army officer, but all he had ever been interested in was music. He had been in the process of taking a post graduate course in music at Liverpool University until circumstances had forced him to leave to take up employment in a bank. He had progressed well in his time there, passing exams with flying colours and working hard to complete his training.

Whilst Carolyn was thinking of John, he was worrying about the problems they were bound to face in America.

"At least we have somewhere to stay when we arrive. The bank has sorted all that out. We need to find somewhere more permanent though. I have to make sure you're safe and occupied, whilst I'm at work. I'm responsible for you now." He smiled sadly. "I can remember the day you were born. I can't believe you'll be fifteen next month. Mum placed you in my arms and I was so proud to be the big brother. We've always had a special relationship, haven't we, love. I promise I won't let you down now."

"You could never do that. Don't be such a dickhead," Carolyn giggled.

"Carolyn!" John spluttered. "Where on earth did a well brought up grammar school girl like you learn words like that? It certainly wasn't at home."

"You'd be surprised what I picked up in care. Don't worry, I'll behave myself. I'll try not to cause you too much trouble. I'm going to look after you. I'm a big girl now," she laughed.

"Yes, and a very pretty big girl too. I really am going to have to watch you. We'll cope, sis, as long as we stay together."

Carolyn slipped her arm through his. "We will, chuck. Not long now and then we can start our new life. I know I'll be fine so long as I have you."

When they arrived at JFK Airport they were a couple of hours going through Immigration, as there was a long queue for non-U.S. citizens. They were interviewed and answered all the necessary questions. The job John had lined up for him made this very straight-forward, but they were tired when they at last walked out of the Airport.

John spotted a line of cabs in front of the terminal and soon they were sitting in a taxi driving across New York City.

The hotel was quite comfortable and their first night in New York passed uneventfully, but Carolyn found it hard to sleep. The noise of the traffic in the street outside and the voices of people, talking in the corridors with their unfamiliar accents, made it difficult to relax.

She wrapped a blanket around her shoulders and looked out of the window at the dark, menacing buildings of the city. *I wonder what the future has in store for us. Things are going to be so different to what we've been used to,* she thought. *Nothing can be as bad, though, as the past year. I suppose life will be what we make it.*

It's like writing a new page. We'll make our own future.

The next day they went to a real estate office and asked for a list of affordable properties for rent. After discussions, appointments were made for them at some of the likely houses in Brooklyn. Thanks to John's planning they were not short of money for the moment. The money from the sale of their family home and the life insurance which they had received following their parents' death was more than enough to give them a good start. They took the subway to the Brooklyn Bridge – City Hall stop and then walked across the bridge. Carolyn was awed by the steel suspension bridge with its double-arched towers and outstanding views.

They strolled over the promenade from where there was a wonderful view of Lower Manhattan and the harbour. They walked for approximately forty minutes before waving down a cab and asking the driver to take them to the properties on the list. After seeing several which they thought totally unsuitable, they found just the one they wanted in Cobble Hill, Brooklyn. It was a nineteenth-century townhouse in a quiet residential area of leafy streets. There were six steps leading up to the front door from the street, with wrought iron banisters either side. The bricks were red and there was a coach lamp fixed to the wall next to the door, the brass around the light, polished and shining. As soon as they walked through the door, and saw the sunlight streaming through the windows in the living room, they both nodded at each other.

"This will do us, John," Carolyn sighed. "I really think we could make this home."

With three bedrooms, it was a little larger than they had intended, but the price was affordable. John looked around the other rooms and decided the House needed some decoration, but they could do the work themselves. The first floor held the hall, a large lounge, the dining room/kitchen and cloakroom. The three bedrooms and a bathroom were located on the second floor.

Once the lease had been signed, the two could not wait to move in and decorate. John only had a couple of weeks before he started his new job so they wasted no time buying paint and brushes and finding furniture and equipment for their new home. Two comfortable sofas were purchased, carpets laid and curtains hung, making the House look cosy and inviting. They both decided on which bedrooms to have, buying a double bed for each room and brightly coloured bedding. For the third or "guest room", as Carolyn called it, they bought two single beds.

John enquired at the bank and found an independent high school for young women close by. He made an appointment for them to visit the school, where Carolyn was asked questions about her previous education in England. He wanted the very best he could afford for Carolyn and felt that she would fit into this type of school. The fees weren't too high, and he explained to the Headmistress that his parents had left them well provided for so the money was no problem. As well as schooling in general subjects, she would be able to take a business course in shorthand and typing. The school also offered extra-curricular activities which Carolyn could get involved with, such as dancing and a library club. It was agreed that provided Carolyn passed the entrance exam she would be accepted as a pupil.

Carolyn sat the examination a few days later and the Principal phoned them to say she would be pleased to have Carolyn start at the beginning of the new term, which was in mid August.

John started his job at the bank, and they soon established a day to day routine. Carolyn knew, however, that he was always conscious, of the dangers in this big city. He fretted a great deal about her walking to and from school on her own.

"Promise me you will always be careful and not talk to strangers. You are so chatty and friendly, I can imagine you talking to anyone, but you mustn't. This isn't Birkenhead, Caro. Please do as I ask and say you understand."

Carolyn nodded and wisely didn't try to argue. "I promise. If anyone tries to talk to me, I'll run all the rest of the way."

She settled in very quickly, making new friends and becoming popular with the teaching staff. Always very keen to learn, she particularly enjoyed the business studies course, which gave her access to the computers in the Information Technology classroom. She joined the library club so that she could borrow books to take home and read at her leisure.

The first six months passed happily for the pair. John enjoyed his work at the bank, and told Carolyn that he too had made new friends. Carolyn coped well with life at school and became an efficient housekeeper. She enjoyed keeping their house clean, always managing to put tasty and nutritious meals on the new kitchen table, where they loved to sit in the evening telling each other the day's news.

Chapter two

One Saturday evening in late December they decided to go for a walk across Brooklyn Bridge at sunset to enjoy the view. Strolling along arm in arm, humming a Michael Jackson song from the album 'Bad', which she had bought for John's twenty fifth birthday in November, Carolyn was never sure how it happened but suddenly a group of five teenagers were in front of them blocking their path.

One of them, seemingly the ringleader, spoke with a grin. "Well now, what have we here? I think we've hit the jackpot. Have you got any money?" The grin faded from his face and he mouthed, "Search them."

Two thugs attacked John. One shoved him to the ground, face first, then he sat astride him, holding him down. The other reached into John's back pocket for his wallet. Another man held Carolyn, forcing her hands behind her back. She yelped in surprise, as the fourth ruffian started to paw her.

"Leave her alone," shouted John, his voice muffled by the dusty pavement.

"What are you going to do about it?" challenged the man holding him down as the other one kicked him.

Carolyn struggled to free her hands as her assailant began to lift her skirt, his hand travelling up her thigh; all the time sniggering and enjoying her terror. She shivered with fear and could feel the bile rising in her throat

"You dirty bastard. Get your filthy hands off me, you gobshite," she yelled.

The dark, greasy haired man gripping her laughed. "You like a fight, do you? Good! That will make it more fun."

"Let me go, you flaming scumbag," Carolyn bellowed, kicking the man's shin. "Help, won't someone help us? Oh, please HELP," she screamed.

Then, as if in answer, two other young men joined in the melee. To Carolyn's relief, they were beating off the attackers. She only had time to take in that they were both tall and that one was black. The two villains who had been molesting her let her go when confronted by the two newcomers, so she was able to go down on her knees to check on John, who appeared to be badly injured.

"Oh, John! John, luv; what have those lowlifes done to you?" she hollered.

She jumped to her feet and began kicking and scratching one of the thugs. "What have you done to my brother, you arse'oles?" she hissed. "I'll punch your lights out."

By now the attackers had taken enough punishment from the two newcomers and the wild banshee that was Carolyn and fled across the bridge.

The white boy spoke first. "You've sure got quite a mouth on you, girl. What, in the name of God, are you two doin' walkin' out here on your own at this time of day? You were askin' for trouble lady and you sure got it."

"I don't know how to thank you; but please help my brother," she cried, the tears streaming down her face. "He's unconscious. They've really hurt him."

The black youth went down on his knees and examined John as best he could. "It's his head. He gotta lotta blood comin' out. Best get him to a hospital quick."

Without a thought for her own safety, Carolyn ran out in front of a car trying to wave it down. She did this to several before a taxi stopped to help. "Please! Can you contact the police and ambulance? My brother's been badly hurt," she shouted hysterically.

Eventually, the emergency services arrived and asked a lot of questions before piling John into an ambulance. The two youths were extremely edgy by now; anxious to leave the scene. Carolyn was having none of this and clearly there were questions the police wanted answered.

"I don't even know your names," she said. "My two white knights in shining armour. Well," she muttered, "I should say my white knight and my black knight. I don't know what I would have done if these two hadn't turned up," she told the glowering police officer.

The two boys gave their names as Jeff Simmonds and Bob Maples and gave an address several blocks from the bridge.

"May I ask where you two were going walking across the bridge? Up to no good, I don't doubt," the officer growled.

Jeff, the white boy, gave a wide infectious grin. "Just admirin' the view, Officer. We often come to do that, don't we bro?" Bob nodded.

"Please, can you let us go? I must be with my brother." Carolyn cried. "Will you come with me so we can thank you properly?"

Both the boys were reluctant to go, but the police officers insisted that they take them all in a squad car.

Once at the hospital, Carolyn was relieved to find John had come round. However, he was very confused and fuzzy. After examination, the doctor reported that he had a few broken ribs and some unpleasant bruising where he had been kicked. Due to a severe scalp laceration he needed to be hospitalised overnight.

Relieved that it was nothing more serious, Carolyn for the first time took a good look at their rescuers. Jeff was tall with dark brown hair and hazel eyes. He looked a strong and handsome young man with a wide smiling mouth. He seemed to grin a lot and joke about almost everything he said. Carolyn could detect, however, that the smile did not always reach his eyes.

Her heart missed a beat as she took in Bob's appearance. He was tall with skin the colour of caramel. Her Dad might have said "two of coffee one of cream." His nose was straight above sensuous and delightfully shaped lips. Long black lashes fringed smouldering, dark brown eyes. Carolyn thought he was the most beautiful man she had ever seen.

As they were about to leave the hospital, the doctor came back to talk to Carolyn.

"I need to make sure, young lady, that you have someone at home to look after you. Your brother has been very concerned about you."

"Oh yes, ta. My neighbour said I can stay at her house to-night. I'll be fine," replied Carolyn, while turning aside and muttering under her breath, "Nosy old sod."

"Is that true, girl? Do you have someone to stay with?" Bob asked, raising his well-shaped eyebrows.

"No, but I can look after myself. I'm certainly not going into flippin' care again, even for one night," was the firm reply.

Chatting between themselves, the boys decided they couldn't leave this young girl to find her own way home, so they said they would take her back there before they went about their business. They were amazed when they walked into the Cobble Hill house. Although merely homely and comfortable in Carolyn's eyes, to Jeff and Bob this was pure luxury. They had never seen the like before and at first felt uncomfortable and ill at ease.

Carolyn had generally led a protected life, being looked after first by her parents and carers and then by John. She always had strong intuition where people were concerned. For this reason she had immediately taken to the two boys, having no fear of them and instinctively trusting them. Her first thought now was that she didn't want to be alone. She was frightened and still shaking from her ordeal on the Bridge.

"Do you have to rush off anywhere?" she asked tentatively. "Because, if you don't, I could do us some supper and I would be so grateful if you could hang around until my brother comes out of hospital."

"What makes you think you can trust us, girl?" Bob asked.

"I have no-one else to turn to and I'm frightened," she said honestly. "I just feel I can trust you. You are my two knights and I need you to stay with me. I don't want to be on my own."

"Okay, Honey. If that's what you want, we can stay a while." Jeff said, raising his eyebrows at Bob, who nodded without speaking, whilst taking in the details of Carolyn's appearance. Her hair was a lovely blend of gold, amber, honey, and tawny brown, springing in wild curls around her face. Her large, emerald green eyes flashed as she spoke, whilst her wide smile lit up the room. He completely fell under the spell of this young and very trusting girl.

Carolyn made up the single beds in the spare room. She found them pyjamas, T-shirts, and jeans belonging to John that she hoped would fit them. She showed them where the bathroom was and where John kept his razor. She even managed to find two new toothbrushes. As tactfully as she could, she suggested that they both take baths as they "didn't smell very fresh," then she went downstairs to make some sandwiches.

A little later on going back upstairs to check if they needed anything else, she found Bob in her room holding a diamond ring which had belonged to her mother. Screaming like a fishwife, she lunged at him kicking him on the ankle.

"Flipping eck! You flaming scally. I trusted you and now you want to rob me. I'm going to use your guts for garters. Give me that ring back now. That was my Mum's ring. It's very precious to me."

Bob hopped around on one foot and Jeff ran in to see what the fuss was all about. Trying to speak through the pain of his burning ankle, Bob shouted "I wasn't gonna rob you, I was just lookin' around and I saw this ring on the dresser. I just wanted to look at it. It's pretty. I ain't seen nothing like it before."

"Listen, Honey." Jeff grinned. "Let's just get one thing straight. We may be poor and we may have gone hungry often. We may have even stole from time to time, but never have we stole from anyone we know. You better take my word that neither me, nor my brother, would steal from you."

"Okay, if you say so." Carolyn shrugged.

"You believe me? You don't think Bob was stealing the ring?" Jeff asked, his face a picture of astonishment.

"I do believe you, yes. Why should you be so surprised?

The two boys exchanged looks and Bob raised his eyebrows and shook his head. "He's surprised because no-one has ever trusted or believed in us before. Up 'till now the only folk we could ever rely on were each other."

"I have to trust you, because you saved me and you are all I have right now. But please don't go into mine or John's rooms unless I say, and make sure you tidy up after yourselves."

They perceived her as a fiery little soul and realised she was not as soft as they had originally thought. They sat round the kitchen table; the supper being eaten in comparative silence. Carolyn was exhausted and eventually said she must go to bed.

"You will still be here to-morrow, won't you? I'll sleep easier knowing you are here. You see, I've never been on my own overnight and I'm a bit scared."

"Give up the chance of a comfy bed for the night? Not us, Honey," Jeff laughed. "We're gonna still be here tomorrow and we'll come to the hospital with you to bring your brother home. Then we'll be off."

The next morning, Carolyn contacted the bank and her school to explain the situation. The three then went to the hospital, where John was now sitting up, out of his mind with worry about Carolyn. She filled him in on the story of how 'her two knights' had come to their rescue, got him to hospital and then looked after her. He was very grateful and felt obligated to them. As soon as John was discharged, they all went back to the House where Jeff and Bob prepared to leave.

"Have you got somewhere to go lads?" John asked.

Jeff and Bob looked at each other and Bob was the first to speak. "We always find somewhere to put our heads down. Don't you worry 'bout us".

John frowned. "You mean you've been sleeping rough?" He glanced at Carolyn who had tears in her eyes, then said, "Listen lads, our Dad had a saying that if someone saved your life, you became responsible for them. Will you stay here with us until we are all on our feet? You'll have to find some work mind. We won't be able to support you if you can't pay your way."

Bob shrugged. "You mean you want us to stay? Really?"

"Yes, we do," Carolyn replied. "We can all help each other. It'll be brilliant. You will stay won't you?" So it was decided.

That evening they sat around the kitchen table, and after supper John and Carolyn quizzed the boys about their past.

Jeff was the first to start talking. "We two have been together since we were eight years old. You have to know that we consider ourselves brothers. We are blood brothers in fact, ain't we Bob?" He laughed, bringing Bob into the conversation. "We cut our thumbs and mixed our blood when we was ten years old."

The boys related how they had met at the orphanage in the Bronx. "That place was real miserable," Bob said, speaking with his eyes staring straight ahead as if he were seeing it all again. "We had to share with eight other boys. We were woken at seven every morning and had to wash all together in one big bathroom. Then we had to make our beds and go to the dining room for breakfast. Jeff and me were always hungry, weren't we?" He glanced at Jeff who nodded and continued the story.

"We had more lessons until lunchtime and then again until we had sandwiches and milk later. We had some free time to follow our own hobbies, like singin', before we went to bed. There was no love in that place. No affection, and no warmth. We had each other though."

John's ears pricked up when Jeff mentioned that they liked to sing. "You enjoy music then, do you? What sort of things do you like?" he asked.

"Motown, Michael Jackson. All the early soul music." Bob told him. "We used to pick up records from the second hand shops and the market. We'd learn the words when we sang along." We enjoy harmonising. The other kids used to like us singin'. Sometimes we sang in the chapel."

"Anyhow," said Jeff "they told us we'd have to leave when we was eighteen. Told us we'd have to make our own way in the world, so we decided not to wait and we hoofed it when we was seventeen. I guess we didn't do so well."

By the time they finished their story, soft-hearted Carolyn was in floods of tears. "You mean you've never had a proper home; never been part of a family? We've been so lucky. Our Mum and Dad loved us very much and we've always had each other. There's us brought up with all that love and you two have never known any. I think that's so sad. I know what it's like to be with strangers because, after our Mum and Dad died, I was in foster homes for a year and hated it so much. I never told you, John, because I knew how angry you'd be, but at that last place I stayed the man tried it on with me. He came into my bedroom and started touching me."

John nearly jumped out of his seat. "Dear God, Caro, why did you never say anything?"

"I dealt with him myself" she said. "I kneed him in the goolies and he never bothered me again."

All three boys collapsed laughing at this slip of a girl. She certainly wasn't the shrinking violet they had originally thought. Bob started to feel something in his heart that he had never felt before. He wasn't sure what it was – admiration, respect – he didn't know. He just knew he wanted to protect this girl from anything like that ever happening again to her. It was in fact, the first fluttering of a love which would stay in his heart forever. From that day he idolised Carolyn.

Later, when Carolyn had gone upstairs to bed, and just the three men were seated round the table, John folded his hands in front of him and leant back in his chair. "I'm glad you're staying, but let's face it we still don't really know each other, do we? I need you both to promise me you will always treat Carolyn with respect. She is the most important thing in the world to me. After our parents were killed in an accident, I vowed that I would always look after her. We were lucky, compared to you two. We had a loving home and parents who cared about us. Being taken into care was the most dreadful thing that could have happened to her. If it takes me the rest of my life I will make it up to her. There are a lot of bad people in this town and it's worried me that I can't always be there for her. Between the three of us, I think we can keep her safe. I'll expect you to look out for her in my absence and to treat her as you would your own sister; always with respect. But understand this; any funny business and you are out. Now, do I have your word?"

For the first time they both saw that the mild mannered, gentle Englishman had a steely side to him. This became more and more obvious over the next few weeks as they realised that although physically he was not as powerful as them, he was so much stronger emotionally and mentally. They both gave their word. Something they never went back on. Their protection and care of Carolyn became the core of their existence, and the affection they received back from her more than made up for any embarrassment either of them may have felt walking her to and from school or the Shops.

Around this time Carolyn started calling Bob 'Robbie'. "It suits you so much better," she said. "My black knight will always be Robbie to me." She was the only one who ever called him that.

Chapter three

John heard of a job at the Bank, doing odd jobs and maintenance, which Jeff was successful in applying for. Under John's eagle eye he managed to carry out his duties without too much going wrong and, in fact, became very popular among the other staff with his sense of humour and handsome looks.

Bob, therefore, walked Carolyn to school, then home, most days. They spent hours talking and listening to each other's stories and problems. He told her of the racial taunts he had often faced and she said, "Remember Robbie, words can't hurt you. Our Dad always said 'Sticks and stones may break my bones but words will never hurt me.' Next time anyone is mean to you just try to count to ten. People like that are just ignorant and let's face it, they're not really important are they? I think only people you care about can hurt you with words. Tell you what, Robbie, there's a song in Walt Disney's Pinocchio. I can't remember it all, but the gist is that Jiminy Cricket tells Pinocchio when he needs him he should give a little whistle, like this:" She started singing the words, pursing her lips to whistle in between,

Give a little whistle!
Give a little whistle!

"So if you are ever in need of me just give a little whistle. If I can hear you, I'll come running to bash anyone who's mean to you."

The two of them laughed and he had visions of being in a situation, such as he had been in many times, when someone called him a black bastard or nigger, and he whistled. He could imagine how well that would go down.

He couldn't speak for a while for laughing. "Oh, you are a wonderful girl. You can always make me laugh."

They linked arms the rest of the way home, singing the whistling song all the way.

A job was eventually found for Bob at The Pink Parrot Club, waiting on tables in the restaurant. It wasn't long before the Manager heard him singing at his work and asked him to sing on occasions for the customers. With more money coming into the House, Carolyn was able to plan meals for them and pay all the bills without worry.

On evenings when they were all at home, Bob and Jeff would often start singing in harmony as they washed the dishes or carried out other tasks which Carolyn delegated. On one of these evenings they were amazed when John joined in with them. He had a wonderful tenor voice which blended in marvellously with their deeper tones. Carolyn was shell-shocked when she heard the three of them together. It was lovely.

John taught them some of the old songs from their childhood that Jack Davidson had sung, such as "Danny Boy" and "Sweet Sixteen".

Bob and Jeff found themselves looking more and more to John for advice. Although only seven years older than them and without the worldly experience they both had, he was wise beyond his years and they were glad of his guidance. He led them without appearing to push or hassle and they found, without realising it, that they were imitating his way of speaking and behaving. They copied his table manners and even his way of walking. John had become their mentor as well as their friend.

One Saturday, Carolyn made a beef casserole ready for supper. Jeff was in the kitchen, so she shouted to him to please put the dish in the oven. An hour later, when she could not detect any delicious aroma emanating from the kitchen, she went to check and found the oven cold.

"Jeff, chuck, didn't you think to turn the oven on before you put the hotpot in?" she shouted.

"No, don't tell me he put it in cold!" John laughed.

"Don't laugh at him, he was only trying to help," she giggled.

They laughed about this story for years to come, and ever after Carolyn always remembered to say "Could you please turn the oven on and put the stew in."

Between them, Bob and Jeff taught Carolyn a few self-defence moves they had picked up over the years. "The knee in the goolies, as you so memorably called them, was a good move, Honey." Jeff said. "But let's look at one or two other useful moves. For instance, if someone grabbed you like this, with their hands round your throat from behind, what would you do?"

"Stamp on their foot?" She ventured.

"Well yes," Jeff laughed. "I daresay that might have some effect, but if you grab their pinkie fingers and bend them back like this, they will have to let go."

"Like this you mean?" Carolyn said as she proceeded to demonstrate on Jeff. "Wow, it really works," she laughed as Jeff shrieked and put his injured hands under his armpits. "I'm sorry," she hooted. "I'm so sorry."

◈

Birthdays had always been important in the Davidson household and Carolyn was shocked to find that neither Bob, nor Jeff, knew the exact dates of their birth.

"We must find out," she said one day. "I'll come with you to the orphanage and see what paperwork they have for you. They must have something on file."

Neither of the boys thought the staff at the home would be very impressed by a sixteen year old girl demanding to see their papers, so it was decided that all four of them would make the trip. John, despite his youth, had an air of authority about him and they felt he would be the best one to do the talking. Jeff felt the hairs on the back of his arms stand on end as they walked into the hated building. Not one to show his feelings, this was not an easy day for him and he held onto Carolyn's hand as they were shown into the office.

Bob was very quiet, remembering the day his father had deserted him. "I don't think I can do this, Honey," he muttered in her ear.

"Yes you can, Robbie; you can do anything you set your mind to. Just stand tall and proud. Let John do all the talking."

John duly explained to the matron the reason for their visit. This lady was very different from the harridan who had made their life so miserable. She smiled at them with understanding, and said she would do anything she could to help them. The matron asked her secretary to bring up from the filing room the boxes from the year they had both been admitted to the Home. First of all she produced a file on Jeff. It contained a birth certificate and details of the various foster homes he had been in since he was three years old, until at eight he had been taken to the orphanage. The certificate told Jeff that his father was listed as "Unknown" and Simmonds had been his mother's name. A handwritten note clipped to the file said that Pauline Simmonds had died in 1975.

"No-body's child, I'm no-body's child..." he started singing under his breath.

Carolyn threw her arms round his waist and said, "You'll always have a family while you have us, Jeff."

"Okay, Mom, thanks." Jeff mumbled.

Next, Bob's file, which also contained a birth certificate, was produced. It named Eve and Benjamin Maples as his parents. His father's occupation was shown as "Mariner." A note on the file said that following the sudden death of Eve Maples, due to an aneurism, in 1978, his father had been unable to cope with the child and had asked the State to take him in temporarily.

There was a last known address listed, but no other information. Bob remembered the tall man who had been his father and felt that nothing new had been learned here.

However he wasn't prepared for Carolyn saying, "Have you thought, Robbie, your father may still be alive?"

"So what if he is?" Bob sighed. "It's obvious he didn't want me. I'm better off without him. Even if he couldn't cope with a young boy, he could still have kept in touch or come back to see me." There was no argument to this and it was a subdued quartet who thanked the Matron for her patience and left the orphanage for the last time.

Walking home Carolyn said "At least we can celebrate your birthdays now," as she tried to lighten the atmosphere. "What a coincidence that your birthdays are so close together in August. Only three weeks between you. Any closer and you could have been twins. Well, not twins exactly, 'cos you're different colours, but you think of each other as brothers anyway…and I'm rambling, aren't I?" She smiled at the three boys' faces, which were by now creased with suppressed laughter.

"How do you do it Carolyn?" John asked. "You can turn any situation around. You are a one off, you are."

Jeff grinned from ear to ear to hear this very English expression. "Oh, you are so right, Dude. There couldn't be two of them. I guess they broke the mould when they made Carolyn."

She giggled and shrugged her shoulders, "Well, John, whilst we're on the subject of birthdays, do you realise you are twenty six next week and we haven't got any plans to celebrate? We really need to do something. What would you like to do?"

John smiled."More than anything else, I would like a nice family meal for the four of us with a few drinks."

He didn't realise what an affect the term "family meal" had on the other two boys. The iceberg in Jeff's stomach melted as if by magic and the immense sadness, which Bob had felt since leaving the orphanage, lifted from his shoulders. Never before could either of them remember being part of a family, and they so much wanted to belong. In less than a year, the affection they felt for this young English couple had grown to the point that they both felt happier than they had ever done before.

Carolyn baked and iced a birthday cake, on which she piped John's name. She spent hours preparing a special roast dinner and laying the kitchen table; decorating it with candles and flowers. Lizzie Davidson, her mother, had been a good cook and had insisted that Carolyn learned from a very early age how to bake and cook.
There was nothing that gave her greater pleasure than watching her family enjoy the fruits of her labours.

Bob had managed to coax a couple of nice bottles of wine from the bar manager at the Pink Parrot. Carolyn had saved a few dollars from the

Housekeeping money with which, when added to the money Jeff and Bob had put together, they were able to buy a silver fountain pen. Just the thing for an up-and-coming young bank manager.

That evening they sat around the table, chatting happily; comfortable and relaxed in each other's company.

"I've got some good news folks," John told them. "The bank has asked me to stay on at the end of the two years exchange plan. We needn't worry any more about being sent home. We can stay as long as we want to, and there should be no problem getting the necessary paperwork for you, Caro, to start work when you finish school next year. I had thought we might have to dig in and live here illegally, but that's not necessary now."

"Do you know what?" Carolyn asked.

"What?" the three boys chorused.

"*The lark's on the wing; the snail's on the thorn;*

God's in his heaven, all's right with the world," she sang.

❧

The visit to the orphanage preyed on Carolyn's mind over the next few weeks. She couldn't forget the look on Robbie's face when the matron had told him how he had been left in the care of the State. It had confirmed in his mind, the knowledge that he had just been abandoned and unloved. After thinking the matter over and over, she approached him one afternoon when they were sitting together in the kitchen.

"Robbie, can I talk to you about something and ask you not to get cross with me?" She said quietly, biting her bottom lip.

Bob was puzzled. Carolyn wasn't usually so reticent about saying what she thought."Of course you can, sweetheart. It looks like it's somethin' serious, lookin' at that stern little face."

Although she had rehearsed what she was going to say, it all came out in a rush of breath. "Robbie you just have to find out what happened to your Dad. We have to go to that address on your birth certificate and find out if he still lives there. In your heart you must want to know."

Bob shook his head angrily."Carolyn, what for? If he had wanted me, he would've come back to find me. I don't need him. I have a new family now. What's past is past. Forget it, girl!"

Carolyn took both of his hands in hers and looked into his eyes. "Dearest Robbie, you know I'd never do anything to hurt you, but I really think this is something you should do. You'll always feel bitter and unsure until you know the truth." She held her breath as she saw the expression on his face change from anger to resignation.

"You're not gonna let this rest, are you girl," he said, tilting his head to one side and smiling at her. Ok then, we'll go, but if he doesn't want to see me that's it. I'm not gonna push it. Like I said, I don't need him. This'll just be a fishing expedition."

They eventually found the address shown on Bob's birth certificate. The lady who lived there had no recollection of Benjamin and Eve Maples, but sent them down the street to see an old lady who had lived there for many years.

The old black woman at first was suspicious of the two of them, especially the young white girl with the funny accent. However, when Bob explained who he was, she asked them into her parlour. She did indeed remember his parents. She was sad to tell him that she had heard that his father had died in some far off place. She didn't know where. She said his mother had been a lovely woman and that Ben had just gone to pieces when she died. She remembered Bob being born and how happy the couple had been.

"At least you know now why your Dad didn't come back for you. He didn't just desert you, Darling Robbie." Tears were streaming down Carolyn's face.

"I should think not," the old lady confirmed. "I'm sure he would've come back for you when he had sorted himself out. Now you're here you can take the box with you."

"What box?" Bob queried.

"The box your Daddy left with me when he gave up the House," she muttered going down on her knees in front of a cupboard to root in the back of it. "Ah, here it is," she said.

She handed Bob a cardboard shoe box which he hurriedly opened. In it was a silver locket, a pair of baby's booties and some other papers, which he put on one side to look at later. At the bottom of the box was a photograph. It showed a young couple with a toddler. The woman was black and very beautiful, but the man was much lighter skinned and his features were so much like Bob's that Carolyn gasped.

"That's your Momma and Daddy, boy;" the old lady unnecessarily explained; "and that's you. That pair loved each other very much, and they were so proud of you. Reckon they'd be even more proud if they could see you now."

They thanked the woman and walked home, hand in hand, in comparative silence.

When they got home, Carolyn for once was lost for words. She scurried round the kitchen making a sandwich for each of them. She pulled two packets of crisps out of the cupboard and put them on the table with a jug of orange juice and the sandwiches. "Come on Robbie. Let's have something to eat, then you can take the box to your room if you want to and go through it on your own."

Bob smiled at her "You don't have to be like that, Caro. I'd rather you went through it with me. You know, this hasn't made me sad. If anything, I'm just happy to know I did come from a loving home once. To know that my Daddy didn't desert me is just so wonderful. But hey, how many folk get a second chance? You and John have given us the home and family we never thought we'd have. I promise you, I have never been so happy."

Carolyn could hardly speak for relief. She had thought this morning may have been a mistake and had worried it would depress Bob. "Oh

Robbie, I'm so glad," she sighed "Come and give us a hug."

They sat at the table eating their sandwiches and Bob was amused to see Carolyn open up hers and start layering crisps inside. "Carolyn what are you doin' with those potato chips?" he laughed.

"You mean you've never had a crisp buttie? Tell you what, you've never lived, lad." She showed him what to do and the pair of them enjoyed their lunch amongst giggles and laughter.

Later they sat down together and examined the contents of the shoe box. The photograph was indeed a find. To actually know what his parents had looked like was marvellous. There were letters in the box which his father had written whilst away at sea. Bob felt almost guilty, as if he was prying, as he read the letters. However, it was obvious that there had indeed been a lot of love between his parents and there were many comments referring to "our baby boy". He knew he would treasure these always and put them back reverently into the box.

The silver locket, when opened, revealed further photos of his parents. "Caro, I'd really like you to have this locket. If it hadn't been for you, I'd never have found these things; never known about my parents. I would've always thought I had just been abandoned," Bob said, holding out the locket to Carolyn.

Carolyn pushed it back into his hand. "No Robbie, you must keep it. Your Mum must have worn it and you must keep it always."

He held the booties in his hands. "Hard to imagine my feet fittin' into these," he laughed.

When John and Jeff came home from work, they were amazed at the news the other two were able to tell them. "Wow, Bro, it must feel good to know your background; somethin' I'll never know," Jeff said.

Bob reiterated what he had said to Carolyn. "Sure, I'm pleased to have all this, 'specially the photo, but I'm pretty happy with my present family too."

John was touched by these words, and even more so when Jeff said, "It's true John. Bob and I may have saved you and Mom, but it's you who turned our lives round that day on Brooklyn Bridge. If it hadn't been for you two, we could well have ended up in the gutter, or prison, or worse."

༺༻

Chapter four

Their first Christmas set the seal for all those to follow. Together, the four did Christmas shopping, decorated the House with trimmings and set up a huge tree in the living room, which was then covered in glass balls and tinsel.

"To think this is how normal people live," Jeff sighed.

This was the first time ever, in his memory, that he and Bob had been part of a family Christmas. The preparations alone were exciting and the boys threw themselves into the wonder of it all, following Carolyn's instructions to the letter.

On Christmas morning there were bacon "butties" all round, while a stuffed turkey cooked slowly in the oven. They all sat round the living room opening their gifts with childlike awe. All the presents under the tree had been carefully wrapped. Perfume for Carolyn from John; a lovely green silk scarf from Jeff, "to match your eyes", and a copy of "Little Women" from Bob.

"You told me it was your favourite book, so I thought you'd like a copy," he said shyly.

"Oh, you are lovely; all of you. Thank you so much." Carolyn was delighted by the thought which had gone into her gifts.

Carolyn gave warm scarves and gloves to each of the boys. As an extra present for Bob she had found a frame for his family photograph. Jeff and Bob clubbed together to buy John a camera.

John was looking quite pleased with himself. They knew he had something up his sleeve, but couldn't work out what it was.

"I've bought a present for all of us" he smiled. A guy at the bank was selling off his piano. I said I'd have it and its being delivered the day after Boxing Day. We'll be able to write our own songs. It's something we always wanted to do."

They sat down to a table groaning with food. John carved the turkey and they all helped themselves to vegetables, roast potatoes, little sausages wrapped in bacon and delicious gravy and bread sauce. They even had sparkling wine.

"This is like the Christmases we used to have at home, isn't it John?" Carolyn sighed." I wonder what Mum and Dad would think if they could see us now."

John smiled at his sister. "I think they would be very pleased to know that we've stayed together and that we're not alone."

"Tell you what Bro," Jeff laughed. "This certainly isn't like any Christmas we've ever had before. A toast to us." They all raised their glasses.

Crackers were pulled and the boys were persuaded to put on the paper hats. John took photographs with his new camera which showed them happy and laughing. It was a wonderful day that bound the four of them even closer together.

"Who would have ever thought that I would end up loving you two scallies so much," Carolyn warmly remarked.

"Honey, I've always meant to ask you, what in God's name is a scally?" Jeff questioned.

"Rapscallion!" John roared. "It's a Merseyside term for rapscallion, or rascal. It's short for scallywag. She's calling you a couple of rascals."

"Well, I've been called a lot worse," Bob laughed.

The new piano, when it arrived, was treated with reverence and awe. The moment it was put into place in the living room and the removal men had gone, John sat down and played a chord, then lazily began to extemporize. Carolyn leaned on the piano beside him, for a moment letting her thoughts drift back with the music to England, to the time when they were young and the brother and sister used to sit around with their Mum and Dad singing along to John playing at the piano.

Bob squeezed in beside her. "Move over," he said grinning. Spreading out his arms in a theatrical fashion he sang in a deep baritone, *"You're my Beautiful Girl, my shining star,*
My heart is yours forever, forever, forever."

"What's that song?" said Jeff. "Sounds great."

"No idea," Bob shrugged, "I just made it up.

John changed key, and went into a slow jazzy mode. "Come on, give me something to go with this." As John's fingers rippled over the keys, Bob closed his eyes and began to sing, improvising as he went along.

Carolyn was spellbound.

Jeff and Bob were astounded when John showed them how he could actually play by ear and write down music. Bob had a wonderful way of coming up with lyrics, whilst the tunes to match the words seemed to come naturally to Jeff and John who put them down on paper.

❧

The New Year came and went. It was 1990. A new year and a new decade. Carolyn would graduate from school at the end of the summer term. Bob was working shifts now at the Club. The manager was pleased with him and said that next year, when he was twenty one, he would let him work in the bar. He still entertained the customers from time to time. Jeff worked the odd evening washing dishes at the club, which meant that they were now all gainfully employed. One of the boys tried to meet Carolyn at the subway and walk her the few blocks home most nights, but now they were all working, it wasn't always possible.

She was sixteen now and very pretty. As a rule she acted older than her years; after all, she had been running a home and looking after 'her family' since she was fifteen. However, to ease her load, they all tried to help with the Household chores.

One evening in March, Bob went to meet her at the sub-way. It had been snowing heavily for most of the afternoon. When Carolyn emerged from the subway and saw the slushy and treacherous pavements, she nearly wept.

"Oh Robbie, I've got my best shoes on. My feet are going to get soaked."

"There's only one thing for it then, Honey, up you get." He turned round and bent down. She leapt on his back, laughing hysterically, throwing her arms around his neck. The piggy-back lasted all the way home to the amusement of most passers-by. There were the usual snide comments from one or two unhappy people, but these were ignored by the two friends.

"Sticks and stones, Robbie, sticks and stones" Carolyn whispered in his ear.

When they arrived home, it was to find both the other boys already making a hot meal with the table set and ready. They were very amused by the tale and this episode was another happy memory which they talked about for many years.

❧❧

Another year passed and soon Jeff and Bob's twenty-first birthdays were looming. Carolyn had been eighteen the previous month and had been wined and dined by the three men at a restaurant. However, after much discussion, it was decided to have a joint party for Jeff and Bob at the House, and each of them and Carolyn and John were to ask friends from work. Carolyn put up streamers and balloons round the walls and spent all week baking sausage rolls, vol-au-vents and quiches. There were sandwiches, cakes and chicken legs and a huge birthday cake with both their names on it. Nothing was too good for her boys. It was a mixed bunch of guests that night. Some of John's colleagues from the bank, who already knew Jeff, were surprised to meet John's black "brother" and his lovely sister. Carolyn had started work in the summer at an office in the city and her new friends from work were bowled over to meet the three handsome men she lived with.

That night was, perhaps, a turning point in the four's relationship. For the first time Carolyn felt the stirring of jealousy in her heart as *her* boys danced and flirted with the girls. As Bob danced around the floor, snuggling up to a particularly pretty black girl from her office, Carolyn had to resist the urge to cut in and dance with him herself. *What am I thinking? I can't be their keeper. Of course they must have girlfriends, but I don't have to like it,* she thought, gritting her teeth.

To take her mind off what was happening, she went over to one of John's colleagues from the bank, Mark, and asked him to dance. When a slow track came on she tried to relax and let him hold her closely as they moved around the floor. She didn't see the looks that passed between Bob and Jeff. Bob, particularly, watched as Mark started to kiss her cheek and then move his lips around to her mouth. She was astounded when she found herself wrenched away from Mark.

"If I see you pawing her like that again, I'll break your fucking neck." Bob yelled in his face.

By now Jeff was standing behind him, waiting to back him up if there was any trouble.

"If I'd known how the land lay, I wouldn't have gotten involved," Mark sheepishly laughed. "Sorry man, I didn't know she belonged to you."

"No!" Bob denied. "She's like my sister. I'm just looking out for her."

"Yes, sure," Mark sniggered as he walked away.

"How could you do that?" Carolyn cried "I've never been so embarrassed in my life. I'm eighteen years old. I had one father and I don't need another thank you very much. Don't ever do anything like that again."

Clearly upset, Bob apologised quickly. "Caro, I didn't stop to think. It was just instinct; just trying to protect you. I'm so sorry."

Secretly, Carolyn hugged herself with pleasure. She hadn't exactly set out to make him jealous, but his reaction couldn't have been more heart-warming.

The party seemed to fizzle out after this incident and people started to drift.

"All that trouble you went to and I had to go and spoil it. I'm sorry, baby." Bob was very subdued.

"Well," Carolyn replied, "it was your party, yours and Jeff's." She patted his arm and shook her head. "I just wanted you to have an evening to remember, but it was a good night, even if it did finish early."

Two nights later, the three boys decided to have a night out together for a proper celebration.

Carolyn declined to accompany them as she said it would cramp their style. They looked so smart when they went out, she almost burst into tears.

"Now, just go and enjoy yourselves, but look after each other," she warned them.

They certainly let their hair down and toasted the birthdays in style, firstly at The Pink Parrot Club, where they were now legally allowed to drink, and then at one or two other clubs.

By 2.00 a.m., when they were still not home, Carolyn had not slept a wink. When she peered out of the window after a knock on the front door, to see a police squad car, her heart somersaulted with fear. She opened the door to find two burly police officers holding the boys up by the collars of their jackets. All three were obviously very drunk.

"Do these three belong to you, lady?" One officer ventured.

"Yes, I'm afraid so," Carolyn said angrily. "Would you bring them in, please. You can just drop them where you like. What on earth have they been up to?"

The policemen were quite amused and fortunately good-natured. "Staggering around, obviously lost, singing "Sweet Caroline." Not bad voices actually. Bit late though to be waking up the neighbourhood. Managed to get out of them that they're celebrating two twenty-first birthdays, and at least they told me where they live. I assume you are sweet Caroline?"

"Carolyn actually," she replied. "Are you going to take any further action or will you leave it to me to sort them out?"

The officer laughed. "I think you will do far more good than us sorting out this lot. No, we won't be taking any further action. Happy Birthday, you guys. Don't give this little lady any more trouble."

The Officers left, and Carolyn tried to wake up the boys who by now were all in various positions on the floor. John was snoring on his back, with a stupid grin on his face. Bob was curled in the foetal position with one hand under his cheek. Jeff, however, was sitting up hiccupping and giggling.

"Gosh, we had a great time, Mom. I wish you'd been there."

"Bloody Hell, I'm glad I wasn't, I might have had to walk away and leave you." Carolyn said angrily.

"You don't mean that, Mom." Jeff muttered and then proceeded to be sick.

"Oh, for God's sake, Jeff! Wait while I get something," Carolyn shouted as she ran to get a bowl and disinfectant. She covered them all with blankets and shoved cushions under their heads, but was so afraid of one of them choking in the night that she stayed downstairs all night in the armchair.

The next day the atmosphere was very cool with the boys almost grovelling in an attempt to atone for their actions. They were all suffering from dreadful hangovers, but got very little sympathy from Carolyn, who kept reminding them that their illness was self-inflicted.

"Oh, never again, Carolyn," John said quietly, whilst holding a damp flannel to his aching head.

"I'll believe you, thousands wouldn't!" She replied.

☙❧☙❧

Chapter five

The next few years passed happily and generally carefree for the friends. The relationship between the four flourished, until Carolyn's two "scallies" could hardly remember when they were not part of this family. They both accepted John as their third "brother". The three of them were inseparable. They adored Carolyn, being very protective and affectionate with her. She was a very tactile girl, always greeting them with a hug. She never treated them any differently from the way she behaved with John. Whilst Jeff's feelings were totally platonic, Bob's were anything but. He had long been in love with Carolyn, but felt he would never be able to tell her of his feelings. He took very seriously the vow he had made to John when they had first been asked to stay. How differently things might have turned out if he had known that his feelings were reciprocated.

Carolyn wasn't sure when she first realised she was in love with Robbie. He was her best friend and confidant; like another brother. The feeling crept up on her so slowly that she was unaware of it, until one day she found herself staring at him and sensations which she couldn't fathom coursed through her body. He was putting up a bookshelf in her bedroom and as his strong, muscled arms held the shelf in place she felt a shiver run down her spine. He had filled out a lot in the years they had all been together, and now, instead of being merely a young, beautiful adolescent, he was an extremely virile and handsome man with a toned and sturdy body. Her eyes paused as they looked from his broad shoulders and then down to his slender waist and hips.

He turned round to smile at her, and her eyes quickly rose to the tempting hollows at his throat. "Does that look straight to you, baby?" he queried. His lovely smile lit up his face and his mouth curled up at the corners showing his even, white teeth. As he spoke, he bit his bottom lip with his head on one side and his eyebrows raised. Carolyn had the sudden desire to kiss that lip. Oh, how she wanted to kiss that lip. She just nodded, looking into his eyes; his beautiful dark brown eyes, and she was lost.

She inwardly shook herself and cleared her throat. "That's just right, thank you."

When he left the room she sat on the bed and took a deep breath. She wondered if she should have said something. However, she felt that a wrong word or move could ruin forever the loving friendship that had developed between them. They were close friends and time spent together was always happy. They confided in each other; sharing their dreams and aspirations. The moment passed and Carolyn followed him down to the kitchen. Still feeling quite emotional, she started to reminisce.

Carolyn told him of the knock on the door the day their parents had died. "Mum and Dad had gone to a party. John and I were watching 'The Sweeney' on television. Two of Dad's police colleagues came to tell us." If she closed her eyes she could still visualise the scene; still feel the horror of what they were saying.

"John, Carolyn, there's no easy way of telling you this," one of the policemen said. "There's been an accident on the M53. There were three vehicles involved. The road conditions were poor. The rain had made the road surface slippery and the front car braked suddenly. The two following cars just piled into it. I'm so sorry, but your Mum and Dad were in the middle car."

Carolyn's head was spinning as she clung to John's arm. She looked up at him, seeing his face drained of colour. She didn't want to hear any more, but she knew before the policeman spoke again that the news was bad. "I'm so sorry," he said again. "They didn't stand a chance. Your Mum died at the scene and Jack died on the way to hospital."

John caught Carolyn as she fell to the floor on her knees, and sobbed as though her heart would break. He knelt beside her, rocking her in his arms, whilst the tears poured down his own face.

Carolyn looked up at Bob. "So you see, Robbie that's how we came to be here in America. John gave up everything for me. I was taken into care and I hated every minute of it. John promised me he would sort things out. He left University and took a job until he could look after me. Then the chance of this exchange with the New York branch came and he grasped it with both hands. I'll never be able to repay him for what he has done for me. Not many men his age would give up their career chance to look after their kid sister."

The tears were still flowing down her face as Bob took her in his arms and held her closely. He closed his eyes and stroked her hair, breathing in the sweet smell of her. She leant back reluctantly and looked into his eyes. "I'm okay, Robbie. Thank you for being so caring. I'd better heat that sauce for the pasta or none of us will be having any supper to-night." Still sniffling, she turned to the cooker and started to heat the sauce she'd prepared earlier.

"Oh, this isn't bad at all. Have a taste," she suggested as she offered the wooden spoon to his lips to try. As some of the sauce dribbled off the spoon, she reached up to catch it on his lips with her thumb before it reached his chin. Unconsciously, she popped the thumb in her mouth and turned back to her cooking, leaving Bob to quickly sit down and say a silent prayer to the table gods for hiding the beginning of his erection.

※

The three men continued writing songs and music. They performed together at the Pink Parrot Club, where Bob was now Bar Manager. Carolyn loved to hear them singing together. Their voices harmonised so well that they could sing anything from gospel to pop, and even incorporated some of the older songs which John had taught them.

They made a tape of one of the songs they had written with John playing the piano and Bob taking the lead vocals. The song was called *Beautiful Girl* and Carolyn thought it was wonderful. The lyrics, which Bob had written, were simple, but when put together with John's haunting melody and the three voices harmonising, the result was stunning.

You'll never know how much you mean to me.
Though, that I love you is plain to see.
You are my reason for living, and all that I do
If only you could love me too.
You may never know just how I feel,
But my love for you is strong and real.
Just one smile can make my day.
Why can't I find the words to say...?
Chorus
You're my Beautiful Girl, my shining star,
My heart is yours forever, forever, forever.
My heart is yours forever.

Don't every worry or have any fear,
You're always safe when I am near.
I'll guard you and keep you away from harm
My darling you're my lucky charm.
Your dear, sweet face is a guiding light,
Even in dreams in the silence of night.
Maybe one day I'll tell you, but as things are,
I'll watch and love you from afar.
Chorus
You're my Beautiful Girl, my shining star,
My heart is yours forever, forever, forever.
My heart is yours forever.

"Oh wouldn't it be wonderful if we could be famous one day?" Jeff sighed. "No more mending locks and washing dishes. We could do what we enjoy most; just sing."

Bob and John agreed that it would indeed be a wonderful thing to be able to concentrate on their love of music.

Without saying anything to anyone, Carolyn sent copies of the tape to several record companies. She didn't hear anything for some weeks and then one day there was an official looking envelope on the doormat. The letter was from a record producer for Neptune Records, named Patrick Donnelly. He said he liked the recording and wanted to meet with the group to discuss where to go from here.

Carolyn was so excited she could hardly breathe by the time all three of the men came home. She took a deep breath and the words came out in a rush.

"Now I know you will be cross with me, but please don't be, because this could really be great and you'll be glad really and ....Oh God, I'm rambling again."

Jeff roared with laughter and spluttered, "For heaven sake, Honey! What have you done now? Come on, spit it out."

She had the attention of all of them now, as she continued excitedly. "Okay, I sent copies of your tape to some record companies. I've had a letter from a producer and he likes you and wants to meet with you."

There was silence for several seconds and then whoops and laughter from the three men. Bob picked Carolyn up and swung her round in his arms laughing.

"Honey, you may just have made our fortune, you lovely girl."

John picked up the letter to read it through several times. "He wants us to give ourselves a name and then call to make an appointment if we want to proceed," he whispered; his voice hoarse with emotion.

"If we want to proceed?" Jeff shouted, his face wreathed in smiles. "As if there was any question. You both want to, don't you?"

It didn't take much deciding. This was a once in a lifetime opportunity. All agreed that John should ring the producer and make an appointment, but first they had to come up with a name. This deliberation did not take as long as expected.

"Well, we're 'Honey's Boys' aren't we?" Jeff smiled.

Carolyn laughed. "Oh Jeff, that's lovely, but it's a bit long-winded. You could be 'The Honeys' though."

They tossed the idea around for a short while and couldn't think of a name they liked better. From that day their professional name was "The Honeys."

No time was lost in telephoning the producer to make arrangements for a meeting. Carolyn insisted that they all dress smartly, but casually.

She took them shopping to buy polo-necked sweaters with new jackets and trousers.

"You'll be able to wear the jackets and pants again; then we can vary the sweaters with shirts," she said excitedly. For John, they chose a powder blue sweater; for Jeff a mint green, and for Bob brilliant white.

On the day of the appointment, she paraded them up and down to make sure they met up to her expectations."Oh my God, you look gorgeous," she giggled. "Robbie, you should always wear white. It looks so good next to your skin." Seeing how handsome he looked, her heart beat so rapidly in her chest that she could hardly breathe.

The offices of Neptune Records were on Washington Street in Brooklyn, so it didn't take long for the excited party to find their way to the impressive building. After asking directions from the doorman, they were soon taking the elevator up to the tenth floor. Patrick Donnelly's secretary met them at the door, ushering them into a plush waiting area. Immediately, Carolyn could feel her hackles rising as the woman postured and flirted with the three men.

Another busty, blond young woman hovered in the office, making Carolyn even more uneasy, as she chatted comfortably with them; fingering her long hair and staring up at Bob with adoring eyes.

"If she drools over them any longer, the spittle will be running down her chin," Carolyn thought to herself. Aloud she said "I believe Mr. Donnelly is expecting us."

The first woman introduced herself as Susan Newton, saying "Susan" with an affected lisp that really grated on Carolyn's nerves. The Siren, as Carolyn had started to call her, was apparently called Bethany and was still gazing at Bob with eyes like organ stops.

"Mr. Donnelly played us your demo tape and we all thought it was awesome. You sounded so wonderful. We can't wait to see what else you can do," Bethany said in a breathless voice. None of them could fail to see the innuendo behind this last remark.

Fortunately, just as Carolyn was about to launch herself at "the Siren", Patrick Donnelly emerged from his office. "Welcome, welcome, young men," he said, holding out a hand to shake each of theirs in turn. "I'd like you to show me what you're made of, and then we can have a chat."

He led them to a recording studio in his suite of offices, where he asked to hear them singing live. He was very impressed by their tape and hoped it wasn't a one off. This was milk and honey to the boys. They had been singing together for so long that it came naturally to them. John sat down at the piano and started playing *Amazing Grace*. The three voices rang out in beautiful harmony as they belted out the words of the lovely song. There was silence for a moment when they finished. Carolyn held her breath, then let it out in a rush, when Mr.

Connelly and his two secretaries, together with other studio workers, clapped and hollered their appreciation.

After they had sung another couple of songs, including *Beautiful Girl*, Patrick sat back in his chair and waved the three men over to him. "Well, you guys, I think you have something very special. There's a contract here for you if you want it. I think we can work together and I think you are going to make me a lot of money. What do you say?"

It didn't take much consideration. Papers were drawn up, whilst Patrick made a phone call to a friend of his who was a manager with a stable of young acts. He also suggested a lawyer who dealt with show-business contracts. Max Hunter, the manager, arrived whilst they were on their third cup of coffee. The two secretaries couldn't stay away and kept appearing with yet another tray of refreshments. By the end of the afternoon, The Honeys had a manager and an appointment with the lawyer to peruse all the paperwork before it was signed. Arrangements were being made for them to cut a recording of *Beautiful Girl* and to make a video to promote it.

As they left the offices, John raised the question of what had happened to Jeff. Minutes later, he came running out to meet them, grinning all over his face.

"Where did you guys run off to? Those girls were waiting to talk to us, but you'd disappeared," he panted.

John raised his eyebrows. "Crikey Moses, Jeff. It doesn't take you long, does it?"

"Long enough to make a date with Bethany. I'm meeting her for a drink after she finishes. She's gonna cook me some supper. Know what I mean?" He nudged Bob and winked. "If you had waited, one of you could have met up with Susan. What a classy chick she is. I was spoilt for choice."

The other three couldn't help laughing at the expression on his face. He looked like a little boy caught in a chocolate factory. Carolyn, however, felt a shiver of apprehension down her spine. *Was this how things were going to be now?*

ೊ

A disc of *Beautiful Girl* was cut and a date arranged to film the video. This would show the three of them standing on a breezy cliff top, singing.

When the chosen day arrived, they were driven to the destination in black Suburbans.

The area was full of cameramen with their bulky equipment, and Max Hunter was waiting for them on the set. There were three large trailers with other numerous vehicles scattered around. A wind machine had been set up and people were scurrying around, setting the scene ready for filming.

The men were ushered to one of the trailers, which they were told they could use as a dressing room and a place to relax. No sooner had they sat down than a pretty young woman, dressed in tight jeans and a clingy T-shirt, poked her head round the door and asked them to go to another trailer for make-up. This caused some hilarity between them.

"Make-up!" Jeff hollered. "I'm not wearing any fuckin' make-up."

Sophie, the make-up artist, laughed good-naturedly along with them before remonstrating with Jeff. "I promise to be gentle, so you don't have to worry. No-one will be able to tell you're wearing any. The camera can be very cruel, and I just need to know that your noses aren't too shiny. I'm sure there's no way we can make you look any more handsome than you already are."

Carolyn felt like a spare part as she tagged along after the boys into the make-up trailer. She watched as a team of nubile young women got to work on the three of them. They spent far too much time, she thought, touching, cosseting and paying them effusive compliments. The men seemed to be enjoying it all. She seethed as even Bob started laughing and joking with one girl. She could see that the three men were flattered by all the female attention, making wisecracks and obviously flirting with their admirers.

When she could stand it no longer, she made an excuse and left the trailer. Finding a sheltered spot, she sat down to watch the proceedings. She felt that no-one saw her leave, but Bob did watch her go and made a mental note to talk to her later about why she hadn't stayed with them. However, the excitement of the occasion was such that all other thoughts vanished from his mind once they were out of the trailer and the filming began.

The three men were positioned standing on the cliffs, looking out across the Atlantic Ocean. The wind-machine was turned on, gently blowing John and Jeff's hair. The collars of their jackets flapped in the breeze. *Beautiful Girl* was played over a loud speaker and they were asked to mime to the words. The harmony rang out with the lyrics touching everyone's heart, particularly Carolyn's. The three singers looked so tall and handsome. With their looks and their sound, they couldn't fail.

How desperately sad, Carolyn thought. *They look as if they are trying to see across the miles; searching for the beautiful girl. I wonder if they ever find her."* She bit her lip and stifled a sob. *Why am I being like this?* she wondered. *I have to shake myself and be glad for them. This is their dream come true, but oh please, God, don't let things change too much*, she prayed.

The record was given air play and suddenly people were buying it. Lots of people.

The Honeys were invited to appear on a daytime TV chat show, where they would perform their song. This sealed their success. Their honesty and humility came over at the interview. Without doubt, they were likeable as well as handsome and talented.

Jeff explained their down to earth attitude, saying: "My Mom always said we should leave our egos on the doorstep."

Carolyn smiled. It had only been last night when she came up with that one, but it sounded good.

After the interview, some of the audience were allowed up on the stage to meet the group. Carolyn gritted her teeth as she watched some of the girls posturing themselves in front of the men, asking for autographs and touching their arms trying to attract each one's attention. They were becoming more confident now; answering questions and talking as if they had always been celebrities.

Gosh, they're loving all this, Carolyn thought sadly. *I'm so pleased for them, but I wish I felt more comfortable about it all.*

When they arrived home, Carolyn began laying the table for four, but John stopped her. "Caro, we're going out for dinner to-night. We made arrangements with three of the girls off the set to take them out. You are included of course."

"Oh!" Carolyn mumbled. "No. You all go and enjoy yourselves. I wouldn't dream of being a gooseberry. I'll be fine. There's a film I want to see on TV anyway."

A few hours later, hearing the key in the latch, Carolyn was surprised that they were so early.

Jeff was the one who put her in the picture. "Light-weights, that's what they are. Those girls were ours for the taking, and what does Saint Bob say? "We'll phone you sometime, girls." Phone you. I ask you. And John, what were you thinking of? Rhea was gorgeous and all over you like a rash. Didn't you like her?"

John laughed sheepishly. "Yes, she was a nice enough girl, but much too forward for my liking. I just didn't fancy her."

"Ah well!" Jeff shrugged. "I guess there's gonna be plenty more where they came from."

༄༅༄༅

Chapter six

Carolyn rushed in through the open doorway, her happy excitement made obvious to Bob, Jeff and John by the exuberant look on her face. "Beautiful Girl's just hit number one on the British Charts and it's climbed fourteen notches this week on the American Top Forty," she gushed. "I just heard the DJ tell the whole world he thinks it will go through the roof in America too."

The three men and Carolyn resigned from their jobs and the boys immersed themselves into their new careers. They were to make an album of their own songs and a tour was arranged for them. They were famous. The public couldn't get enough of them. Carolyn, of course, travelled with them, and everywhere they went there were girls; beautiful girls.

The first stage of the tour was in Los Angeles. They travelled first by plane and then by limousine whilst the band and roadies went ahead by coach. Still new to all this luxury, they were in awe of their surroundings when they booked into their hotel that night. They had been given two suites, each with two bedrooms. They spent the evening together in one of the suites, all dressed in the hotel's white fluffy bathrobes, sipping champagne and giggling with happiness.

"This is the life. I was meant to live like this," John said as he threw himself backwards onto one of the beds.

The next morning they went to the theatre to do a sound check and rehearse for the evening's performance. They were introduced to the other acts on the bill. The theatre was enormous; the auditorium surrounding the stage on three sides. They were a little subdued at first and Carolyn realised this was down to nerves. This was bigger than they had ever imagined.

That evening the atmosphere was electric and there was a hush until the M.C. announced, "And now ladies and gentlemen, here's who you have been waiting for...The Honeys."

The three ran out, took up the microphones and began to sing. It had been decided to start with an upbeat number that had the audience clapping and singing along. They followed with a few older songs, including *Danny Boy*, sung in harmony; some of their own numbers that had become popular from their album and finally *Beautiful Girl*. The audience went wild, standing and clapping so much that they had to do an encore. The boys ran off the stage, bowing and waving to their fans.

Carolyn was waiting for them with tears in her eyes. "Oh I'm so proud of you. You were wonderful."

The group were mobbed as they left the theatre: mainly by girls who wanted to touch them, talk to them or just see them close to. Autographs were written and photographs handed out. Carolyn watched and smiled, but she knew life would never be the same again.

An after show party had been arranged back at the hotel, where the acts mingled with invited guests. Carolyn tried to be a part of the celebration. She didn't want to be a killjoy, but she had a sense of foreboding and a headache that just wouldn't lift so she excused herself and went to bed.

She didn't realise until the next morning that John hadn't come back to their suite, but deduced later that the three had held their own party with three girls in the other suite until the early hours. She had expected that something like this would happen, and understood that young men would not be able to resist what was being offered to them. However, her heart was sick with jealously when she thought of Robbie with someone else.

After breakfast the tour party took their leave and set off for their next appearance. This, then, became their way of life for the next two months. Carolyn learned to keep quiet and not to criticise the men where women were concerned. How could she? They had to make their own mistakes and she didn't have the right to say anything, did she?

One incident, however, stayed in her mind, when Bob took her on one side at their hotel in Philadelphia. "Caro, I need to talk to you. Just in case you hear this from anyone else, there's been a lotta drug use going on at these gigs. I just wanted you to know that none of us have been involved or tried anything stronger than a spliff."

Carolyn was horrified but nevertheless pleased that he had told her the situation. "Oh Robbie, promise me you will never try drugs, even cannabis. I couldn't rest if I thought you were getting involved in that sort of thing. Please promise me."

"I promise you, sweetheart," he said, hugging her. "If I am ever tempted, I will just think of your face when you're angry. That would be enough to put anyone off."

She hugged him back and said, "Oh you! You mustn't even joke about it. So many people we meet seem to be high on something. I know the temptations are out there, especially when you have the money to pay for things, but that's something I couldn't cope with."

Jeff poked his head round the door and said, "This sounds a serious conversation. What's goin' on?"

Carolyn turned round to face him and took both his hands in hers. "Jeff, I've just made Robbie promise something and I'm going to ask you to do the same thing."

"Anything, love. Just name it," Jeff replied.

Carolyn put on her most serious face and looked him in the eyes. "Jeff, promise me you will never be tempted to try drugs of ANY sort. Please promise me. That's all I ask."

"Okay, Honey. That's not too hard. Drugs are for mugs. Oh, sounds like a cue for a song."

"Never mind the jokes, Jeff." She couldn't help smiling. "Please just promise me."

"I promise," he replied.

"Do you think John has ever thought about it?" she worried.

"No." They assured her. John had been most vocal in his derision of those snorting cocaine and using heroin. There was no way John was ever going to be tempted.

The tour was very successful and sealed their popularity with the public. They were the flavour of the month and could do no wrong. There were good times and bad times for Carolyn. It wasn't that they didn't include her or were less affectionate towards her. Quite the contrary, they always made a fuss of her, being still as caring and affectionate as ever, but they were so independent now, and still the women came and went. That was the hardest part. The three men had their pick of the most beautiful girls around. Everyone seemed to want to be seen on the arm of one of the Honeys.

Carolyn had spent ages choosing a dress for an award ceremony they were to attend. The dress was emerald green and strapless. The bodice was fitted and the skirt long and sleek with a split up the side. She was twenty three years old now and felt very grown up. She had her shoulder length hair taken up off her neck into a chignon and wore a simple jade pendant which the boys had bought her for her twenty first birthday.

The effect was stunning. When she walked into the room and turned around, John took a deep breath. "Sis, I've never seen you look so beautiful. You make me feel so proud."

Jeff, too, was bowled over by this elegant Carolyn and laughed. "Wow, look at you, I can't believe this is my Mom. You look a million dollars, doesn't she, Bob?"

Bob smiled and nodded. Yes, she does," was all he said, before he turned and walked out of the room.

Carolyn didn't realise that his heart was too full of love to speak. He was completely knocked out by her appearance, but couldn't find the words. The moment for her was ruined and she just went through the motions for the rest of the evening. The situation was made even worse, when, after the ceremony, she saw her Robbie leaving with a gorgeous young girl. At the door he turned to smile and wave at her.

She started to realise, that if she was to have any happiness in her life, she had to stop mooning after what she couldn't have and try to make the most of the situation. *Okay*, she thought. *What's sauce for the geese is sauce for the gander.*

At the next show-business party they attended, she fortified herself with a few drinks before making a beeline for the dance floor. It wasn't long before she was asked to dance and for the rest of the evening she never sat down.

She had been dancing with one nice-looking man for some time and so was in his arms for the slow records at the end of the evening. His name was Howard something. She hadn't caught his surname, but he was quite tall and not bad looking. When he suggested they go on to a club and get to know each other better, she didn't object. She sent a message to John to tell him she was alright, but not to wait up for her, and then left with Howard.

It was nearly five o'clock in the morning when Carolyn eventually arrived back home, only to find all three men pacing the floor with worry.

"Where on earth have you been all night, Carolyn?" John fumed.

"For goodness sake," she replied. "I'm twenty three years old. You have to let me live my own life. You all enjoy yourselves and expect me to sit like a vestal virgin with my mug of cocoa whilst you tomcat around. Well, things are going to change now."

Bob was incandescent with rage. "You stupid girl! Don't you know what could have happened to you? It's different for us, we're men."

"Oh, yes," she sneered, "and you know your own tricks best, don't you? Yes, I know what could have happened to me. What makes you think it didn't?"

There was silence in the room as she stomped off to bed. They might not have been so hard on her if they had known she had spent the best part of the night fighting off Howard and had travelled home alone in a cab.

∞

The family decided that their Cobble Hill home was no longer suitable for them and they should move to a more fashionable district in Manhattan. With the help of an exclusive real estate agent they were able to move into their new apartment shortly after Carolyn's twenty fourth birthday. All were sad to leave the old house that held so many happy memories.

Carolyn cried as they drove away for the last time. Looking over her shoulder she sighed, "I wonder if any of us will ever be as happy as we were in that house."

"Of course we will, love," Bob said, holding her hand. "We just have to start making new memories."

Another tour followed, with more parties and more deception, as Carolyn gave the impression she was having a wonderful time playing the field. In truth, although she had many admirers, she never met anyone she wanted to be with. She laughed at their jokes, flirting and dancing so no-one would have guessed that it was all an act. Many nights she came home late to the hotel, insinuating that she had been with a man. The truth was that she always made an excuse to go home on her own.

She sat through films in late-night movie theatres, often watching the programme through twice, before calling a cab. She thought she would come to feel better about things, but she didn't. She felt so depressed and miserable all the time that it started to show.

John, Bob and Jeff were all concerned about her, wondering what the problem could be. They agreed that perhaps they had been neglecting her and resolved to spend more time and effort ensuring that she knew she was part of their success. She was so dear to all of them. They were upset to think that her despondency might be due to them.

Bob, particularly, was kicking himself. His love for Carolyn was so overwhelming that he had felt it necessary to take a step back from her in order to maintain a semblance of normality when he was close to her. There were times, when they were talking, that he felt an urge just to take her in his arms and tell her how he felt. In the back of his mind, however, was the vow he had made to John all those years ago. They were still very close, but he shuddered when he thought of the hurt look in her eyes when he chose the company of other women rather than spend time with her. This though, had been his safety net. He was twenty seven years old with all the needs of a man. The feelings in him which were aroused by Carolyn had to be assuaged in some way.

One day Jeff sought her out, saying, "Honey, come and talk to me. Tell me, darlin', what's troubling you? I can't bear to see you like this."

With tears streaming down her face she replied, "Oh, Jeff, I know I'm being really selfish, but I just want to go home. I want our old life back. I so miss what we had."

"We'll be going home soon, darlin'." Jeff assured her sympathetically.

"We can't go home. Home's not there anymore. I feel as if I don't belong anywhere now." Carolyn wept.

"Oh sweetheart, you belong with us wherever we are. You always will. Why are you being like this?" He couldn't understand why his beloved

"Mom" was so unhappy. They had everything they had ever dreamed of; no money worries and a way of life they could never have envisaged. He was to go over and over this conversation during the next few months wondering if he could have said or done anything differently.

Things came to a head for Carolyn on one of the last nights of the tour. She had been with the men at a party in the hotel, but had left early, going back to her room where she had read and watched television for a while. Starved of company, when she heard movement from the next room she thought she would join them for a nightcap. She knocked on the door and after a while Jeff opened it. Over his shoulder she could see a couple of scantily dressed girls, one of whom was lying on a bed in Bob's arms. He sat up quickly when the door opened and looked straight at her before he lowered his eyes in embarrassment.

"You can't come in, Baby," Jeff said sheepishly. "Go to bed, love, and we'll see you in the morning."

Carolyn stepped back into her room as if she was sleepwalking. She knew beyond doubt now that her love for Robbie was so deep it was all consuming. "How much can anyone take?" she muttered to herself. At least, before fame had taken him away from her, they had spent time together, talked, and enjoyed each other's company.

Now it was just too heartbreaking to be around him. She had always felt that there was a certain chemistry between them, binding them together. *How could I have been so wrong?* she thought, as she paced up and down like a caged wild animal. *I know we've never spoken of anything like that, but he's always been so caring and loving with me. I just thought that one day...*

She began to cry then and once she started she could not stop. All the pent up emotions of the past few years surfaced. By the following morning, having not slept a wink, Carolyn had decided on a course of action. She had to go way and make a new life for herself. But first, she would have to find out what his real feelings for her were. *Well, chuck, I guess its make or break time,* she thought.

❧

They returned to their new apartment at the end of the week. All three of the men commented on the fact that Carolyn was very pale, quiet and listless. There was none of the usual backchat and laughter. They would have been more concerned had they known how she filled the next few days. As if in a daze she carefully packed a couple of cases. She sorted out timetables and booked a flight for London on the following Friday morning. So that she could not be followed easily, she booked the flight from Chicago and intended to take a domestic flight from Newark Airport to Chicago. Now, if her last attempt failed, she was ready to leave.

At first, she thought fate had lent a hand, when John and Jeff both decided to go out on Thursday evening. If they were surprised by her hugs when they left, neither of them commented. Carolyn had always been tactile with them all and they were used to her displays of affection, but she squeezed first John and then Jeff as if she didn't want to let them go. "Just have a lovely time and look after each other," she said, smiling at them both through her tears.

"Whatever's the matter, Sweetheart?" John asked when he saw her tears. "If you don't want us to go out we won't. You've only got to say."

"Don't be so silly" she replied. I'm just a bit tired. I'll probably have an early night. Go on. Off you go."

After they had left, she sat next to Bob on the settee. He had his arm around her shoulders whilst they watched the television for the next hour or so. Well, Bob watched the film that was showing. Carolyn's mind was certainly not on the movie. She wondered how and when to make her move. All she was conscious of was his strong arm around her and the broad shoulder her head was resting on. She could smell the clean, fresh scent of his cologne in her nostrils; hear his quiet breathing as he sat relaxing next to her.

When the film ended, Carolyn stood up and walked over to the window. The apartment was on the seventh floor and the people in the street below looked like ants. It had been raining heavily and the traffic was quite busy as cars and cabs moved along the wet street, taking people who knew where. *Just a normal evening,* Carolyn thought to herself.

As if on cue, Bob came to stand behind her with his arms wrapped around her shoulders and his face against hers as they looked out of the window. "Look, Robbie, a shooting star," Carolyn cried. "We should make a wish."

Bob smiled, "O.K. but we mustn't say what we're wishing for."

Oh God, please let this work. Carolyn thought.

She turned around in his arms. Knowing her intentions, she was unable to look him in the face. Her eyes were drawn to the lovely hollow at the base of his throat. Instinctively, one hand touched his collarbone, her fingers tracing a path across his skin. She felt a pulse throbbing and couldn't resist the urge to let her lips rest there for a brief moment, breathing in his smell and feeling the warmth and softness.

Bob held his breath, closing his eyes in ecstasy at the sensations her attentions evoked.

Feeling bolder when he didn't turn away, Carolyn let her hand travel to the back of his neck. Holding the other hand to his cheek, she brought his face down to hers and kissed him; gently at first and then more firmly.

He moaned as his arms tightened around her; crushing her to his chest and returning her kisses with a passion that made her senses reel with joy.

Suddenly, he pushed her away with such force that she fell against the wall. "What are you doing?" he shouted. "This is so wrong, girl. How could you ever think I would feel that way about you? This is like incest. I feel sick."

"Robbie, you kissed me back. I know you did. Just tell me you don't want me," she wept.

"I **don't** want you girl. Now get out of my sight," he yelled at her.

For a brief moment their eyes met; two hearts entwined as they crashed and burned together in torment. Carolyn's heart exploded in her chest as she ran from her own pain. She did not see Bob hold out his arms with a sob before sliding down the wall; the fragments of his broken dreams running down his face into his hands. She could not know the effort it had taken for him to reject her. She was the love of his life; his darling girl, but he knew she wasn't for him. He would never be good enough for her. He had to be strong. All that mattered was her.

In the early hours of the morning, no-one heard Carolyn slip out of the apartment, leaving a letter addressed to John on the table.

The following morning, Jeff was the first to go into the kitchen to make coffee. Finding the envelope on the table he took it along to John's room with his cup. "This is Carolyn's writing, John. It was on the table. What's she doin' writing to you?" He was alarmed to see the colour drain from John's face as he read the letter inside. Without speaking, he passed it to Jeff, who read through without comment.

"My Darling John, I know you will never understand my reasons for doing this, and I can't fully explain. All I can say is that I have been very unhappy lately. Everything has changed and neither you nor Jeff or Robbie really need me

anymore. I can't bear not to be needed. I have to go before the situation destroys me. I am going to try to make a new life, but it has to be on my own. Your future is here now, with the boys. I'm so pleased you have found success and a secure future.

The only other thing I wish for you is that you are happy and have a marvellous life. You will always be my wonderful brother. I will watch your career with pride and with love. The three of you have been the centre of my life for a long time and have looked after me so well. I know it is not going to be easy to be on my own. I will miss you all and think of you every day of my life. Please tell my darling boys that I will never stop loving them, and if you could just tell Robbie I'm sorry, he will understand. My love always, Carolyn."

The two of them raced to her room. The bed was neatly made and an inspection of the wardrobes showed that much of her clothing was missing.

They pushed open Bob's door. He had finished off a bottle of rum before staggering to bed and was bleary eyed, but when he saw their faces he knew that something was dreadfully wrong. "What is it? What's happened?"

John was heartbroken. "She's gone, Bob."

"Gone? Gone where?" Bob managed to get out.

John shook his head "I don't know, mate. Jeff; show him the letter." Jeff passed Bob the letter, which he read through twice.

"Nooo!" Bob shouted. It was a terrible sight to see this big, strong man's shoulders racked with sobs as the tears poured down his face.

All three were in a state of shock. Jeff said haltingly "I knew there was something wrong. I knew she was unhappy. She told me as much at the end of the last tour." He repeated the conversation he had had with Carolyn. "I honestly thought she would be okay once we came back here. I should have told you; done something. We might have been able to stop her. Bob, what does she mean when she says to tell you she's sorry?"

With tears still streaming down his face, Bob looked from one to the other of them. "This is nobody's fault but mine. Guys, I've been in love with her for years; almost from that first day: but I made a promise to you, John, all those years ago, and I've always kept it. Most of the time it was enough just to be near her and to know that she loved me, even if it was as a brother. However, lately, I started to realise she had feelings for me. It came to a head last night and I knew how you'd feel about it so, God help me, I rejected her. I guess she must have already been planning to leave but took one last chance. Looking back, she's been acting strangely for weeks."

John was aghast. "For fuck's sake, Bob. That promise I extracted from you was ten years ago. You were strangers to me. Now we are as close as brothers could ever be. There's no way I would have objected to you two being together. You are a fine man and I'm so proud of the way you've turned out. Why on earth did you think I'd object? Because you are black? God, Bob; when in all these years has your colour ever been an issue with any of us?"

Bob closed his eyes and bowed his head in sorrow. *What had he done?*

By the time they had pulled themselves together to try to track Carolyn's movements, she was long gone and on her flight from Chicago to London.

☙❧☙❧

PART TWO

1998

LONELINESS

Chapter seven

Carolyn's thoughts were far away as she sat on the train taking her from Wallasey to Liverpool. This last twelve months had been the loneliest and most miserable of her life, but things were starting to come together now.

When first arriving in London, she intended to settle there and find a home and job, but she realised very quickly that she was never going to fit in. London was a metropolis; a melting pot of people from all over the country and all over the globe. It was one thing to be amongst strangers and totally alone, but she realised she would be more able to cope if at least she was amongst her own kind of people. Therefore, after a month of burying herself in her hotel room and crying all the time, she travelled up to the Wirral.

It wasn't difficult to hide her identity. She changed her surname from Davidson to Davis and opened a bank account in that name. Her share of her parents' legacy had accrued interest and together with money which the boys had insisted in paying into her account, she was not short of money. She had arranged Bank Drafts to be raised in New York and these when paid into her new account, came to a respectable amount.

She went through the motions of organising her new life with a cold efficiency she had not thought possible. Gone were the laughing eyes and in their place was a sad, haunted look.

She found a house in Wallasey to rent that suited her requirements. It was a dorma-bungalow with an open-plan lounge, and a kitchen. There were three bedrooms upstairs and a bathroom. Although probably larger than she needed, it was comfortable and bright.

"If I have to be miserable and lonely, I may as well be miserable and lonely in comfort," she muttered to herself as she signed the lease.

The decoration was clean and the owner had laid new carpets throughout, so having purchased a bed and a three piece suite, she was able to move in almost immediately and start furnishing the rest of the House. This kept her occupied for another month as she trawled the second hand and charity shops for other items of furniture and kitchen equipment. She bought new bedding and other linen and colourful scatter cushions for the lounge. When everything was in place, including new curtains and rugs, she sat down to admire the effect. Whilst she had been kept busy, somehow her mind had been able to cope but suddenly the silence was intense. *So this is it then,* she thought. *Just me and my memories.* The tears were never far away, but she knew if she didn't get a grip of her emotions she was not going to be able to cope.

Every morning, her first waking thought was of her boys and at bedtime she always said "Goodnight my darlings," to the photograph on her bedside table. This showed the four of them smiling and happy as she wanted to remember them.

An advertisement in the Liverpool Echo showed an Agency recruiting Secretaries and Administrative staff to work in the City and surrounding areas. Carolyn applied and was successful. She had been working for the Agency for eight months now and it suited her that she was never placed for long periods in any one firm. She didn't want to open up to people, and she found it easier to keep quiet about her past if she didn't work too long with the same people. Merseyside people were friendly, but she found it difficult not to pour out her troubles when people lent a sympathetic ear.

At present her assignment was in a Solicitor's Office in the City. She was covering for one of the permanent secretaries who was on maternity leave. Carolyn was very efficient at her job. Because she had no social life and kept to herself, she was able to give full commitment to whatever task she undertook. She didn't smile much and didn't join in the laughter and gossip with the other girls. One day she was having a sandwich at her desk when one of the other secretaries, called Sue, hovered over her desk.

"Carolyn, it's my birthday today and some of us are going to the pub after work for a drink. Would you like to come with us?"

All that awaited Carolyn at home was a cold empty house and a microwave meal, so with trepidation she agreed to accompany the group to a wine bar near the office.

Her heart began to thaw a little as the friendly colleagues toasted the 'birthday girl', and she found herself joining in their conversation.

Perhaps that's what happens, she thought. *You don't get over things. You get used to them, and without realising it life goes on.*

She sat up quickly when she heard one of the girls saying "Now, how many tickets shall I ask for? It'll be a sell out, so we need to be on the ball. Carolyn, we're going to see The Honeys in Manchester next month; would you like to come with us? We're going to hire a mini-bus."

Carolyn felt as though her tongue was stuck to the root of her mouth. *Oh my God,* she thought, *See them; hear them sing.* Aloud she managed to get out. "Yes. Yes, I would please. Yes, you can count me in."

Sue was very excited at the prospect of seeing her idols. "Wow! They are all so handsome. I can't wait. Which one do you fancy most, Carolyn? I think I'm in love with Jeff. I dream about him."

Carolyn smiled and thought; *you and a few million others darling,* but just said, "They're all lovely."

On the night of the concert, Carolyn thought she would be sick with excitement. She would see her boys and best of all she would see her Robbie. When they ran out onto the stage she was frightened to take her eyes off their faces. They were all so special; so smart and handsome. How proud she was of them. She tried to take in how they all looked. John was John; still her lovely, gentle brother. He didn't seem to have changed. Jeff was as handsome as ever and still smiled a lot. Robbie seemed so serious and brooding.

Oh God, do you still miss me as much as I miss you? she thought. After a few opening numbers, her Robbie stepped forward and his voice rang out with the words of his new song.

"I look for your face in the morning sunrise; I search for you in the evening breeze.
In a crowded place, I look around, but you're not there, you're not there.
Will I ever see your face again, will you ever come to me.
I look for you in the stars my love, my only love.

Where are you now my love?
Do you ever think of me?
I swear by the heavens above
My heart will never be free.
Where are you now my dearest friend?
Do you still feel this tie?
I'll love you until life's end
Yes until the day I die."

Although the words and melody burned themselves into her brain and heart, because of the way they had parted, Carolyn failed to realise that, to Bob, they mirrored the separation between the two. He sang with sadness and poignancy, making her so emotional that she could not prevent the tears cascading down her cheeks.

The second of Robbie's singles was equally as sad and haunting.

"My life might have been so happy with you by my side through life.
But only in my dreams my darling, is the love I might have had.
Can I never be happy, can I never be glad?
Will I always dream of the love I might have had?"

When the group harmonised on their final number, and ran off the stage, Carolyn wanted to run after them and beg them to let her go home with them. Instead, she stood up with a heavy heart and followed her colleagues out of the theatre. Their excited chatter was just background noise in her head and she thought she was going to faint. They were very concerned to see the tears running down her face.

"Didn't you enjoy the show?" Marie asked her.

"Of course I did," Carolyn managed to say. "They were wonderful. Just reminded me of someone and made me very sad. I'll be O.K. soon."

"Oh, Carolyn's got a mystery love." Sue laughed. "I thought you were drooling over Bob Maples, the way you were looking at him."

Carolyn smiled and nodded in agreement. She couldn't speak. *If only they knew,* she thought. She was relieved to get home, shut the front door behind her and finally give way to her emotions. "Oh my darlings, I'll always love and miss you and you'll never know," she cried.

That was when she decided to send Birthday cards and Christmas cards to them throughout the year. Provided they were posted out of town, the postmark would not give away her locality. At least then, her memory would be kept alive and they would know she hadn't forgotten them.

That first concert was a turning point for Carolyn. A whole year on her own and she had a house, a job and a life of sorts. She had seen "her boys" and knew they were well and still together.

The following week, Carolyn joined a keep-fit class at the local Leisure Centre. She made new friends and started going out on the odd evening. She even went on a couple of dates, although these men were kept at arm's length. Carolyn always dreaded the time when they would drop her off outside the House, as there was always the goodnight kiss or the groping hands to contend with.

Carolyn had never driven a car. There never seemed the necessity, as there was always someone to drive her where she wanted to go, but she realised that if she wanted to be totally independent, she would need to be able to drive. She booked with a local firm to have lessons two or three times a week. When she failed her test the first time she was very disappointed. The second time, however, she passed. She was so pleased with herself that she went out and bought a car straight away. She chose a second-hand, maroon coloured Suzuki Grand Vitara which caught her eye. The mileage was low and it had obviously been well looked after. *The world is my oyster now, she thought.* She loved driving round the Wirral and spent hours on the promenade at New Brighton; sitting in the car watching the waves beating against the embankment.

Although never totally happy, Carolyn found herself filling her days. Instead of moping around the House in her spare time, she would be out either visiting friends or driving around exploring. Four of the girls she had met at the keep-fit class started meeting up once a month in each other's houses for a meal and a bottle of wine. This became a regular event and, although at first reticent about opening up to people, Carolyn found herself telling the girls a little of her background, leaving out the fact that the men were in fact the famous Honeys, and just intimating that unrequited love had made it necessary for her to leave. *Well,* she thought, *it is the truth really.*

Her boys were never far from her mind. It was impossible not to be reminded of them. *At least if someone died, or you split up with them, you wouldn't be constantly reminded of them by their voice coming on the radio or their face on the television,* she thought on one dull wet day in December. In fact, Carolyn couldn't help herself. She bought every music paper and scoured the glossy magazines hungrily for any mention of them. She bought their new CD when it was released and trawled the music channels on the television to catch a glimpse of them singing. She bought a computer to look for anything connected with them.

She gladly accepted when one of her new friends, Anne, asked her to spend Christmas Day with her and her husband. It was not a time to be on your own. The previous year she had only just arrived here. Christmas had come and gone in abject misery.

She carefully selected a Christmas card to send to the boys and sent it off in good time. Strangely enough, she actually felt happy as she posted it, but the feeling soon passed. She could not give them an address, so they would not be able to contact her. She had written in the card:

"To my Darling John, Jeff and Robbie. Hope life is being kind to you and that you are all well. I caught one of your concerts in England. It was wonderful. I am so proud of you. I miss you. All my love always, Carolyn."

She tried to imagine them receiving the card. At least they would know she was safe. She was sure they would want to know that.

Chapter eight

Carolyn may have been very surprised if she had seen just how much the Christmas card meant to the family. When she fled, she left a huge hole in all their lives. The week after her departure was frantic. The three men tried to track her movement at the airports, checking all the flights from New York to England. However, despite their celebrity, they kept hitting red tape. 'Customer confidentiality' became the most annoying phrase in the English language.

"Bloody Jobsworths," John fumed. "Surely they can at least tell us if she was on any of the passenger lists."

They didn't think to check the domestic flights and, therefore, missed the fact that Carolyn had in fact flown to Chicago before taking a flight from there to London. However, this information would have done them little favour, because, by this time Carolyn was lost to them in the huge city.

They hired a renowned Private Detective Agency to try to find her, but the information that she had at last been traced to London came too late. All three flew over to London and questioned the staff at the hotel where Carolyn had stayed. Some of the staff remembered the lovely, sad girl who stayed there, but no one knew her destination when she left the hotel. She apparently did not leave her room very often, and always looked as if she had been crying.

Bob sat down and covered his face with his hands. "Oh my God, she would've been so frightened. That first night, at Cobble Hill, when she asked us to stay, she said she'd never spent a night on her own. Since then we've always been around. She's never had to fend for herself before. How will she cope?"

John shook his head sadly. "We Davidsons are a strong breed. I know she'll find the strength. It's just hard to imagine what she's doing. Oh, I miss her so much."

Jeff still blamed himself for not doing more when he noticed she was so unhappy. He felt the bottom had dropped out of his world. Carolyn was his sister, his mom and his friend. She had helped make him what he was to-day and suddenly he didn't know how he would cope without her. The three were very subdued when they flew back to New York.

Whether he was searching to replace the love and stability Carolyn's leaving had taken from his life was never clear, but a few months later, Jeff started seeing Nicole Saunders. Nicole was very beautiful with naturally blond hair. She was a photographic model with an amazing figure; always impeccably dressed in the latest fashion. She impressed Jeff with her sparkling personality; chatting animatedly in company, attracting men to her like flies. Always very ambitious, she wanted fame and money. She didn't care how she got it.

Jeff was at his most vulnerable when she set her sights on him. Usually a man who liked to play the field, he found himself drawn to Nicole, who was at her most vivacious and charming in his company. Within weeks he had proposed to her and she started planning the wedding of the year. This was to take place in November, which coincided with the anniversary of Carolyn's departure. A very fashionable venue was booked and all the arrangements were in place.

Although not immediately apparent, Nicole was a racist. She hated Bob with a vengeance and was very jealous of the closeness between the two men. She was uncomfortable in his company and tried to avoid any contact with him. She realised, however, that she was on a hiding to nothing when she tried to persuade him to have John instead of Bob as Best Man.

"Nicole, darling, you have to realise that Bob and I are brothers in every respect except parents. I think the world of John, but he'd never expect me to ask him over Bob. There's no way I'm gonna change my mind. I don't understand why you don't get on with him. Bob's a great guy and we've been through a lot together."

In the end, Nicole had to give in and everything was in place for the big day. One of the glossy magazines, "Stars To-day" had paid an enormous fee for the exclusive rights to publish photographs of the wedding. After their honeymoon in the Caribbean, they moved into their new home, a huge luxurious penthouse in Manhattan.

John began dating one of the secretaries from the Office and Secretarial agency which they used. Her name was Annie and she reminded him a little of his beloved sister. Unlike Carolyn, Annie was petite and shy, but at the time, she was what John needed to take his mind off his constant worries. He had someone who hung on his every word to look after again. Whilst he still missed Carolyn, like Jeff, he realised that he needed to move on.

Bob, on the other hand, could not move on. Every waking moment he thought of his lost love. When he closed his eyes he could see her face. He felt he would never be whole again and the verses he wrote for his songs all expressed his feelings and emotions.

> *"I can't close my eyes without seeing,*
> *the time you were here in my life.*
> *Your voice is in my mind saying that you care*
> *But I threw away a love so rare, so very rare.*
> *Could we have made it together? Could I have made you my wife?"*

After waking himself up one night shouting her name he sat up and wrote,

> *"Sometimes in the dead of night, I wake and wonder why,*
> *Your name is still upon my lips, spoken like a sigh.*
> *Did I call you, did you hear me, or was it just a dream?*
> *Are you happy, are you sad, will I ever know?*

Life's so lonely without you; why did you have to go?"

John and Jeff had written wonderful melodies to the verses and the three were in the process of recording them for their new album.

Bob still played the field, enjoying the company of beautiful women, but now he was moody and serious most of the time. He made sure he never saw the same woman more than a couple of times, so his emotions were never involved.

This, then, was the situation in New York when Carolyn's Christmas card arrived. Only Bob and John now lived in the apartment and it was John who went through the morning post. Fan mail was now dealt with by the secretarial agency and was redirected, but since their mail had increased to vast proportions, they had devised a code which, when written on the envelope, meant that the contents should be dealt with personally. This system had been in place for a few years, so Carolyn was aware of it. However, John immediately recognised his sister's handwriting and pounced on the envelope.

"Thank God, she's safe," he said passing the card to Bob.

"Oh Darling, where are you?" Bob muttered as his fingers traced her handwriting and he lifted the card to his face. "I wonder which concert she went to. If only we could have known she was there."

"I suppose we must assume she could be at any of the British concerts next year when we go over," John acknowledged. "Perhaps we could say something, make an announcement, or somehow give out a message to her."

Bob was pessimistic. "Let's face it, John; if she doesn't want to be found, she won't be."

"But Bob," John persisted, "If she knew how you felt about her it could make all the difference."

Bob shrugged "If she came to a concert, she will have heard the words I wrote for her. Surely she must know what I'm saying; must realise what they mean. We've got to accept that she may have made a new life by now. She may have met someone else and be happy." He felt as though his heart would break all over again at the thought.

They phoned Jeff to tell him about the card and he hugged the news to himself. He had already seen the other side of Nicole and realised that the information would be of no interest to her. After all, it wasn't about her. At the first opportunity he dashed round to the apartment so he could see and hold the card for himself.

"If only she had given us an address. It would be so good to be able to hear her voice and talk to her, even if she didn't want to come home," Jeff commented. He left the apartment reluctantly. Nicole had arranged another photo-shoot with Stars To-day Magazine which was to show the two of them relaxing in their luxury apartment. Never a man to flaunt his wealth, and still very aware of his background and roots, the whole idea was abhorrent to him.

How different life was now. *Carolyn was right*, he thought, *we were never so happy as when we were all together in the Cobble Hill house.* Nicole, however, was obviously very contented with their way of life and so he felt obliged to fall in with her plans.

So, life in New York carried on pretty much as before for the next few years. John eventually married Annie, and although it wasn't the society wedding arranged by the Simmonds, it was a happy affair.

A photograph and report of the wedding appeared in the international press. Rather than choose between his two friends, John decided to have two 'Best Men', so both Jeff and Bob acted as the Groom's attendants. They were happy for him as Annie was a gentle soul who helped John accept the fact that his darling Carolyn was lost to him.

Bob now lived alone in the apartment, but threw himself into song-writing and personal appearances. He was now popular in his own right, so as well as still appearing as one of the Honeys, he occasionally did solo concerts. Constantly living and working on his own, he was lonely, growing increasingly moody and introverted; wearing a soulful, sad expression on his face.

It was at his suggestion that the three men decided to extend their field of work to helping other acts get a start in the business that had been kind to them. They began going to showcases and signed up a few young acts who they thought were capable of making a career in show-business. Their own manager, Max Hunter, encouraged them with this and once acts were signed up, he was able to find bookings for them.

They decided to move again; this time into a condominium penthouse. It was in two parts with a large living area, which they named the House and the other, which they called the Shop. Time spent discussing decor and furnishings while making arrangements meant time spent together, and the men were never happier than when they were together. The Shop housed their own recording studio, music room, and offices. Their new company was called "M., D. and S. Productions," and new acts on their books were able to cut their first discs in the Honey's own studio. The main disadvantage of the new apartment was the fact that Bob lived there alone. He hated the silence and the loneliness and spent as little time as possible at home. He employed a housekeeper, a plump, motherly woman called Bess, who came in each day and cleaned for him. She kept his food cupboards stocked, and there was always a casserole or pasta dish in the fridge ready for heating.

The men employed a Personal Assistant, Stella Baldwin, who very efficiently looked after their day-to-day diaries, bookings, and arrangements for their personal appearances and tours.

Each of them received birthday cards from Carolyn the second and third years after her disappearance. They had arranged with the people who moved into their old apartment to forward on any correspondence displaying a U.K. stamp to the new address. The first time a card arrived for Jeff before his birthday in August, Bob was a nervous wreck whilst he waited to see if he would receive one three weeks later. It was the year they were both thirty and sure enough Carolyn had remembered this.

When Bob's card arrived he was elated and sat down to savour the moment when he opened the envelope. *"Dearest Robbie,"* she had written. *"Just wanted you to know I was thinking of you. Hope you enjoy your birthday. Saw you on T.V. at the Awards. Please stop wearing those shades indoors. You'll break your neck! All my love, Carolyn."*

He smiled through his tears. *She can still make me laugh, even when she isn't here. Oh, my wonderful girl, where are you*? Bob never wore dark glasses indoors again.

۞۞

Chapter nine
2000

The Millennium celebrations came and went, with Carolyn remembering the time ten years earlier when Robbie had given her a piggy-back home in the snow and she told him to "Give a little whistle" if he needed her. *I wonder if he ever thinks of those times*, she thought. *I was so happy then; I wish I'd never sent that rotten tape off. Still, I suppose eventually he would have met someone and left me. You can't make time stand still.*

In August, she carefully chose birthday cards for Jeff and Bob's thirtieth birthdays, and again in November found a suitable card for John. Having seen all the details of the weddings in the glossy magazines and newspapers, she was unsure whether Jeff and John would receive theirs, but it made her feel better just to write and post them. The note she added to Bob's card was following a television programme which showed him at an award dinner, walking up the red carpet and into the luxurious hotel wearing dark glasses.

"Oh, take them off, Robbie; take them off. You look a prat!" she shouted at the television screen.

Carolyn was still meeting up with her friends each month for dinner and looked forward to the evenings, when they sipped wine and chatted comfortably together. The five went to the keep fit class each week and had occasional nights out at the theatre in Liverpool. Other nights she would visit Anne or Anne would come around to see her.

In March of the following year, Carolyn bought a caravan on the Isle of Anglesey in Wales. She wanted somewhere to escape to, where she could spend time walking and be alone with her thoughts and memories. It was a lovely spot on the headland at Trearddur Bay, amongst the heather and the gorse. Carolyn found more peace walking around the headland and sitting on a large rock looking out at the Irish Sea than she had enjoyed in almost three years. She called the rock her "Thinking Rock," spending ages thinking about how much her life had changed and planning her way forward.

She befriended the girl who owned the caravan next to hers. Irene was on her own too, so they spent evenings together, cooking meals and chatting. Whilst discussing their past lives, she still found it impossible to be totally honest. She confided in Irene that she had fallen deeply in love with someone when she lived in America, but that her love had not been returned.

"For years he was my best friend and I'm afraid that was all I ever was to him; but I adored him and always will," she sighed. "It's just that no-one can ever measure up to him." She laughed, mirthlessly. "Pity me. I'm a twenty eight year old virgin with no sign of the situation altering. I bet there's not many of them around. It's just that I've never wanted anyone else."

Carolyn still worked for the secretarial agency, and now found her services being requested by firms she had previously been assigned to. At one of these offices, she met Ian Walker. Tall and stocky with dark curly hair, he seemed pleasant enough, so when he asked her out one evening, Carolyn accepted. Ian was in his late thirties and divorced. Their first date, at a wine bar in Liverpool, passed quite enjoyably. Ian was very talkative so sitting and chatting with him was easy. When he saw her home in a taxi, she managed to persuade him to stay in the cab and leave her at the door without much difficulty.

When Ian asked her out again, she agreed. They dined at a popular Chinese restaurant in Liverpool's Chinatown and, once again, Carolyn found his company agreeable and quite entertaining. She hadn't told him much about her past, but now found herself telling him that she had lived in America for ten years, and that her three brothers, from whom she was estranged, still lived there. He told her some amusing stories, but it became apparent that his main interest in life was himself and what he intended to do with his life. He was incredibly ambitious and obviously thought he would go far in the insurance world. Once again, Ian dropped her off at her front door and she managed to persuade him that she was too tired to invite him in for a coffee, so he reluctantly left after a goodnight kiss.

However, she was conscious of the fact that if she wanted a normal life, she wouldn't be able to keep men at arm's length forever. On the third date, therefore, she accepted Ian's invitation to go back to his flat in West Kirby where he was to prepare a meal for her. *Oh my God, she thought, what am I letting myself in for.*

He cooked quite a decent pasta dish with salad and garlic bread, and they drank two bottles of wine with the meal. Carolyn helped wash up, then they sat on the comfortable settee and Ian put some records on. The second album was one of The Honey's. Carolyn was feeling quite tipsy, so when Robbie's voice started to sing, *"I look for your face in the morning sunrise, I search for you in the evening breeze,"* the haunting melody sent her senses reeling.

Ian took her in his arms and started to kiss her. His hands were everywhere and somehow she was in another place, with someone else. She imagined that this wasn't Ian, it was Robbie. Before she realised it her blouse had been removed and his hand was moving up her thigh. She made no complaint as she closed her eyes and let the sensations waft over her. She was in Robbie's strong arms; her face buried in his neck, his warm breath on her cheek, his fingers pulling and kneading her breasts.

"Come on Carolyn, let's go somewhere more comfortable," Ian said as he pulled her up from the sofa to lead her to the bedroom.

She had time to register the two glasses with the bottle of champagne in a bucket of ice by the bed, and realised that this was well planned.

Then the rest of her clothes had been removed and he was on top of her.

Carolyn had started to sober up by now. This was no longer Robbie; it was a stranger, but she knew it was too late to stop what was happening to her. He pushed his fingers inside her, then entered her without further hesitation, tearing into her delicate skin; moving and panting. The whole experience was unpleasant, painful and over very quickly. *How do people say they enjoy it?* she thought, as she turned over in the bed and curled up in a ball. She just wanted to cry and thought to herself, not for the first time, *Oh Robbie, why didn't you want me. I know it would have been so different with you*

Ian sat up in bed and opened the bottle of champagne, the pop from the cork making Carolyn jump with surprise. "Here you are sweetheart, mind the bubbles don't go up your nose," he said pleasantly. As she turned round to face him, he handed her a glass and offered her a cigarette. She shook her head without speaking and sipped at the champagne, trying to hold the threatening tears back.

"You didn't tell me you hadn't ...you know...done it before Carolyn," he said sheepishly. I'm sorry if I hurt you. I'd have taken things slower if you'd only said something."

Carolyn was touched by his concern. She shrugged her shoulders and tried to appear nonchalant. "It was fine, Ian. It was good. A girl's got to start sometime." With a smile which did not reach her eyes she repeated, "It was good, but you better phone me a taxi. Work to-morrow, you know, and I can hardly turn up to the office in my evening gear, else people will be talking.

Once home, she stood under the shower, trying to block out the images in her mind. *If I'm going to have a normal life, this is how it has to be from now on. It will be easier next time.*

Carolyn saw Ian on a few more occasions, and slept with him a further time, but she knew she couldn't carry on with the relationship, especially as she came to realise that Ian was becoming very keen on her.

Trying to be as kind as she could, on their last date, she told him some of the truth. "Ian, you're a lovely man, but I can't go out with you anymore. There's someone else, you see. I love him very much, but there are reasons I can't be with him. It isn't fair to give you hope, when there can't be any future for us."

"You say you love someone else, Carolyn, yet you were a virgin when we met. You must know how I feel about you. I'm starting to fall in love with you and I know I could make you happy if you'll only give me a chance," Ian pleaded.

Carolyn knew she had to be firm and make a clean break. The fact that he was falling for her made it even more imperative that she finish with him before his heart was broken. She knew too well how that felt and she couldn't do the same to Ian. "I'm so sorry, dear, but this is how it has to be. I know you'll meet someone who deserves you one day and you will forget all about me."

She stopped accepting dates and only went out with men when in other company. Soon her nickname became "The Iceberg," and it was a challenge amongst some of her male colleagues to see who could thaw the ice.

Carolyn decided she was quite content to be on her own and not accept second best, because whoever it was, they could only ever be second best to her. What she felt for Robbie was so special that she could never love anyone else. He had been her best friend as well as the love of her life, and she knew that she would never get over him.

One of the secretarial assignments was with an American import and export firm in Liverpool. Carolyn had already spent two sessions there, when she was asked back in the spring of 2002. She found that two Americans from New York were now working there on a temporary management transfer. Patrick Owen and Mike Hughes were pleasant enough to work for. However, Mike was black and although he looked nothing like him, together with his voice and his New York accent, he reminded Carolyn so much of Robbie that she wanted to burst into tears every time she was near him. She was totally uncomfortable in his company, and it didn't take long for him to pick up on this.

One day when Carolyn was in his office taking dictation, he put his pen down and sat back in his chair. "Miss Davis," he said "I can't help but notice that you have a problem with me. Believe me it wouldn't be the first time, but your obvious repulsion of me is beginning to get on my nerves. Now if you really can't stand to work with me I think we need to ask the agency to find you another post."

Carolyn was horrified. *Oh My God, he thinks I'm a racist*, she realised.

"No, Mr. Hughes, I know what you're saying and you are so wrong," she spluttered. "Okay, I do have a problem with you, but it isn't what you think. Perhaps one day I can explain, but for now, please forgive me. I've been acting stupidly, and it won't happen again."

That night she took stock of the situation. *It's been four years and I still go to pieces at the thought of him. What's happened to all my resolutions to be independent and get on with my life?* After that she tried to be more pleasant in the office, although her heart still broke every time she heard Mike's accent and caught sight of him out of the corner of her eye.

That summer, whilst at the caravan, Carolyn and Irene sat watching a televised Honeys' concert at Madison Square Gardens in New York. They watched in silence as the tears poured down Carolyn's face when the group ran onto the stage. After a few songs, her darling Robbie looked straight at the camera and said, "And this one's just for you my Darling, my Beautiful Girl."

The Honeys started singing their first ever hit, *Beautiful Girl*.

"Oh Irene, no!" Carolyn cried in anguish. "That was their first song. The one that made them famous. I was a part of all that and now he's met someone and he's dedicating it to her. I can't bear it."

Her grief was so intense that she didn't even notice the little whistle he gave at the end of the song, and so completely missed the message the three of them had tried to send to her.

Irene was perplexed. "What are you talking about, Luv? You've been crying all though the programme. What do you mean; you were part of it all? You knew the Honeys in America then?

Carolyn could not hold back any longer. The whole story came gushing out, amongst the tears and hiccups. She told Irene about her "darling brother" and how they had met her two "scallies" soon after they arrived in America. Irene was spellbound listening to the story of how this strange but loving family had evolved.

"You see, Robbie was always very special to me. I loved him as my best friend for years, and then one day, I realised he was the most important person in the world to me. This amazing feeling struck me like a thunderbolt. I don't know what I expected really. I just felt that one day he would see how much I loved him, and that he would feel the same way. Then, when they hit the big time, everything changed. The three of them, including Robbie, became public property. Oh God, Irene, the women swarmed round them like flies, and didn't they just love it. To cut a long story short, I threw myself at him one night and he rejected me. He said he didn't want me; that it felt like incest. So you see, I ruined everything. If I could only have accepted that he loved me as a sister and as a dear friend I could have still been a part of his life. But no! I had to go and spoil it all with my jealousy, and there was no going back after that. Now it looks like he's fallen for someone."

Irene had kept quiet through Carolyn's story and now she took her hands in both of hers and spoke softly. "Don't you think they will all have been worried about you? Your brother especially. Is there no way you could have let them know you were alright?"

Carolyn nodded; the tears still streaming down her cheeks. "That's why I started sending cards. I don't know whether they still receive them, or even whether they still care. Well, of course I know John will. I feel really bad about him, but they are the three musketeers now and it had to be all or nothing."

She said her goodnights and went back to her lonely bed in her own caravan. "That's it then. It really is all over," Carolyn sobbed into her pillow that night. "All three of them are happy and have found love. I was so pleased for John and Jeff, but I can't be glad for you Robbie. I know I'm being selfish, but I always felt that one day you might change your mind. How can I carry on?"

After that day Carolyn sent no more cards. She tried to harden her heart, and in doing so once more lost her lovely sparkle and the laughter in her eyes. She still socialised with her friends and spent time at the caravan, but even these simple pleasures seemed to have lost their allure. She threw herself into work, spending more time alone; reliving the past and pondering her lonely, empty future.

※

Whilst Carolyn was trying to rebuild her life in England, things were steadily falling apart in New York.

Jeff and Nicole's marriage started to crumble before their second anniversary. Nicole loved the lifestyle of being married to a Superstar, and enjoyed accompanying the group to various events, concerts and dinners. She adored the show business parties, where she could mix with other stars. Never one to stay in the shadows, she was always in the foreground of photographs. Nicole made sure that she hosted similar events at their apartment where she could put on fabulous buffets and invite the top people to her home. Jeff hated every minute of this lifestyle. He only wanted love and a home of his own so couldn't believe how shallow and selfish Nicole was.

He tried at every opportunity to still spend time with Bob and John who, because of their closeness, tried to be supportive to their friend. Neither of the men liked Nicole, but were reluctant to let Jeff know how they felt, as they thought he still cared about her. Most of the time Nicole ignored Bob, and on the few occasions she spoke to him she was patronising and often offensive, but never in Jeff's hearing. Bob knew Nicole had been unfaithful to Jeff on several occasions, but could not bring himself to tell him. Everyone else in their circle knew about her infidelities, but Jeff seemed either to turn a blind eye or wasn't aware of the situation.

In fact, Jeff did know and had come to the conclusion that he no longer cared what she did. He had started drinking far too much and even dabbled in cocaine; although, remembering the promise he had made to Carolyn all those years ago, he did not make a habit of this.

֍

In 2001, Annie found a lump in her breast. She did not tell John at first, keeping the secret to herself. However, it didn't take long for John to realise that something was troubling her as Annie's normally cheerful, smiling face was pale and serious. When, finally, he managed to press the information from her, he was horrified that she had not had the lump checked out.

"Annie, love, why on earth didn't you tell me sooner? It's probably nothing, but we need to get you to a doctor and have you examined. I don't want to take any chances, dear," he remonstrated with her.

Annie had obviously been worried and was relieved when John took control of the situation. "I just didn't want to bother you. I thought it might just have been a mastitis swelling which would go down, but it hasn't. Like you say, it's probably nothing."

John immediately phoned their doctor and arranged to take Annie that afternoon. She was given a thorough examination and sent to a specialist clinic for further tests to be carried out. When the surgery phoned the following week to say that all the results had come back, a further appointment was made with Dr. Ferguson. John and Annie sat in front of the doctor's desk, holding hands, whilst he read through the notes in front of him.

John's heart sank as he saw the serious expression on Dr. Ferguson's face. He knew before the doctor spoke that the news was not good. "There is no easy way to tell you this, Mrs. Davidson, but the biopsy has tested positive. You have an aggressive form of breast cancer and we must operate and remove your breast as soon as possible."

John bit hard on his bottom lip and took a deep breath. "You have caught it in time, though, haven't you, Doctor?" he asked.

The Doctor nodded, but still unsmiling replied, "I have no reason to believe otherwise. I am very hopeful that we can contain this with the appropriate treatment."

Annie was booked into the private clinic for the following day and went home to make arrangements and pack a suitcase. As soon as he was on his own, John phoned Bob to put him in the picture.

"Bob, mate, this hasn't half shaken me," he said, once he had fully explained the situation. First Carolyn leaves us and I just thought I was getting on with my life; now this happens. I just have a really bad feeling about this."

Bob was upset for his friends. "Oh, John, that's terrible, I'm so sorry. Give my love to Annie."

Following a mastectomy and chemotherapy Annie seemed to be making a good recovery, much to the relief of John and the other men who had become very fond of the quiet, gentle girl. It was a worrying and stressful time; John wishing so many times that Carolyn could have been with him to talk to and support him. However, by the spring of 2002 it was apparent that the disease had returned in Annie's other breast, so she underwent a further mastectomy and more chemotherapy.

Once the treatment was finished, they found themselves sitting in Dr. Ferguson's consulting room looking at the man's serious face. "This feels like déjà vu," John thought bleakly.

The doctor shuffled his papers, and then walked round the desk to take Annie's hands in his. "I'm so sorry, my dear lady. We knew this was an aggressive form of cancer and it has now spread into your lymph glands and bones. I have to tell you there is nothing more we can do for you. I'm afraid the prognosis is not good."

John felt his tongue was stuck to the roof of his mouth and he could not speak. However, Annie smiled sadly and said, "I think I knew that before you told me, Doctor. One knows one's own body, and I knew I wasn't getting better. How long do I have?"

"It could be up to a year or as little as a few months. Our main aim will be to keep you comfortable and pain free."

John found his voice at last and demanded that they have a second opinion. Dr. Ferguson agreed that this would be arranged, but confessed that he knew the result would be the same.

They drove home in a daze; Annie clinging to John's arm in the limousine as they sat silently side by side. As they were pulling up to the door, Annie turned to John, saying, "Dearest John, I want you to make me a promise. I'll say it now, and then we won't talk about it again. We'll just make the most of the time we have left. Thank you for making me so happy. I love you very much and I don't want you to be sad and lonely. I want you to try and find your sister and one day you can tell her about me. I want you to marry again. That would be the biggest compliment you could pay me."

John couldn't speak; he just took her in his arms and held her closely, whilst the tears poured down his face.

He stopped performing in order to spend as much time as he could with Annie. Their relationship had always been comfortable and companionable. Whilst never passionate or fiery, their marriage was nevertheless happy. He knew he would be lonely and lost without her. He booked a holiday for them both with Annie's parents in Los Angeles.

It was very hard telling her mother and father that they were going to lose their daughter, but John felt they should have their chance to spend time with her before she was too ill to travel. They were, of course, devastated; nevertheless, the memory of that two weeks would be treasured by the people Annie would leave behind.

※

It was left to Bob, therefore, to carry the flag of the Honeys over the next year. He found himself doing more and more solo concerts. They did, however, all sing at Madison Square Gardens in New York in 2002; an event which was filmed to go around the globe. They put into operation a plan to send Carolyn a message in the hope that she would see and understand how much they needed her. It was John's suggestion that Bob should dedicate their first record to her. "She'll realise you are telling her you love her. She's bound to contact us," he said hopefully.

Nicole was beside herself with curiosity and pressed Stella, the P.A., to try to find out who the mysterious woman was that Bob was referring to. However, Stella was not a party to the men's confidence either, and so could not shed any light on the situation.

That year there were no birthday cards and no Christmas card. At a time when all three were at their lowest ebb, this came as a bitter blow. "You understand what this means, don't you?" Bob sighed. "She's met someone and she's putting us out of her mind." His heart once again crumbled into fragments at the thought of Carolyn married to a stranger somewhere. *She's probably living the life I wanted for her, but I don't think I can bear it,* he thought.

Once when in bed with a beautiful young girl, she started to call him "Robbie". His passion cooled immediately and he jumped out of the bed. "No-one calls me that, do you hear me. No-one!" he shouted. His ardour was well deflated and he sent the lady home in a taxi.

He was so unhappy; he even contemplated taking his own life. He was lonely and miserable, but the knowledge that both John and Jeff needed his strength, kept him going, and in Carolyn's absence he was all they had.

At the end of the year he travelled to the United Kingdom to fulfil a couple of commitments which had originally been booked for the three Honeys. Publicity had been altered to inform the fans, and despite them now being solo concerts, all four venues were sell-outs.

An Aide, Harry Martin, travelled with him. Harry worked for an agency that for some time had supplied the Honeys with assistants, security men and drivers, as required. All three of the men trusted as well as liked Harry and always requested that he be on the team when recruiting. Harry, a widowed, retired New York Police Department Captain, was black with chiselled features and generous moustache. He had what John described as a "lived in face". Harry was a very wise man with a quiet and thoughtful nature.

He seemed to ponder well before answering questions, but he was always truthful and loyal. Bob was very happy to have his company on the flight to Britain and on the rest of the tour.

The tour was booked to start in London; move on to Cardiff, then Birmingham and end in Manchester. At each venue, Bob wondered whether his Carolyn might be in the audience, and if she was, whether she would be alone. Before one concert, Harry had noticed how lost in thought Bob was, as he was getting dressed for the performance. "Wanna talk, son?" He said. "Someone's really hurt you haven't they."

Bob gave a mirthless laugh. "Not her fault, Harry. But yes, there's only been one love in my life and only ever will be."

Harry shrugged. "Why don't you tell her then?"

Bob shook his head sadly. "Because I don't know where she is. Believe me, if I did I'd make sure she knew how I felt, but I don't think she cares anymore."

Harry noticed a tattoo on Bob's breast, above his heart. It showed an outline of Brooklyn Bridge with the name *Carolyn* in an arch over the towers. Bob noticed Harry looking at it and said; "One of these days I'll tell you the story, but yes, that's my lovely girl. Her name's Carolyn."

The last concert was in Manchester, and Bob couldn't shake the feeling that Carolyn was somewhere nearby. He could feel the hairs on the back of his neck standing on end and was so sure she was there in the audience, that once again he dedicated *Beautiful Girl* to "His Darling".

After the show, as he stood talking to Harry and some of the musicians, his eyes were attracted to a C.C.T.V. monitor. It showed the outside of the theatre as people were leaving. It was pouring with rain; most of the fans were dashing to shelter in taxis and waiting cars. All, that is, except for one girl who was walking out of the theatre as if she was in a daze. Suddenly, there she was; the camera showing her beautiful face with the tears streaming down her cheeks as she walked out of the door and into the wet street. She hesitated briefly, taking a big sigh as she turned, looking straight into the camera and into Bob's eyes.

Bob had never moved so fast. He rushed passed the crowd of people shouting, "Harry, quick it's her." Harry ran after him and they flew through the now empty theatre. Apart from the security men and several fans waiting for a glimpse of their idol, the street was deserted. Bob desperately tried to describe Carolyn to the security men, hoping to find which way she had gone, but despite running up and down the street, there was no sign of her. Harry hailed a taxi and they scoured the surrounding streets for over an hour, but it was hopeless.

The only comfort Bob had from the incident was that she had been on her own and she had looked so very sad. *I shouldn't be glad she's miserable*, he thought. *But, oh my Darling, are you still missing me as much as I miss you?* Back in his lonely hotel room, he phoned first John and then Jeff with the news that he had seen her. "I only saw her for an instant. She looked well, but so unhappy. Does this mean she's living in Manchester, John, do you think?"

John was elated that Carolyn had been spotted, but didn't hold out much hope of it helping them to find her. "She could be, but the only thing that's for sure is that she is up North. I still feel she would have gone back to Merseyside. You mark my words Bob, she's around Liverpool somewhere."

Bob stood, staring out of the hotel window; his mind seeing again his Carolyn's face on the TV monitor. It was as if, for a brief moment in time, she had looked into his soul and shared his pain. Surely she must still have feelings for him to be so upset. If only he could tell her how he felt. She was the love of his life; his soul mate. Bob travelled back to New York reluctantly. *So near and yet so fa*r, he thought.

He spent that Christmas with John and Annie, and put off returning to the lonely apartment so was still staying with the couple in the New Year when Annie took a turn for the worse. He was a great comfort to both of them during her illness and was able to give them support and help whenever he could. When Annie died in the spring, both Bob and Jeff were all that kept John going. They helped with all the arrangements, and were there to stand either side of him at the funeral. A photograph of Bob and Jeff holding a devastated John by the arms and looking at

Annie's coffin was in all the international press, so John found himself inundated with letters of sympathy from people wanting to share his grief.

After they had cleared Annie's possessions and settled her affairs, it was agreed that John should move back to The House, so his clothes and belongings were moved to the condominium. Jeff found himself wishing he too could move in with them and spent most of his free time there. However, John decided firstly to spend a couple of months with Annie's parents in Los Angeles and so once again Bob found himself alone, apart from visits from Jeff.

❧❧❧

Chapter eleven

Carolyn had indeed been at the concert in Manchester. She sat enthralled as Bob went through his set of numbers, clapping and cheering with the rest of the audience. She couldn't take her eyes of his dear face the whole time. He looked so brooding and serious, and she wished he would smile more. Even after all these years, Carolyn failed to miss the relevancy of the words of the songs. Now that she imagined he was in love, her mind could only take in the fact that he was singing to someone else, never dreaming she was the one in his mind and in his heart.

"Sometimes in the dead of night, I wake and wonder why, your name is still upon my lips, spoken like a sigh," he sang with heartbreaking sadness. Once again he introduced the song *Beautiful Girl*, saying "and this is for you my Darling, my beautiful girl."

She must be here somewhere, Carolyn reflected sadly. By the time Bob had left the stage and the theatre started to empty, she could hardly see through her tears. *Why do I torture myself so?* she thought. She stumbled out into the street and hailed a taxi to take her to the station, where she caught the train back to Liverpool and then home, oblivious to the panic she left behind at the theatre.

※

Another Christmas passed without any celebration. Carolyn spent Christmas Day again with her friends, but she put up no tree or decorations at home and was glad when the festive season came to an end.

She realised now that she should never have run away, but it was far too late to turn the clock back. She pondered, *I was miserable before, because of my jealousy over all the women, but at least he was still in my life. I've missed both my other darling boys getting married and I don't know if I have any nephews or nieces. I was loved and cared for. That would never have changed. Oh what have I done? All I have now are memories, and I'm so lonely and unhappy. If I hadn't been so weak and jealous, I could have still been with them. I could still have at least been a sister to all of them. Oh Robbie, I'd rather be your sister and friend than nothing at all.* The tears came again then, and she was so desperately sad she couldn't face work the following day so phoned the agency to take sick leave.

Another New Year passed and spring came. In New York Bob and Jeff were supporting John through the last stages of Annie's illness.

Carolyn spent weekends at her caravan in Anglesey and during the week continued to work for the agency doing temporary placements. In May of that year she found herself once again at the American import and export firm. The staff made her welcome and she herself was pleased to see the familiar faces. The people who worked in the office had long ago accepted the lovely, sad-faced girl. She was never spiteful or vindictive; always having a pleasant word for everyone. She was an enigma to them as she had never talked about her background or family.

Carolyn was surprised to find herself working for Mike Hughes. She had thought, after her previous time at the office, that she would be the last person he would request to work for him, so she felt she had to say something when she was first called into his office. "Mr. Hughes," she started.

"I think it's about time we dropped the formalities, Carolyn," he said.

"Okay, Mike." Carolyn nodded. "I feel I owe you some sort of an explanation, and I want to try to explain why I seemed so strange with you on my last assignment here. You see, it was absolutely nothing personal, but you remind me so much of someone I care about and that was what unnerved me. I lived in New York for ten years you see, and my family still lives there, but I don't see them anymore. I know it will sound strange to you, but one of them is black. Your colour, your voice and accent; even your mannerisms remind me of him. It just made me so sad."

This was the last thing Mike had imagined, and he was immediately sympathetic but still puzzled. "You say one of your family is black?" he questioned.

"Yes," she replied. "Someday I'll tell you the whole story, but you'll just have to make do with that for now."

"Just one more thing. What's his name and where does he fit into your family?" Mike asked.

Carolyn took a deep breath and replied, "I call him Robbie, and you could say he's my brother." *There*! She thought. *From now on that's what I have to remember he is.* She turned just before she left the office and sadly said, "I have three brothers, you see. Okay, only one of them had the same parents as me, but we always thought of each other as a family."

Mike was to remember this conversation a couple of weeks later when he was urgently called to the main office. Carolyn had apparently almost fainted, and was sitting in a chair with her head down, sobbing as if her heart would break.

"What on earth has happened?" he asked the other girls, who were trying to console the obviously very distressed Carolyn. One of the girls, Connie, showed him a newspaper photograph. It showed the three famous "Honeys" at a funeral. John Davidson was in the middle, looking gaunt and heartbroken. The funeral was that of his wife. Bob Maples and Jeff Simmonds were either side of him, holding him as if he would fall without their support.

Connie spoke first. "We were just saying how terribly sad this photo was, and how devastated and lost they all look. Then when Carolyn came to look at it she almost passed out. We just can't get her to talk. Do you think we should get a doctor?"

Mike stooped down and took Carolyn's hands in his. "Carolyn, what is it? If you don't tell us, we can't help you. What's the matter? What does the photograph mean to you?"

Through her sobs, Carolyn stuttered, "Mike, it's them. I should have been there. How could all that have been going on and I wasn't there for them. My poor John. Oh God, what can I do?"

Mike told the girls to help Carolyn into his office and sat her in a comfortable chair in the corner. "Someone make some tea or something please," he said. When the other staff had left the office, he once again stooped down and asked, "You said it's them; did you mean your brothers? Those three aren't brothers surely?"

Carolyn nodded. "They are, Mike. Oh, not in the biological sense, but that's how they think of each other. My name is Davidson not Davis, and John is my real brother. We met Robbie and Jeff soon after we arrived in New York. They had never had a family, and that's what we became. Its fifteen years since we all met, and those three have always been so close. I should have been there when they needed me. I might have been able to help. Oh God, just look at their faces in that photograph. I left them nearly five years ago, because of my jealousy and insecurity. The only person I considered was myself; I regret it so bitterly. What can I do?"

Mike was shocked at the revelation. "Well you should get in touch with your brother. You need to let him know you are here for him. You have no choice now. Do you have an address or phone number?" He asked.

Carolyn shook her head. "No, I did have an address, but since then John and Jeff have been married and Robbie has someone, so I think they must have moved. I used to send Christmas and Birthday cards but I don't anymore and I don't even know whether they ever received them, except…"

"Except what?" Mike asked. Carolyn told him of the note she had put in Robbie's card about not wearing dark glasses indoors.

"You know I've never seen him wearing them indoors since, so he may have had that card," she said seriously.

Mike couldn't help smiling. "In that case you have to try writing to John at that last address, and keep your fingers crossed. Do it to-day Carolyn; you can forget work, just type a letter and post it to-day. We could check out their Web site too."

Mike wasted no time in finding the Web site on the Internet, and sure enough there was a book of condolence for fans to leave messages to John. "What a lovely idea," Carolyn said. She didn't know what to type, but knew it had to be a personal message which he would understand if he ever saw it.

"Give our e-mail address here," said Mike; "otherwise you may find all sorts of weirdoes contacting you if you give an address or phone number."

She wrote, *"Dearest John, I heard about Annie and I am so very sorry. Do you need me? Love to my two scallies. Carolyn."* Mike was amused when he read the message over her shoulder. "Well," she commented. "At least he will definitely know it's from me."

Mike left her in his office to type a letter to John, which she found very difficult to do. The office junior was then sent to the Post Office to make sure the letter was sent that night. There was nothing more she could do. Carolyn was not to know that the sheer volume of letters and sympathy cards was so great, that John never actually received her letter. The note left on the Web-site was similarly overlooked. John was still in Los Angeles, and although he looked from time to time at the messages of condolence on the Web site, he failed to read the one from Carolyn.

When a month had passed with no reply to her letter, and no e-mail on Mike's computer, she was out of her mind with worry. "I just don't know how to contact them anymore. What can I do?" she asked Mike one day.

"Well" he said, "You are just gonna have to write to one of the others. Go on; sit down and get cracking. At least you will be doing something."

So the decision was made. She had to write to Robbie. This letter was even harder than the one she had written to John, but she knew she had no choice.

She wrote;

"*My darling Robbie, I read of the death of John's wife in the paper and I am desperate to contact him. I've written to him, and left a message on your Web-site but I've had no reply and I don't know what to do. Robbie, I'm so sorry I spoiled our special friendship. Can you ever forgive me? Not a day goes by when I don't think of you. I miss you so much. I don't know whether you will ever get this letter; but if you do and if any of you need me, just give a little whistle. My love always, Carolyn.*"

At the bottom of the page she typed her mobile phone number. As before, she wrote the last known address on the envelope and asked for it to be forwarded. She also added the personal code, which she remembered. Once again, the letter was taken to the Post Office, for mailing that evening.

Chapter twelve

It took three weeks for Carolyn's letter to reach Bob after being forwarded to the new 'House'. John was due home any day and Bob was looking forward to seeing him.

Seeing the writing on the envelope, with its Liverpool postmark, he couldn't wait to rip it open and read the letter. When he saw the telephone number at the bottom, he couldn't believe it. He could speak to her, hear her voice.

His hands were shaking as he dialled the number and whistled the old Jiminy Cricket tune gently into the phone. There was silence at the other end, then he heard,

"Robbie, is that you? Robbie, speak to me."

"Hi!" he managed after a long pause.

A sigh and then, "How are you Robbie?"

"Same as I've been for the past five years," he said.

"Oh God, Robbie, just to hear your voice; I can't believe it." There was a pause before Carolyn said, "Please tell me about John. How is he coping?"

Bob found his voice and said, "He's coming through it now. It's been a bad time for him and, yes love, he did and still does need you. Now for God's sake give me an address where we can find you. No more messing around, please."

She gave him her address in Wallasey. He sighed and took a deep breath of relief. *He knew where to find her, at last.*

"Tell me about Jeff; is he happy?" Carolyn asked.

"No baby," Bob sighed. He's miserable. He's trapped in an awful marriage. But that's a long story. Sufficient to say he needs you too."

"And you Robbie. Do you need me even a little bit?"

There was silence, then what sounded like a sob.

"Robbie?" Carolyn repeated.

In a hushed and fretful voice he said, "I need you most of all. I've missed you more than you'll ever know. I've missed you every minute, of every hour, of every single day for five years. Not a day has gone by when I haven't thought of you. Carolyn, I thought I was doing the right thing by you all those years ago. We need to talk, baby. Please let me come over and meet with you."

"You know where I am now," she said.

Again there was silence for a moment before he said, "I'll make arrangements and come as quickly as I can. I'll phone you again soon."

Bob quickly phoned John in Los Angeles. "Sorry bro, I'm not gonna be here when you come home, but I know you'll forgive me when I tell you the reason. I know where she is, and I'm gonna try to bring her home."

John was beside himself with joy. "Oh thank God, Bob. Don't mess it up, will you."

Bob was puzzled. "What do you mean John?"

John sighed. "This is your chance mate; you know you two should have always been together. Just tread carefully and bring her home."

Bob asked, "You mean I'd have your blessing?"

"God, Bob, there's no-one I'd rather see with my sister." John laughed. "You are the only man I would trust her with, knowing how you feel about her. I know you would always cherish her like no-body else ever could."

Bob was touched and delighted by his friend's faith in him. "I'll just have to play it by ear, John. After all I don't know what I'm going to find. She could be living with someone, married, or have commitments." He called Jeff, who was equally delighted by the news, to ask him to keep an eye on John in his absence.

Carolyn sat for a good ten minutes with the phone still in her hand. She was going to see him, talk to him. He had said he needed her. When she had composed herself she went to Mike's office. "It's Robbie; he's phoned, and he's coming over to see me," she said breathlessly.

"Result!" Mike smiled. "Pardon me if I'm totally out of order here, but judging by the expression on your face, those aren't exactly sisterly thoughts you're having."

Carolyn shrugged. "They're going to have to be, Mike. You see, through my jealousy I lost everything. At least he said he's missed me and needs me. That has to be enough for now. If he'll accept me back as his sister, I can live with that. I'll have to."

Carolyn was packed off home. She bustled around the House cleaning, tidying and making up the bed in the spare room. Bob had given her no indication when he would be coming and she sat on the edge of her chair with her mobile phone in her hand waiting for it to ring. She had just decided to go to bed when he phoned.

"Darlin', I've booked a regular, scheduled flight from New York to London and then one to Liverpool. Unless there are delays, I should be at John Lennon Airport by mid-day to-morrow. I'll phone you when I land. Will you book me into a hotel please?"

Carolyn was breathless with joy. Her heart was hammering in her chest, and she was sure he could hear it. "Robbie, I'll meet you at Liverpool Airport, and you're not staying at any hotel; you're staying with me. I'll see you to-morrow. I'll be there at noon." She spun round and round in the room, hugging herself; her face a picture of joy. "I will! I'll see him tomorrow!" It just seemed too good to be true.

She rose at the crack of dawn and made a cottage pie with grated cheese on top. Her cottage pie had always been one of Robbie's favourites in the old days.

She couldn't decide what to wear, and changed four times before she decided to dress casually in jeans and a pretty lemon-coloured sleeveless blouse. One last look around the room, to make sure everything was ready. The cottage pie was in the oven on a low light and the table was laid. Next time she came home, Robbie would be with her. The journey to the airport would take about an hour, but there was no way she was going to be late, so dead on half past ten Carolyn jumped in her car and set off.

Sure enough, Carolyn was early and stood around hopping from foot to foot waiting for the time to pass. The internal flight from London was on time and at twelve noon Carolyn was standing at the barrier, her eyes glued on the passengers trooping through.

At first she thought he had missed the flight and her heart was heavy, then suddenly he came around the corner into her sight. Their eyes never left each other as he walked towards her, passing through the barriers. Then he dropped his bags and she was in his arms. Not a word was spoken; they clung to each other as if frightened the other would disappear. He leant back and they gazed at each other; Carolyn taking in every detail of his face. He had hardly changed, except for looking a little older; there were worry lines where there used to be laughter lines. He had grown a moustache and closely-clipped goatee which suited him. He was still her Robbie; so tall, so handsome.

Bob saw the same beautiful girl he remembered and had loved for so long. Her face hadn't altered and she'd grown her lovely, chestnut-brown hair to shoulder length. He wanted to stroke it and run his fingers through it. Her emerald green eyes were awash with tears.

He realised that he too was weeping and they clung to each other again.

"Can we get out of here, Darlin'?" he asked. In a daze, Carolyn paid the parking fee and led him across the road to the car. They tossed Bob's bags in the back and climbed in. "So, my girl is drivin' now," he smiled.

Carolyn giggled. "Well it was needs must. I had to learn to be independent."

Somehow, the years of separation did not exist. They slipped back into the old comfortable companionship as if they had seen each other only yesterday. On the drive home, Bob told Carolyn of Annie's long and bravely fought battle against her illness. He told her about Nicole and her seemingly hypnotic hold over Jeff. He tried to put into words how lonely he had been and how much he had missed her.

"When I said on the phone that I was the same as I've been every day for five years, I meant just as miserable and lonely. The sunshine went out of my life when you left, Carolyn."

Carolyn did not want to break the spell of this lovely time, so instead of asking Bob about his new girlfriend, she told him about her work, the caravan and how she had tried to make a new life for herself.

She parked the car in the drive and ushered him into the living room. Take your bags upstairs. You are in the back bedroom next to the bathroom. There's hot water so just come down when you're ready and we'll have something to eat."

Bob did as he was told, but shook his head as he came back downstairs. *All this small talk,* he thought. *We're skirting around each other like strangers.*

They sat at the kitchen table and Carolyn served up the cottage pie, which Bob ate as if he hadn't eaten for a week. "Slow down, Robbie, there's plenty more," she laughed.

"Oh Caro, I can't remember when I enjoyed anything so much. You know, in a lot of ways I wish we could just turn the clock back and be sitting round the table in Cobble Hill. They were happy days weren't they, Darlin'?"

Carolyn smiled sadly. "I wish I had a pound for every time I've thought along those lines; both before I left and since I've been here on my own."

As they washed up together, Bob put his arms around her. "Please Darlin', just turn round and look at me. We really have to talk."

"Here it comes," Carolyn thought. "Now he's going to tell me about her, and I'm going to have to pretend to be pleased for him or I will lose him altogether again. I'm not going to let that happen."

Just then the phone rang and Carolyn rushed into the living room to answer it. "Hi, Mike. Yes he's here and everything's fine. Oh, that's great, thank you. See you Monday then."

Bob had followed her, and with his heart in his mouth asked, "Boyfriend?"

"Boss," Carolyn replied. "He said I can have to-morrow off, so I don't have to go into work until Monday. I don't have a boyfriend." Bob had been holding his breath since Carolyn had answered the phone; now he exhaled noisily in relief.

"Robbie, when are you going to tell me about your girlfriend?" Carolyn asked now, with a heavy heart.

"What girlfriend? Do you know something I don't know, baby?" Bob queried.

"The one you keep dedicating songs to. I saw the concert at Madison Square Gardens. I was at Manchester too, when you dedicated *Beautiful Girl* to her."

Bob closed his eyes and put his head back, taking a deep breath. "Carolyn, come here and listen to me. No, don't interrupt," he added as she started to speak. "I have to tell you all this while I have the courage. By the way, I saw you on the CCTV at Manchester, but you'd gone by the time I ran out of the theatre. You were crying, Darlin'. Was that why? Because you thought I was with someone?" Carolyn bit her lip and nodded.

"Right," he started. "Here goes! Carolyn, think back to that first song. Who do you think was my Beautiful Girl? I wrote that song for you. Do you really mean you never had any idea how I felt about you? I love you more than I can ever say, my Darling. I've always loved you; almost from the first day I met you."

The sparkle came back into Carolyn's eyes, as she smiled joyfully up at him. *He loves me.*

"Haven't you ever listened to any of my songs? Every one was dedicated to you. Those words came from my heart. I've got to explain about that last day. You will never know how hard it was for me to push you away. All those years I looked after you and protected you, not just from other men, but from myself. The number of times, I wanted to hold you, kiss you, make love to you, but I couldn't. The night John asked us to stay, all those years ago, Jeff and I both made a vow to always respect and take care of you. Oh, but for years I loved you so much, Carolyn. I didn't have any idea you felt the same way until that last day. I didn't think I was good enough for you. You deserved so much more. I wanted you to have a nice life, with a respectable white man and live in a nice suburban house with two or three nice white children. I wanted you to be happy, Darlin', and all these years that's how I've tried to imagine you, and yet all the time a little bit of me died every time I thought of you with someone else. But I had to give you that chance." He paused and took a deep breath. "Did you move on, Caro? Have you been happy?"

All the time he had been talking, one of Carolyn's hands had crept around the back of his neck. The other caressed his face whilst her eyes stared into his, no longer hiding the depth of her feelings from him.

"Not for one single day," she cried. "Oh Robbie, I've always loved you too. I've never stopped loving you." Carolyn smiled through her tears. "Are we stupid or what? All those wasted years, Robbie; I should have had the right to decide for myself."

"Yes, you should. I knew that after you'd left. That was the worst day of my life; when I realised it was my fault you'd gone. Can you ever forgive me for what I said on that day? I knew if I'd been stronger we could have been together; especially when John released me from that vow and both boys said they would have supported us. As it was, I made everyone's life hell."

"Those dedications, by the way." Bob smiled. You must realise by now they were for you. I even whistled our message at that concert, but you didn't come."

Carolyn explained how she had mistaken the meaning of the songs, and in fact had not heard his whistle. "Robbie, I thought you'd fallen in love with someone. It was like losing you all over again. I was so miserable, my brain just didn't function properly."

He put his hands either side of her face, his thumbs caressing her eyes, her cheeks and mouth. "I love you so much, Caro."

She smiled, "I love you too."

Their first kiss was magical; his lips covering hers, lightly at first, becoming more demanding and passionate. Carolyn's heart leapt with joy as she melted in his arms.

As if by mutual consent, they sank down onto the sheepskin rug in front of the fire. Time had no meaning. Nothing else mattered as he carefully undressed her, and then quickly pulled off his own jeans and shorts. His kisses rained over her eyes and face; trailing down her neck. He was so gentle and tender, her senses reeled; she felt lifted onto another plain. He marvelled at her breasts as his lips and tongue played with her nipples. His hands did wonderful things as they parted her legs, his fingers stroking her like an act of worship as he made sure she was ready for him. Then he was inside her and they were moving together. She climaxed and so did he; both calling each other's names in joy and love.

"Oh Robbie," she sighed. "I never knew it could be like that."

"You okay, my love?" he asked, holding her to him and kissing her nose.

"Oh yes, much more than okay," she smiled. "Let's go to bed and do it again."

They both started to laugh, all the tension and unhappiness in both of them evaporating with the sound of their laughter. Still giggling, she pulled his T-shirt over his head before they ran up the stairs, holding tightly to each other. "Robbie, you've still got your socks on," Carolyn spluttered as he dragged off one sock and then the other, before picking her up and depositing her onto the bed.

This time Robbie's kisses were more urgent, as his mouth moved from her lips to her neck, sucking her ear lobes; his tongue licking her skin and tasting the sweetness of her. She moaned with pleasure as his fingers moved gently from her shoulders, down her spine to grip her hips whilst his lips moved to her breasts, arousing her nipples until she was nearly screaming with delight. She wrapped her legs around him as he entered her and her orgasm was so strong she felt as though the earth really did move. As he felt her climax he let his own orgasm take him to heights he had never experienced before.

Sometime later Carolyn noticed the tattoo on his breast, which spelt out her name over the outline of Brooklyn Bridge. "When did you have that done Robbie?" she gasped.

"About a year after you left, Darlin'. I was just feeling so miserable. I was passing this tattoo parlour and thought I'd have it done."

"Did no-one ever notice it?" she enquired.

Bob nodded, "Oh yeah; a number of ladies."

"I don't know that I'm going to like this. What did you tell them?" she ventured.

"He smiled into her eyes. "I told them it was the lost love of my life. Somehow it acted as a spur. They all thought they could be the one to replace you, but no-one could ever do that. There was never any room for anyone in my heart but you, girl. One day we can talk about those five years, but for now, the past is the past and we have the future to think of."

"No, Robbie," Carolyn argued. "I need to tell you about those men you thought I was sleeping with in America."

"What do you mean, 'thought'?" Bob asked.

Carolyn looked sheepishly at him. "I never did. I mean, I just wanted to make you jealous. I just pretended I was sleeping around, but I wasn't."

Bob looked bemused "You were trying to make me jealous? Well you sure succeeded, girl. Oh, Carolyn, you mean that last day, I could have been the first?"

The rest came out in one long breath. "Yes Robbie, but that's not all. I've only done it twice since with the same person and I didn't like it. It hurt and there was no pleasure in it for me. I really didn't know how wonderful it could be. So you see you are the first as far as I'm concerned."

Bob shook his head and smiled through his tears. "Oh, as John would say, you really are a one off, my beautiful, darling girl. I love you so much."

Practically she muttered, "Should I be concerned after all those women, Robbie?"

He laughed "If you mean what I think, Darlin', I've always been very careful. You're quite safe."

Carolyn kissed the corners of his mouth. "When you say '*DAHLIN*' it's like a caress. It's wonderful." Her fingers touched his collarbone and traced the path across his skin, first explored all those years ago. She felt the pulse throbbing in his throat and kissed it, nuzzling his neck under his chin and sighing. "Do you know; you have the sexiest clavicle. Last time I did that you ended up throwing me across the room. I always wanted to bury my face in your throat; nuzzle it and kiss your neck. Your throat is like a magnet to my eyes. Stop laughing and lay still."

Bob tried to put on a serious expression. "Carolyn if you had one wish what would it be?"

"Oh, that's easy," she sighed. "To always be with you for the rest of our lives, and never to be separated again."

"Caro, do you think…" He stammered.

"What, Robbie? Come on. Spit it out," she replied.

"I always imagined doing this on Brooklyn Bridge, but what the hell!" He jumped out of the bed, naked as the day he was born, and knelt at the side clasping her hand in his. "Will you marry me, my dearest love?"

"Oh yes, yes, yes," she said, throwing herself into his arms.

"Do you really think we can do it? Can it really happen; you and me married?" he said.

Carolyn looked into his eyes and smiled. "Why shouldn't it? We've wasted all these years; let's not waste any more time."

Bob held her closely to his chest. "Caro, I swear to you that I will never knowingly hurt you. I will spend every day for the rest of my life making you happy, but promise me you will never, ever leave me again."

She kissed him gently. "Robbie, wild horses won't get me away from you now I know you love me. I swear I'll never ever leave you."

"No more loneliness," he sighed. "Sounds like a good title for a song. Okay; let's do it. I don't want to wait. How soon can we get married?"

"I don't know my love, but I know someone who will know," she said, quickly getting dressed. She phoned Anne, who was a Registrar of Births, Marriages and Deaths, and who would able to give her the information she needed. "I'm getting married Anne, and I need to know how to go about it."

Anne gasped. "That was quick, I only saw you last week and you hadn't met anyone. You were still going on about Robbie."

"Yes well, you will never believe it, but he is actually here and we want to get married."

Anne was delighted and happy for her friend. She told her that anyone subject to immigration control would need to make initial arrangements through a designated office, the nearest one being Liverpool. They no longer would need a special license, but he would have to live here for seven days before making arrangements, and they could then be married sixteen days later. There was nothing to stop them getting married in Wallasey, and in fact, Anne said she would be delighted to marry them herself. That meant they could be married in three weeks.

They phoned John and Carolyn sat, biting her lip, as Bob explained that she was there with him. "There's someone here who wants to talk to you, Bro," he said as he passed the phone to Carolyn.

"John, can you ever forgive me?" she asked, her voice shaking. "I'm so sorry for giving you all that heartache and for not being with you when you needed me. I wish I could have met your Annie, and been there to support you. Oh, John, please say you understand and aren't too cross with me."

John was completely overjoyed to talk again to his adored sister. "Carolyn, my dear, dear girl; all I care about is that you are here, at the end of a phone, talking to me. I have so much to ask you. Where have you been? What have you been doing? Please come home, Carolyn. It would make me so happy to see you."

"I'll explain everything, dear. I am coming home, John, in about three weeks. I've got some sorting out to do here first. There's something we both want to tell you. Robbie and I are going to get married. Here have a word with him," she said, passing the phone to Bob.

John was so happy for them both, he could hardly speak. Finding his voice, he said "Bob, mate, this is a very happy day for all of us. We are going to be a family again. You know what this means, don't you? You will actually be my brother-in-law." They laughed happily together.

Next they phoned Jeff, who broke down when he heard her voice. "I've missed you so much, Mom." he said.

"Going away was the most selfish thing I have ever done," she told him. I should have been there for all of you, but I promise I will somehow make it up to you."

※※※※

Chapter thirteen

The next few weeks passed in a flurry of activity. Carolyn resigned from the agency and gave Mike's firm notice of her intentions to leave. One of the girls at the office, June, was getting married in a few months and asked Carolyn about the possibility of taking over the lease on her house. After some formalities with the Landlord, this was arranged. June was happy to take all the furniture and fittings, so Carolyn was saved the hassle of having to empty the house. She left at the end of the week, promising to call and see everyone before the wedding.

Carolyn took Bob to stay at the Caravan where she was able to show him her "Thinking Rock," and take him on some of her previously lonely walks. She introduced him to Irene and they all shared a meal, laughing together as Irene recounted the numerous times she had listened to Carolyn talking about "her Robbie." They invited her to the wedding, and spent a happy time discussing their arrangements and telling Irene about their plans for their life together.

The three of them decided to keep the caravan to use when they were in England. Irene would let it out or use it as she wished whilst they were in America. Money was not a problem now, so they could send any necessary ground rent over regularly. After discussion between themselves, they asked Irene if she would like to have

Carolyn's car as a gift when they left for America. She was touched and pleased to accept.

※

All the arrangements had been made for the wedding, with paperwork sorted for Bob between the American Embassy in Liverpool and the Register Office. Anne took Carolyn shopping in Liverpool to buy an outfit for the wedding. As she only intended to get married once, she decided on a traditional wedding dress. She chose a strapless oyster-coloured satin gown, with a skirt that fell straight to the floor from underneath a ruched bust accented by rhinestones. She bought a small spray of silk flowers for her hair. To complete the ensemble, she found a pair of plain, oyster-coloured satin shoes with stiletto heels, which perfectly complimented the dress.

When they went to the jewellers to choose wedding rings, Robbie surprised her. "I want you to have an engagement ring, darlin'. You can have whichever one you like."

The jeweller brought out tray after tray of expensive rings. There were huge diamonds and other precious stones, but the one that caught Carolyn's eye was a diamond ring in the shape of a daisy. Each petal was a separate diamond shaped around the main stone. Her eyes sparkled like the stones in the ring as she slipped it on her finger to try.

"Robbie, can I have this one, please? Look how it shines. I love it."

Robbie smiled lovingly, cocking his head to one side. "Caro, wouldn't you like a bigger stone. I said you can have any one you want, and of course you can, but there are some much fancier ones here."

Carolyn shook her head. "No, I don't want a fancier one. Some of these are far too big and gaudy for my taste. I'd be afraid to wear them. Please, can I have this one? It was made for me and it even fits."

"Of course you can, my darling, if that's what you want. If you're happy, I'm happy." They chose their wedding rings and left the shop holding hands, giggling like a pair of teenagers.

That evening, Robbie booked a special meal for them at a local restaurant. Leaning over the table, he took her left hand in his, placing the engagement ring on her finger. "Now, we're officially engaged, my love, and very soon we'll be married. Please don't ever stop loving me, Carolyn. I could never cope without you now."

"That will never happen, Robbie. You are everything in the world to me. I'm the happiest girl in the whole world."

※

Carolyn called in to see Mike and the other people at the office where she was delighted to be presented with cards and a huge bouquet of flowers. Only Mike knew who "Robbie" really was, but all the staff made a fuss of her, admiring her engagement ring. Everyone wanted details of her wedding dress and future plans. She didn't know how to start to thank Mike for all his help and sympathy, but she did extract a promise from both him and Pat Owen that they would contact her when they went home to New York. They were both given a number to ring and a code to quote to ensure she would receive the message. In the meantime, she invited both of them to the wedding.

She took Bob on a tour of the Liverpool waterfront, visiting Albert Dock with all its quaint shops and museum and then to Cavern Walks and other tourist spots made famous by the Beatles. She pointed out to him the lovely skyline of the Cunard Buildings and Liver Buildings with the two huge, stone Liver birds on top. The birds are chained down, as folklore has it that if the Liver birds fly away Liverpool will cease to exist. They visited the old offices of the White Star Line, where the Titanic was registered and where people queued waiting for news of the fateful sinking. Everywhere they went, Bob was amazed how friendly and helpful people were. Although he was recognised on a few occasions, despite his sunglasses and baseball cap, people were good-natured and chatty without interfering with their tour.

The next day, Robbie asked Carolyn to show him her old home, where she and John had such a happy childhood. They drove to Prenton, past Tranmere Rovers Football Ground; where on Saturdays during her youth, the roar of the crowd would reverberate around the area. "Dad would always complain that he could never find a space to park the car when there was a match, because people used to park all along our road," she laughed, remembering. She turned into a terraced road and slowed the car down. "Do you see that school? When I was ill or off school myself for any reason, I used to listen to the children playing in the yard at break-time. Wherever I am now, if I close my eyes and remember, those are the two sounds that bring my childhood back to me; the roar of the football crowd and the children laughing and shouting in the schoolyard."

She stopped the car and pointed over the road. "That's our house, Robbie. Oh gosh, it doesn't look any different. They've still got Mum's hydrangeas either side of the door and they're in bloom. She was so proud of them." The door and windows had recently been decorated, and the emerald green paintwork, catching the sunlight, looked bright and cheerful. There were sparkling white nets at the windows and the red stone steps had been scrubbed until they shone.

Carolyn sighed, sadly. "I'm so glad you asked me to bring you here, Robbie. I didn't think I'd be able to face it, but it was such a happy house until that terrible accident and I'll be able to think of it now without just remembering the bad times."

Bob hugged her and smiled. "I'm so glad you shared this with me, baby. I can see you and John here when you were kids, and imagine what it was like. However, that curtain keeps twitching. I think the present occupier is wondering why these strange people are parked opposite their house starin' at it. I think we should make ourselves scarce before we get asked to move on."

They both giggled as Carolyn started the engine and they drove back to Wallasey, stopping the car on New Brighton Promenade for a short time to watch the waves beating against the embankment.

Bob took her in his arms, holding her closely. She put her head back and looked lovingly into his eyes. "Robbie Maples, you are so special. I am a very lucky girl."

He shook his head and he sighed. "Carolyn, I'm so afraid that you are going to turn around one day and realise that I'm not so special. Why are you laughing, girl?"

"Because, my love, you will always be special to me. You'll always be my Robbie, and nothing will ever change that."

∽∽∽

Bob had one commitment to fulfil in London; a charity concert, which had been arranged for some time and was at the Royal Albert Hall. This raised the discussion as to why he was doing solo concerts. He explained that this had arisen due to the other two men being "off the planet" for the past twelve months.

Carolyn was not impressed. "No, I'm sorry, but this is wrong. You three have always been a team. You need to get them to pull together again."

Bob shook his head. "Things have drifted Caro. We are still close, but I've needed to work to keep sane. "I suppose they've both had too many other things on their minds. You really have no idea how bad things have been, baby. Perhaps now you're back, we can pull the old firm back together."

Carolyn pulled a face. "Robbie, has all this been my fault? I can't help feeling responsible when you tell me how unhappy you've all been. Oh God, Robbie, I really was only thinking of myself when I left you all. It's a wonder you don't all hate me."

Bob put his hands on her shoulders and sighed. "Baby, no-one could have foreseen what was gonna happen. Jeff may still have married Nicole. Okay..." he laughed as Carolyn shook her head crossly. I know you'd probably have had something to say about it, but at the end of the day, it was his decision. As for Annie dying, Caro. Surely you can't be blaming yourself for that too? You've always told me you thought our fate was mapped out for us, and I think you're right. We were meant to be together, and now we are. So stop all this self-recrimination, honey, and let me see that lovely smile again.

Carolyn travelled down to London with him, where they had been booked into a hotel. *What a difference from last time,* she thought. *Now we are together, and neither of us need ever be miserable again.*

At the sound check that afternoon, Bob introduced her to Harry as "his girl." Although always courteous and efficient, Harry was definitely cool with her. He had seen so many other girls with Bob. However, after a while he detected the difference in the way Bob was acting. He smiled and laughed a lot. Harry realised he had never seen him like this; he actually seemed happy.

The penny eventually dropped and Harry asked, "It's her, isn't it?"

Bob laughed. "It certainly is, Harry. Will you look after her for me while I'm busy?"

Harry agreed, so he and Carolyn watched the concert together. He was amused when she linked her arm through his as they stood watching the show. It had been a complete sell-out and she was so proud of her Robbie. The songs now held certain poignancy as she listened to the words. Only Harry and Carolyn noticed that the heartbreak was missing from his voice. After the show, the pair asked Harry to stay in England until after the wedding so he would be able to be there.

Carolyn watched Robbie as he talked to fans and other visitors back stage. He was composed and smiling; holding conversations with all these people as if he had been in the public domain all his life. He excused himself to join her when he saw her watching him.

"What is it, baby, you look so serious? He said putting his arms around her. Closing his eyes, he put his head back with a sigh. "Oh, just to have you here. If you only knew what that means to me."

She kissed his neck and nuzzled her face under his chin. His arms tightened around her so that she felt breathless. "You would tell me if there was something wrong, wouldn't you?" he asked.

"Oh Robbie, it's just that you are so confident now; so self-assured and, well, grown up. I'm frightened you will realise that you don't really need me. Are you sure this is what you want?"

He kissed the tip of her nose. "Baby, I have never been more sure of anything in my life. Nothing is more important to me than you. I'll never have to pretend with you. I can be completely myself, because you know me better than anyone in the world. Remember, you're my Jiminy Cricket, girl". They both smiled at his reference to Carolyn's story about "Give a little whistle" all those years ago.

※

The last night in the House together before moving out, they lay and held each other closely while they made plans for the future.

"I never knew I could be so happy, Robbie. I thought a loving marriage was never going to happen for me. Who would ever have thought that things could change so much in just a few short weeks. I love you so very much."

Bob smiled tenderly into her eyes. "I want us always to be as happy as we are now. To always have this wonderful feeling. This love we have is so special. I promise you, I will always try to keep you as happy as you are to-day and to never knowingly hurt you."

"Robbie, tell me one thing." Carolyn asked.

"Anything my love," he replied.

"Feeling how you did about me, how did you manage to keep your hands to yourself for all those years?"

Bob roared with laughter. "Oh Carolyn, don't ever change, my darling. You could always make me laugh. Well, in answer to your question; my love for you has been all consuming for most of my adult life but somehow I used a lot of self-control. Remember that piggy- back? Your thighs were around my back, your arms around my neck and your lips whispering hot air down my ear. You didn't know what you were doing to me, girl."

"Oh, you are a lovely man, Robert Maples. I'm so lucky. Don't you ever change either," Carolyn laughed.

෴

They had booked a suite at the Crowne Plaza Hotel in Liverpool, where Bob stayed the night before the wedding. As a surprise for Carolyn, both John and Jeff had flown over to meet him and were already booked in at the hotel. Theirs was a joyous reunion, as the knowledge that they would see their dear Carolyn the next day was a wonderful healer. John and Jeff felt more positive and happy than they had for some time.

Carolyn was staying at Anne's house and early the next morning, John phoned her on his cell phone to wish her happiness. "I'm so sorry I can't be there with you, sweetheart. I would have loved to be able to give you away, but I'm sure you'll understand how busy I am. It's just not been possible to leave here."

John was mortified when Carolyn started to cry. "Of course I understand, especially after the way I've let you down. It's okay, really it is."

John muttered, "Alright love, I'll be thinking of you both." He turned to the other men and sighed. "Bad idea, lads! Now she thinks I don't care, and I've made her cry on what should be the happiest day of her life."

There was only one thing for it. A taxi was arranged to take John through the Mersey Tunnel to Anne's house.

"You'll have a couple of hours with her before she needs to leave," Bob told him. "Just make sure she's smiling when I get to the Register Office. We'll keep Jeff in reserve; at least we can still surprise her."

When John arrived at Anne's house he found Carolyn still in her housecoat, with her two other friends, Irene and Sue, having her hair put up in a sweeping style. When John was shown into the room she nearly fainted with shock.

"John, is it really you? Oh John..." she shouted as she threw herself into his arms.

He smiled into her eyes. "Did you really think I could stay away? Oh Carolyn, how could I not be here to give you away? Who else could do that?"

Carolyn was so proud to introduce her lovely brother to the girls.

They sat and talked for over an hour. John was able to tell her a little of Annie and how sad a time it had been.

"I wish you could have met Annie, Caro; you would have liked each other. We weren't together very long, but I loved her. She was such a good person and so brave, even when she knew she wasn't going to get better. All she worried about was how her parents and I would cope after she was gone. She left me a letter saying how happy she had been with me. She said I shouldn't give up hope of finding you. Annie was very fond of Jeff and Bob too; especially Bob. He used to sit and talk to her. He was with us when she died. Carolyn, I honestly don't know what I would have done without those lads. They have been so good to me and it's their strength that saw me through."

"Oh John, you'll never know how badly I feel about not being with you. I know Annie and I would have been friends. She sounds lovely and I'm so sorry you had to lose her. Was Jeff's wife any help whilst she was ill?" Carolyn asked.

"Nicole? No! Nicole said she didn't like to be around sick people, so she just stayed away. Annie was always uncomfortable with her anyway. Nicole had this way of making her feel inadequate and insecure. I know you would have liked Annie, but I'm not so sure you'll like Nicole, Sis."

Carolyn frowned and pulled a face. "I'll be ready when I do meet her. Don't you worry about that, John."

Very soon it was time for Carolyn to re-do her make-up and put her gown on. When John saw her he couldn't help shed a tear.

He sighed. "You were always beautiful, Caro, but I don't ever remember seeing you as beautiful as you look to-day."

"Let's hope my Darling thinks the same," Carolyn laughed.

Then it was time to leave. John and Carolyn sat in the back of the limousine, holding hands all the way to the Town Hall. Anne, Sue and Irene had driven ahead so that Anne could sort out the formalities.

Carolyn's other friends arrived; Helen, Jackie, Carol, Mike and Pat and were introduced; then there he was, her darling Robbie. He looked so handsome in a pale grey suit with a buttonhole in his lapel and a huge smile on his face. Behind him was Harry, an equally big grin adorning his face.

"Any regrets, Darlin'?" he asked, spinning her round.

"Only one," she sighed. "I wish Jeff could have been here. That would have made everything perfect; the icing on the cake."

"Just as well I decided he couldn't get married without me as Best Man then," a voice at her shoulder said.

She threw herself into Jeff's arms. "I can't believe it. First John and now you. I think I've died and gone to heaven."

Jeff put his head back and laughed with joy at seeing his beloved "Mom" again. Just then Anne appeared at the door to ask them all to go into the Wedding Room. Everyone entered except Carolyn and John who then walked in to the strains of the wedding march.

The ceremony passed in a daze. Here she was marrying the love of her life and her darling brother and "other brother" were here with them. What could be more perfect?

The girls made sure plenty of photographs were taken both in the wedding room and on the grand staircase at the Town Hall. They had booked a sit-down dinner in a private room at a local hotel.

It was only when they were all sitting down chatting that Carolyn noticed how gaunt and pale Jeff looked. Once again she felt guilty for having not been there for him, and vowed to herself that she would help him try to sort things out with this Nicole woman when she went back to New York.

With lots of tears and promises to keep in touch, Carolyn and her new husband, together with John, Jeff and Harry, climbed into the limousine which took them to the hotel in Liverpool.

That night in their hotel room, the lovers lay entwined in each other's arms going over the surprises and other events of the day. "How on earth did you keep that to yourself? I hadn't a clue John and Jeff were over here. That was the best wedding present you could have planned. This is the happiest day of my life. I want to always feel just as I do today and I want you always to look at me the way you looked when you saw me in my wedding dress. I love you so much, Robbie."

Looking into his beloved's eyes, he kissed the tip of her nose and said "I'll try to make sure you're always this happy. I've heard couples say this feeling doesn't last for too long, but I'm gonna make darn sure it does for us. As for looking at you the way I did to-day; my Darling, you have always been the most beautiful girl in the world to me and you always will be. You are my life and I adore you."

Some time later, Bob passed Carolyn a piece of paper. "This is another wedding present. It's not quite finished yet, and I have to work with John on the tune, but I wanted you to see it to-day."

Bob had written a song called *No More Loneliness*. Underneath the title he had written,

"To my Darling Carolyn on our Wedding Day".

The lonely years have passed my love, and we are here as one.
We never again will feel the hurt and sorrow of being alone.
Today two hearts united forever; two halves became a whole.
You will always be my everything; my body and my soul.

No-one can know how I have missed your lovely face, your smiles.
Your laughing eyes have haunted my dreams from far across the miles.
But now we will be together, forever come what may.
I promise you will never have to cry or regret this day.
For I will love you 'til the end of my life;
My Dearest love, my darling wife.

෧෧෧෧෧

PART THREE

2003

NEW BEGINNINGS

Chapter fourteen

It was a very different Carolyn who travelled back to New York with her new husband and their brothers. This Carolyn was stronger and far more confident than she had ever been before. She was secure in the knowledge that she was loved by the man she adored, and felt she could face anything. Bob, too, had changed almost overnight from the unhappy, lonely, embittered man he had become. He, also, had gained in confidence. Now he was calm, happy, contented and couldn't wipe the smile off his face. After all, his wildest dreams had come true and he had married the love of his life; his darling girl.

Before they had left the hotel, a courier had brought them a package containing a small album of their wedding photographs, which Anne had printed off on her computer. John had booked them first class from London Heathrow, so their flight was comfortable and happy and seemed to pass quickly. Carolyn was delighted with the luxury, which was a far cry from her previous experience of flying. She chatted away to the other passengers, who were amused by her and delighted to be travelling with the famous Honeys.

The three men went to the lounge for a drink, leaving Carolyn to watch a film. She was just nodding off when she found Jeff sitting alongside her. She had been waiting for a chance to talk to him alone, and was pleased he had taken the initiative. He took her hand in both of his and smiled at her. "How's my best girl? I've missed you, Mom."

Carolyn smiled back at him. "I know, Jeff, and I've missed you too. I meant it when I said I realise how selfish I've been. I was only thinking of myself. My jealousy and insecurity only made everyone miserable. I promise I'm going to make it up to you somehow."

Jeff shook his head. "No darlin', it hasn't been your fault; none of it's been your fault. Everyone has to be responsible for their own actions and mistakes, and I've just made one mistake after another. You know you were right that time when you said home was Cobble Hill. I've never been happy since we left that house. You know what I've missed nearly as much as you? The laughter! All the laughter seemed to disappear when you did. Instead, came the fame, the fortune and Nicole. Somehow none of it was as important."

"Oh Jeff," Carolyn said. "At least if I'd been there, you could have talked to me. I should have been there for you. I've only got to look at you to see what a horrible time you've had. Tell me about Nicole, Jeff."

He gave a mirthless laugh. "Well, I think I did love her once, Honey. We're still together, but I'm not sure why. Every time I suggest that we separate, she gets vindictive and threatens to take me for every penny. She doesn't love me, but she loves being married to a celebrity. She adores the parties, the publicity and the money. I know she has lovers. She doesn't really hide it any more. I haven't exactly been faithful either, but I think I've had every excuse. I just don't know what to do. I just don't seem to have the courage to make that final stand."

Robbie had told Carolyn most of this, but she was still horrified to see how her big, strong Jeff had become a puppet in the hands of this woman. "Jeff, dear, the money doesn't matter. A good lawyer will iron that out, but even if she took your last sixpence, surely peace of mind is more important. Dump her, sweetheart and come home to us."

"Oh Honey" Jeff smiled, "No-one has ever been able to make me smile the way you do. We could always laugh together, couldn't we? I have a couple of confessions to make, whilst I have you to myself. I've been drinking far too much. I mean, really far too much, but I promise I'll do something about it now you are back. The other thing is; and I feel guiltier about this than anything; I have sort of dabbled in cocaine."

Carolyn was appalled. "Oh Jeff, what do you mean sort of dabbled? Are you an addict?"

Jeff shook his head, "No, baby, and do you know why? I was tempted, believe me, darlin', but I could see your face begging me never to take drugs, and that's what stopped me. I haven't touched any charlie for months, and I vow to you here and now that I never will again."

Carolyn sighed with relief. "We've got to get you away from her Jeff, before she destroys you.

No-one hurts one of my boys this way. That woman's got a shock coming; she hasn't met your secret weapon yet." Jeff put his head back and laughed, properly, for the first time he could remember.

"You'll see, Jeff," Carolyn continued, "We'll all find the happiness again we had at Cobble Hill. I'm going to make sure of it."

Jeff nodded. "I believe you can do it, Honey, but please beware of Nicole. She is not a nice person, believe me. It's so wonderful to see you two so happy and I don't want anything to spoil that. You have no idea what he was like when he found you'd gone. He never stopped loving you, you know?"

Before long the pilot announced that they would be landing in around half an hour. Carolyn was able to watch the descent from the window. Bob had returned to his seat and held onto her hand as she excitedly waited for the plane to come to a halt. Soon they were preparing to go through the Immigration control. Because they had only just been married, Carolyn's passport was still in the name of Davidson, so she had to queue with other non-US citizens. John had long ago adopted dual-citizenship so went through Passport Control with Jeff and Bob. The three men waited for ages, and started to be concerned as to whether there were irregularities with Carolyn's papers.

Meanwhile, Carolyn was sitting chatting quite happily to the Immigration Officer. After the usual formalities had been carried out and all the paperwork completed, Carolyn said she had just married an American citizen and hoped she wouldn't have to queue on her own next time she came back from abroad.

When she told the Officer who her new husband was he was very impressed and commented, "Bob Maples, eh? Well, he is one of our national treasures, I'll have you know."

Carolyn nodded. "He may well be, but he's my treasure too now."

Bob stopped one of the British contingent as they came out of the Immigration area. Have you seen my wife? Can you tell me if there's a problem in there."

The man laughed, "No problem at all, mate. Last time I saw her, she was showing all the officers your wedding photographs. She's a hoot, isn't she, your wife?"

The three men were still laughing when Carolyn emerged, wearing a baseball cap someone had obviously given her, singing "*I'm an alien, I'm a legal alien; I'm an Englishwoman in New York*".

They were in this happy frame of mind when, after retrieving their luggage, they went out into the Arrivals lounge, and saw Nicole, surrounded by photographers.

Jeff started giggling, and whispered, "I kinda forgot to tell her about the wedding, so she must have arranged all this to greet your sister, John. It's another good excuse for her to be in the papers, but just wait till she finds out Carolyn has married her favourite guy."

The four were still in such a good mood, even Nicole couldn't spoil the moment. Jeff made a big show of kissing her on the cheek and said, loudly, "Hello darling, how nice of you to come and meet the newly-weds. Let me introduce you to the new Mrs. Maples."

Carolyn gritted her teeth and grasped Nicole by the shoulders to give her a hug. Nicole by now seemed to have turned into stone with shock. She couldn't speak without stuttering, and the smile she attempted for the cameras became more of a grimace. "Why didn't you warn me," she hissed at Jeff.

Carolyn took stock of Nicole. She was indeed very beautiful, with long blond hair extensions, which she kept shaking over her shoulder. She was very slim but shapely; dressed to kill in skin tight, black leather trousers and a designer blouse with a plunging neckline. The stiletto heels of her Jimmy Choo shoes were so high that Carolyn wondered how she could possibly walk in them. Even her large handbag must have cost a fortune. Carolyn could certainly see what had attracted Jeff to her. She was gorgeous, but very flashy.

Harry and two other security men, who had arrived with Nicole, ushered the five out of the terminal to the waiting car. As Carolyn was about to climb in, Harry whispered in her ear, "Watch her, Carolyn; she's poison."

Carolyn nodded and said under her breath, "Don't you worry about me, Harry. Let her underestimate me. When I'm ready, she won't know what's hit her. I'm not the walkover she expects." She hugged Harry and kissed him on the cheek. Thanks for everything. Will we see you again soon?"

"I've no doubt we'll meet again soon," he said, helping her into the limousine.

Nicole sniffed as they settled into their seats. "Carolyn, dear, I hardly think it's fitting for you to be so familiar with the hired help."

Carolyn smiled sweetly and replied, "Oh, Nicole, I'm so sorry if I've offended you already, but Harry is actually my friend and I'll treat him as I see fit."

The car drove to the Simmonds' home first, where the two alighted. Jeff's face looked so sad that Carolyn jumped out of the car after them and threw her arms round him. She whispered in his ear, "Hang in there, Jeff, we'll talk again tomorrow. It's going to be all right, I promise." She turned to Nicole and smiled sweetly, saying, "Nice to meet you Nicole, love," before hopping back into the car.

She looked from Robbie to John before bursting out laughing, saying, "Oh tell her to go suck another lemon. Gosh, she's got a face like a smacked bum."

The limousine pulled away again and soon they were driving across Manhattan towards the condominium. The skyline had dramatically changed since Carolyn had last been in New York, by the loss of the twin towers. They talked about the dreadful events of that day and could all remember what they had been doing when the awful news had reached them.

Before they reached home, John turned to Carolyn with a serious face and said, "Sweetheart, Bob, Jeff and I have been talking and we want you to know that you are now officially a part of our team. We are going to make you a Director of M., D. and S. Productions so you'll have equal voting rights with the three of us. We also want you to know that this is now your home and we want you to change anything at all you don't like, either in the" House" or the Shop. You've only got to say and it'll be done."

Carolyn was really touched by this thoughtfulness. "Oh, that's a lovely welcome home for me. Thank you so much. I know I'm going to be happy here; I just can't wait to see the House."

The car pulled into an underground car park where they alighted and took an elevator up to the top floor. The two men laughingly threw the main door open with a flourish and ushered Carolyn into the Shop. She was to find that this consisted of a secretarial office with computers, and a larger office, which doubled up as a meeting or conference room. There was a music room with a piano in the corner and a fully equipped recording studio. There was also a large storeroom, and a kitchen and cloakroom. These rooms all opened into a corridor, which ended with a further door leading into the House.

A striking blonde, blue-eyed woman of medium build came out of the office when she heard the voices. She was very elegantly dressed in a smart business suit and her hair and make-up were faultless.

"Ah Stella", John said. "We would like you to meet my sister, Carolyn, who is also Mrs. Robert Maples." There was silence whilst Stella registered this information. Like Nicole, she had been aware that Bob had gone to England to bring John's sister home, but had been completely unaware of the real reason for John and Jeff's sudden decision to join him.

Since being appointed Personal Assistant to the Honeys, Stella had inveigled her way into their lives in such a way that she had become invaluable to the smooth running of the operation. Nicole had never been a threat, and indeed the two women had found themselves as allies on more than one occasion. In fact, the only thing Stella and Nicole totally disagreed on was Bob. Seeing the lifestyle which Nicole enjoyed, Stella had been planning to be Mrs. Maples herself if she played her cards right. She had enjoyed her position as "Queen Bee", and on first meeting Carolyn was horrified to think she was not only going to lose her place as First Lady but would also lose any chance with Bob.

It was natural, therefore, that Stella took an immediate dislike to Carolyn. The feeling was, in fact, mutual. It was hate at first sight for both of them. Carolyn could feel the hairs on the back of her neck stand on end. *This one's trouble*, she thought to herself. *Talk about the gruesome twosome. Nicole and Stella make a lovely pair; I don't think*!

Bob asked Stella, "Do we have any engagements coming up Stella?"

Managing to hold herself in check, she replied, "Only a Showcase in a couple of days. There are six acts for you to see at The Greyhound Club."

Oblivious to the emotions churning in Stella's breast, Bob turned to Carolyn and commented. "You might enjoy that, Darling. Your first engagement for M.,D.and S. Productions."

Stella gritted her teeth and smiled, but as soon as the trio had left the office she picked up the phone and dialled Nicole's number.

Before opening the door into the "House," Bob swung Carolyn up into his arms.

"What are you doing Robbie, you daft lummock," Carolyn squeaked.

Bob laughed joyfully, "I'm going to carry my Darlin' over the threshold like any decent husband would."

Carolyn's first impression of the living accommodation was how surprisingly bright and roomy it appeared. There was a lovely open-plan lounge with three comfortable looking sofas in soft cream coloured leather. The carpets, drapes and scatter-cushions were in terracotta and mustard. The windows were from ceiling to floor and looked out onto a vast balcony from where the Manhattan skyline could be seen in all its glory. At one end of the lounge was a dining area with a large table and eight chairs.

There were three steps up to the kitchen, which had a wooden balustrade looking down onto the lounge. In the middle of the kitchen was, wonder of wonders, a lovely wooden table just like the one they had sat round happily for so many years at Cobble Hill.

"Oh," Carolyn squealed. "Please tell me that's OUR table."

"It is, Darlin', it is," Bob replied. "It's sort of a piece of family history, and we went to a fair bit of trouble to get it back. Do you like it all, Baby?"

Carolyn could hardly speak, she was so happy. "Oh it's just wonderful, I love it. Let me see the bedrooms now."

John and Bob both escorted her through a further door into a corridor, from where there were four large en-suite bedrooms. One room was John's which he had decorated to suit his masculine taste. Another was kept in reserve for Jeff when he wanted to stay, and the third was a guest room.

The fourth room had been Bob's and, at his request, John had called in an interior designer and had the bedroom and bathroom completely redecorated. The bedroom was light and airy, with plain cream carpets and mint green and mimosa bedding. The wallpaper was cream with a shiny pattern and the drapes and scattered rugs were mint green and mimosa. The whole effect was lovely and Carolyn caught her breath in delight.

Bob, too, was delighted with the new decoration but said, "Darlin' if there's anything at all you don't like, you must get it changed. This is your home and we just want you to be happy."

Carolyn threw her arms around his neck and smiled into his eyes. "Oh Robbie, John, you are so good to me. I don't want to change anything. I absolutely love it all. We are going to be so happy here. It feels like home already."

They had hardly had time to see everything when Jeff arrived. "Sorry folks, I couldn't stay away. Would it be O.K. if I stayed here tonight? Nicole is going out anyway, so she won't miss me."

Carolyn hugged him tightly. "Jeff, you will always be welcome here and the sooner we have you back with us the better. Come and see our lovely bedroom." She pulled him back down the corridor to see the newly decorated room. When they walked back into the kitchen it was to see Bob taking a large dish of lasagne out of the oven whilst John was laying the kitchen table, putting a bowl of salad and garlic bread out.

"Oh God, I'm famished where did that come from? It smells delicious." Carolyn asked, taking deep sniffs of the mouth-watering dish.

John smiled, "Good old Bess has left it all ready for us. You'll meet her to-morrow, love."

The four sat round the kitchen table and enjoyed their first family meal together for nearly five years. It was as if the clock had been turned back as they reminisced and laughed together like old times.

Tiredness eventually got the better of Carolyn after the journey and the excitement of coming home. Seeing her eyes drooping, Bob once again scooped her up into his arms and carried her down the corridor to their bedroom.

"Oh I'm so happy, Robbie," she whispered as she rained little butterfly kisses on his neck.

He tenderly laid her on the bed, saying, "Come on now, get undressed and into bed, because if you carry on like that you won't be getting much sleep, girl. I'll go and make some hot chocolate and I'll be with you very soon."

By the time he returned, however, Carolyn was fast asleep. As he climbed in beside her, she turned over into his arms reaching for him, and they slept that way, entwined together.

They were still in that position the next morning, when Jeff knocked and, getting no answer, went in with cups of coffee for them. He left the cups on the bedside table and laughing, said to John, "You should just see those two. They look like the Babes in the Wood. Honestly, it does my heart good to see them so happy."

༺꧁꧂༻

Chapter fifteen

It was mid-morning before Carolyn eventually rolled out of bed. Bob had left a note on the pillow telling her to take her time. He would be in the Shop talking to Stella and the other men about future commitments. Carolyn showered and dressed before she went through to the kitchen to find some breakfast. Standing at the sink, chopping vegetables, was a plump Italian looking woman. Tears were streaming down her cheeks as she sobbed and muttered to herself.

"Whatever is the matter, love?" Carolyn queried, putting her arm around the woman's shoulders. "You must be Bess. I've heard so much about you. Come and tell me why you're upset." Carolyn ushered Bess to a chair, poured two cups of coffee and sat down beside her. "I'm Carolyn, by the way. I think you have probably heard I was coming, but you mightn't know that Bob and I were married in England."

Bess stopped sobbing long enough to stare at the kind lady stroking her hand and smiling at her." You two are married, and you are Mr. Davidson's sister too?"

Carolyn laughed. "Yes, Bess I am. I want us to be friends, so you have got to start by telling me what's upset you."

Her tears began again as Bess tried to explain. "Oh, Ma'am, I try my best, honest I do, but it just ain't never good enough. I never know if I'm still gonna have a job at the end of the day, and I sometimes fear coming in. Miss Baldwin, she always threatenin' to replace me; always findin' fault. Just now she told me the new missus won't want a fat, ugly thing like me hangin' round and will probably tell me to go."

Carolyn could feel her hackles rising. "Well, Bess, I suppose I'm the new missus. I think you've got a lovely face, and your lasagne is to die for, so there will be no more talk of you leaving. I need you to show me the ropes and help me look after these three men. I certainly can't manage without you."

Just then, Stella appeared in the lounge and ran up the three steps to the kitchen. "How often have I told you, Bess, not to sit round drinking coffee when you should be working? Carolyn, you are going to have to keep this one in order."

Carolyn was shocked by the fact that Stella had just walked in to what was now her home, without so much as a by your leave. She was also amazed at her total lack of professionalism in reprimanding an employee in front of her. "Stella, I think in future it would be better if you concentrated on your administrative duties and left the domestic arrangements to me," Carolyn said in her most authorative manner.

Bess gazed at her with respect and adoration in her eyes, which by now had stopped their tearful flow. Stella muttered something under her breath, but did not argue with Carolyn. She could see immediately that Carolyn was not going to be the shy "kid sister" Nicole and she had been expecting. No walkover here then!

When the men eventually came through to the House it was to find Carolyn and Bess chatting comfortably together as they discussed Bess' workload and menus. "Do you know, you lot, that you have never actually given Bess any proper work instructions? Now there are three of us; often four here, we may need to get Bess some assistance for cleaning here and in the Shop. She has a formidable area to cover, especially when we're all here."

Carolyn raised her concern about access to the House from the Shop, and asked that a buzzer be put on the dividing door. "No-one should be able to just walk in here except us four. I mean we could be doing **anything!**" Carolyn commented.

For some reason, all three men seemed to find this amusing. "What exactly did you have in mind, Darlin'?" Bob asked.

Carolyn raised her eyebrows and tried to look cross. "Well, it's true. You don't know what we might be up to, and I didn't mean **that!**"

All four were by now in fits of laughter.

☙❧

After lunch, Bob suggested he take Carolyn for a drive. "There's something important I want to do," he said mysteriously. She was surprised to find the car approaching Brooklyn Bridge, where Bob found a parking area and they left the car to walk hand in hand across the bridge.

When they reached the spot where they had met all those years ago, he turned to her.

"Now don't think I've gone mad, but I promised myself if I ever found you again, I would do this. It's a little late in the day now, but what the hell," he said, laughing as he went down on one knee in front of her. "Darlin', I adore you. Will you marry me? I'm on a safe bet here because you can't say no now, but I'm asking you again anyway." Cars were passing with horns honking and good-natured laughing shouts out of car windows.

"Oh get up, Robbie, you lovely, lovely man," Carolyn laughed, throwing herself into his arms. "If you hadn't already made me the happiest woman in the whole world, I'd marry you all over again, but it was a wonderful idea coming here. What a lot has happened since I met my two knights. Robbie, there's a man watching us. He's coming over." Her voice dropped to a whisper as the man in question approached them.

"Caro, I'd like you to meet Justice of the Peace Arnold Pettinger. I asked him to meet us here for a reason." Then turning to the stranger he explained, Mr. Pettinger, this is my wife Carolyn. Do you think you could carry out my request now please."

The man nodded and whilst this exchange was proceeding, Carolyn was watching open-mouthed, wondering what on earth was happening. Bob took her by the shoulders, kissed her on the nose and said, "Darlin' we're about to be married again; here on Brooklyn Bridge."

"Oh Robbie, only you could have thought of this," she said through tear-filled eyes.

They held each other's hands whilst the Justice of the Peace said the words over them. When he said "I now pronounce you man and wife," Carolyn turned in Robbie's arms and they kissed long and deeply. Passers-by were obviously amused by the exchange but apart from a few wolf-whistles and cheers, no-one interrupted the proceedings. When Carolyn looked around, the Justice of the Peace had disappeared.

"I bought you this baby," Bob said, taking a small box out of his pocket. In it was a gold eternity ring set with diamonds. "It'll fit between your engagement ring and wedding ring, and I know it'll fit. See what it says inside." There, engraved in the gold were their initials, C. and R. entwined, next to BB 1988.

"When did you have this done, Robbie? You haven't had time since we got to New York?" she asked him.

"I had it done in Liverpool, my love, from the same jeweller we bought the other rings from. I was just waiting for the right moment."

"Oh Sweetheart, I just didn't think I could be any happier, but this is just the most wonderful surprise. Thank you my dear love; thank you."

They walked back to the car in a daze of euphoria and drove across the bridge and into Cobble Hill, where they briefly parked opposite their old home. A young couple came out of the house and walked arm in arm down the street laughing.

Carolyn smiled "Oh look, Robbie, perhaps a little of our laughter was left in the house and it's making other people happy. You do know that happiness in a house stays like an aura, don't you? I'm going to make sure we have that same laughter and happiness in our new home." They drove back home reminiscing about their old life and chatting happily about plans for the future.

Entering the Shop, it was to find Stella with a very aggrieved face, having found the lock and buzzer on the dividing door. Carolyn hugged herself with glee and it took all her self control not to make a sarcastic comment, but she managed to restrain herself.

A couple of days later, it was the Showcase at the Greyhound Club. Harry had been asked to drive Carolyn, John, Bob and Stella to the club where they would meet Jeff and Nicole, who would not miss this opportunity to meet with other celebrities and press. It was early afternoon when they set off and the sun was streaming through the windows of the car as they drove across New York.

"What a lovely day it is. Not really an afternoon to be in a smoky old club, but I guess we'll have to put up with it," John commented.

The club was packed with producers and agents who had been invited to the Showcase. There were six acts on the bill who were mingling and chatting to interested parties. Carolyn noticed how cosy Nicole and Stella were together. She was left in no doubt about whom they were talking, as they both kept glancing her way and smirking. Carolyn could feel her hackles rising, so when Stella crossed over to them and asked if there was anything they required, Carolyn spoke up, smiling at her.

"Some coffee would be very nice, please Stella. Mine's white with no sugar, ta." Stella was seething. You could almost read her mind, Carolyn thought. I bet she's dying to say, "Who do you think you are, giving me orders?"

John too, was reading the situation, so when Stella turned to him, ready to make a comment, John said, "Yes, same for me please. Anyone else want coffee?"

The acts weren't due to perform for another hour, and eventually Carolyn found herself getting bored standing around listening to the conversations. She saw Harry out of the corner of her eye and made her way over to him. He was about to join some other minders and roadies in the courtyard of the club for a "smoke" and coffee. She followed him and sat down on the low wall next to Harry who introduced her to everyone. She happily chatted with the group. Never one to stand on ceremony, and not yet used to the high life, she respected everyone for who they were not what they were. Her Dad had always said, "Remember, you are as good as everyone else but you are no better than anyone else." Both John and Carolyn had always tried to live up to what they had been taught.

Harry asked her how she was getting on with "The Rottweiler". She chuckled and said, "Do you mean Vinegar Drawers? God, she's poison isn't she? She certainly doesn't like me." Everyone started laughing. Stella was well-known.

As the laughter echoed around the yard, Stella and Nicole appeared at the door and Nicole beckoned Carolyn over.

"Oh Lord" she muttered under her breath "It's the gruesome twosome." Once more there was laughter from the group, which did nothing to wipe the frowns off the faces of the two women. Carolyn got up and walked over to them.

"Carolyn, dear," she whispered, "I've already pointed out to you that you shouldn't be so familiar with the hired help. The way you behave reflects on all of us and you'll be giving the Honeys a bad name. I really cannot understand what a well brought up English girl sees in that black piece of trash you've married anyway; unless it's his fortune you're after. However, it would seem that maybe that's where your preferences lie, if you prefer the company of that black agency-man out there to your own kind."

Carolyn was beside herself with rage. "Black piece of trash!" she roared. You called my husband a black piece of trash. How dare you speak like that about him? You're nothing but a fortune-hunting trollop who doesn't care who she drops her knickers for. Unfortunately, you're my sister-in-law until such time as your husband sees sense and dumps you. Until then, you and I will just have to put up with each other."

Nicole's mouth fastened back into a sneer as she hissed, "Sister-in law? No, I will never accept that, as I'll never accept this stupid idea that those two are brothers. You are not, and never will be anything to me."

Seeing Stella smirk at this tirade, Carolyn turned to her and barked, "And as for you, Stella; be absolutely sure that, if you value your job, you'd better learn which side your bread is buttered." She turned and flounced away from the pair.

As she walked away she heard someone ask the women who the English chick was. Nicole's reply was priceless, and enough to ensure that the two would never again be civil to each other, let alone friends.

"Oh, her! That's the new Mrs Maples; although I'm not sure who is screwing her, him or my husband. Neither of them seems to be able to keep their hands off her."

Carolyn gritted her teeth in anger and had to bite her tongue not to retaliate. She continued to walk, her head held high, whilst inwardly seething at the unjust comment.

It was time for the acts to start their sets. The first five were in no way exciting or outstanding; then, two Italian looking, young brothers started to sing. Nerves were obviously getting the better of them as they kept forgetting their words, although their voices and harmony were excellent.

Carolyn bent forward and queried "I might be able to help. Would it be okay if I go and talk to them?"

The men were delighted that she should want to get involved. "Of course, love, do whatever you think necessary," John said as the other two nodded their agreement. They, of course, were pleased to include her.

She went onto the stage and took the brothers on one side. "What's the problem, boys? Is it just nerves, or something else?" It turned out that it was the first time they had sung in public. They had previously only sung at family gatherings for their mother and other family. They had been persuaded that they had talent and should audition to see if they stood a chance of a career. Carolyn quickly thought of an idea. "How would it be if you pretended I was your mum? "I'm going to sit over there and you are going to sing just to me. Forget everyone else in the room. You can do it."

She put a chair at the front and asked for the lights to be lowered in the club. The lads started singing again. This time their voices were pure and clear. The harmony was wonderful making it obvious how good they really were. The Honeys quickly signed them up, before anyone else had the chance, arranging for them to come to the Shop to cut a disc and sort out their future.

Bob put his arm around Carolyn's shoulders, and whispered, "Darlin' I'm so proud of you. You knew just what to do. What an asset you're gonna be." Carolyn was happy that at least she had been able to make her mark.

She didn't tell the men of her confrontation with Nicole and Stella, but was amused when they arrived home and Bob said, "Oh, Stella terrifies me. When she corners me she makes me feel like a naughty boy standing in front of the matron again."

Carolyn laughed. "I know what you mean, but remember; she works for you, not the other way round."

༺࿐༻࿐༺

Chapter sixteen

Stella continued to go out of her way to make life as unpleasant as possible for Carolyn, who did her best to ignore the sideways glances and under-the-breath comments. She was particularly surprised, therefore, one afternoon, when Stella buzzed and was admitted into the apartment. The three men were in the Recording Studio with one of their acts, and Carolyn was alone in the lounge.

"Carolyn, can we please bury the hatchet?" she ventured. Carolyn was so astonished at first that she could not reply. Stella continued, "I really would value your help and advice, you know. I feel I have been most unfair to you, and I would like to make amends. Will you let me try please?"

Big-hearted Carolyn could do nothing but nod. This was the last thing she had expected. "Stella, please come in and sit down. Would you like some coffee?" She managed to get out.

For at least an hour, Stella and Carolyn chatted together. Although still very wary of Stella's motives, Carolyn was delighted to think that life could be more pleasant if Stella and she were able to communicate.

"Look, Carolyn, I'm supposed to be going to a personal appearance with Bob to-morrow. Instead of going ahead with him, why don't you come with me a little later and I can show you the ropes. It will give us an hour to look at some of the files in the office and you can familiarise yourself with things. Then sometimes you can go by yourself with him, and sort out whatever is necessary. John and Jeff have separate commitments to-morrow and won't need me, but there are times when I feel I need to split myself in two. It would be so helpful if you were more involved."

Carolyn couldn't believe her ears. Stella was actually asking for her help and including her in the arrangements. "I'd be pleased to do anything to help, Stella. I really would like to be involved. You know, there's nothing worse than feeling useless and lately I've felt a bit like a spare part." Carolyn confessed.

That evening, Carolyn told Bob how friendly Stella had been and told him of the arrangements for the following day. He was to appear at a youth club to present some awards. Later in the day, he was to visit a children's hospice where he would talk to some of the children.

"That's fine, Darlin'. I'll go on my own to the youth club and you can both meet me there, before we go on to the hospice. Just beware of that one though. I'm not sure she can be trusted."

After breakfast the next morning, John left first to meet Jeff and view another promising act. As Bob went to leave, Carolyn flung her arms around him; kissing and hugging him.

"Goodness, girl, whatever did I do to deserve this?" he laughingly asked, whilst hugging her closely to his chest.

"Just wanted to remind you how much I love you and that I'm missing you already," Carolyn laughed.

Harry was driving Bob to the youth club, and they arrived in good time for the presentations. The youngsters were all on their best behaviour; very excited to be meeting a real superstar. Bob made a big fuss of all the children as they came up for their prizes and awards. He showed interest; spending time with each one, listening to what they had to say, and giving them advice. When all the youngsters had been seen, Bob was shown into an ante-room where refreshments had been arranged. He was surprised when he looked at his watch to see how the time had passed. There was still no sign of Carolyn and Stella.

He went over to Harry and asked, "Any sign of the girls, Harry? I'm a little concerned, because they should have been here an hour ago."

Harry shook his head. "No sign, Bob. Have you tried ringing?"

Bob tried ringing the "House first," but there was no answer. He tried ringing Carolyn's cell-phone, but again there was no reply. He frowned, "I can't understand it, Harry. I'm starting to get really worried now. Come on Darlin'," he muttered under his breath, "Please answer the phone."

Just then, Stella walked in, looking rather sheepish and subdued. Bob immediately confronted her, asking where Carolyn was.

Stella took a deep breath, "Bob, I don't know how to tell you this."

A knife twisted in Bob's heart. "Stella, what on earth are you trying to say?"

Stella explained that she had found Carolyn in tears after he had left. "Bob, that girl is in pieces. She said she'd made a terrible mistake coming back and, although she loves you, she can't cope with this life. She told me she didn't think she could make it work. She feels she has only one option, and that's to go back to England. She explained how she left last time. She was going to book a domestic flight from JFK to Chicago, then get a flight from there to England."

Bob's first reaction was to laugh. "No, Stella, you're making this up. Carolyn would never leave me now. You're just being spiteful. I don't believe you."

At that moment a text message came through on Bob's phone. "Ah thank goodness. It's from her," he said. However, as he read the message the blood drained from his face and he couldn't breathe. The text said, "Darling, I will always love you, but this really isn't going to work. I have to go. Please forgive me and try to be happy."

He tried to phone her back, but the cell phone had been turned off. There was still no answer on the landline. He sat down in a chair before his legs gave way, holding his hands to his head. "I don't understand any of this. She needs me as much as I need her. We have to be together. Please let me be dreaming this."

Harry quickly took charge of the situation. "This doesn't ring true to me, Bob. From what I know of Carolyn, there's no way she'd leave you like this." Neither of them, however, could explain the text message.

"Come on, son," said Harry. "We'll go to the airport just in case. Stella, will you let the hospice know we won't be coming to-day."

The traffic was heavy as they crossed New York to JFK Airport. Bob sat on the edge of his seat all the way, cursing the slow moving line of cars. When they reached the airport, they ran into the terminal. Bob found the flight desk for Chicago, which was deserted. A flight had recently been checked in and left. There wasn't another one for a couple of hours.

"Please, could you have a look at the flight list for me? I need to know if a Carolyn Davidson, or a Carolyn Maples was on that plane," Bob managed to say. "She's British. Has an English accent."

The attendant recognised Bob, and although at first reticent about giving any customer details, she eventually agreed to look at the passenger list.

"Sure! There was a C. Davidson on board and I do remember her, strangely enough. She was quite chatty and she did have a British accent. She was dark haired and very attractive, but she looked so sad. I remarked on it to Sally, didn't I Sal?" she said turning to the other attendant behind the desk, who nodded in agreement.

Bob was completely devastated. "This just isn't happening. No, my Darling, please don't leave me. You swore you'd never leave me. I can't live without you."

By the time Harry managed to lead him back to the car, Bob was distraught and walking like a zombie. "What did I do wrong, Harry? What did I do wrong?" he kept muttering, over and over again. "I couldn't love her more. I would have done anything she asked of me. Oh God, what did I do wrong?"

As they parked the car in the underground car park, he complained of pains in his chest and looked very ill; his skin ashen and clammy. Harry was afraid he might be having a heart attack. Bob stumbled though the Shop, his breath coming in shallow gasps, and gave Harry his key card to open the door into the apartment.

A surprised Carolyn jumped up and ran to them. "Oh my God, Robbie! What's happened? You look terrible."

Bob couldn't speak for relief. He held her to him as if she might suddenly disappear. Harry explained what had happened and suggested that they call the doctor out to check on Bob as he did indeed look dreadful.

"I thought you'd gone, baby. I thought you'd left me; but you're here. You're here," he muttered into her hair as his arms tightened their grip.

Carolyn was perplexed. "I've been here all morning," she said. "Stella disappeared while I was looking through the files in the office with her. I couldn't get an outside line on the phone and I can't find my cell phone anywhere. I just had to be patient and wait for someone to come home, because I didn't even know where the club was you'd gone to.

Carolyn quickly phoned John on Bob's phone. She just told him that there was an emergency and Bob wasn't well. He said he would call the doctor and be straight home.

Whilst Harry checked out the phone line, Carolyn and Bob clung to each other. Bob's breathing had now gone back to normal and the grey pallor was gradually leaving his face.

"My darling, darling boy, I would never hurt you like that. I realise now what a terrible mistake it was when I left before, but now we're together, I just couldn't manage without you. You must have faith in me, however bad things may seem. Trust me, my love, and I promise I'll always trust you. Let me see this bloody text I'm supposed to have sent. Oh, how wicked," she exclaimed as she read the words. "I can imagine how you felt when you read this."

Harry came back in, followed by the Doctor, who Carolyn thanked for coming, informing him that thankfully, it didn't seem quite as serious as had first appeared.

He insisted, however, in checking Bob over, and Carolyn left them to talk to Harry. "Carolyn, the main phone has been unplugged in the office. That means there would be no connection in either the Shop or the House," Harry said angrily. "On my life, this has been well planned and executed. Whoever did this must have stolen your cell phone too."

John and Jeff arrived and were shocked when they heard details of what had occurred. It all seemed like a nightmare. It seemed impossible that someone could play such a terrible trick on Bob. Thankfully, the doctor was able to report that Bob had suffered a panic attack and that his heart seemed strong. It had been frightening, but not serious.

Carolyn kept shaking her head in disbelief. "That anyone who knows how much we mean to each other could do something like this. It just beggars belief. Stella obviously was lying so it had to be her, but why? What could she hope to gain? She must have realised we'd know she was involved. Let's face it, though, she couldn't have done it by herself. She was there when Robbie got that text and it certainly wasn't her at the airport. So, that brings us to who? Well, I'm sorry Jeff, but there's only one other person evil enough to be a part of this charade."

Jeff nodded, "Nicole! You're right, it couldn't be anyone else. She's been seething since she found out we'd made you a director, and she's always hated Bob. Sorry Bro."

When Harry had left, with thanks from all of them, John phoned their lawyer, Joseph Abrahams, to find out if they had any chance of prosecuting the two women. They all felt that Nicole and Stella shouldn't get away with causing so much misery for Bob. When he arrived, Joe was sympathetic. However, he felt that although, obviously they could sack Stella for gross misconduct, there was no recourse to prosecution.

There was no proof that it was her who disconnected the phone and had stolen the cell phone. Nor could they prove she was connected with the airport spoof. Although it was highly probable, it was only conjecture that Nicole was involved. He suggested that the best course of action was to make sure Stella could do no more damage by sacking her and trying to write the whole affair off.

Joe Abrahams had been the Honeys' lawyer for about four years. In his early forties he was of medium height with dark hair peppered with grey. He came from a working class background, but had worked hard to get through school and better his life. Now a trusted lawyer with a good reputation, he had always given the trio good advice. He was a likeable man with a pleasant personality. Carolyn found herself warming to him.

"Right," she said, standing up. "How would you all feel about me taking over the hiring and firing? It would give me so much pleasure to be the one to sack the bitch. Would you trust me to deal with this situation?" This was a side to Carolyn the men had never seen before. "Nobody hurts the people I love and gets away with it," she said in a steely voice.

No-one opposed her. They could see from her face that she was resolute in wanting to sort things out. They all knew that when Carolyn was determined, nothing would stand in her way.

She set her plan in motion, and phoned Stella to come in and collect her things. Pulling no punches, Carolyn made it clear that it was the end of the line for her. She asked Joe to be on hand to deal with any implications concerning the work contract.

When Stella arrived, she met her alone in the office. Carolyn stood with her arms folded. "Come on Stella, I need to know your motives for all this. Why did you do it? There's only us here. Spill the beans."

Stella smirked. I just felt you were far too smug with yourselves. We were doing fine until you came on the scene. I could have had Bob. If I had beckoned he would have come."

"In your dreams," Carolyn hissed.

Stella shrugged her shoulders. "Well, I had already been offered another job and I wanted to leave a parting gift. If nothing else it must have come as a nasty shock to Bob. The look on his face when the text came was priceless."

"Yes, the text," said Carolyn. Did you take my phone? Come on Stella. It was Nicole texting wasn't it? And the airport incident. She would have only had to wear a wig and put on an English accent. Not very difficult."

"Prove it." said Stella.

Carolyn shrugged, "You know I can't prove it, but just between you and me; it was her, wasn't it?"

Nicole smiled. "Yes I took the damn phone, and of course it was Nicole. She hates you as much as I do".

"Why, Stella? Why all this hate?" said Carolyn.

Stella laughed mirthlessly. "You just weren't wanted, but we realised you were here to stay. That didn't mean life had to be easy for you."

"Well, you realise you won't get a reference, don't you?"

"I don't need one, my dear. The person I am going to be working for has been trying to head hunt me for as long as I can remember. He needs no reference. He's absolutely delighted to get me."

After Carolyn called Joe through, he settled all the necessary paper work and financial details with Stella, before she left for good.

When Joe and Carolyn went back through to the apartment, Carolyn took a micro-recorder out of her pocket. "I pinched this out of your drawer, John. Well, we may not be able to use this legally, but at least it may come in useful in the future. For a start Jeff, you have to divorce Nicole, she's poisonous."

She played the recording back and there was silence for a moment. "If nothing else we could prosecute Stella for the theft of your phone," said Joe.

Jeff said, "This is the jolt I've been waitin' for. Set the ball in motion for me, will you, Joe. Mom, can I come home?"

The tension evaporated as they all laughed. Carolyn said, "Some good can come of this. I want the laughter back in our lives. I want this to be a happy home with good and happy people round us. Can I make one or two suggestions?" she asked, not waiting for an answer. "Firstly, you do need a P.A. I can take over the admin for a while until we find one, but I don't know enough about your contacts and business to do it on my own."

Joe said, "I hope I'm not talking out of turn, but my wife is out of work at the moment and I'm sure she would help until you find someone permanent. She has a Business Degree and has worked as a P.A. before. To be perfectly honest, she had to leave her last job because of personal problems. You see, ours is a bi-racial marriage. I'm Jewish and my wife is black. what a combination,eh? Anyhow, we are happy together. We said to hell with everyone else, but she was so unhappy with the bigots she was working with we decided to retire her. She is bored silly and I know would be delighted to help out."

Carolyn suggested that he ask his wife, Pam, to come to see her in the morning.

"Next," says Carolyn. "I think it is absolutely ridiculous that a successful group like yourselves needs to constantly use agencies for staff. I'm not saying you should go as far as some of these guys. Robbie's told me about one mega rich Rapper who travels with a personal tailor, his own cook, wardrobe manager and barber as well as his many aides. What I am saying is that firstly, you should have your own aide to drive and take care of you, and perhaps a secretary to be in that office at all times. Are you all with me so far?"

There were shrieks of laughter, particularly when Bob said, "Well I'm certainly not going to oppose you while you're in full throttle. You're scarin' the hell out of me." The laughter continued as Carolyn and Bob hugged each other.

"I think I have a good idea who you have in mind for our aide," said John, "and I couldn't agree more."

"Harry it is then," they all said in unison.

They suggested Carolyn phone him and she broached the subject immediately. "Harry, we've decided we can't manage without you, will you come to work for us permanently, please."

Harry didn't have to think twice about it. He immediately agreed to the proposal.

"No-one's ever said **please** would I work for them before," he said chuckling. "It would be a pleasure and an honour to work for you." Carolyn asked him to come in the next morning to talk over the details.

That night, Bob had a nightmare and woke up calling for Carolyn. She understood how badly the incident had hurt him and, realising the depth of his feelings for her, knew how she would have been in similar circumstances.

"Oh, my dearest love, I'm here. I'll always be here," she cooed, as she held his head to her breast. He was shaking and the sweat was pouring down his face.

"It just made me realise, Caro that I couldn't live without you now. You're my life."

Carolyn kissed his brow and whispered, "I know Darling, but you see we are two halves of a whole now. "We both need each other to exist and together we are a formidable pair. Just let anyone try to separate us again and I'll knock their block off."

Despite himself, Bob laughed. "I don't know about knocking blocks off, but if anyone ever tries to take you away from me, I'll break their fuckin' neck."

"That's never going to happen, Robbie, because people might try, but they'll never succeed," Carolyn smiled.

Bob looked serious. "I just feel we haven't seen or heard the last of those two. I don't think they've finished with us yet."

Carolyn nodded, "You could be right, Darling. It makes it even more necessary for us to be on our guard and trust each other, so if they do try anything we'll be ready."

Chapter seventeen

Early next morning, Carolyn spent hours in the office going through the appointments diary and looking through files to familiarise herself with the business. Carolyn had to admit that Stella was very efficient, as the systems were faultless and easy to follow.

Pam, Joe Abraham's wife, arrived at the same time as Harry. Carolyn heard them laughing together outside the door and liked the sound. She went to the door and after greeting Harry, she introduced herself to Pam, then turned to say, "You go through, Harry, and talk to the boys. They can tell you what they want you to do. But don't go without popping in to see me."

Carolyn quickly took in the details of Pam's appearance. She was slim, of medium height, wearing a very smart, navy blue, pin-striped suit and white blouse. She had an open, attractive face and Carolyn was immediately fascinated by her radiant smile. Her voice was educated and she spoke quietly, but distinctly.

Carolyn smiled at her. "My word, you do look nice, Pam. You make me feel scruffy in my jeans and T-shirt."

Pam leant forward and spoke as if relaying a secret, "Well you see, I was trying to create a good impression."

Carolyn roared laughing. "Well you've certainly done that, Pam. Anyone who can make me laugh is okay in my book."

The two women sat down and were soon at ease with each other. Carolyn thanked Pam for agreeing to help and gave her a rough outline of the task that lay ahead of them. Within a very short time they were laughing together like old friends.

Meanwhile, Bob and John were giving Harry the low-down on his new job and agreeing terms with him. He already knew them well, so he was delighted to be a part of their team. They asked him to make some suggestions for security and put any ideas forward to them.

Carolyn brought Pam through and introduced her to John and Bob, and the five talked together whilst Bess made a large pot of coffee and passed round some of her home-made cookies.

"I want to make a suggestion right away, if I'm not speaking out of turn," Harry started to say.

John interrupted him quickly. "Harry we are putting you in charge of security. We know we've been lax, mainly because we value our privacy so much. Please feel free to make any suggestions you think appropriate."

Harry suggested that the dividing door should be fitted with a number pad; the combination only known by designated people, and changed weekly. He also thought it would be a good idea to have a spy hole in the outside door so that callers could be checked before being admitted.

It was agreed that Harry go ahead with these measures. Seeing the benefit of this sort of discussion, Carolyn suggested that they should have a weekly meeting whenever possible to iron out any problems and make sure everyone knew what was going on.

After Carolyn and Pam had gone back through to the office, taking Harry with them, John shook his head laughingly. "By God, she's going to keep us on our toes, isn't she? She's working like a Sergeant Major. No more slacking for us any more, me old mate."

Bob too, was laughing "Tell you what, John; I'll go a step further. I'll bet you ten dollars, she'll have Jeff back livin' here before the end of the day."

Just then, there was the sound of the door opening and a clatter as cases and bags were carried in by Harry and a cab driver.

"Sorry, mate, I'm not taking that bet," John chortled, as Jeff's voice could be heard in the passageway.

Carolyn came in, arm in arm with Jeff, "Look whose here. I told him to come home soon, but I didn't think he'd pack that quickly. Isn't it marvellous? We're all back together again. It will have to be a very special lady who takes you away from me next time. I'm going to vet every single one."

The sound of their laughter echoed in the room, and as Carolyn went back through to the office, she felt her heart warm to the sound.

"Oh, Pam, things really seem to be coming together at last," Carolyn said and continued to tell Pam some of the problems they had all had to face. "So you see, it's wonderful to hear them all laughing together again. It makes me so happy."

The two women spent the rest of the afternoon working their way through the filing system and computer programmes. They continued in this way for the next few days and found they enjoyed each other's company and worked well together. By the end of the week, they were firm friends.

At the first staff meeting, they used the conference room and the six sat around the table. Carolyn and Pam were able to report on their progress, and Pam was asked if she would be prepared to stay on permanently as their Personal Assistant.

She was elated. "Oh I couldn't be happier; thank you. To be honest, the last week has been so delightful; I would gladly keep coming in without pay, just for the pleasure of it.

Carolyn punched her gently on the arm. "Pam, don't let them hear you say that. They'll have you working for buttons." She turned back to the others and said, "We've been discussing the possibility of an assistant P.A. being appointed too, and a Secretary. That would ensure that there'd always be someone available to sort out any problems and accompany all of you to concerts and other commitments."

John turned to Carolyn and asked, "Sis, how would you feel about carrying on in charge of all this side of the operation? You don't have to spend all your time working. Just pop your head in here each day to sort of keep the lid on things. You can be the main signatory on our cheques and sign any other necessary official documents. We'll always be on hand if you need us, but it would take a lot of pressure off us."

Carolyn was ecstatic. "Oh, yes please. I want to be useful and feel needed. I'll enjoy working with Pam too."

As the men walked back to the House, Bob remarked, "Oh, it's good to see her gettin' involved in all of this. She needed a purpose. Caro's never been one to sit on the sidelines. She's enjoying this so much and I'm glad she's made a friend out of Pam. It worried me that she'd left all her girlfriends in England. It'll make the world of difference her having another woman to chat with."

Meanwhile, the girls had wasted no time, and were putting adverts out for the two new staff whilst they discussed the type of people they were looking for.

"My priority is people we can get on with, Pam. I don't want any miserable faces, and we'll have to be on our guard against people just wanting to work here because the boys are famous." Carolyn commented.

Pam and Carolyn visited the agency which had been used before, with a view to asking if they had anyone suitable on their books who was looking for a permanent position. Due to a misunderstanding, they found themselves sitting in a full waiting room with others waiting for job information and placements.

Sitting between them was a young man who assumed that they, like him, were waiting to be interviewed. He was very chatty and friendly, offering them candy from a crumpled packet. He looked to be in his mid-twenties, being of medium height and build with brown hair and brown eyes. He was intrigued by Carolyn's English accent, questioning her about where she came from. He was very "into" the Beatles, wanting to know all about Liverpool and the Cavern. Carolyn chatted quite happily to him, telling him about her background, but leaving out the fact that she was related to three superstars.

"Look at you, a rose between two thorns," she laughed.

"No," he said, "a thorn between two roses." "What are two lovely ladies like you doing in a dump like this? You both look far too good for any job you're likely to get in this agency." He introduced himself as Tony Fox.

Carolyn queried, "Have you any Irish in you Tony, because I'm sure you've kissed the Blarney Stone?"

The three laughed loudly and in the full but silent room there were disapproving looks. Tony told them he was looking for a job which would use his organisational abilities. He had been working in an office but wanted to get out more and meet people.

The girls were called in to the office, where they were greeted with more respect when they said who they were and gave their reasons for being there. The woman in charge said she would send details of available secretaries and staff with P.A. abilities.

In the lift down, Carolyn voiced her doubt that anything would come of the visit, but after a moment, said, "Do you know what I'm thinking Pam? The nicest, funniest young person I've met in a long time is sitting up there waiting to be offered a job."

Pam laughed, "Now girl, don't be jumping into anything you may regret."

"Well at least let's ask him in for an interview. That way we can find out what he can actually do," Carolyn said.

They waited outside the building, sitting on a wall until Tony appeared. "Hello lovely ladies. Did you have any luck?" He asked sitting on the wall next to them.

"More to the point Tony," Carolyn said, "Did you?"

Tony's mouth turned down at the corners. "No. Only boring old office jobs. Someday, someone will see my worth," he replied.

Carolyn took a deep breath, and asked, "Have you ever thought of working in show business? Would you be interested in an interview for an Assistant P.A. job with a singing group? I can't promise you anything at this stage, but it might be worth a try."

She didn't go into any details of who she was referring to and what her position was. In fact she gave him the impression that she was the office Manager. She introduced Pam as the Personal Assistant, and asked him how he would feel having a woman boss, as he would have to defer to Pam in all things. He said he had no problem with this, and arrangements were made for him to go to M.,D. and S. Productions at the Shop for a formal interview.

Over the next few days, several prospective secretaries, together with two or three hopeful Personal Assistants, including Tony, were invited in for interview. The girls whittled the secretaries down to two; Rosie Metcalfe and Penny Ashworth. Both were given an assignment on the computer. Rosie was definitely the more efficient of the two, but both Carolyn and Pam were drawn to Penny with her lively personality and infectious giggle. Penny was about twenty years old with blond hair and blue eyes. She blushed a lot and it appeared that her parents were quite strict and kept her under close control. She seemed quite old fashioned in both her dress and manner. Carolyn was concerned that Penny's parents might be uncomfortable about their daughter working in the show business world, and asked the girl if she would like her to phone or visit them to put their minds at rest. Up to now The Honeys' name had not been mentioned and it was intended to wait until they were able to introduce them, before divulging who she would be working for. Penny was delighted to be offered the position. She loved the set-up at the Shop and was intrigued by the mystery surrounding her new employers.

The prospective Personal Assistants were then interviewed, but none of them would have been suitable. After the third person, a young man, left the office, Carolyn shook her head glumly.

"Goodness, if he was made of chocolate, he'd eat himself, wouldn't he. It must be wonderful to know everything. I think he'd end up trying to take over the whole operation in a week. Right! Let's see what Tony is made of. After that lot, I've got high hopes."

Tony sat down stiffly, obviously on his best behaviour. Carolyn smiled at him. "Tony, let us get one thing straight before we start. When we asked you to come in to see us, we knew nothing about your ability to do the job. That's what you've got to get over to us now. No, we asked you in because we took a liking to you; you made us laugh. You don't need to go all self-conscious and formal on us now. Just be yourself, and we'll get along fine."

"Wow, thank goodness for that. I can take this broom out of the back of my shirt now." Tony laughed.

Carolyn sat back in her chair and said, "Now, Tony, just chat normally to us and tell us about yourself, your background, home life, hobbies, everything."

Tony told them about his office career and produced some references and certificates. He said he was twenty five and still lived with his parents, but if he got the job he would be looking for an apartment to start off on his own. He liked meeting people and was into all sorts of music and listed some of his favourites. When he mentioned The Honeys, especially Bob Maples, it took Carolyn all her self control not to spill the beans.

"I've never done any P.A. work, but honestly I'm a quick learner and I'd love to have you as my boss, ma'am," he said, smiling at Pam.

"There you go, I knew he'd kissed the Blarney stone," Carolyn tittered. "Tony, is there anything you want to ask us or tell us?"

Tony licked his lips before saying quietly, "You have both been so great with me, and I want you to know that I will accept anything you decide without question, but please, please give me a chance. I know I could do this job."

Carolyn looked at Pam and raised her eyebrows. Pam nodded, and as they were both obviously of one mind, Tony was offered the position immediately.

Carolyn phoned Penny's parents, who appeared pleased by her concern. They said they realised they couldn't wrap her in cotton wool forever, but were comforted by the fact that Carolyn had wished to speak to them. Penny and Tony were asked to come in the next morning to meet their "Principals" and be shown around the rest of the Shop.

It was the following day, therefore, before either of them met the Honeys. Tony and Penny were sitting around the conference table with Pam when Carolyn ushered the men into the room.

"Meet your new Assistant P.A. and your Secretary. This is Tony Fox and Penny Ashworth. Tony you can close your mouth now."

It took a good minute before Tony could speak. He was, as Carolyn put it, totally "gobsmacked". His first words sent them all into hysterics.

"God, I've died and gone to heaven. Will someone pinch me, please." It had never occurred to either Tony or Penny that the people they would be working for would be so famous. They were overwhelmed by their down to earth natures and "unstarlike" attitudes. They were even more surprised and impressed to find that Carolyn was not only married to Bob Maples but was John Davidson's sister. When she said that Jeff Simmonds was her brother-in-law, this was all too much to take in.

"I'll explain all that at a later date," she giggled.

Harry came in and was introduced as "our Lovely Harry". This later became a standing joke with the office team, who always referred to him as L.H. Harry hadn't a clue what the initials stood for, but the banter between them was always enjoyable and good-natured.

It didn't take long for the two young people to settle into their new careers. The men would often tease Penny, who blushed and giggled continuously, but her standard of work was excellent. No-one could find fault with her. She enjoyed working for these "lovely men" and told her mother she would have "paid to let her work for them."

Tony fitted in well from the onset. He was bright and funny, getting on with everyone. He was very keen to learn, and nothing was too much trouble for him.

Over the next couple of months, all the inherited problems were sorted out. A new phone system was installed with private lines directly into the House. Each week meetings were held, which everyone who was available would attend. So followed a period of contentment and calm.

Harry's suggestions were put into operation, and as a final gesture Carolyn asked him to have a plaque made for her. She told him that years ago, she had said to the men, the evening before their first television interview, that egos should always be left on the doorstep. "I want that message over our front door," Carolyn told him. So Harry had a big metal plaque made for her, which said,

"Everyone is welcome in our home, but please leave your egos out here."

Chapter eighteen

It was the first evening for months that Carolyn and Bob had been on their own in the apartment. Jeff was out on a date and John was visiting some old friends. "Let's just have a lovely quiet evening in front of the T.V. We can cuddle up on the sofa, snog, and send out for a pizza," Carolyn said cheekily.

They ordered their pizzas, then talked about the past few months and how happy they were. People said that when one of them went out of a room, the other was on pins watching for their return.

"I'm so happy, Robbie. I never dreamed I could be so happy," Carolyn said, tracing his eyes and nose with her fingers. "Do you know? Your face is the dearest thing in the world to me."

Bob held her closely to his chest, and kissed the tip of her nose. "Darlin', I'm almost afraid to let you out of my sight, in case I wake up and all this has been a dream. I have to pinch myself to believe you're mine. This has been the happiest time of my life, and I will never be able to express in words just how much I love you."

"Show me then, my love," she sighed, leaning back against the cushions.

Their kiss was long, deep and loving; his fingers caressing her back, and moving up inside her sweater to fondle her breasts. "Oh, baby, I know I'm possessive but I can't bear the thought of you with anyone else. Promise me you'll never stop loving me," he whispered in her ear.

Sometimes, even now, he woke in the night shouting her name, and Carolyn had come to realise just how much their separation had affected him. Knowing how unhappy she had been, she was able to appreciate the depth of his feelings.

"I really don't mind, Robbie. I just feel so secure and safe knowing you love me so much. When we first got together, it frightened me that I wouldn't be enough for you. I'd had so little experience; whereas you'd played the field and had all those beautiful women in your bed. It still worries me at times that you'll wake up one day and realise what you've been missing."

Robbie smiled tenderly at her, "My dearest love. Okay, I've been around the block a few times, but I have never, ever loved anyone but you. "That makes the difference darlin'; loving you as I do and knowing you love me makes every time special to me. Anyhow, baby I haven't heard any complaints from you yet. You're always hot for me. I couldn't ask for more," he laughed wickedly, his shoulders shaking.

Carolyn blushed. "Oh, I never knew loving could be so wonderful. To think of all the time we wasted when we could have been making whoopee." He kissed her with such love and tenderness that she felt as though her heart would burst with joy.

Because they were both so taken up with each other, the sound of the buzzer from the intercom on the downstairs door made them both jump.

"Ooh, that'll be our supper. I'll be right back, just hold that thought, baby." He spoke into the intercom to query the caller, and when he heard the reply, pressed the button to open the door into the building.

Bob went through the dividing door, leaving it open and looked through the spy hole. When he saw it was the pizza delivery man, he started to open the door, but it was thrown open, knocking him backwards. Two men wearing ski-masks and wielding guns pushed him and the pizza man down the passageway into the apartment.

Carolyn jumped up and ran to Bob, horrified at what was happening. One of the men grunted, "Tie them up." The other one grabbed Carolyn, proceeding to tie her hands behind her back, and then her ankles, with cable ties.

Bob was incandescent with rage and fear for her when he saw what was being done. "Take your dirty hands off my wife," he yelled as he lunged at the man.

His companion lifted his gun and shot Bob in the chest. "The pizza man made a run for the door and the same man shot him in the back.

Carolyn watched Bob fall to the floor, as if in slow motion. It felt as though she was turned to stone for a few seconds, then it hit her like a sledgehammer. This was happening, this was real. Robbie had been shot! She screamed, "No! No,

Robbie. ROBBIE! Oh God, Oh God, what have you done to him?"

He was bleeding profusely from the wound in his chest and she shuffled across to him, falling onto her knees.

"Oh Robbie, my Darling, stay with me. Please don't leave me," she sobbed, putting her face to his.

He was just holding onto consciousness, but she could see how serious things were. The blood was pouring from his chest and his skin had gone an unhealthy greyish colour.

At this point the thieves were scurrying round the apartment collecting up valuables, but Carolyn no longer cared what they took. All she cared about was the fact that her darling Robbie was apparently bleeding to death on the floor. When the robbers had what they wanted they left, leaving the doors wide open.

Bob managed to whisper, "Darlin', you're gonna have to try to get help."

Sobbing, Carolyn asked, "Robbie, what shall I do?"

He muttered, "Can you get to the phone. You really need to try. Knock it onto the floor if you can."

Carolyn managed to move along on her bottom and she knocked the phone off the table onto the floor with her feet. She tried and tried to dial with her chin, her teeth, her nose but it was impossible.

Frustrated, she managed to rock the table until a pen dropped onto the floor. After several attempts, she picked the pen up in her teeth and tapped in 911, then tapped the hands free button. Sure, enough a voice was at the other end.

"My husband has been shot," Carolyn screamed. "Please send someone."

The operator was infuriatingly efficient and slow, asking for the address, then said, "How bad is your husband? Can you look at his wound?"

Carolyn was frightened by the look of him, but replied, "He's bleeding very badly and he's unconscious now."

The operator asked, "Can you put pressure on the wound?"

Carolyn howled with frustration. "Hells Bloody Bells! I'm tied up here. My hands and feet."

The operator told her, "Help is on the way. They should be with you any minute. Try to stay calm."

Sobbing with fear, Carolyn lay across Bob to try to put pressure on the wound, all the time muttering to him, willing him to hang on. "My dear, dear love you can't die; please be strong."

The ambulance arrived and the medics tried to assess his condition. It was immediately obvious that he was in a bad way. John and Jeff arrived home at the same time, to find flashing lights outside the building and police everywhere. They were recognised and admitted to the apartment where they immediately took in the situation and were horrified to see Bob and Carolyn in what looked like a blood bath. They were relieved to find that the blood Carolyn was covered in was not hers.

John sank to his knees besides Carolyn, as her ties were cut. Her wrists and ankles were raw and bleeding, where she had strained to free herself. Her sobs were dreadful to hear as she tried to get back to Bob, who the medics were trying to assess. "Let them do their job, Sis. What in God's name has happened here?" John muttered as he held her tightly. Carolyn was mumbling incoherently about the pizza man and the gun, but all she could focus on was what was happening to Robbie.

Jeff tried to get some information from the paramedics. "How bad is he? He is gonna be okay, isn't he? Oh Jesus, tell me he isn't gonna die."

One of the paramedics shook his head sadly. "It's not looking good I'm afraid, but we need to get him to hospital right now to give him any chance at all. He'll be given every care, I promise you."

The ambulance took Bob to hospital with Carolyn sitting beside him, whilst a police car rushed John and Jeff after the vehicle.

Bob's heart stopped in the ambulance and he had to be resuscitated, so by the time they reached the hospital Carolyn was almost fainting and nearly fell into John's arms. After Bob was examined, the three were told that an operation would be needed to remove the bullet but it would be touch and go as it was very close to his heart.

Jeff was distraught and just stared blankly out of the window. Bob was his brother in every respect and he could not imagine life without him. They had always been there for each other, but this was a battle Bob would have to fight himself. There was nothing he could do to make things better.

John also was close to tears. He kept saying over and over, under his breath, "Come on lad, you can do it." This had all happened so suddenly, at a time when things had seemed to be on the up. He had been moving on and getting back into living a normal life for the first time since Annie's death and now they could lose Bob. He looked across at Carolyn. She had brought so much happiness back into their lives and this was her reward.

Carolyn was out of her mind with shock and worry. She just stared into space, seemingly muttering to herself. In fact she was praying over and over again, "Please let him live".

John phoned Harry, who soon arrived at the hospital, running through the corridors to join them. He had tried to secure the apartment, but the police refused him access whilst the crime scene was investigated. However, he was able to contact Pam and the other office staff to inform them of the situation. He tried to rally the family with words of comfort, but nothing could reassure them until they knew the outcome of the operation.

Publicity started to drift out and Jeff made a statement to the press outside the hospital, saying how poorly Bob was. He said that Bob's wife and family were with him. Someone said, "His children?"

"No!" Jeff cried, "His wife, his brother in law and me. Bob and I have been together since we were eight years old. Is that family enough for you?"

The press and television people were sympathetic, as they could see how upset he was. The men phoned Pam and Tony and asked them to let people know the situation.

The atmosphere at the Shop the next morning was very subdued, as Pam, Tony and Penny tried to keep going whilst being very worried. Fans and friends sent many messages and presents, and there were phone calls all day, including some from England, where Carolyn's friends had heard the news on the television. It seemed bad news did indeed travel fast.

The police were everywhere, investigating the crime scene; looking for fingerprints and anything which would point them towards the gunmen. The pizza delivery man had been killed immediately, so this was in fact now a murder investigation.

Bob's operation took several hours but the surgeons successfully removed the bullet. His heart stopped again whilst in theatre and once again he was resuscitated. The family were told that his recovery would depend on how he survived the next twenty four hours. They were able to sit with him, whilst Harry tried to keep everything together.

He said, "He is stronger than any of you. He'll fight this, just keep talkin' to him."

Carolyn put her face to his and whispered, "Robbie, my Darling, I love you so much. You know I couldn't manage without you. You promised me you'd never leave me. Please, please get better."

The four took it in turns to stretch their legs, but each one could only stay away from the bedside for a short time. Carolyn stroked Bob's forehead and held his hand tightly. She was too frightened to let go.

It was the following morning before she felt a slight answering squeeze to her hand, and suddenly he started to choke on the intubation tube. Carolyn pressed the emergency button, and a nurse ran in immediately, calling a doctor to remove the tube.

Before passing out again, Bob slurred, "Carolyn did they hurt you?"

The relief in the room was palpable. There were sighs and a few more tears, but no-one could help smiling to think that his first thoughts were of Carolyn.

John and Jeff make a joint statement to the press. "He seems to be out of danger, thank God. It's typical of the man, that despite being shot near the heart, losing gallons of blood and stopping breathing twice, his first thoughts were for his wife. He wanted to know if she had been hurt. We would like to thank everyone for their messages. It has meant a lot to us to know people cared so much."

Once Bob was out of danger, John and Jeff went home to shower and change. Carolyn refused to leave Bob, so Pam took a change of clothing and some toiletries to her. Back at the Shop, the office staff phoned round all the friends in America and England, giving them the good news.

The police were still in the apartment and so, after packing a few necessities, John and Jeff arranged to stay in a hotel close to the hospital for at least one night. They booked a room for Carolyn, hoping that they might be able to convince her to have a good night's sleep, but there was no persuading her to leave her Robbie.

"No, I want to be here when he wakes up again, and he'll rest easier knowing I'm with him," she insisted.

John and Jeff were very concerned. "Yes, Sweetheart, but what about your rest? You'll be no good to him if you make yourself ill." Carolyn promised she would think about herself to-morrow.

That night, after the nurse had made her evening round, she climbed into the bed beside Bob and cuddled up to him.

"I'm here, Darling, right here. Night night, God Bless. Just get better for me. I love you so much."

Chapter nineteen

Over the next few days, the improvement in Bob was amazing. His strong constitution, together with the desire to be up and about, contributed to his recuperation. By the end of the week the doctor had promised the family that, if this continued, he would be able to go home in a few days to continue his convalescence.

The Police had now left the apartment, and John, Jeff and Carolyn had been able to return home. However, Carolyn, particularly, had found it very traumatic walking back into the House and seeing where the shooting had taken place. She started to shake at the unwelcome, frightening memories. It was clear that the incident had left its mark on Carolyn, as she was pale with dark rings under her eyes. Despite the fact that Bob was out of danger, she burst out crying at the slightest thing, and was off her food.

Bess was very worried about her beloved "missus". She tried to tempt Carolyn to eat with home-baked cookies and her favourite lasagne, but Bess's kindness only made Carolyn more upset. "Oh Bess, you are kind. Thank you." She blubbered. Bess just gathered her up in her motherly arms and patted her back.

"Come now, you gotta stop this cryin' and start makin' yourself pretty to see that lovely man of yours. He won't be happy to see those red eyes, and a man likes to have somethin' to hold onto child. The way you're goin' on there won't be none of you left to hold."

"You're absolutely right, Bess. I have to pull myself together. Robbie's going to be fine. I just have to keep telling myself that. But, Bess, what would I have done if I'd lost him?" she asked, her big green eyes wide with horror at the thought.

Bess was so worried about Carolyn that she took the first opportunity to go into the office and talk to Pam. "Perhaps if you talked to her, woman to woman like, she might feel better 'bout things. I don't think she feels able to talk to her brother and Mr. Jeff, in case it upsets them."

Pam had actually been thinking along the same lines and so, when Carolyn was due to come in for her morning stint in the office, Pam phoned through to the House."Carolyn, would it be alright if I came through to see you. I could do with a girly chat. Put the coffee on, babe."

They sat either side of the kitchen table, holding the steaming mugs of coffee, relaxed and comfortable in each other's company. "What did you want to talk about, hon?" Carolyn asked.

"I just wanted to see how you were getting on. We haven't had much time on our own since the attack. How are you coping with it all?"

Carolyn shrugged. "I'm fine, Pam; absolutely fine." Then, "Ooh, no I'm not. Not really. Every time I close my eyes I see him falling to the floor, his blood running down his chest. His eyes were staring at me with shock, Pam. Then I see him lying there and the ambulance men working on him. I thought he was going to die. I honestly thought he was dying." By now the tears were pouring down her cheeks and she stopped talking to blow her nose and wipe her eyes. Pam handed her some tissues from the box on the table, but waited for her to continue talking.

"Then he did die. In the ambulance, his heart stopped, and I thought, *Oh God this is it; I've lost him.*" She hiccupped and gave her nose another loud blow.

Pam took both her hands in hers over the table and leant forward. "But he didn't die, did he, Carolyn? They brought him back in the ambulance and again at the hospital. You didn't lose him. He's getting better and stronger every day. Soon he'll be coming home. You have to be positive and look forward to the future, because you do have a future together now. You did everything you could. You managed to get help to him and he is on the mend. Try to focus on that, dear."

They talked together for some time before Pam suggested that Carolyn go back to bed for a couple of hours and try to get some sleep. To her amazement, instead of seeing the shooting when she closed her eyes, she saw Robbie's face smiling at her. She did sleep, cuddling his pillow to her, and awoke feeling more refreshed than she had in a long time. The talk to Pam had really helped her see what was important. They'd come through it and everything was alright.

❧❧

Bob was going home the next day and there was a lot of chatter round his bed as they discussed how he was going to be spoilt and pampered. John's face was serious for a moment as he said, "Something we are all going have to address, folks. We can't chance this sort of thing happening again. Harry has been talking to Jeff and I about taking on more security staff, and with your agreement, that's what we intend to do."

He called Harry into the room, asking him to explain to Bob and Carolyn what had already been discussed with Jeff and himself. Harry said he thought it was crazy that these "superstars" only had him to look after all of them.

Bob sighed and shook his head. "You know, Harry, we'll all be eternally grateful for this fame and the fortune it has made for us, but we never wanted to live in a goldfish bowl. One thing my wife always taught us was that we should keep our feet on the ground and remember where we came from."

The other three agreed with Bob's comments. John shrugged and said "Well yes, we've had a good run haven't we? On the whole we've been able to live normal lives and yet still enjoy the nice things in life. At least Bob and I have. I can't say the same for you, Jeff, when Nicole was around." They all laughed at this reference to Nicole's love of publicity. John continued; "However, after what's just happened, I think we should seriously consider Harry's suggestions."

Harry managed to persuade them that it can be a wicked world, and he felt it was crucial that they took steps to ensure the safety of all of them. It wasn't only in their working life that security was necessary, but also in their private lives. He felt that in future they should have an aide with them at all times. He said that meant at least another two men; three if Carolyn was included. This would also allow for someone to be on night duty and for days off.

They discussed the possibility of making the storeroom in the Shop into a rest room with a bed. The family agreed with all Harry's suggestions, but insisted they did not want "bouncer" type thugs working for them. "If we have to put up with this we need to choose the right people," John said.

They asked Harry to start making enquiries, at his old agency and also at the N.Y.P.D. to see if any police officers were retiring or looking for a change of career.

The next day, Bob was wheeled down to the car in a chair. The press had somehow learned that he was being discharged so there were several photographers and reporters outside. Bob briefly asked the press to thank everyone who had sent messages and flowers. There was a lovely photograph in the international press showing Jeff pushing the chair, with Carolyn on one side holding Bob's hand and John the other, with his hand on Bob's shoulder. All four were smiling and, although Bob was still gaunt and weak, it was obvious to all that he was well on the way to recovery.

Bob's parting shot to the press was to say, "Someone once said, *What doesn't kill us makes us stronger*, and I feel that's what's happening here."

"You seem to have come through it alright, Bob," one reporter remarked.

Carolyn could not restrain herself from saying, "Oh he's definitely getting better; he's started answering me back."

The reporters and photographers were still laughing as the car drove away, taking the four home.

※

Carolyn was so pleased to have her Robbie home again and started fussing around him like an old hen. "Oh God," she remarked, "You'd better change my name to Chucky Mary. I hope you're making a note of all this, because I'll expect the same attention if I'm ever not well."

A sofa was made into a day-bed, complete with cushions, pillows and blankets. Bess and Carolyn waited on him hand and foot and made sure that everything he might need was to hand. At night, Carolyn nestled up to him and they whispered lovingly to each other before they slept.

Harry had arranged interviews with several promising candidates, which were to take place in the week following Bob's return home. They all agreed that Carolyn should be on the panel with John, Harry and Pam. Jeff was to stay in the apartment to keep Bob company. Towards mid afternoon they were disheartened and frustrated. So far, all the applicants had been just the sort they did not want. Huge men most of them, with bland faces and little intelligence. "How can we spend all our time with people like that," Carolyn commented.

"I have a feeling you may approve of the next guy," Harry remarked. Pete Harrison was a retiring police sergeant Harry knew. He was due to retire on Friday from the New York Police Department because of his age and an old sports injury to his knee, which although not debilitating made him unfit for active duty. Pete was in his mid forties, married with a couple of children. He had brown hair, which was receding; was tall and well built. Carolyn's face lit up when he walked in. He looked so normal after the previous disastrous candidates. Because of his present job, he was well used to unsociable hours, so this didn't present a problem to him. Neither did the fact that a great deal of his time would be spent waiting around for one or other of the employers.

John asked him to step into the outer office for a moment and quietly phoned through to Jeff to ask him if he could spare a moment to meet one of the candidates. He came through and was introduced to Pete. It appeared that in fact Pete was quite desperate for a job as he had nothing lined up and had a family to support. Harry said he felt they would be lucky to get him as he had a good reputation at work.

It only remained for Bob to meet him, so Jeff took him through to the apartment. As they left, he whispered to John, "That guy outside doesn't look half bad. He certainly looks the right sort anyway."

John relayed this information to the others saying, "Perhaps things are looking up at last, shall we wheel him in?"

This last candidate of the day was Martin Brewer. His C.V. showed that he had fifteen years military experience, including time spent with Counter-terrorism and with Special Operations. Marty was black, in his early forties and of medium height. Carolyn's first impression was, *what a dour man*. He seemed serious and unsmiling. The panel had a great deal of difficulty in getting him to talk about himself. It appeared that he had led a very hard and lonely life, having no family.

One of his references stated that he was an "intensely loyal man to anyone he considered worthy of his loyalty." This wasn't an easy interview, but there was something in this man which touched each of the panel members. There was a quiet dignity about him, and although he didn't offer any information about himself, he answered each question with consideration and openness. John asked him to wait outside, whilst the four talked about him. Carolyn and Harry thought it worth taking a chance on him. John and Pam were not so sure.

"Do you think he ever smiles?" John commented grimly.

Tony poked his head round the door to remind John he had an appointment. He was to honour one of Bob's commitments at a Boys' club, which would only take an hour, but he needed to leave in the next ten minutes.

Carolyn smiled. "I've got it, John; get Mr. Brewer to drive you and you can see how he works out. It will give you a chance to make up your mind properly and we'll go with whatever you decide." So it was agreed, with Marty and John going off together to the Boys' club.

As they were leaving, a detective and a uniformed officer arrived to have another word with Carolyn and Bob about the shooting incident. Carolyn went with them into the House, where Jeff and Bob were still chatting comfortably with Pete. It happened that Pete and the uniformed officer were old friends, having been at the Police Academy together. Pete explained why he was there, and the officer, Bill, said, "Good luck Pete, you deserve a break."

Jeff took Pete back to the office, whilst Carolyn and Bob were questioned once more. Bob was baffled. "I really don't know what more we can tell you guys. The gunmen were wearing ski-masks and gloves, so we can't give you any description."

The Detective leaned forward, conspiratively, and said, "You know, we sometimes find that if we leave it a while and ask victims again, their minds are clearer and they can remember things which didn't seem important before."

Whilst Bob shook his head, Carolyn took a deep breath before she spoke. "I'm a policeman's daughter, you know, and our Dad always said it was the little things that are important. I've been thinking a lot about that night, and I think I did notice one or two things. Okay, for a start they were both white."

"How on earth could you tell that?" Bob asked.

"They had light eyes, maybe blue or green. I can't be sure." Carolyn commented. "The one who tied me up was about the same height as me, and the other one not much taller, so about five foot eight inches. One was stocky and the other was thin. I think they both had Bronx accents, because they talked like you and Jeff when I first met you. Well, that's about it, but you never know, it may help."

The officers were impressed and thanked Carolyn before leaving. "If you think of anything else, however small, just ring the precinct," the Detective said.

As Carolyn was showing them out, Harry came into the corridor, having been told by Pete of Bill's presence. "Hello Red, nice to see you. I've just heard you'll be another ex-police officer in the employment queue from Friday. You wouldn't be interested in talking to us about a job would you? Carolyn, meet "Red" Power; so named because of his red hair and complexion."

Whilst the Detective chatted to Penny and Tony, "Red" was ushered in to meet Pam and without any preamble was offered one of the vacant posts.

Bill "Red" Power was retiring following an injury sustained in the line of duty and would have a pension, but felt he was too young at forty two to retire completely, so was delighted to accept. He was married with one daughter. As with Pete, his wife was well used to shift work and unsociable hours.

Meanwhile, John was finding that Marty was a different man in a one to one situation. Whilst still serious and quietly spoken, he opened up more to John and, without going into much detail, was able to tell him some of his experiences. He had indeed led a violent and unhappy life, but never turned away from his duty in his service to his country.

As they were driving home, he turned to John, who was sitting beside him. "I feel I must be totally honest with you, Mr. Davidson, before you make a decision on me. I'm a recovering alcoholic. Haven't had a drink now for over a year and hope I never will, but the temptation is always there."

John took stock for a moment before replying. "Thanks, Marty, but you realise I have to tell the others this. It isn't something I can keep to myself. However, I'm willing to take a chance on you, providing Bob and Jeff agree. My name is John, by the way and I think we'll get along just fine. But Marty; if you ever let me down, there mightn't be a second chance."

When they returned, John told the others what he had decided. Marty was introduced to Jeff and Bob, who seemed to bring the man out of himself. He even managed a smile when he was offered the third post, subject to checks. The new security men were told that Harry would be their immediate boss. Arrangements were in hand for the alterations to the storeroom. A bed, table and chairs had been ordered to make it into a rest room which could be used by the men, where the night staff could rest their heads. A kitchen and bathroom had already been installed in the Shop area.

꧁꧂

Pam pushed open the door of her apartment and shouted, "Joe, I'm home," before throwing herself into the easy chair and kicking off her shoes.

Her husband appeared from the kitchen carrying two steaming cups of coffee. "Ooh, my baby looks tired. Had a busy day, Pammy?"

"Yes I have, but it's been fun. We've been interviewing for security staff. I've brought the details home, because John asked if you'd do a check on the three men we've chosen, and then draw up their contracts. Two of them are pretty straight forward. The third may take a little more time."

Joe pulled a stool up in front of Pam and lifted a dainty foot onto his knee. "Forget about work for a little while, I'm gonna give you a nice foot massage," he said, proceeding to kneed the sole of one foot and then the other.

"Ooh, that's so good. Mmmm, Mr. Magic Fingers," she sighed in ecstasy. How's your day gone? Did you get chance to speak to your Momma about comin' over at the weekend?"

Joe shook his head. No, I haven't had chance. All hell broke loose in the office to-day. I've been so busy that, to be honest I didn't give this weekend a second thought. I'll phone her this evening. Now, I picked up a lasagne and some salad from the deli, so no cooking to-night. There's a bottle of nice wine in the fridge and we can eat as soon as you're ready."

The Abrahams' apartment was furnished with bright autumn colours, mahogany tables and wall units. With two working people living there, it was never totally tidy, but had that lived in, comfortable look of home.

Since working with Carolyn and having something to fill her days and focus on, Pam had once again become the girl Joe had fallen in love with. She was happy and motivated. Their marriage had been a love match, with much opposition from both families and from their friends. Initially, in the first throws of passion, none of this had seemed to matter, but as time went on they had found the isolation chilling and lonely. Arguments had started to creep in to their otherwise placid relationship and Pam had grown depressed and moody. Things had come to a head when Pam had started to be bullied at work. Usually so strong and outspoken, this had been more than she could cope with, so they had decided she should leave. Sitting at home, day after day, did nothing to raise her spirits and once again their marriage suffered. They had actually started discussing a trial separation when the opportunity had risen for Pam to help Carolyn. Joe thanked the powers that be for the chance, which had made such a difference to them.

Pam closed her eyes, enjoying the experience of Joe's strong fingers stroking and massaging her feet. One eye opened, and she smiled as his hands travelled up her legs, to her calves and then proceeded up her skirt. "Oh, you're such a bad boy. Takin' advantage of a poor, tired, helpless woman. Mmm, that's nice. Don't stop. How about you and I defer supper for an hour and have a little lie down."

Without further preamble, Joe stood and taking her hand pulled her up from the chair. "I think that would be a very good idea. Poppa's just in the mood to please his lady."

Chapter twenty

The new staff soon became part of the everyday life and routine of the family. Bob's health and strength continued to improve, so Carolyn settled back into normality. She was very happy, but since nearly losing him for good, Robbie had become even more precious to her. She was afraid to let him out of her sight.

"Surely things have to go right for us now, Darlin'," he said one day to her. "In just a few months, there seems to have been one crisis after another."

Jeff's first divorce hearing was due to be heard the following day, and he was on edge worrying about the settlement he knew Nicole would demand. "I just know she's gonna try to bankrupt me. She's gonna hold out for the maximum she can get."

When they were alone, Carolyn turned to Bob and asked "Do you feel like a little trip out tomorrow, Robbie? I want to go with Jeff to this hearing and I don't think it would go down too well if I went on my own."

Bob was puzzled. "Why do you wanna go? They won't let you into the hearing anyway; and why would it look bad you going with him?"

Carolyn took a deep breath and told him about what Nicole had said at the Showcase, the first week they had been back in New York. "If I go on my own with Jeff, it will add fuel to her rumour-mongering that there's something going on between us. Besides, I have something up my sleeve."

Bob was furious to hear of Nicole's comments, and very curious as to what Carolyn had in mind, but she just winked and tapped the side of her nose. "I know we won't be able to go into the Hearing with him, Robbie. At least we can wait for him and be there to give him our support."

The next day, the three waited in the corridor with Joe Abrahams for the Hearing to begin. Nicole had not yet appeared, and Carolyn was tense, waiting for the opportunity to put her plan into motion. When she did at last make her grand entrance, Nicole flounced past the four with a smirk on her face. As usual, she was accompanied by a photographer and dressed as if she was going to a grand function, instead of a divorce hearing.

Carolyn saw her walk into the ladies cloakroom, presumably to make sure her hair and make-up were perfect. W*onderful,* Carolyn thought. *This is my chance.*

"Won't be a mo' lads," she muttered, as she followed Nicole into the cloakroom.

Nicole turned around from admiring her face in the mirror, when she saw Carolyn standing behind her. "I don't think it's a good idea you being in here. What do you want?" she asked nervously.

"Oh, you know; when you've got to go, you've got to go." Carolyn replied. "How are you keeping, Nicole? I've often wanted to ask you if that wig made your head itch. Watching the C.C.T.V.," she bluffed, "I must say you suit blond hair better than dark. You might be able to disguise your hair, but you'll never be able to disguise that miserable face or your slutty walk. Did you really think no-one would recognise you?"

Nicole, by now, was looking decidedly uncomfortable. "I really don't know what you're talking about, Carolyn. You can't pin anything on me."

Carolyn enjoyed Nicole's every facial expression as she took the tape machine from her pocket. "Oh but I can, Nicole. What with the C.C.T.V. (remember, the camera never lies), and with this tape, I've got you banged to rights. You see, your crony, Stella, was most helpful in explaining what had happened that day, and I've got it all here, including my dear, details of your clever texting and impersonation of me. You know, I think the press would be over the moon to have both tapes, don't you? Be an end to your celebrity days though. The Honeys are on a roll just now with the public, what with Bob getting shot. I don't think it would make you too popular if people knew how you hurt him."

Nicole's face had turned from puce to white. She could see her lifestyle and the little popularity she had, fading before her eyes. "What do you want?" she hissed.

"What I want," Carolyn said firmly, "is for you to go easy on Jeff. Just take what you are entitled to and don't try to ruin him. I swear here and now, that if I think you have gone even a dollar over the top, both the C.C.T.V. tape and this audio tape will be in the hands of the press by the end of the day."

Without waiting for a reply, Carolyn turned on her heels and, with head held high, walked out of the cloakroom and back to Bob, Jeff and Joe. The Hearing was due to start and it wasn't long before those involved were called into the chamber. Carolyn and Bob took a seat outside and Carolyn quickly whispered to Bob what she had said to Nicole.

"You minx," he stuttered. "You mean she actually believed you about the camera?"

Carolyn shrugged "Well, we'll soon know, won't we. Anyhow I think it was worth a try. That woman's so up herself, all she'll be worried about is her reputation."

Jeff and Joe appeared in what seemed a very short time, Jeff beaming from ear to ear. Carolyn nudged Bob when she saw the smile. "I don't believe it," Jeff said. "She was actually reasonable. She seemed reluctant to push it any further."

The amount of the settlement seemed enormous to Carolyn, but Joe assured them that it was the least she could have expected. As Nicole walked passed them, the look she gave Carolyn was purely malicious and, despite her victory, she could feel the hairs stand up on the back of her neck.

Oh, she thought, Robbie was right; *we're not finished with her yet.*

Harry and Marty were waiting outside for them and ushered them into the car away from the waiting cameras and pressmen. It wasn't until they arrived home and Joe had left, that Carolyn and Bob told Jeff, and a laughing John, about Carolyn's "meeting" in the cloakroom with Nicole.

"Oh Honey, that's outrageous. You're truly amazing," Jeff roared.

Carolyn smiled, "I promised you I'd help sort things out and it's only what she deserved. Let's hope she leaves it at that and stays away from all of us. I just never want to see her again."

The four opened a bottle of champagne to celebrate and toasted their future. It seemed that at last things were going right for them.

❧

Bess still came in most days and now stayed until tea time. Her niece had been drafted in to help, especially with keeping the Shop clean, and on Bess' days off when she prepared meals for the family. Carolyn was Bess' idol and could do no wrong. "The missus" always praised where praise was due and made a fuss of the motherly woman. She now loved coming into work and the apartment was spotless. When she wasn't busy in the office or out with the men, Carolyn enjoyed getting involved with the cooking, and showed Bess how to make their favourite cottage pie and other English dishes.

Most Sundays, the four loved to sit down to a family roast dinner, when Bess would leave everything prepared for Carolyn to cook the meat and vegetables. There was usually an apple pie or something equally delicious for afters. Whichever security man was on duty was often invited along. This was usually either Harry or Marty, as Pete and "Red" were usually given Sundays off to be with their families.

Carolyn was enjoying her time spent in the office each day. Tony's funny sense of humour and the banter between him and the three girls was a source of real pleasure. *What a difference, from when I first arrived here,* she thought. Penny had come out of her shell, gaining confidence and maturity under the influence of the two older women, whilst Pam and Carolyn had become closer still in the aftermath of the shooting.

The three new men had all been accepted as part of the extended family and had all become fond of their employers. Harry was, of course, still treated with affection and respect by all. However, he was still puzzled by his new nickname. "Morning L.H.," Tony and Penny would shout, as he popped his head round the door each day.

Harry had taken Marty under his wing and the two had become close friends. Neither had any family and it seemed natural, therefore, that the two should spend time together. As had been hoped, Marty had accepted these four as being worthy of his loyalty and although still very quiet most of the time, everyone felt blessed when they were the recipient of one of his rare smiles.

At one of the staff meetings, which now had grown to include any of the aides who were on site, Pam read out a letter from a children's hospice. It was the same institution which Bob had been diaried to visit on the day of Nicole and Stella's cruel confidence trick.

The matron, Cathy Fellows, reminded Bob that he had promised to make new arrangements to visit and said that the children kept asking her about him. She wondered if it would be possible for him to become a "Friend of the Hospice", which would entail visiting occasionally. Some of the children were staying for respite care, whilst others were desperately ill and would never leave the hospice. Carolyn thought it was a lovely idea to get involved, and asked Pam to make arrangements for her to visit with Bob.

When they arrived on the first occasion, Cathy met them at the door and ushered them through to the day lounge, where respite children were sitting around in chairs. We call these the walking wounded," Cathy said as a way of introduction. "They have been so excited at the thought of meeting you."

Cathy Fellows had been matron of the Hospice for nearly ten years. It had become her life since she had lost her husband two years ago. She had a nine year old son, who she adored, but apart from him she had no other interests besides the welfare of the children in her care. After her husband's death, she had discovered that he had been unfaithful to her for some time and her confidence had been rocked so much that she had a deep mistrust of most men. She was an attractive woman in her mid thirties, with fair hair and blue eyes. Carolyn was immediately attracted to her and thought what a nice woman she was.

Bob and Carolyn spent time chatting with the children in the day room, and then asked if they could perhaps visit some of the bed-ridden children. Many of them were obviously very poorly, but a kind word and a little time spent holding hands seemed to be a great comfort, not only to the children, but also to relatives who were visiting. This then became a regular date for Bob and Carolyn, who made a point of popping in to the hospice at least once every couple of weeks when they were available.

܀

Now Bob was back in good health, the Honeys had started working on their new album. This was a compilation of mainly new songs, including *No More Loneliness,* which Bob had written for Carolyn on their Wedding Day. They spent many hours in the recording studio with musicians, sound men, the producer and other staff.

Over the next couple of months, therefore, Carolyn saw less and less of Bob and the other two men as they were always exhausted when they eventually finished work each evening. Bedtime was always Carolyn's favourite time of the day. She and Bob would curl up together and he would tell her about different incidents which had occurred during the day in the studio, whilst she would recount office gossip or bits of trivia from her day. It was the only time of the day that they were ever truly alone, and whilst they loved having Jeff and John living with them, they treasured these moments spent in each other's arms. Their love-making was still wonderful and passionate, although many times during these busy months Bob would fall asleep from sheer exhaustion, just holding Carolyn closely.

The four had been invited to a party at a hotel to celebrate a friend's fortieth birthday. Carolyn bought a new dress for the occasion and felt elated when all three men made a fuss of her appearance.

The dress was black; ankle length with a halter neck, plunging neckline and split up the side of the skirt to the thigh. It made her feel very sexy. At the party, Bob could not take his eyes off her. His gorgeous, darling girl looked wonderful. The chemistry was mutual as she watched her handsome husband across the room dressed in his black tuxedo.

Oh boy, she thought. *Don't men look great in dinner jackets!*

He caught her eye across the room and walked across to her. Darlin'," he whispered. "That dress is absolutely stunnin', but I can't wait to see it on the bedroom floor. You don't know what you're doin' to me looking like that."

Seeing the whispers and smouldering looks between the two, Jeff laughed, "Come on you two, get a room."

Carolyn blushed and slipped her hand into Bob's. A few minutes later, she excused herself and went out to the ladies' room, then, giggling under her breath she crossed the foyer to the reception desk. "I'm feeling a little tired and could do with a lie down. Do you have a room free by any chance, just for the afternoon?" she asked the Receptionist.

Ever the soul of discretion, the receptionist took payment with Carolyn's debit card and handed her a room key.

Feeling very daring, by now, Carolyn went back into the party room and whispered in Bob's ear, "Darling Robbie, if you meet me in room ten, fourth floor, you may see something to your advantage."

Bob watched as she sashayed out through the door, throwing him one of her dazzling smiles over her shoulder. After a decent interval, he followed Carolyn out of the room and took the elevator up to the fourth floor where she was waiting for him. Sure enough, the black dress was in a heap on the floor. She was giggling with glee as he picked her up and deposited her on the bed.

The dinner jacket, shirt and trousers ended up on top of the dress as he quickly kicked his shoes off in his rush to join her on the mattress.

"Just look at those awful curtains, she squealed. How could anyone have chosen them?"

"I'm not looking at any bloody curtains, girl," Bob sighed as he kissed her, his arms holding her closely; whilst his long fingers fondled her breasts and moved down to hold her bottom and stroke between her legs until she was breathless and panting for him to enter her. He teased her and held back, kneeling and pulling her up so that she was facing him on the bed, whilst his kisses became more and more urgent.

Both of them were so engrossed, that neither noticed the flash of a camera which, for a second, lit up the mirror behind the bed. Nor did they hear the door quietly close.

At last, Bob laid her down and entered her, bringing them both to a climax which left them both feeling totally sated.

Sometime later, when they rejoined the others at the party, the two of them were giggling like a couple of conspirators.

"That was nice, wasn't it?"Carolyn whispered.

Bob smiled lovingly, "Oohh! Wasn't it though? Surprises are always the best."

༺๏๛๏༻

Chapter twenty one

Before releasing a single from the new album, the Honeys had to make a video. The single was to be *What is Love?* It was about the different types of love between family, friends and lovers. The producer of the video, Philip Carter, was a very clever man, who always managed to bring the best out of people. He and Carolyn got their heads together and came up with a "story" to fit the vocals.

The opening setting was a park, where a family with Mum, Dad and kids were playing and laughing. The camera then scanned to The Honeys kicking a ball around, which was something they had done for years. They almost forgot they were being filmed, and the enjoyment was obvious on their faces. In the background their voices would ring out with the words of the song. After a while, they flopped down on the grass. They saw three young boys rapping, so they stood up and went over to them. Some "Rap" had been incorporated into the song. This was done on the record by Jeff and Bob, as John was completely hopeless, but it was felt he needed to look to be a part of it on the film. The three guys started the rapping; copying the movements of the three youngsters, but John couldn't speak for giggling. As the other two carried bravely on, the tears were running down his face as he shook with mirth. By the time the section was finished the three of them were holding onto each other because they were all laughing so much. Every facial expression was caught on camera.

The third and last section saw the three men walking down the street at night and going into a club, where they were allocated young women to sit on their knees.

Carolyn, watching from the wings, found this very amusing but, referring to the lady on Robbie's knee, whispered to the producer, "Bloody hell, Phil, where did you find her? I've seen better legs hanging out of a nest."

He laughingly said, "Do you think you could do any better?"

She surprised him by saying, "I do yes."

Without making any comments to the group, she took her trousers off, leaving her in a shirt blouse which just about covered the essentials. She rolled the sleeves up to just below her elbows and turned up the collar. Whilst the make-up attendant quickly powdered her nose, Phil called the other young lady off, and Carolyn walked onto the set, draping herself on her husband's knee. The look on Bob's face was pure astonishment. The camera also managed to catch the amazed look on both John and Jeff's faces. The chemistry and smouldering looks between the two lovers was also captured.

With the Honeys' voices reaching the finale of the song, the three were about the leave the club, and whilst the strains of the music came to an end, Bob's face could be seen scanning the club for the lady. (He was actually looking around for

Carolyn). As they reached the doors he glanced around one more time, and there she was at his shoulder. He smiled broadly at her and she left the club with him. The final scene was of them walking hand in hand in the park.

When they saw the finished video they were delighted. Phil had created a masterpiece. He had managed to incorporate all the laughter of the "Rap" and the enjoyment of the soccer, showing the affection between the three men. The club section was a wonderful finale.

The expressions on Bob's and Carolyn's faces seemed to tell a story of lovers meeting and the words of the song said the rest. When released, the single was a great success, reaching the top of the charts.

However, forever afterwards, every time they performed this number on stage, and started to rap, John raised his eyes to the sky and they all laughed. He never managed to master it. It was always a popular number, and soon the audience was already laughing as soon as they heard the opening chords of the song.

∽⁕∾

Life was good, and the Honeys were back on top where they belonged. Carolyn arranged an auction to raise money for the children's hospice. They called on show business friends to help and some of the men were "auctioned" as a date. At the auction Jeff and John met Cathy Fellows, the matron from the children's hospice, for the first time. John, particularly, was immediately attracted both by her looks and her dignified and efficient manner. She was different from the usual women he met and in fact didn't recognise him until Carolyn introduced her "darling brother".

The next day, John phoned Cathy and asked her out for dinner, but she refused. She was not impressed by his fame and fortune. He persisted over the next few weeks, sending her flowers and phoning her. Eventually, he couldn't get her out of his head, so he paid a visit to the hospice.

As he walked into the entrance hall, Cathy was in the process of talking to the family of one of the sick children. Not wishing to intrude, he stood patiently looking at some of the photographs which adorned the walls. They were all of children who had been patients at the hospice. John was struck by the smiles and glowing faces of these lovely children, some of whom he knew would no longer be alive.

Cathy's voice at his shoulder startled him and he turned to smile at her. Whatever are you doing here, Mr. Davidson?"

"I wondered if I could change your mind about coming out for a meal with me sometime," John replied; his usual self-assurance rattled by the feelings which washed over him as he looked into her eyes.

Cathy was busy, and at first didn't want to make time for him, but his gentle and charming manner eventually melted her reluctance so she stopped work and made him a cup of coffee. She saw that he was very down to earth and so like Carolyn in personality that she couldn't help liking him. Eventually she agreed to spend the following evening with him, and he arranged to pick her up from her home.

Carolyn was delighted when John told her he was to take Cathy out on a date. She had become very fond of Cathy during the visits which she and Bob made regularly to the hospice and thought she was just what John needed.

※

One afternoon, when Carolyn walked back into the House, after spending time in the office, all three men were in the lounge looking very serious. In fact, Bob's face was thunderous as he caught Carolyn's eye. When she approached them, he handed her a photograph and what she saw made her gasp with horror. The photograph was obviously of her, naked, in the arms of a man, who was most definitely not her husband.

Carolyn could hardly speak. This was just too horrible to comprehend.

"It's me… How? … I don't understand," she managed to mutter. "It's me!" she said again louder. She looked pleadingly into Bob's face, her eyes wide with horror.

Bob laughed mirthlessly. "Well at least that's somethin' we can all agree on."

John turned to her with disgust on his face. "My God, Carolyn, what have you done?"

A howl, like an animal in pain came from Carolyn's mouth. All she could think was, *This was it. This would part them where a bullet couldn't.*

"John, you really think... Oh my God, John. Knowing how I feel about him, how can you think I would be capable of that?"

She couldn't look at her darling Robbie. She was too afraid what she would see in his face. She could feel the bile rising into her throat and knew she was about to be sick, until he spoke.

"Of course she wouldn't. Are you crazy John? No, this is what we've been waiting for. This is their vengeance. I don't know how, but these photographs are obviously fakes. They say revenge is a dish best served cold."

Carolyn turned to him and instead of the hate and disgust she had expected, all she saw was love and realised that he believed in her.

"But Robbie it's me. How can it be?"

Bob took her by the shoulders. "Darlin', I don't know how or when, but remember what we said. Trust and have faith. I do trust you, so that means these are fakes and we'll get to the bottom of it."

Carolyn closed her eyes and swayed against him. "But you looked so angry, Robbie."

Bob dried her tears with his fingers "Not with you, my Darling. I'm angry with the low-lifes who think they can split us up. Why can't we just be happy? Why do all these things keep happenin' to us?"

Carolyn ran to the bathroom, where she was violently sick. After splashing cold water on her face she went back into the lounge, where a shamefaced John shook his head.

"I'm so sorry, Caro. It was just reaction when I saw them."

Bob put his hand to her face. "Baby, are you alright? You look so pale."

Carolyn straightened her back and shook the hair from her face. "I'll be fine, thank you Robbie. Right! Now you've all had a good look at my bare boobs, let's have another look at this photograph."

The tension lifted with her outrageous comments and Carolyn took the photograph to the window where she studied it for a moment.

"Well, I think we can work out where and when, but I really don't know how. Robbie, look at these curtains. Do you remember them?"

Bob shook his head, "I can't say I do, no. I've been looking at that photograph for half an hour trying to see something familiar."

Carolyn held the photograph out to him and pointed again at the curtains. I think I said something like, "Look at those awful curtains," and you said, "I'm not looking at any bloody curtains, girl."

Bob let out a gasp. That party; the hotel room. But no-one could have known what we were going to do. Unless we were followed."

Jeff interrupted. "Will someone please tell us what you're talkin' about?"

Carolyn quickly related the story of how she had come to book a room at the hotel. "And you two can take the smirks of your faces," she said crossly.

"But who in heaven is this man, Robbie? I mean, look at my face. There's only one man who could put an expression like that on it. Oh for heaven's sake look at his reflection in the mirror. Look at that mark on his chest. It's just where your tattoo would be; only it looks as if it's on the opposite side. It has to be you. They've lightened your skin and added a different face. We need to know who would be capable of doing something like that."

"We're going to have to ask Harry and the team if they can help us." John said. "Caro, that means we're going to have to show them this photograph. This isn't something we can deal with ourselves. Will you be happy with that?"

"Not happy, no; but you're right John. We can't deal with this ourselves and I want it sorted. Someone is going to pay for this." Carolyn said angrily.

John called the security staff who were on duty. Harry, Marty and Pete came in and Carolyn reluctantly let them look at the photograph, saying

"Just one snigger, or even one smirk, and you're all fired."

Bob told the men what they had been able to figure out, and asked if they could come up with any ideas. Pete remembered a similar case he'd been involved with, and had a suspicion who the photographer might be. He said he would check first with his old precinct to see if they had anyone else on their books.

"Leave it with us," Harry said. "We'll investigate and let you know if we find anything."

After calling on one or two people on their list, the three men paid a visit to a private investigator, who was also a photographer, and who had been prosecuted in the past for falsifying photographs. The man, Freddie Tyson, was definitely shifty and was not able to hide his discomfort at the presence of these three big, stern men who were obviously not going to leave without finding out what they had come for.

Marty surprisingly took charge of the situation. "Harry, Pete, perhaps you'd like to wait outside whilst I have a chat with this punk. As ex-cops, I'm sure you'd be reluctant to use violence to find out the truth, but believe me, I have no such scruples."

Harry nodded, pushing Pete out of the room in front of him. The look on Freddie's face was one of pure terror as he turned back to the unsmiling Marty.

"Now Freddie, are you gonna tell me what I want to know, or am I gonna have to whup yo' ass," Marty hissed as he started to roll up his sleeves.

The threat alone was enough to start Freddie talking. It appeared that two women had come to see him and asked him to tail Mr. and Mrs. Maples to find something which could be used against them. It hadn't been difficult to follow them as they were nearly always together, but he had almost given up finding anything detrimental until the day of the party. He had seen Carolyn ask for a room key and had followed her up to the room. She had left the door ajar, and he had slipped into the bathroom before Bob had arrived. He had taken only one photograph from the bottom corner of the bed, which showed them both kneeling, facing each other. You could see their reflection in the mirror behind the bed. It had been perfect, and he had left the room without either of them detecting his presence. It had been a simple matter to alter Bob's appearance and produce the fake image.

He was able to give them the name from the signature on the cheque which had been paid to him. Nicole Simmonds had given him a very large sum for his trouble. Details of addresses and another name, Stella Baldwin, gave the men all the proof they needed.

To make sure that they had all the necessary information, Freddie was forced to sign a confession to his part in the affair, naming the two women who had paid for his services.

When they went back to report on their findings, Harry insisted that Bob and Carolyn report the whole affair officially to the police. "You have to put a stop to those two witches here and now. The only way to do that is to prosecute them. If you don't, you'll always have them hanging over you like a bad smell; then one day they'll do something so evil you won't see it coming and they will truly harm you."

Somewhat reluctantly, the official complaint was made. Unfortunately, it meant an even wider audience for the offending photograph, but even Carolyn could see sense in the decision.

"Flipping heck! I don't know why I just don't charge a dollar a look and be done with it. Is everyone in New York going to see Carolyn Davidson Maples in all her glory, or what!"

The investigating detectives promised to be totally discrete with the photograph and were able to report by the end of the day that both Stella and Nicole, together with Freddie Tyson, had been arrested. Bail was to be agreed, and the family would be kept advised of future developments.

༺◈༻

Chapter twenty two

John had taken Cathy out for dinner on a couple of occasions and enjoyed her company. He had found it very difficult to start dating again after Annie's death. At first he felt awkward and unsure of himself, although this was never apparent in his demeanour. John always had a presence about him, which gave the impression of confidence. He seemed to know what to say and do in any situation; always having the answer to problems. This meant that he was constantly the one to turn to for advice, so he had always been the backbone and quiet strength of the family. This aura often hid his gentle and kind nature.

On these dates with Cathy, the two found each other comfortable and easy to talk to. Before long they knew almost everything about the other's life and past. John told Cathy about Annie's illness and how Bob and Jeff had been such a support to him during that very difficult time. He told her of his love for his sister and how much it meant to him that she was married so happily to Bob and had come home to them.

"Carolyn will probably never know how hard it hit me when she left, and I can never dwell on it too much, because she feels bad already about not being here for all of us. She's brought joy back into our lives, despite attempts from some pretty evil people to split her and Bob up."

He told Cathy about Stella and Nicole, relating their two confidence tricks.

"Perhaps now that everything is out in the open we can have some peace and a chance to move on and be happy. That's all the four of us have ever wanted really, to be happy. Okay, so we live in a bit of a cocoon, surrounded by people who care about us, but what is important to all of us is the family. That's something outsiders have always found hard to grasp."

Cathy had become very fond of this quietly spoken Englishman. The more he talked about "his family" and how much he cared for them, the more she saw the other, gentle, compassionate side of him. She loved the story of how the four of them had "found each other" and become so close, and was moved to tears by the tale of Bob and Carolyn's love which had survived their separation, against all odds.

Cathy in turn was able to tell John of her late husband's infidelity and how hurt she had felt on finding out about his mistress after his death.

"She actually turned up at his funeral. I didn't know who she was until she introduced herself. They'd apparently been sleeping together on and off for about three years. There I was, the grieving widow with a seven year old son and up she came to tell me all about their sordid little affair. It nearly destroyed me, John. I didn't think I would ever be able to trust a man again."

"And now?" John asked. "You must feel there is something here between us, Cathy. Its early days, but I know I've got feelings for you, and I'm sure you don't altogether dislike me." This last remark was made with a shy smile on his lips and raised eyebrows.

Cathy sighed. "If we're being honest with each other, yes I know I could be very fond of you, John; but we'll have to take this slowly because my head's all over the place where you are concerned."

John took her hand across the table, "Cathy, we will take it as slowly as you like. In the circumstances, it would be a mistake for either of us to rush into something that wasn't going to work out. We've both had heartbreak one way or another. I wouldn't want you to think I could just forget about Annie and move on without looking back from time to time. We weren't together all that long, but she was a sweet girl. I loved her, and she deserves to be remembered."

Far from making Cathy uncomfortable, John's words made her feel even closer to him. She realised how vulnerable he actually was.

"You and Carolyn are more alike than you realise you know. The two of you have always been the strength of that family, and when she wasn't around, you had to take all of it on yourself, didn't you? You say you couldn't have coped without Jeff and Bob when your wife was ill; but they would never be the men they are now, if you hadn't moulded them and given them a purpose. I do know you are appreciated, however. Bob talks of you so warmly and with such affection."

On their fourth outing, Cathy suggested that John should meet her son, Bradley. Up until then,

John had only ever got as far as the door to Cathy's apartment and had never presumed to be invited inside. It was with a certain amount of trepidation, therefore, that he accepted Cathy's invitation to supper and was introduced to the nine year old, who glared at him over wire rimmed spectacles. John had thoughtfully brought along a couple of the latest computer games, together with a bouquet of flowers for Cathy. Nothing, however, could raise a smile from Bradley who answered every question with a sniff or a shrug.

Uh, uh! John thought. *I'm going to have my work cut out here.* He didn't, however, give up trying to make conversation and find a point of communication, so by the time Cathy announced it was Bradley's bed time, John was thoroughly exhausted.

"He just doesn't like me, does he?" John sighed.

Cathy laughed, "Of course he likes you. He's got a Honeys' poster on his wall and he's always playing your CDs and dancing to them. He is so old fashioned for a nine year old. He's just jealous, because he's had his Mom to himself for so long. Please be patient. I'm sure he'll come around when he realises how nice you are."

John felt his heart swell at this last remark and it encouraged him to put his arm around Cathy's shoulders and draw her to him for a long and lingering kiss. She didn't resist; kissing him back with a passion that surprised and delighted him.

"Just how slow do I have to take this, Cathy?" John whispered in her ear as they reluctantly sat back.

Cathy exhaled and smiled at him. "If I'm not being too forward, not too slow, John. Will you stay with me to-night? But please be patient. There was only ever my husband before and..."

John kissed her again, on her lips, on her neck and her ears. "Cathy, it's been a long time for both of us, but trust me and everything will be wonderful. Bradley isn't likely to appear any minute is he?"

Cathy giggled girlishly. "No, he never wakes up. He'll be in the land of nod having sweet dreams."

Cathy led John to the bedroom, where they almost tore the clothes from each other. John couldn't believe the way the quiet, efficient, ladylike Cathy, suddenly turned into a sexy and passionate tornado.

Her hands caressed his shoulders and his back as he kissed her deeply, his tongue probing and tasting the sweet corners of her mouth, then down her neck as he breathed in her heady perfume. She rolled on top of him and sat astride, taking his hands and placing them on her breasts as she lowered herself on to his erection, moving and moaning all the time. Wanting to take charge, John tossed her back onto the bed and, still joined together, they both reached climax at the same time.

Much later, as they lay in each other's arms John puzzled, "Cathy, your husband must have been mad looking elsewhere. You're sensational, and I know I said we would take this slowly, but Cathy, you really are special."

※

Back at the House, Carolyn was a little concerned when John had not returned home by the time she and Bob were going to bed. It wasn't unusual for Jeff to stay out all night, but it was very unusual for John. Bob laughed, "Darlin', stop worrying. He was going to Cathy's for supper and he's probably staying over.

Carolyn's face was a picture as she bit her lip and smiled knowingly. "Oh, I do hope you're right, Robbie. Wouldn't it be lovely if they made a go of it? They're so well suited, and I do like her. Ooh…"

Bob kissed the tip of her nose "Caro, don't be buyin' a wedding hat yet. Just let them find their own way and don't even think of interfering."

"As if I would." Carolyn said, still smirking.

※

Out of the blue, Bob announced that he was taking Carolyn on holiday.

"Do you know, we have never had a honeymoon? We've been married nearly two years and never had a proper vacation. Just look what's happened in that time. All the traumas most people don't have in a lifetime. How would you feel about a couple of weeks on a beach somewhere, just the two of us?"

They excitedly discussed their options and, after searching the Internet, decided on a luxury cabin on the beach in the Maldives. They would be completely alone, except for maid service each day. They could either eat at the main hotel, or meals and other requirements would be brought to the cabin on request. As they had no commitments for the next few weeks, they were to leave in a couple of days.

"We'll ask John to pop into the hospice for us, while we're away" Bob said cheekily. "I'm sure he won't mind."

The holiday was just what Carolyn and Bob needed to recharge their batteries. What with Stella and Nicole's evil tricks and Bob being shot, their first couple of years together would have rocked a less strong couple but their trials had, if anything, brought them closer together.

When they were shown to their cabin, Carolyn couldn't contain her glee. The water lapped the white sand only yards away from the cabin terrace. Coconut palms shaded the patio outside the door, where there were sun beds as well as a table and chairs. The inside of the cabin was cool and airy with a huge bed and a sitting room area.

"Oh my God, Robbie, it's so beautiful. I've never seen anything like it. Look at that sand and the water is so blue and clear. Oh darling, I love it, I love you. Ooh... I don't believe it." Carolyn gabbled as she spun round and round with her arms held out wide and her eyes like organ stops.

Bob caught her in his arms, laughing and spinning round with her before kissing her. "We've come a long way since Brooklyn Bridge, haven't we, darlin'? We could never have imagined we'd ever be able to afford a vacation like this. I want this to be so special for you, Baby."

"It already is, Robbie. Right, let's get our cozzies on. Last one in the sea is no good; chop him up for firewood," she shouted excitedly in a sing-song voice.

They hurriedly changed into their beachwear and ran into the sea, hand in hand, shrieking with laughter. The water was deliciously warm on their skin and it wasn't long before the new trunks and bikini were discarded in the sea. Bob's hands caressed her back and buttocks as he held her to him and kissed her ardently. He lifted her up so that her legs were around his waist as he entered her and took her with passion and without regard for the water lapping around them.

Sated, they ran back to the seclusion of the cabin where they dried each other lovingly. Wearing fluffy bathrobes which had been left for them, they raided the fridge to find a feast of cold chicken, ham and cheese. There was salad, fruit and fresh crispy bread.

"I think I've died and gone to heaven. Robbie, pinch me. Ouch not that hard, you scally."

They had always been close and at ease in each other's company, first as friends and then as lovers. The two weeks, doing nothing but lazing around in the sun, swimming and making love, was a magical, precious time to them both. Most evenings they walked hand in hand up to the main hotel, where they dined and chatted to other holidaymakers. Then they would amble back to their cabin where they sat on the terrace to talk or make love under the stars.

The night before they were due to return to New York, they lay in each other's arms listening to the gentle sound of the waves on the beach.

"Oh, I've enjoyed this couple of weeks so much, Robbie," Carolyn sighed. "It's been so relaxing and uncomplicated. Can we please come back again someday?"

Bob tightened his hold on her and breathed in the lovely fresh smell of her hair. He kissed her as she turned her face up to him. "Darlin', this will be our haven from now on and whenever we need a break, this is where we'll come."

John and Jeff were pleased to see them on their return. It seemed that everyone had missed them, as all the staff made a point of popping in to see them, commenting on how well and relaxed they both looked. Carolyn couldn't wait to quiz John on how he was getting on with Cathy and was pleased to know they were still spending a considerable amount of time together. Bradley seemed to be coming round and had even gone so far as asking John's advice on homework.

※

One afternoon, Carolyn had gone on ahead to a Showcase with Pam. They had heard there was a young man with promise who they all particularly wanted to hear sing. The Honeys were due to meet the girls at the theatre, and were to follow on after making a personal appearance which had been a long-standing commitment.

The traffic was so bad that the car taking the group from one venue to another was delayed and Carolyn found herself on her own with Pam, when the young singer took to the stage. There was no disguising his talent, and Carolyn could see that one or two other people were showing interest in him, but no-one had as yet approached him.

She leant forward and whispered to Pam, "We can't sit back here, Pam, can we? If we delay we're going to lose this signing."

Carolyn wandered down to the front of the stage and beckoned the young man over to her. His name was Simon and though lacking in confidence, he had that certain something which made him special. Carolyn talked to him for a while and asked him how he would feel being signed to The Honeys' Production Company. Simon was delighted and Pam immediately sorted out the paperwork for him to sign.

A short time later, Bob, John and Jeff came puffing through the doors to be met by a Producer leaving the theatre.

"You're too late if you were coming to see Simon Barr singing. He's been signed up."

"Ah well, que sera, sera. Let's pick up the girls and go home." John sighed. "Who signed him up, mate?" he shouted after the producer.

The man turned with a frown. "Some British chick. Never seen her before, but she was too quick for the rest of us. In like a shot she was."

John turned to look at Bob and Jeff, whose faces were wreathed in smiles.

Bob's shoulders were shaking. "That's my girl. To quote one of your comedians, John, "That gerrl's my werrld." This last comment was made with a pseudo-scouse accent.

The three men were laughing so much by the time they reached Carolyn and Pam that they could hardly speak.

Carolyn waved the contract in front of their noses as she was hugged and congratulated on her speedy actions. She lapped up their praise and was elated to think she had actually sorted out the deal herself.

First a lovely holiday and now this. Things were actually going right for them for a change.

ཪ᠊ᥦᥨᥦ᠊ᥩ

Chapter Twenty Three

The euphoria didn't last more than couple of weeks, because Carolyn started to feel poorly. First of all she had pains in her abdomen and pelvis; then in her shoulder. She started feeling nauseous all the time and was actually sick with diarrhoea. She felt dreadful and decided she must have caught a bug or had food poisoning. None of the others had any symptoms, however, and when she was still suffering after a couple of days, Bob and the other men were really concerned. They were due to travel to Las Vegas in two days for a show and it was obvious that Carolyn would not be in any state to go.

Bob insisted on taking her to their doctor, the day before the trip. He examined her but was puzzled by the symptoms. "I have a suspicion of what it could be, but I'm not going to commit myself without further tests. I'm going to have to admit you to hospital, I'm afraid. There is no way you are going to Las Vegas."

Bob was adamant that the concert should be cancelled, but Carolyn would not hear of it. "People are depending on you, darling. Think of all your fans who have bought tickets and all the folk involved in the performance, like the band and other theatre staff. There's no way I'm going to let you cancel. I'm only having tests and probably won't know anything right away. We can keep in touch by phone."

Bob was due to take her into the hospital in the morning before going to the airport. Both John and Jeff tried to argue, alongside Bob, that they cancel the trip to stay with her, but Carolyn kept steadfast in her decision, insisting that they go. The next morning, Bob took Carolyn to the hospital and kissed her before reluctantly leaving.

"Remember, I can come back if you are at all worried. We're leaving Marty here to keep an eye on things, so tell him immediately if you need me."

They were taking the three other aides with them and both Personal Assistants. At the door, Bob turned and blew Carolyn a kiss. She managed to keep a brave smile on her face until he had left. As the door closed, the mask fell from her face and she started to cry. She had never felt so ill in her life and knew there was something terribly wrong.

Further tests showed that Caroline was having an ectopic pregnancy, and the doctor explained that a baby was growing in her fallopian tube. "If action is taken quickly it might be possible to carry out keyhole surgery or use drugs, but if the ectopic ruptures the fallopian tube will have to be removed under general anaesthetic. I do recommend that we take you down to theatre now and try the keyhole surgery, before you get any worse."

Carolyn knew that if the Honeys were aware of the true situation they would come back to New York immediately. As much as she yearned for Robbie to be with her, she didn't want to ruin the arrangements for the concert, so she insisted that they wait until it was over. Bob phoned often, so each time she spoke to him Carolyn managed to lie and say she was fine and there were no results yet.

He phoned before the Honeys went on stage and Carolyn hid the fact that she was starting to feel worse. The pain was very severe and she was feeling faint. The Doctor was starting to get very angry with her.

"Mrs. Maples, it is imperative that we operate immediately. If we don't, I cannot be responsible for the consequences. Every minute you delay, you are putting yourself at risk and making our job all the more difficult."

Carolyn realised she could not delay any longer, so she made the nurses promise that if her husband phoned later he was to be told she was asleep and not to be disturbed. Under no circumstances were they to tell him she was having an operation. Marty visited as Carolyn was being prepared for theatre and found her in tears. She was pleased to see a friendly face, and couldn't imagine how she had ever found this man dour and miserable. He sat with her whilst she waited to go down for the operation, and held her hand as she explained to him about the baby.

"This wasn't planned, Marty, but isn't it so sad that our baby can't possibly live. Robbie doesn't even know he was nearly a Daddy."

Marty tried to comfort her and be philosophical. "If it wasn't meant to be, ma'am, nothin' is gonna change things."

Carolyn squeezed his hand. "Please don't call me ma'am, Marty. Just be my friend. That's what I need you to be right now. Please promise me that if anything goes wrong, you'll tell Robbie how much I love him."

Suddenly the pain became much worse and she was doubled up in agony. Marty pressed the button and the nurses came rushing in, followed by the doctor. It seemed that the fallopian tube had ruptured and there now wasn't a moment to lose. By now Carolyn was very poorly indeed and she was rushed into theatre. She was bleeding internally and her blood pressure was erratic.

When the concert in Las Vegas was finished, Bob phoned but was given the arranged story by the nurses. No-one seemed to be able to give him any information on the test results and he started to be suspicious, sensing there was something very wrong. "I just can't understand it. Why can't anyone just tell me what's goin' on?"

John also was very concerned and tried to contact their own doctor. As it was quite late they couldn't get in touch with anyone who could tell them the situation. It was if a curtain had come down and no-one would tell them what was happening. Now they were really worried. "They say she's asleep, but surely if she was just in for tests they wouldn't have needed to keep her in overnight," Bob fretted.

Jeff seemed to be the only one to keep his head. He phoned their man on the spot, Marty, on his cell phone. Although Marty was loyal to Carolyn he felt the men should know the situation and he told Jeff that Carolyn was in theatre. "I don't want to panic you guys, but I think you should be here. She was in a bad way when they took her down."

Jeff was dismayed. "Just tell me, Marty; is she in any danger?"

Always a man of few words, Marty told him, "Yes."

Bob could hardly contain himself. "Jeff, for God's sake what did he say? You asked if she was in any danger. Tell me what's happening."

Jeff quickly explained the situation to Bob and John. After that, no time was wasted. Jeff asked Pam to arrange for a private plane to take them back to New York immediately.

Bob kept in constant communication by cell phone with Marty, who tried to explain to him about the baby. They were still talking when Carolyn was wheeled back into the ward.

"I think she's okay, Bob, but they won't tell me anything," Marty told him.

Marty heard Carolyn mutter "Robbie," and going to the bed, he put his phone to her ear.

"Someone here wants to talk to you."

"Darlin'," Bob said "It's me, my love; I'll be there soon. I should never have left you. I should have been there."

She muttered, "Robbie, we were going to have a baby. I've lost our baby."

All Bob could think about was that his Darling needed him. "We'll talk about it later, but for now please just get better. I won't be long; I promise." Marty assured him he would phone the minute there was any change.

Bob shook his head in disbelief. "It was a mistake you know. I should never have married her. None of these terrible things would have happened if I hadn't married her."

John put his arm around his shoulders. "Don't talk such rot, man. Your only mistake was not marrying her sooner. No-one could love her more than you do. We know that. Sure, some terrible things have happened to you since you've been together, but none of them have been your fault. Now come on, be positive. You've got to stay strong for our girl."

By the time the men arrived at the hospital, Carolyn's condition had stabilised. The doctor explained the details of the ectopic pregnancy. Unfortunately because of the delay, the tube had ruptured and had to be removed. She had been lucky, because once the fallopian tube had ruptured, causing internal bleeding, she had started to go downhill fast. This would mean they would not find it easy to conceive another baby, although it was not to be ruled out. Even though this one had not been planned, the news was devastating to Carolyn who felt she had let her Robbie down. She had lost a lot of blood and was very weak and weepy.

Bob stroked her cheek with his fingers and said, "A baby would have been lovely Darlin', but I can exist and be happy without one. What I can't exist without is you. You are everything to me. My reason for living. When I knew your life was in danger, I couldn't concentrate on anything but you. Those five years when you went away were the most miserable of my whole life. At least before you went, you were there; you were my friend. I could see you, talk to you almost every day. Somehow I survived those years without you. Now, though, since we've been together, it would be unbearable, absolutely impossible, for me to go on without you."

It took some weeks before Carolyn could come to terms with their loss. Although it had not been planned, she had lost a baby. Unfortunately it is true that when we hurt we take it out on those closest to us, and Carolyn found herself snapping at Bob and the other men; finding fault with everything they tried to do.

She acted as though she couldn't stand Bob to touch her; flinching and turning away from him in bed, even when he just wanted to hold and comfort her. Her coldness was hurtful, but he tried to be understanding; hoping that the crisis would pass so he would have his beloved girl back.

After a few weeks, when her head started to clear, Carolyn realised how dreadful she had been to Bob and felt she should try to explain how she felt. "Robbie, we need to talk," she started to say when they were alone one afternoon. "Robbie, I never meant to hurt you. It's just that with these awful things happening to us, I'm starting to be afraid to get up of a morning, in case something else happens."

Bob misunderstood what she was trying to say, and his heart sank. He had felt over the past few weeks that she had cooled off so much that she must have stopped loving him. His voice breaking, he said, "This sounds like a parting of the ways speech coming, Carolyn. Please don't tell me that you don't love me anymore. You name it; anything, and I'll do it; but please let this be something we can sort together."

When she saw the expression on his dear face and realised how much she had hurt him, something inside her snapped. Sobbing, she stammered, "How could you even think such a thing, my dear, dear love. I could never stop loving you. I was just going to ask you to be patient with me for a little longer. I can't explain why I've been such a cold bitch. I mean, we didn't even plan for a baby, but losing it after everything else that has happened, just knocked me for six and I started to feel I couldn't cope any more. Yes, Robbie, it was bad losing the baby, but when you were shot and I thought I was going to lose you, that was the very worst time of my life. Lately, I've been frightened you might turn to someone else, and I think that would kill me. I just haven't been able to pull myself together, but oh, Robbie, never think I could stop loving you. You're my life! You're such a lovely man. You've never harassed me; never said an unkind word in all this time. I just don't know what I did to deserve you."

Bob held out his arms and Carolyn melted into them. He hugged her for a moment and then pushed her shoulders gently away from him whilst he looked into her face. "Carolyn you have to stop shuttin' me out, Darlin'. These bad things have been happenin' to both of us. It was my baby too and I think we've both been grieving on our own instead of together. You really frightened me, you know. I was sure you felt you just didn't wanna be with me anymore. I couldn't cope with that, and I would never, I repeat NEVER turn to someone else. Now come here."

He pulled her back to him and held her so tightly that she gasped. She lifted her face up to him and he kissed her gently and tenderly. That night, in bed, she turned to him, and whilst they still didn't make love, it was the start of their journey back to normality.

Over coffee, one morning, she told John how she felt. "Do you know, John, he has never pressured me. Never blamed me. He is the kindest, most considerate husband. I've been an utter bitch over the past month or so; sniping at him, being miserable, and he's taken it all without complaint. How many husbands would be like that?"

John shook his head "Why on earth would he blame you?"

"Well,"' said Carolyn. "Remember the story from when we were in the Maldives, and Robbie seemed to get broody over a little lad we got to know. One day out of the blue he said, "Darlin', have we left it too late to start a family?" and I nearly choked on a packet of crisps. Well I got to thinking that was what he must want and

"Darlin'" came off the pill without discussing it with him. I went back on it when we came home, but of course the deed had been done." Also, there was the delay letting them operate. At the time, it seemed the right thing to do; but, oh God John! Don't you realise if they'd caught it right away, the tube wouldn't have ruptured and there wouldn't have been all that panic."

John took hold of her hand. "Sweetheart, he knows all that, but if you had seen the state he was in when Marty said your life was in danger. That was all he really cared about. He is just so grateful you're okay. Nothing else seems important."

She shrugged and said "I think we both realise too, that having a baby would have caused major changes to our lives. I wouldn't have been able to travel with you or come to all the concerts and functions. I know it sounds selfish, but I don't want to be a stay at home wife. I want to be with him all the time. We wasted too much time and I'd be too insecure left at home with hours to think and worry."

John smiled, "Surely you don't think he would stray if you weren't there. That's never going to happen."

"You know," she said "Robbie is always apologising to me for being possessive and jealous, but when it boils down to it I'm the same. I just try to bottle it up. No, I really do trust him, but at least if I'm there, the girls tend to keep their distance."

"You are a funny old thing," John laughed.

Carolyn looked sad for a moment. "Still, it would have been nice, really, wouldn't it? A baby I mean. I hadn't really even thought about a baby until then. Now, I keep wondering what it would have been. Oh, drat, I don't know what I want do I?"

John hugged her and silently thanked God that his sister seemed to have come out of the depression which had seemed to engulf her for weeks.

Strangely enough he had a similar conversation with Bob, who admitted that had their baby lived, he wasn't sure how he would have coped with their lifestyle.

"I need to be with her, and if that had meant staying at home and helping, then I would have. John, I waited so long for her, I'm not sure how good I would be at sharing her with anyone, let alone a full time commitment like a baby. However, it would have been quite nice in a way, wouldn't it?"

༻⭒༺

Chapter Twenty Four

John was still seeing Cathy on a regular basis, so far as their careers would allow. Working with sick children meant that Cathy had no set hours, as she worked whenever she was needed at the hospice. She always stayed the night when a child took a turn for the worse and so was on hand, personally, to comfort bereaved parents. A very compassionate and caring person, Cathy was perfect for the work that she did so well. John had come to care very deeply for her and their relationship was made even more interesting by her fiery, passionate nature.

John's marriage to Annie, whilst being happy, had never been a passionate one. Annie had come along at a time when he needed someone to care for and look after. She had been a gentle, quiet girl and he had loved her, but this new relationship was so different and exciting that he found himself counting the hours to the time he could be with Cathy again. Her outward demeanour was so calm and ladylike, with never a hair out of place, always giving the impression of being efficient and business like. Behind closed doors, however, it was a different story and their lovemaking was adventurous and electrifying.

John couldn't decide if he was in love or in lust. He only knew that he was truly happy for the first time in years. His world had turned upside down when Carolyn had left He had met

Annie, and then Annie had died. He had only started to get back on an even keel when his sister returned to them. However, those he loved most had been hit by one disaster after another and, being the man he was, John had felt the pain they were suffering himself. Now, hopefully, the dark days were over.

Carolyn and Bob were happy and totally devoted to each other. Jeff had regained his strength and sense of humour, which had been so severely battered during his marriage to Nicole.

Now, John had started to make time for himself, and Cathy was a perfect partner for him. Bradley was becoming more approachable and accepted John as a friend rather than someone trying to steal his mother away. He even, on a couple of occasions, phoned John to ask him advice on his homework. Sometimes, Cathy and Bradley joined the family at the House for Sunday lunch and John was encouraged by the fact that Cathy and Carolyn were so comfortable together. Even Jeff, a self-titled "connoisseur of women" had only good comments to make about Cathy, who said that "Jeff could charm the knickers off a nun."

Carolyn and Bob still visited the hospice every couple of weeks, and had become very popular with the children, especially the "walking wounded"; some of whom called them Uncle Bob and Auntie Carolyn. Bob thought nothing of getting down on the floor with the smaller children and playing along with them.

Carolyn had now fully recovered from her depression following the loss of her baby. She had thrown herself back into work, finding the company of Pam, Tony and Penny therapeutic. One thing she particularly loved was the laughter which the four shared as they happily worked together. The four Aides also had become an integral part of the team. Carolyn never forgot how kind Marty had been to her when she was in hospital and she wouldn't hear a word said against him. "Do you know, that man sat and held my hand for hours and let me cry all over him, without a word of complaint."

In August, Carolyn decided to cook a special dinner for Bob and Jeff's birthday celebration, which they usually tried to hold together. Cathy was unfortunately working and couldn't come, but Carolyn asked Harry, and Marty, who would be on duty that night. Carolyn in her usual thoughtful way asked Harry if he would like to stay the night.

"It means you can relax and not go home late to an empty flat. Marty will be in the security bedsit, so you'd better have the guest room, because we don't want people talking if you both stay in the same room." This was said amongst laughter from those present, at the very thought of anyone daring to talk about Harry and Marty in that way.

Harry put his head on one side and narrowed his eyes. "I've got a 357 Magnum here, which says NO-ONE will be talkin'. Okay?"

A second single from the album had been released, which was *No More Loneliness*; the song Bob had written for Carolyn on their wedding day. This had shot to number one, quickly becoming a favourite for couples to use at their own weddings. In September, there was to be a big awards dinner, where The Honeys had been nominated for three awards.

Carolyn had a new gown made for the occasion and had insisted on taking Cathy with her where she paid for a similarly beautiful one for her stunned friend. Cathy's was to be pale blue chiffon attached on one shoulder, leaving the other shoulder bare, and had a draped skirt. The colour was very becoming with her blond hair and fair complexion and she was delighted with her appearance in the full length mirror.

"Oh Carolyn, it's beautiful. I've never had a dress like this before."

Carolyn smiled. "It's you who's beautiful, Cathy. John will adore you in that dress. Now how about mine, what do you think of this?"

Carolyn's dress was of pale apricot silk, having a low cut neckline with crystal straps which carried on down the side and underneath her breast. The flowing material seemed to follow the contours of Carolyn's body and the effect was totally sensational. The two girls were thrilled with their purchases and couldn't wait to get dressed up on the night of the dinner. A beautician came to the apartment to fix their hair and make-up.

Bob could hardly speak when he saw how wonderful Carolyn looked and spun her round in the lounge in front of John and Jeff. "Just look at our girl. Doesn't she look a million dollars?"

Cathy was staying the night, and Penny was to child mind Bradley for them, so when Cathy appeared in her lovely blue gown, she was similarly feted and the men agreed how lucky they were to be escorting two such beautiful ladies.

"Hell, I wish I'd asked someone to be my partner now. I feel like Billy-no-mates," Jeff grumbled.

Walking down the red carpet outside the hotel, Carolyn put her arms through Bob on one side and Jeff on the other, then the five walked into the ornately decorated arena where the dinner would be served, followed by the presentations. Carolyn never ceased to be amazed and overawed by these ceremonies. Cathy, who had not been to anything of this enormity before, was bowled over and star-struck by the many famous faces already seated at the round tables scattered about. They were ushered to their table, where they were to join three couples. Jeff found himself sitting next to a lovely girl who was with a record producer, vaguely known to The Honeys. The other two couples were not known to them, but Carolyn soon had them all chatting quite happily together.

The young lady at Jeff's side, Cindy Matthews, seemed very pleasant and friendly. She was wearing a midnight blue dress with a fitted bodice and plunging neckline, which accentuated her curves. Her raven black hair was taken up into a chignon, which emphasised her long swanlike neck. Jeff could not take his eyes off her. When Cindy went to the powder room, Carolyn accompanied her and they chatted together comfortably. Cindy was the producer's secretary and her boss apparently expected her to go with him to the dinner as part of her job. However, she told Carolyn that he was a most unpleasant man and she was struggling to be nice to him.

"He is so rude and arrogant. His hands keep touching me at every opportunity; patting and rubbing."

"Ugh," Carolyn shuddered. "Half Roman and Russian eh?"

"Excuse me?" Cindy puzzled.

Carolyn giggled. "You know, roaming hands and rushing fingers. I hate men like that."

Cindy shook with laughter. "Oh I'll have to remember that one. He's so full of himself. I wish I hadn't come now, but it was such a temptation to see all the stars. I'm so glad to have met you and The Honeys. What lovely men they are. They all seem so down to earth and approachable. You would never imagine they were so famous."

Carolyn swelled with pride at the compliment and commented, "They're never any different, Cindy. Yes, they are three lovely men, and I'm so lucky to be a part of their lives."

After the meal came the important part of the night; the Awards. The first category the Honeys had been nominated for was "Best Single". When they were announced as the winners for *What is Love?* the audience erupted with applause as they ran up on to the stage. Everyone knew what a bad time they had suffered, with John's wife dying, the shooting and then with Bob and his wife losing a baby, and so it was all the more poignant that they should be the recipients of this award.Their next nomination was for "Best Video", the video of *What is Love?* bringing them a further award.

When it came to "Best Visually Entertaining Act", and they were once again called up onto the stage, the three men received a standing ovation. The Master of Ceremonies was Philip Carter, the same producer who had made the winning video, and he commented that these well deserved honours were down to the fun and laughter brought to the Honeys' shows, which made them so enjoyable.

He called The Honeys the *Three Musketeers*, and said, "I feel we should also pay homage to their *D'Artagnon,* who was the inspiration behind the winning video and in fact appeared in it."

The audience were a little puzzled by these comments, until John took the mike and whilst thanking all involved said, "Phil has mentioned our D'Artagnon, and I feel I must tell you a little more about her. The lady in question is in fact my darling sister, who is also Bob's wife. She is not only the lady who started us off on our career and named us, but she has been the inspiration for nearly all our songs and the one who has made these awards possible. She has brought the laughter back into our lives and we love her very dearly. I would like to ask her to come up here with us for a few moments."

Carolyn was so shocked at first she couldn't move from her seat, until she found herself almost lifted from the chair and jostled to the front of the stage where she was led up the steps to cheers and loud applause. Phil, the Master of Ceremonies, announced cheekily "Ladies and Gentlemen, I give you The Four Honeys."

The applause did not stop until the four were back in their seats, and Carolyn realised that the tears were streaming down her cheeks. "Oh, I can't believe you just did that. It was such a lovely thing to say. You've made me so happy and I love you all very much."

Bob took out his handkerchief and wiped the tears from her eyes. "Darlin', if you're happy, I'd hate to see you when you were sad," he said tenderly.

The rest of the evening passed in a blur as everyone chatted. Questions were asked about Carolyn's involvement in The Honeys' career and some of the story of her romance with Bob was related.

Meanwhile, Jeff was becoming very interested in Cindy and kept trying to draw her into conversation, much to the annoyance of her dinner partner and boss. The man in question, Wesley Dunford, was well known in the music industry as a ruthless and mercenary producer, whose only interest was in self-promotion and money making. Money had, in fact, changed hands, to ensure his place at the table with the Honeys, as he saw this as good publicity for him and his company. He had invited his secretary along to the dinner, so that he would have a beautiful lady on his arm, and appear a man about town. He felt it demeaning to himself that she should be paying more attention to another man and made his displeasure clear to her.

Jeff tried several times to persuade Cindy to give him her phone number. Come on what harm could one date do? Say you'll come to dinner with me."

However, his reputation as a womaniser was well known and although attracted to him, Cindy was adamant in her refusal to see him again. "Jeff, it's been lovely meeting you and I've really enjoyed talking to you, but I feel things are better left like this. Truly, you would soon see that I'm not your type."

Jeff was not used to being turned down. Women generally fell at his feet and couldn't wait to be asked out. What was he doing wrong here? He did, however, notice Cindy and Carolyn exchanging numbers and promising to have lunch together so he made a mental note to get round Carolyn later on. At the close of the evening, Cindy appeared to leave with Wesley, but later, when Bob went to the men's room he saw her standing by the door on her own. She told him that her boss had left her to find her own way home, so she had called a cab, but it was very busy and one had not been forthcoming. Harry was waiting to drive The Honeys home so Bob arranged for him to drive Cindy the short distance to her apartment and then return for them.

༄༅༄༅

Chapter Twenty Five

Jeff was furious to hear that Wesley had abandoned Cindy and promised to give him a piece of his mind next time they met. However, he was secretly pleased to think that she had, in fact, gone home alone.

The next day, he used this as an excuse to wheedle Cindy's phone number from Carolyn and phoned her to ask if she had got home safely. He repeated that he would like to see her again. "How about lunch? You wouldn't be in too much peril from me in the middle of the day now would you?"

She finally agreed to have lunch with him the following day and they met at a cosy Italian restaurant which Bob and Carolyn often frequented. Despite herself, Cindy found that the conversation flowed easily between them as Jeff related to her the story of his family. He told her how two young guys with no future met an English boy and his kid sister. Suddenly the world had become a better place for them.

"Those two gave us all they had of themselves. They accepted us and became everything to us. Most women I've known have been unable to accept the special relationship between the four of us. Carolyn is my sister, mother and one of my three best friends. I will always love her. Same applies to John and Bob." Jeff told her how jealous Nicole had been and how she had always hated Bob. "When we were youngsters in that orphanage, he was all I cared about. We looked out for each other then and we still do. As far as I'm concerned he's my brother. How could a woman be jealous of a friendship like that?"

Cindy was disturbed by her feelings for this "new" Jeff. Surely this wasn't the same person everybody had warned her about. This didn't seem like a man who notched women up on his bedpost like trophies. She started to confide in him, a little, about her background. Cindy had been badly hurt in the past and for this reason was reluctant to get involved with someone who had the power to hurt her again. Reluctantly at the end of a lovely lunch, she stood up, thanked Jeff and, although she wouldn't make any definite arrangements, promised to go out with him again some time. She insisted that he call her a cab and that she would find her own way home.

This was a completely new experience to Jeff. He was certainly not used to women playing hard to get and he couldn't stop thinking about Cindy. "Man, she has sure got under my skin," he moaned to Bob and Carolyn. "What more can I do? I've tried every persuasion in the book. I can't even send her flowers, because she won't give me her address."

Carolyn pulled a face and put a finger to her lips. The thing is, Jeff, we love you, but we know how you treat most of your girlfriends. I like Cindy, so I'm not going to encourage this if all you want to do is make a point, take her out a few times and then drop her. She isn't your usual type and I'm worried in case you're just looking at this as a challenge."

Jeff sheepishly took a deep breath and then exhaled slowly. "No, Honey, that's not how I see it. I really do like this girl, but how am I ever gonna be sure if I can never get to know her?"

Carolyn nodded. Okay then, ask her for Sunday lunch with us. You could sort of drop in the fact that you've never asked anyone before. I think she might be quite impressed by that."

Cindy was amazed and pleased to be asked. She was happy to meet Cathy again and meet her son, Bradley. Harry also was invited, as it had become a regular thing for whichever aide was on duty to join them for lunch. Cindy immediately saw the closeness of the family group and far from being put off by this, she found it endearing. She loved the way they all bantered with each other.

Bob had them all laughing, recounting the first day they had all met and Carolyn had kicked him on the ankle. Honestly, I limped for a week. There was blood and everything."

Carolyn threw her napkin across the table at him, laughing. "Oh, take no notice of him. He just wants the sympathy. Anyone would think he was a young weakling instead of a big strapping lad. Really, Cindy, you mightn't believe it now, but Robbie and Jeff were a pair of thugs when I met them."

"THUGS!" both Bob and Jeff shouted and nodding at each other they stood up, lifting Carolyn, still on her chair, and deposited her, shrieking, on the other side of the room, where they left her. The laughter was infectious and Cindy felt so blessed to be part of this lovely family, if only for the afternoon.

At the end of the day, Cindy offered to call a cab, but Harry was asked to run her home and Jeff went with them. At least he knew where she lived now. She invited him in to her apartment to tell him how much she had enjoyed herself.

"I can understand how you feel about your family. They're all so special, Jeff. But I've got to ask you if you aren't just a little bit jealous of Bob and Carolyn. I mean, you obviously love her so much."

Jeff shook his head. "Not in that way, Cindy. But, yes, I would give the world for someone to look at me the way Carolyn looks at Bob. Just to be so sure of each other and know beyond any doubt that you had something that would last forever. Cindy, I really would like us to get to know each other better. Can we do that please? I think we could have something special here."

"Okay, Jeff," Cindy said shyly, "But let us promise to always be absolutely honest with each other. Please, don't make any promises you can't keep; don't make any declarations you don't mean" Jeff drew her to him and kissed her warmly on the lips, then turned to leave.

"I have things I should tell you, if we're going to be honest with each other. There are things in my past which I've never told anyone. You don't have to go Jeff," Cindy said.

"Cindy, I know you're not gonna come without some baggage. I have baggage too. When you're ready, you can tell me. For now, let's just get to know each other." He pulled her to him again and this time his kiss was passionate and more demanding. "Give me five minutes to send Harry home, and I'll be back" he whispered.

When Harry arrived back on his own Carolyn was euphoric. "Oh, ain't love wonderful. I just hope he treats her well, because I really like Cindy. How about that, eh! We could start our own group "The Three C's"

Bob couldn't calm her down, or pour water on her excitement.

"Oh Robbie, all I want is for both John and Jeff to be as happy as we are. Well, no-one could ever be as happy as us, but you know what I mean; and I'm rambling again..."

※

The following week, Bob announced that he was taking a month off as he wanted to take Carolyn home to England for a holiday to see all her old friends. Coming out of the blue, this was a wonderful surprise for her and she feverishly started phoning around and buying presents for everyone.

Accompanied by Marty and Pete, they booked in at the Crowne Plaza in Liverpool, where they had stayed last time, and using this as a base they spent some happy days revisiting Wallasey and New Brighton. They called on Anne and the other girls who had been Carolyn's friends when she had needed them so badly. A supper night was quickly arranged, where the girls met up to discuss old times. They were brought up to date with all the traumas and excitement that had occurred since their last meeting.

They were agog to hear all the details of the shooting incident, and how close her darling Robbie had come to losing his life. They were sympathetic and understanding when she told them the story about losing the baby. When she related the tales of the two wicked tricks played on them by her "arch enemies", Nicole and Stella, you could have heard a pin drop. Carolyn told them that both Nicole and Stella had received suspended sentences and ordered never to contact any of the family again. If either of them ever tried to harm Carolyn, Bob or either of the other men, then both women would be sent to prison.

"I just hope I never see either of them ever again. They really are a pair of witches" Carolyn told the girls.

Bob and Carolyn visited Irene at her home in Runcorn, again repeating all the stories of their short but eventful married life. They said they would love to visit Anglesey whilst they were in Britain, and although October, it was lovely Autumn weather, so it was arranged they would stay at Carolyn's old caravan for a week and meet Irene there for a few days.

"Doesn't this feel like a come down after all the luxury you're used to now?" Irene laughed when they met up at the caravan site.

"God no! It's just so normal. Now and again that doesn't do any harm you know. I was very fond of this place and used to find it soothing when I needed healing."

They walked round the cliffs and sat with their arms around each other on Carolyn's old 'Thinking Rock'.

"Do you know, Robbie; I used to sit here, thinking of you, and missing you so much. That was such a sad time for both of us wasn't it? Robbie, I've always loved you and when you came and found me I loved you, but I love you even more now. "Does that make any sense?"

Bob smiled. "Darlin' that makes perfect sense to me, and I love you too; more than ever." That night they lay in each others' arms and their lovemaking was even more intense and passionate than ever.

The fresh air was very invigorating and the beauty of the area, with the heather and gorse in all their splendour, gave the two lovers the peace and tranquillity that they needed to renew their strength and recharge their batteries. When they returned to Liverpool, they were amused to find that Marty and Pete had spent their time exploring. They had visited the famous Albert Dock and also been on a Beatles Tour of the City. The usually quiet Marty was full of praise for the hospitable and friendly people they had met.

"I've never been made so welcome anywhere I've been. Do you know, you've only got to walk in a bar and people actually start talking to you?"

Carolyn was delighted and had to agree that Merseyside people generally were friendlier than anywhere else she had ever visited.

Soon it was time to return home, with promises from Anne and Irene that they would meet up and arrange a shopping trip to visit Carolyn and Bob in New York before Christmas.

"Just let us know when you can come and we'll make all the arrangements. All you need to do is get on the plane." Bob told them.

❧

Carolyn was delighted to be able to entertain her two friends in New York for a week at the beginning of December. Anne and Irene shared the guest room at the House. They were introduced to Pam and the other staff; also to Cathy and Cindy. The girls, spent their days shopping and touring New York. They were interested to know that Central Park had in part been inspired by Birkenhead Park, which one of the architects, Calvert Vaux had visited. They went to the top of the Empire State Building and admired the view from the roof of the Rockefeller Centre, where they were dazzled by the number of shops and restaurants housed there. They even went for a ride on the Staten Island Ferry. This was a half hour ride across New York Harbour and from the ferry boat they had a wonderful view of Manhattan and the Statue of Liberty.

Bob arranged evenings out for them to Broadway shows and meals at lovely restaurants.

They were able to go to one of the Honeys' performances towards the end of their week's stay and although they had, of course, seen the group on television, neither of them had seen a live show. They were impressed and delighted to be treated as honoured guests, especially when they were ushered backstage after the show.

The evening before Anne and Irene were due to fly back to England, Carolyn sat on one of the beds in their room chatting to them. Irene had noticed that Carolyn was looking a bit pale and had commented to Anne that something was wrong. Carolyn was adamant, however, that nothing was worrying her.

Anne wasn't going to let it drop. "Come on love, something is bothering you. It can't be Bob, because he is still obviously as much in love with you as ever and you with him, so what is it. Aren't you feeling well?"

Carolyn took a big sigh and blew the air out through pursed lips. Promise you won't say anything." Both girls nodded. "Well, it's silly really. I had just hoped that I might be pregnant again. I was a few weeks late and I'd started to get excited, but it turns out I'm not, and I'm really disappointed. After the ectopic pregnancy thing, they told us I might have trouble conceiving. It was just with being late. I was hugging the idea to myself. It's no big deal, honestly. I have a lovely life and I couldn't be happier.

Life suddenly seemed very quiet once her two friends had been seen off at the airport and

Carolyn and Bob returned home. Preparations were underway for Christmas and, as usual, Carolyn wanted to make sure everything was perfect for the family to enjoy the festivities.

∞§∞

A party had been arranged on Christmas Eve for all their staff and close friends. The House had been decorated like a fairy grotto with a huge Christmas tree standing in the corner, decorated with tinsel and glass balls and surrounded by presents. Caterers had organised a fabulous buffet, and the table was groaning with food. Carolyn had a new outfit for the occasion and was pleased with Bob's reaction when he saw her in the emerald green strapless dress. The colour was so very flattering to her chestnut hair and complexion that he gasped.

"Wow, my Darling, you'll knock them dead in that. Reminds me a little of another dress you wore once, years ago. Do you remember my love? It was before you went away and I was so bowled over I couldn't speak."

Carolyn remembered the occasion when she had been hurt so badly by his apparent lack of interest in her lovely new dress. So he had noticed after all. How strange life was.

Cathy and Cindy had already arrived when they walked through to the lounge, where Bradley was excitedly telling John of his good report and grades from school. Soon everyone else started to arrive. Bess proudly introduced her husband, who the family had not met before. Her niece was accompanied by her young man who was similarly introduced. Pam and Joe arrived, followed by Pete and "Red" with their wives, Fern and Tricia. Harry was ushered into the room by a laughing Tony and Penny, then finally Marty wandered in sheepishly, hanging around in the background, only to be pulled into the group by Carolyn. Champagne was poured and music played; the atmosphere in the room was soon carefree and relaxed. Tony and Penny started the dancing, then Pam and Cindy kicked off their shoes to strut their stuff on the floor.

Carolyn looked around the room at all these dear people. "Robbie, only a few years ago the four of us knew none of these people and now they are all such a big part of our lives. We're so lucky to have found them all. I love you very much. Thank you for making me so happy."

PART FOUR

2006

LOVE UNLIMITED

Chapter twenty six

Cathy and John's relationship was by now accepted as being for the "long haul". John found an apartment, just around the corner from the family home, which they furnished together. Whilst luxurious and wanting for nothing, it was comfortable. Cathy was delighted with the result. Bradley had his own room, which contained all he could ever desire in the way of computer and entertainment centres. He adored John; looking up to him in a touching and endearing way.

Carolyn was sad to see John move out of the House, but was very pleased at his obvious happiness with someone she considered a friend.

The day they moved in, Bradley spent the night with the family, whilst his mother and John sorted everything out. As they were unwrapping some of the china from Cathy's old home, John turned to her, smiling. "Cathy, let's get married. I'm still old fashioned enough to think we should be married if we're going to live together. You know I love you, sweetheart. If not just for me, for Bradley's sake; let's get married."

The suggestion had come from nowhere and, whilst pleased, Cathy was stunned. I love you too, John, but let's just wait a little longer. I'm not saying no; just not yet. When we get married I'll feel I should leave the hospice and I'm not ready to do that yet. I want us to have a family; a brother or sister for Bradley. I'm asking you to please be patient a little while longer."

"Alright then, Cathy, but let's compromise here. Can we at least get engaged? I really want this." John went down on one knee and holding her hand said, "Darling Cathy, I love you very much. Please, will you marry me one day, when you are ready?"

Cathy laughed; her eyes flashing as she pulled him to his feet. "Dearest John, of course I will." He pulled her closely to him and kissed her long and hard before whispering in her ear, "Let's cement this decision shall we, and christen our new home."

Within seconds, their clothes were in a heap on the floor and Cathy pushed John into a chair before sitting astride him. She moved her hips seductively, throwing back her head as he caressed and licked her breasts. Then he was inside her and she moved faster until they were both panting and moaning with ecstasy.

Some little time later, as they lay together in the new, huge, Emperor-sized bed, John held her in his arms as they cuddled up together. "Cathy, this is a very happy day for me. A couple of years ago I thought I'd never be happy again. You've brought me so much joy, and I couldn't love Bradley more if he was my own flesh and blood. To-morrow, my dear, you and I are going to buy an engagement ring fit for a Queen. I won't stand for any arguments."

Carolyn couldn't contain herself when they broke the news to the family the next day. She jumped up and down like a two year old, first hugging John, then Cathy. Bob and Jeff patted

John on the back, and hugged Cathy with delight at the news, whilst Bradley giggled with delight, and threw his arms around the newly engaged couple. Cathy had chosen a solitaire diamond which shone as she lifted her hand one way and then the other to display the beautiful ring.

"A party: we must arrange a party to celebrate your engagement. What would you like to do? Would you prefer to have some friends here or have a formal party somewhere?" Carolyn asked with excitement.

"Oh, Carolyn, we don't want to make a fuss." Cathy said hurriedly. What I'd really like is for the seven of us to have a nice meal together at our new apartment. That way we'll have an engagement and housewarming party in one. We'll make it into a dinner party and christen our new dining table. Oh I'd love that."

The dinner party was a great success and a happy, joyful occasion. The family was growing, and no-one was more pleased than Carolyn.

⁂

Cindy was very quiet on the way home in the limousine. She and Jeff had become very close over the past few months and he was concerned by her pallor as the car came to a stop outside her home.

"What is it Cindy? Aren't you feeling well?" Jeff asked her, as he took her key and opened the door.

"I know, when we first got together, you said you weren't bothered about my past before I met you, but seeing everyone so happy to-night has made me realise that I must tell you about things I've tried to push out of my mind for years. I love you, Jeff, and I need you to understand me. The only way you ever will, is for you to know about my past." Cindy poured them both a nightcap and took a deep breath before telling Jeff her story.

※

Cindy had been the eldest of three girls, there being five years between her and the next eldest, Muriel, then a year later Hope the baby was born. Her family had come from Bethlehem, Pennsylvania. She was a very pretty child with raven hair and brown eyes. Cindy didn't like to remember much about her childhood. Her father drank and had been a bully, constantly beating her mother who at first had tried to protect her three daughters from the abuse which she had to endure night after night when her husband came home. Cindy's ears would ring with her mother's cries and pleas but the girls learned from a very young age that you didn't interfere, because if you did you usually ended up bruised and beaten too.

Cindy had been eleven when her father first turned on her. She came home from school one day to find that her mother was shopping and her two siblings were both out. Her father was in the kitchen in a foul mood.

"Where's your fucking mother, bitch? She knew I'd be early to-day and need feedin'. I've a union meeting to go to and I want my dinner now."

Cindy felt her knees trembling, but tried to placate her furious father. "I think Mom was gonna buy you something nice for your dinner. I'm sure she won't be long Daddy."

He wouldn't be appeased. "I'll have to make do with a sandwich. Make me one now if you're capable, you lazy cow."

"Daddy, you've had a lot to drink. You shouldn't be driving to a meeting," Cindy had rashly muttered."

He turned on her in a blind rage. "What did you say? Are you talkin' back to me girl? How dare you question me?" As he was shouting, he was undoing his leather belt from around his waist, and slowly he slid it out and wound it around one hand. Next minute she felt a searing pain as the belt hit her across her shoulders. Again and again the strap came down.

"Daddy, Daddy, you're hurting me," she tried to scream, but his free hand slapped her across her mouth.

"Now, make me that sandwich, before I lose my temper altogether," he ranted.

Cindy did as she was told, and breathed a sigh of relief when her father left the house. She was so frightened and sore; all she could do was run to the bathroom where she stood under the shower, trying to wash the awful images away from her body and her mind. The skin on her shoulders and back was stinging and her lip was split and swollen. Despite being afraid of her father, she tried to broach the subject with her mother but found her unbelieving and cold. She supposed her mother was only too pleased to have avoided her usual beating and let somebody else, even her young daughter, take her place for once.

So began the nightmare years for Cindy. At least once a week, her father would manage to get her on her own and the abuse would continue. He used her as a punch bag whenever he lost his temper. He would pull her hair and use his belt as a strap on her tender skin. On one occasion he actually broke her arm and it was necessary to lie to the staff at the emergency room. Cindy was far too afraid of her father to tell them that he had twisted her arm until it snapped, so said she had fallen down the stairs.

Her mother appeared to turn a blind eye to the whole situation. Indeed on many occasions she would accompany her husband on one of his drinking binges, leaving Cindy to feed her young sisters their evening meal and put them to bed. More often than not they had to make do with a sandwich of bread and jam, because there was no other food left for them.

Cindy was fifteen before she had the courage to tell a teacher, who insisted she report her father to the authorities. The kindly woman remembered the numerous times Cindy had made excuses for various cuts and bruises she had come to school displaying. By then Muriel was ten and Cindy knew that if she didn't take some sort of action her little sister would soon be suffering the same torment she had been tolerating for four years.

Things happened quickly then. The three girls were taken into care and put into foster homes and both her parents were prosecuted for cruelty and neglect. Cindy never saw or spoke to either her father or mother again. Her mother had let her down as much as her father and she hated them both.

The foster family she found herself living with were kind, but Cindy was ambitious and wanted to make something of herself. She had to make sure she was never subjected to anything so humiliating or hurtful ever again.

When she was sixteen, Cindy decided to leave school and took a job at a local ice-cream parlour where she made enough money to be able to dress in the latest fashion, albeit on a budget. She bought make-up and other fancy things which she had always craved but never been able to afford.

She was always very much in demand with the local boys, but was very choosy about who she accepted dates from. None of them could understand why this beautiful young girl was so cold and undemonstrative and was never prepared to let any of them kiss or pet her.

She still saw Muriel and Hope on a regular basis, saving all her affection for the times she spent with her two young sisters. They too were now happily settled, both with the same family who had said they would like to adopt the sisters. Cindy was pleased for them as they were still both young enough to have a happy and loving childhood. Something which she had never known.

When she was eighteen, Cindy met Gavin Richards. He was twenty three and had three brothers, two of whom were in the Bethlehem Police Department. Vernon, a traffic cop, was just twenty one, whilst Joe, the eldest, was twenty eight and a detective in Vice. Joe had been married but was now divorced and had his own apartment. The other brother, James was at University training to be a lawyer, whilst Gavin wanted only to be on the stage. He had been in all his high school productions and had then gone on to a theatrical College where he had studied singing, dancing and acting. At the time he met Cindy he had done some minor parts in various television productions, but was "resting" and had taken a job at the ice-cream parlour..

Cindy and Gavin became good friends, chatting comfortably together. For the first time in her life she found she could laugh and talk to someone whilst being herself. For a long time, they were just friends but eventually he took her home to meet his family. She was overjoyed by the love and camaraderie between the brothers and their parents. Never having been part of a normal family, she couldn't get enough of their company. She found herself included in all their celebrations and was invited along for Thanksgiving and Christmas dinners. The only fly in the ointment was Joe, who never really seemed to like Cindy. It was as if he could see right through her, realising that her feelings for Gavin were purely that of a friend and that he was her ticket to be part of the family as a whole. Over the years this discomfort seemed to grow to such an extent that by the time Cindy and Gavin were talking marriage, Joe could no longer hide his distaste for her and avoided her whenever she was at the House.

Muriel and Hope were in time adopted by their foster family, and eventually moved away. Cindy felt that it was in their best interests to sever all contact with them, and although it broke her heart to do so, she felt they deserved a new start and a happy life. She tried to cut them from her mind, the way she had buried her parents in the far deep recesses of her brain. The only time she thought of them now was in nightmares.

She had never told Gavin of the torture she had endured and neither was he aware that she had two younger sisters. Gavin was kind and gentle so she found she could relax and trust him. She had told his family that she was an orphan who had been put into foster care. Cindy felt that this story made her more special, and that was what she wanted to be to Gavin's family.

Eventually the two married and found a smart apartment which they furnished gleefully with colourful curtains, cushions and second-hand furniture. At last Cindy felt she had arrived. She had a place of her own and hoped ultimately to start her own family, but in the meantime her parents-in-law, James and Vernon, were always made welcome. Cindy joked that Vernon could smell her oven door opening from three blocks away as he always seemed to turn up when dinner was being served. He would often stop by with his partner in their squad car for a coffee break. Only Joe kept his distance and this made Cindy very sad because she was quite prepared to accept him as part of her family.

Gavin was starting to find more jobs acting and had some work appearing in television commercials. He went to auditions all over the state and even in New York, so they were delighted when he was accepted for a small but important part in a six month run of a Broadway play. They opened a bottle of champagne and toasted his success.

"At last I'm on my way," he shouted, picking Cindy up and spinning her round the room.

"You deserve it, Gavin. You've worked so hard for this," Cindy laughed.

She felt close to Gavin, in a way she had never thought possible. He was a very popular young man; liked because he was so down to earth and level-headed whilst always being considerate and kind.

He was still her best friend and, she cared for him very deeply, but she could never really have said that she was in love with him. She felt that part of her heart had been damaged so badly by her evil father that she could never give herself completely to any man.

Gavin found an inexpensive boarding house in New York where he stayed whilst performing. Every couple of weeks he had two days off together and he would take a Greyhound bus home to Bethlehem. Whilst he was away, Ma and Pa Richards would ask Cindy round for regular meals and Vernon continued to call regularly to see her. She loved the banter she had with him and called him her "baby brother".

One spring day, when the apple blossom trees were in bloom and the sun was shining, Cindy was shopping in the town when she saw a crowd gathering outside the main precinct. Gavin was in New York, and Mr and Mrs Richards were in Harrisburg, nursing Grandma Richards, who was very poorly, having suffered a stroke. There were ambulances and police cars everywhere and there was an uneasy atmosphere charged with apprehension and foreboding. Cindy approached a bystander to ask what had happened.

"A cop's been shot. Stepped in front of the gunman, he did, to protect a woman."

Cindy was frozen to the spot. "Do you know his name? Has anyone said his name? Can anyone tell me?" she frantically asked the onlookers.

"I think someone said it was Richards," a helpful woman spoke up.

"Oh my God, Vernon," she screamed as she ran, pushing her way to the front.

"You have to stay back lady," a uniformed police officer told her as he held onto her arm.

"I think it's my brother-in law," Cindy sobbed. "Please let me go to him. Is it Vernon Richards, do you know?"

"No ma'am, it's his elder brother, Detective Joe Richards, but I guess that still makes him your brother in law."

Cindy let out a gasp of breath with relief, but this was short lived when she took in the scene in front of her. Joe was on a stretcher being lifted into the ambulance and looked very poorly indeed. The kindly police officer ushered her through, where she bent over the man on the stretcher and took his hand in hers.

"Momma," he muttered.

Whilst the police officer who had helped her explained to the paramedic who she was, she found herself lifted into the ambulance behind the stretcher. Before the ambulance doors closed, Cindy shouted to the police officer.

"Will someone please try to contact Vernon and James, his other brothers. My husband, Gavin, is working in New York but I'm sure he will want to be here. I haven't an address for his parents, but one of the boys will have it."

"Momma," Joe muttered again.

The paramedic nodded to Cindy, "Just agree with him, ma'am. He needs reassurance right now."

Cindy took Joe's hand in hers again and the next time he said "Momma" she said, "I'm here Joe. Momma's here."

When they arrived at the hospital, Joe was assessed then rushed down to surgery to remove the bullet which had lodged in his chest. He had lost an enormous amount of blood and it was touch and go whether he would survive, but eventually he was brought back from the operating theatre and put to bed in a private ward. By now Vernon and James had arrived and the three of them were told by the doctor that if all went well over the next twenty four hours, he should survive although it would be a long road to recovery.

Vernon and James were amused when Joe, despite being partly unconscious, once again grabbed hold of Cindy's hand.

She was surprised by the strength in his grasp but pushed his hair back with her free hand and said, "Momma's still here, Joe. You're quite safe now." She sat that way right through the night and into the early hours of the morning, until she was so stiff that her hand had pins and needles. Just as daylight started to filter through the windows, Mr. and Mrs. Richards rushed through the door into the ward together with Gavin, and they gathered at the bedside just as Joe opened his eyes.

As Cindy let go of his hand she was the first person he saw. Who the fuck let her in?" were his first words to the startled family.

An exhausted Cindy went to sit out in the corridor, where Vernon joined her. He'll be mortified, sis, when he finds out you sat with him all night. He didn't mean it you know."

"Of course he did," Cindy said laughing. "I think we can safely say he's on the mend, and that's all that matters."

◈

Cindy broke off from her story to stand up and pour two more drinks. Jeff hadn't said a word all through her narrative and was looking very serious.

"Why did you never tell me about your childhood, and the small fact that you'd been married? Did you think I'd judge you; that I wouldn't be sympathetic about that evil bastard's treatment of you? I'm so very sorry you grew up having to cope with all that. My poor darling; you should have told someone much sooner about what was goin' on. You have two sisters you never see. That must surely prey on your mind? But Cindy, I'm concerned about the fact that you hadn't told me you'd been married. Why did you keep that from me? You said you'd been very hurt and that was why you were so reluctant to get involved. Was it your husband who hurt you?"

Cindy smiled, sadly. "I'll finish the story, Jeff, and perhaps all your questions will be answered. Then you can decide if you still want to be with me."

Chapter twenty seven

Cindy hunched her shoulders and took a large swig out of her glass. "Jeff, I've never felt about anyone the way I feel about you. I want you to believe that before I continue. I don't want to lose you, but I can't live a lie any longer. When you've heard it all, you'll perhaps understand why I haven't told you this before."

Jeff sat back in his chair and waited to hear the rest of Cindy's story.

⁂

It was agreed that as soon as they knew for sure Joe was out of danger, his mother and father would need to return to grandma's sickbed, which would cause a problem as to who would care for Joe. It looked as though the best plan would be for him to go into a police nursing home for a month or so until he was fit enough to return home, but Cindy wouldn't hear of it.

"Nonsense," she said. "There is no way one of my family is going into a nursing home while I'm capable of looking after him. He can come home with us. We can arrange for a nurse to come in every day to do what is necessary. I will manage."

Although Gavin was not entirely happy with the plan, due to the fact he would have to return to New York and Cindy would have to cope on her own, he understood the sense of the arrangement, so it was agreed. All that remained was to tell Joe. Fortunately, because of his weak state he was not strong enough to argue for long, so as soon as he was able to be discharged, he was taken home to the apartment and put to bed in Cindy and Gavin's spare room. At the end of the week, Ma and Pa travelled back to Harrisburg and Gavin bussed back to New York; all the time hoping that his understudy had not done too good a job in his absence.

It was arranged that a nurse would come in each morning to dress the wound. He would also wash and shave Joe. It wasn't going to be easy, with the friction which still existed between the two, especially on Joe's part, but Cindy was determined she was going to make it work.

Early the next morning Cindy poked her head around the bedroom door. Joe's face was ashen and she could see something was desperately wrong.

"What's wrong, Joe?" she asked.

"I wanted to use the bathroom. I tried to get up and couldn't. I didn't make it." He looked so ashamed, she couldn't scold him.

"Come on, Big Bro. Let's get you off that bed and into some dry clothes," she said softly. Muttering words of encouragement, she let him lean on her whilst she helped him to the bathroom, where she insisted on taking off his wet pyjamas and helping him into the shower.

"I'm not looking, you daft thing. Just be careful and don't fall," she told him.

Cindy wrapped him in fluffy towels, and led him into the living room where she held onto him while he put on clean pyjamas; then she sat him in a chair with a blanket round him. She turned on the television, and then went back to his bedroom where she stripped the bed, remaking it with clean linen. When she returned to the living room, Joe stuttered as he tried to apologise for all the extra work he had caused.

"Joe dear," Cindy smiled. "I know you've never had a very high opinion of me but you're Gavin's brother and in my eyes that makes you my brother too. There should be no embarrassment between brothers and sisters. Just remember that whilst you're staying here. Try to relax and feel at home."

When the nurse paid his daily visit, Joe was relieved to find that Cindy had not related the episode to him and said as much to her.

"Joe, no-one needs to know what passes between us while you're ill. That's just between the two of us," she smiled.

Joe was still quiet and withdrawn for a few days. It was obvious that the shooting had not only disabled him physically but had taken away his confidence and independence. This was very hard for a man who had always been in control and on top of things.

One night when Cindy had got up to make a milky drink because she couldn't sleep, she heard sobbing as she passed Joe's room. As she opened the door the weeping stopped, but she could tell Joe was holding his breath. Cindy didn't say a word. She just lay down on the bed next to him, putting her arm around his shoulders so that his head was on her breast. The sobbing started again but he didn't pull away from her, and eventually he fell asleep in her arms. She had gone to her own bed before he awoke in the morning and the incident was not mentioned by either of them when she took in his morning coffee.

Little by little the tension between the two lessened and by the time Gavin came home for his two days' break he was delighted to hear the two laughing together as he entered the apartment. Cindy threw herself into his arms with pleasure at seeing him. He entertained the two of them with stories of the play and the cast in New York.

"This girl is driving me mad making me watch quiz shows and do crosswords with her," Joe laughed. Thank goodness for some masculine company. Vernon calls in most evenings, but he always seems to want to rush away somewhere with someone."

They all laughed together at the vision of Vernon and his wild social life. Their youngest brother seemed determined to date every attractive girl in Bethlehem and the names of his conquests rolled of his tongue like a telephone directory. Gavin couldn't believe this was the same Joe who had been so miserable and depressed only two weeks ago.

"I have to confess, Gav, I was so very wrong about Cindy. She's been unbelievably kind to me, especially considerin' how I treated her.

Nothing is too much trouble for her and she's been patient and tolerant of my black moods; never berating me. Not once has she lost her temper or criticised me. The girl's a saint, man. She has made me realise that life is still worth livin'. When Samantha left me, my confidence just hit the floor and I guess I thought all women were just in it for what they could get. I'm so glad to be proved wrong about Cindy. I feel, though, that I should move back to my apartment as soon as possible. It's an awful lot to expect of her. Even with the best will in the world she must be longin' to see the back of me."

Gavin couldn't have been happier. Joe had always been his favourite brother and it had been difficult over the past few years to see the conflict and tension between him and Cindy. "Joe, you can stay here as long as you need to. Cindy, come in here sweetheart," he shouted to his wife who was in the kitchen. "Cindy, Joe's in a hurry to move back to his apartment. Do you think he could cope?"

Cindy tut-tutted and shook her head. "No way, sunshine. You're only just startin' to get stronger. I'm not letting you go anywhere until I'm sure you're fit. Anyhow, I'd miss my big bro now," she laughed. It was very lonely for me with Gavin working away and you aren't bad company when you set your mind to it. I especially enjoy watching the quiz shows with you. You enjoy them don't you Joe?" she said with tongue in cheek as she winked at Gavin.

And so, when Gavin returned to New York, Joe was still a fixture in the apartment. As he became stronger he was able to do small jobs around the place for Cindy and the two of them talked about everything under the sun, from politics to show business. Joe told her about the breakdown of his marriage to Samantha and how he had come home from work one night to find one of his friends in bed with her.

"I thought the world was comin' to an end, Cindy. I never thought that girl would cheat on me. There were no signs. God knows how she kept two men happy, but it appeared she had been seeing him for months. I just couldn't take it. The marriage was over from that moment."

Joe was very like Gavin physically. He had the same straight nose and full, sensuous lips. He was tall and handsome but in a far different way. Whereas Gavin's face was very good looking in an almost perfect, sensitive way, Joe's face had character and was tougher. Anyone looking at Detective Joe Richards would know right away that he was a man to be reckoned with and not a man to mess around. He showed authority and immediately, without speaking, demanded respect.

Cindy couldn't help comparing the two and without realising it at first, it was Gavin who came off worst in the comparison. Gavin was gentle and sweet, but often indecisive and quiet. Joe's masculinity oozed from him. His sexuality and powerful personality were always evident. As Joe's health improved Cindy became more and more aware of the chemistry she felt every time she was close to him.

She found herself telling Joe things she had never been able to tell Gavin. She told him about her dreadful father and what he had done to her. She described the horror of realising how alone she was with no-one, not even her mother to turn to. By the time she came to the part about her two sisters and their adoption the tears were pouring from her eyes. All the memories and feelings which she had tried to bury came to the surface and she thought she would never stop crying. Joe held her in his arms, the way she had held him just a few weeks earlier. He didn't speak; he just stroked her hair and held her closely whilst she sobbed. When the tears stopped, she turned her face to him. It seemed the most natural thing in the world when his lips came down on hers and he kissed her, first gently, then passionately.

As his tongue pushed itself into her mouth, she responded with a passion she did not think possible. Their kisses opened a dam which could not be closed. Without thought for the consequences, Joe peeled off her blouse and bra and kissed and sucked her nipples until she thought she would scream with delight. Then they were both naked, and his hand was between her legs bringing her to a climax such as she had never experienced with Gavin. When he entered her she moved with him; astonished to feel again the fireworks and amazing joy of another climax as he too reached fulfilment and collapsed on top of her.

For a while they just lay and held each other until Joe was the first to pull away. "Oh my God, Cindy, what have we done," he whispered.

Cindy was still in a daze from their love making. "Joe, it was wonderful. I think I love you. I know now I married the wrong brother. We have to be together. We have to tell Gavin."

Joe jumped to his feet with horror on his face. "Are you mad, woman? Gavin is my brother. He must never know what we've done and it can never happen again. He trusted me with his wife and gave me the hospitality of his home. Oh God, this is how I repay him. Promise me you'll never tell him about this. I could never look him in the face. I have to go now."

Cindy watched numbly as Joe packed his belongings into a bag and phoned for a cab. When he turned to Cindy it was with tears in his eyes. "You must realise Cindy that this is it. This is as far as it goes. In different circumstances, Sweetheart, I would never walk away from you, but I have to be the strong one now. I'm not gonna be the one to break my brother's heart."

Then he was gone. The apartment seemed quiet, empty and very lonely. Cindy sat on the floor hugging her knees under her chin. Everything was different now. It was all spoilt. The lovely family she had surrounded herself with no longer seemed important. How could she go back to living with Gavin? How does one revert to bread and jam when you've tasted caviar? She laughed to herself grimly at the comparison.

Time to once again lock away things she didn't want to think about. All the memories which had surfaced to-day had to be re-interred and all thoughts of Joe; wonderful, passionate, loving Joe, had to be buried with them. The strange thing was she didn't feel bitter, because she knew it had taken courage and loyalty for him to leave. But as he had said, "This is as far as it goes."

By the time Gavin came home again she was able to shrug her shoulders and carry on as though nothing had happened. She had already made excuses on the phone for Joe leaving, saying that as he got stronger they had started to get on each others' nerves, and it had been decided that he was fit to go home.

By the end of the month, Cindy had missed a period and knew without doubt that she was carrying Joe's child. This was an impossible situation. There was no-one she could tell or ask for advice, but she knew there was no way she could bring this child into the world. After much thought and many tears, she made an appointment at an abortion clinic, booking herself in for a termination.

Everything would have gone smoothly if Gavin had not returned unexpectedly and found Cindy curled up asleep on the sofa. She had been given some pills at the clinic which would bring on a miscarriage. The doctor had warned her that she would have cramps and should lie down when she got home. A sheet of instructions had been given to her and this was open on the table. When she opened her eyes, it was to see a horrified Gavin reading the paper. She looked away from the hurt in his eyes.

"Cindy what have you gone and done. We were going to have a baby? Why didn't you want it"?

Cindy stammered and held her hands out to him "Gavin you don't understand. I can explain. I just wasn't ready to have a baby."

Gavin's usually pleasant and smiling face turned into a hard mask as he grimaced with pain. "You weren't ready to have a baby? Didn't I get a say in this? I always knew you didn't feel as strongly as me, but sweet Jesus, why did you do this to me? Why couldn't you have told me? We could have worked it out."

There was no possible way Cindy could tell Gavin the truth. There was no reasonable excuse which would sound feasible and understandable; nothing she could say which would make him feel kinder towards her. She knew this was the end of her marriage. The end of her dreams of belonging.

When Gavin returned to New York, Cindy packed up all her personal things. Before leaving the apartment, she wrote a long letter to Gavin saying that she was giving him his freedom and that if he divorced her she would not contest it. She drew some money from their joint account and said that one day she hoped he would find someone deserving of his love. Then she booked a greyhound bus to St. Louis and left Bethlehem.

When she was settled, she had sent an address to Gavin where mail could be forwarded and had half hoped that he might follow her and try to persuade her to go home. However all she received were the divorce papers dissolving their marriage. Like all the other episodes in her life, her marriage to Gavin and her love for Joe were just two more incidents to be locked away in the secretive drawers of her mind and never mentioned again.

She took a secretarial course whilst working in a bar at nights and studied computers and office management. By the end of a year she was able to fill a post as a Personal Secretary. Three years after leaving Gavin, Cindy moved to New York to take up a job as Secretary to a Record Producer. It was whilst working for this firm that she met Jeff.

ಸಿನ್

In telling the last part of her story, Cindy had found it impossible to look at Jeff, but now she turned, breathing in deeply as she looked into his eyes. "So you see, Jeff, I'm damaged goods. You're very quiet, Jeff. Surely you must have some questions; want to tell me what you think about it all."

"I just don't know what to say, Cindy. What a dreadful childhood for any little girl. I thought I'd had a rough time of it, but I don't know how you coped with all of that. I had no-one at all, except Bob, when I was child, but I think having no family is better than the one you had. I can understand your need to be part of a loving family though. All my life, that's been the most important thing in the world to me. To belong and have people who care about me. I wish I'd been around in those days for you to talk to. I wish I could have been there to help.

However, I know you told me that you'd been hurt, Cindy, but this... I accept you had a terrible childhood, and I'm real sorry about that, but all the rest... All this time you let me think you'd never been married. You should have told me about Gavin. I would have accepted that; but sleeping with your brother-in-law for Christ's sake, and having an abortion. I just can't get my head around all of that. It's just too much for me to take in. I made one enormous mistake when I married Nicole. That relationship was based on lies from the beginning. I don't want to go down that road again."

"I just wanted you to know everything, Jeff. Apart from telling Joe about my childhood, I've never spoken about the rest of it to a living soul. I really did think I loved Joe, but I know I was wrong to do what I did and I think about that little baby every day of my life. I thought having a termination would save my marriage, but instead it destroyed it. Please try to understand. I've kept all of this inside me for so long. My parents, my sisters; then Gavin, Joe and the baby. Meeting you and getting so close to you and your wonderful family has been the happiest time of my life. I knew one day this would all come out and I felt I should be honest with you now rather sometime in the future."

"Ah yes," Jeff whispered, "My family. You must realise that you could have destroyed your family if the truth had come out. To me that's the most unforgiveable thing. To come between two brothers like that. I need to think about everything you've told me, Cindy. I really need to go away and work out if we still have a future here."

He stood up and walked slowly to the door where he turned. The devastation on her face was plain to see. His heart lurched to see the hurt and pain in her eyes; the tears streaming down her cheeks as she held out her hands to him.

"Jeff, please try to understand," she wept.

"You'll have to give me some time, Cindy. I'll call you," he said as the door closed behind him.

Chapter twenty eight

No-one could understand why Jeff was so quiet over the next few days. It was obvious that something was bothering him. It became apparent when he stayed in for three consecutive nights that there was a problem between him and Cindy. With John no longer living at the House, Jeff's demeanour was very noticeable, but Carolyn and Bob were unsure how to approach him over the situation.

This was the state of affairs when Carolyn found Bob and Jeff, looking very serious, with a letter open on the kitchen table. "Whatever's the matter? Has something happened?" Carolyn asked.

Bob looked at Jeff, biting his lip and taking a deep breath, then turned to Carolyn. "Darlin', we promised not to keep any secrets from each other and we never have. I'm not gonna start now. This has been a complete shock to me. I just don't know what to do about it."

Jeff looked away as Bob handed Carolyn the letter and she started to read it. It was from the Social Services Department and was quite formal.

"Dear Mr Maples, A child by the name of Daniel Fuller has been placed in the care of Social Services and is at present living in one of our children's homes. It would appear that his mother recently died, and as her partner was leaving the area, the child had no other relatives. The enclosed letter was amongst the child's

possessions. I should be grateful if you would inform me of your intentions regarding Daniel."

Carolyn put the letter down and turned to Bob, with a puzzled expression on her face. "Darling, who is this boy and what has it got to do with you? What was in the other letter?"

Bob handed his wife two sheets of handwritten paper and she read it without comment. Now and again she gasped and glanced up at first Bob and then Jeff, before reading the letter to the end.

"Dear Bob, You probably won't remember me. We had a very brief affair in 1998, when I was working as a backing singer on your tour. I had a baby in May the following year. He is your son. I'd never win prizes for being a mother, Bob. In Danny's short life he has had many 'uncles'; none of them good role models. Sometimes I have found him an encumbrance to my ambitions and have shown it. I know I haven't got long to live and the one thing I can do for Danny now is put him in touch with his father. I know my present partner won't want him. I hope you will find it in your heart to accept him into your life, but if you cannot do that, please help provide for him and see he has the right schooling. I've never asked you for anything in all the seven years of his life. Please do the right thing now. He has always known who his father is." It was signed *"Debbie Fuller."*

"Oh my God," Carolyn managed to get out before flopping into the nearest chair. "This has come from nowhere. I thought things were going too smoothly. What is it they say about the past always being there hiding, waiting to bite you on your bum? What are you going to do, Robbie?"

Bob shrugged his shoulders and sighed. "I'm so torn here, baby. You know you're the most important thing in the world to me, and I'd never do anything to hurt you, but somewhere there's a little boy, just like I was, wondering if his daddy will ever come for him. What shall I do?"

Carolyn leant forward and took his hands in hers. "Well first of all, you need to have DNA tests done. You don't know for sure he is your son. This woman says she's had loads of men in her life. Who is to say she isn't lying about this because she knows you're rich and famous? We need to go and see him; talk to him." Then seeing he was still looking worried, "Stop looking so tragic. You have a son. You must be a little bit curious what he looks like."

Bob shook his head in disbelief at her reaction. "Aren't you cross; worried? Don't tell me you aren't upset about this."

Carolyn pulled a face and blew the air out of her lips with a whoosh. "Why should I be cross? I knew you'd not been a monk when I married you. I'm surprised a few other women with children haven't crawled out of the woodwork. Let's face it neither of you have led blameless lives. Maybe the time has come for you to pay the piper. If he is your son, we are going to have to make sure he's put with a loving family and has everything he needs. You will have to be financially responsible for him. I'll phone this Social Services lady and make an appointment."

Whilst Carolyn was making the call, Bob poured himself and Jeff mugs of coffee then sat down again at the table. "Isn't she just amazing? I thought she'd raise the roof when she read that letter."

Jeff smiled and sipped at his coffee. "She's too sensible for that, Bro. She knows all that happened before you two were together. How could she possibly hold it against you? You've been completely open with her and that was the best thing you could have done." As he spoke, Jeff gasped and closed his eyes, taking a sharp intake of breath.

"What is it, Jeff? " Bob asked at the sudden change in Jeff's expression.

"I'm just beginning to realise what a complete and utter fool I've been, Bro. What I've just said to you, about something that happened before you got together and being open about things. I should have been telling myself that, Bob. I may have lost a wonderful girl through being a hard, cold bastard. Without going into detail, Cindy told me something from her past which I didn't like, so instead of giving her sympathy and understanding, I walked out on her like a prize idiot."

"Jeff, what have you turned into? Why have you become Holier than Thou? Neither of us is beyond reproach. Christ, when I think of the way you and I used to live. Have you forgotten the time when you were snorting coke at any God-given opportunity, and drinking so much you couldn't remember things the next day? Have you forgotten about all the women you and I bedded, because I haven't. What if you've got children out there you don't know about? Look what's happenin' here to us now. If I handle this wrong it could really harm what I've got with Carolyn, and I can't let that happen. Remember what it was like in that orphanage, Jeff. Don't you think I want to run down to that home and wrap my arms around that little boy? I want to tell him his Daddy's come for him and bring him home, but I can't do that. How can I bring another woman's child into Carolyn's home?"

"I'm sorry, Bro," Jeff remarked. I'm bothering you with my problems and you have far more on your plate. You know my feelings about family and how important it is to be loyal and look out for each other. What Cindy told me went against everything I believe in and I over-reacted. I should have accepted that she was being honest with me and let the past stay where it belonged. I don't know how I can make it up to her, but I have to try."

"Do you love her, Jeff?" Bob asked.

"Yes, I know that I do, and I'm gonna have to put things right, but first we need to sort out this problem of yours."

"Well, I'm gonna say something to you that I've never said before. No-one has ever blamed you, Jeff, but it was you who brought that bitch, Nicole, into this family and she nearly destroyed it. When you find someone as special as Cindy that you really care about, you should grasp at the chance of happiness. Cindy's a lovely girl and whatever baggage she has in her past, it can't be worse than your own old lifestyle. Go get her, Bro, even if you have to crawl over hot coals. But remember this. You have to be as honest with her as she's been with you."

※

The visit to the Children's home was arranged for the next morning. Bob was very quiet in the car and held onto Carolyn's hand tightly. As they drew up outside the building he turned and smiled at her. "You've been so wonderful over all this darlin'. I don't know how to thank you for not screaming at me. You had every right to. This little boy is my problem, and I want you to know that whatever happens, you will always come first."

"Oh stop it, you daft bugger," Carolyn said. "Since when have your problems not been mine? Anyhow, I've stopped thinking of him as a problem. He's a seven year old boy and it's up to us now to step up and be responsible for him in whatever way we need to be."

They were ushered into a large sitting room by a gushing attendant who was over- awed to be meeting Bob Maples. Mrs. Partington, the Social Services Advisor was already there sitting next to a small boy. She jumped to her feet and shook hands with both of them before turning to the child.

"Do you know who this man is, Danny?" she asked.

"Yes, it's my Poppa," he replied, his large, liquid brown eyes gazing up at Bob with adoration, and something that looked like fear."

Danny was slim and small for his age. Although being lighter skinned than Bob, he was so like him that Carolyn gasped. His features were identical from the straight nose to the full lips. To make the similarity even more alarming, he stood with his head to one side, biting his bottom lip, just as Carolyn had seen her beloved Robbie do countless times before.

Bob bent down so his face was the same level as the boy's. "Hello Danny," he said quietly, holding out his hand. Danny took the proffered hand in his and shook it like an adult. Carolyn could see that the child's long fingers matched Bob's, and once again she took a large breath and exhaled through pursed lips. Bob turned and introduced her to his son, saying, "This is Carolyn, my wife. Shall we sit down, Danny, and you can tell me a little about yourself."

Mrs. Partington nodded at Danny to take a seat, saying to the couple, "I've been told he hasn't had much to say since he's been here. He just sits quietly all the time, not mixing with the other children. He jumps at loud noises and seems frightened of his own shadow."

Bob gently took the boy's hand in his and spoke in a quiet, kindly manner. "Danny, what did your mother tell you about me?"

Danny sat with hunched shoulders and spoke haltingly. "My momma said you were my poppa and I had a poster of you on my bedroom wall. I used to talk to you."

Bob had to swallow hard before he could speak. "You used to talk to me, Danny? That must have been a very one-sided conversation eh? What else did you used to do?"

"When I came home from school I had to have my dinner and then go to my room and be seen not heard. Momma didn't like me being in the way when she had friends round. When she was drunk she moaned at me and sometimes she hurt me, so I used to tell you about it."

Bob gasped, "She used to hurt you? What did she do, Danny?"

Mrs. Partington lifted the back of Danny's T-shirt and asked him to turn around so Bob could see his back. She lowered the waist of his jeans to show scars, which looked like cigarette burns, on the top of his buttocks."

"Oh dear God, who did that to you boy?" Bob said angrily.

"Momma," the boy whispered. "She told me she wished I'd never been born. I shouldn't say it, but I liked it better when she got sick, because she was nicer to me then and wasn't so mean to me. I used to sit with her and tell her what I'd done at school. She told me more about you and said I would meet you one day. Uncle Jim said he'd look after me, but after Momma got taken to the hospital, he said he had to go away. Then he told me Momma had died." His wide eyes were darting around the room from face to face as he talked; the words being spoken rapidly.

Carolyn had been sitting quietly through this whole exchange, but she felt she had to say something to this poor, lonely little boy, and she stood up and knelt in front of the child. "Would you like us to come and see you again, Danny? Perhaps we could go out for the day sometime. You be a good lad now, and we'll see you again very soon."

He nodded and watched as they said their goodbyes and left the room. They promised Mrs. Partington they would be in touch as soon as the results of the DNA tests were known, and that, whatever the outcome was, they would arrange for whatever finance was necessary to be available for the child's keep and education. She was able to tell them that Danny's mother had died from cervical cancer and that apparently her illness had been fairly rapid.

After they had climbed into their limousine and collapsed back into the seats, Carolyn turned to her husband with tears in her eyes. "What a lovely little boy. You're not doubting that he's your son, Robbie?" His features, his facial expressions; everything about him. He's your dead spit. He's yours. I've no doubt whatsoever. What a dreadful life he's had. Whatever happens, and whatever you decide, we have to play some part in that child's life, Robbie; see him from time to time."

Bob just nodded and squeezed her hand. His heart was too full to speak, and his instinct was just to rush back into the home, pick Danny up, and never let him go. This was never going to be easy.

※

Whilst Carolyn and Bob were getting to know Danny, Jeff was frantically trying to get hold of Cindy. He had left numerous messages on her answer phone at home, and also on her cell phone, which appeared to be switched off. A call to the office where she worked did not produce any helpful information. Cindy had apparently phoned in sick a few days earlier but had not given any details.

Feeling very concerned by now, Jeff called for an aide, and it was Pete who drove him round to her apartment block. The doorman let him into the building without any preamble, recognising him from his previous visits. After knocking on the door of the apartment for several minutes, and calling her name, Cindy's next door neighbour, Thea, came out to see what the noise was. She too was familiar with Jeff and was pleased to be able to confide in him that she had been troubled about Cindy for a couple of days now.

"Mr, Simmonds, I haven't seen Cindy at all. It's most unusual, because she usually drops by for a coffee and a chat now and then. To be perfectly honest with you, I've been really worried about her."

Jeff's heart missed a beat. "Thea, do you by any chance have a key to this apartment?" The concerned woman nodded and agreed that they should both go and make sure that everything was alright.

The apartment was tidy, as always, but there was no sign of Cindy. Nothing seemed to be missing in her wardrobe. Her nightshirt was on the bed, where she had left it. His messages were still on the answer phone, so obviously they had not been played. Some dishes had been washed and left in the drainer in the kitchen. The whole place was like the Marie Celeste. Where was she?

"Thea, I'll leave you my number. Please, will you phone me if Cindy contacts you? I just can't imagine where she is, but she's gonna need some of her clothes soon, whatever she's doing. I need to speak to her urgently."

Thea agreed to let him know as soon she had any information and he went back to the House with a heavy heart. Surely history wasn't going to repeat itself. However, the fact that she didn't appear to have taken anything with her meant that her absence hadn't been planned. He decided if he didn't have any news by the next day he would report her as a missing person. In the meantime he asked Pam to make discreet enquiries to see if anyone knew where Cindy might be.

༄༅༔༅༄

Chapter twenty nine

The next morning, Jeff still had no news of Cindy's whereabouts and was becoming increasingly alarmed. The Honeys were to lay down some tracks for a new signing of theirs in the studio and so during a coffee break Jeff took the opportunity of putting his friends in the picture.

"To be honest, I'm worried to death. It's just strange that no-one seems to know where she is. I phoned the local precinct this morning and reported her missing, but quite honestly I don't think they took me too seriously. You could hear the silence the other end of the phone, especially when I said we'd had a fall out. They were probably thinking 'just another lover's tiff'. I didn't want it all over the press, so I didn't give my real name. I only said I was her boyfriend."

John, being the practical one, offered the suggestion that they ask Pam to phone round the hospitals. Jeff went through to the Security room, where Harry was chatting to Marty. He asked them if they had any ideas, and Harry offered to make a few enquiries.

It was two days later before Jeff received a message from Thea, Cindy's next door neighbour, asking him to contact her. He visited her at the first opportunity and she told him her news.

"Cindy telephoned me this morning. She's in hospital, Mr. Simmonds. She was mugged and her purse stolen. She banged her head on the sidewalk and she's had something called 'Retrograde Amnesia'. The hospital didn't know who she was for a couple of days until she came round and they've kept her in for observation since. She phoned to ask me to take her in some things. She said she had a friend with her, so she's not on her own."

Jeff was relieved that at last there was some news, and at the same time puzzled as to who the "friend" could be. "Thea, if you can pack up the things she needs, I'll take them in to her and make sure she's okay. Thank you so much for getting in touch with me. I was real worried about her."

The kindly woman produced a bag which she had already packed, and sent her good wishes for a speedy recovery. Jeff lost no time in picking up the biggest bouquet of red roses he could find, together with a huge box of expensive chocolates, and then had Harry drive him to the hospital. He had no difficulty in finding the correct ward and knocked before poking his head round the door.

Cindy was sitting up in the bed, looking very pale but beautiful to him. However, sitting on the bed was a strange man, and he was holding her hand. There was no doubting the pleasure in her eyes at seeing him, but neither could she hide the hurt and disappointment that still lingered there.

"Hi, how're you doin'?" He asked. "I've only just heard what happened or I'd have come sooner. I've been trying to get in touch with you for days. Are you okay?" As he spoke he glanced questioningly at the man on the bed, still holding Cindy's hand.

"Jeff, thank you for coming. This is my ex brother-in-law, Joe. Of all the coincidences in the world, he's working for the NYPD now and heard about my attack on his police radio. He thought it was too much of a coincidence for there to be two Cindy Matthews so he came to see if it was me."

Jeff shook hands with the tough looking detective, whilst secretly wishing he could wipe the grin of his smug face. *Of all the times for this guy to re-appear.*

"I recognise you. You're that singer, aren't you? Part of a group, if I remember rightly. I've seen your face a million times, but I'm sorry, I can't remember your name."

Cindy laughed, "It's Jeff Simmonds, Joe. Jeff's a friend of mine. Oh, those roses are gorgeous. Thank you. What's new? I feel so out of touch with being stuck in here. Joe, would you see if you could find a vase for me please."

As soon as Joe had left the room, Jeff took up the hand that the other man had been holding and blurted out, "Cindy, can you ever forgive me for the way I behaved. I've missed you so much, baby. I love you; please believe that." Before he could continue, Joe had returned, followed by a nurse who took up the bouquet and proceeded to arrange the roses in a vase.

Cindy's eyes had filled with tears as she stared at Jeff. *If only he'd told me that when I unburdened my soul to him.*

She smiled at him through her tears. "Jeff, thank you so much for coming. I'm not sure of my plans when I get out of here, but I'll let you know. Give my love to the family, especially Carolyn. I'll call you."

Jeff couldn't believe what he was hearing. *Surely she must have misheard him. She hadn't even commented on what he had said.* "Cindy, we need to talk. I have so much to say to you. Can I come back later?"

Joe stood up and pointed at the door. "I think you heard what she said, dude. She said she'll call you."

Jeff turned at the door, "Cindy, I do love you, darlin'. I really don't want to lose you. I'm not gonna give up." He walked out of the hospital with a heavy heart and made his way home.

Meanwhile, Joe was feeling very confident as he sat down again on the bed, smiling. "You've done the right thing, Cindy. I'm gonna look after you now. We've talked about what happened after you left Bethlehem and I know I really let you down. I can make up for it now though. Gavin's married again and settled with a couple of kids. He'll have to accept that we're together. We needn't ever tell him about what went on before. When you have this baby, we can bring it up together. I suppose that guy is the father?"

"Yes, Joe he is, but he doesn't need to know that. As for us being together, our time has passed. I did love you, Joe and I'd have gone to the ends of the earth with you if you'd have asked me, but I've moved on. I don't know whether I'll ever be able to forgive Jeff for the way he behaved, but I do love him. He's the one I want to be with, and only time will tell whether we can work things out. Until I'm sure, I'm not going to tell him about the baby. One thing I'm sure of though. I'm going to have this baby and I'm going to love and take care of it; on my own if I have to.

⁂

Carolyn could not get Danny's little face out of her mind. His frightened eyes and the scars on his back haunted her dreams. What had a seven year old boy done to deserve such a horrible start to his life? Bob had been tied up for the past week; involved in the recording studio with the other men and their protégé. The feelings she had were so strong that one morning, without telling anyone else, she phoned to make arrangements, and then asked Marty to run her to the children's home. It was the school holidays so there had been no problem when she asked if she could take Danny out for a few hours.

When she arrived, Danny was in the same lounge where they had originally met him. He was sitting on the edge of a chair; his hands folded in his lap, and his shoulders hunched. "Hiya, Danny. Do you remember me?" Carolyn asked gently.

"Yeh. You're married to my Poppa," the little boy replied, with a face so serious that Carolyn could hardly restrain herself from hugging him.

"I am, yes. I wondered if you'd like to come out for a little trip with me. Is there anywhere you'd care to go? What sort of things do you like?"

The little boy shook his head, whilst his fearful eyes stared into hers with apprehension. "I don't mind where we go." Then with a sigh, after a few moments contemplation, "but I like animals."

"That's great then, I know just the place we can go. In Central Park, there's a pond with ducks and swans and there's also a Children's Zoo. Would you like to feed the ducks and some other animals? My nephew, Bradley, tells me you can cuddle the rabbits if you want to, and they have sheep and goats as well."

The child's face lit up at the prospect, and he nodded excitedly. "Oh, yes please. I would like that. My Mom would never let me go to the zoo."

Carolyn smiled, "Well, there's a bigger zoo as well, but we better leave that for another day. Come on then me laddo, get your coat on."

Danny giggled as he was helped into his anorak. "You talk funny. Are you foreign?"

"Mmm, I suppose I am, yes. I come from a place called England, which is far across the sea. I'll tell you a little more while we're out."

"Okay, can we go now?" he asked, almost jumping up and down in his anticipation of this wonderful outing.

Carolyn poked her head around the door of the kitchen and asked if there was some stale bread they could have, to take with them to the duck pond, then she took the child out to the car, where he was introduced to a startled Marty as "her friend, Danny". She asked Marty to take them to Central Park; first stop the Pond.

She had asked Bess to prepare some sandwiches before leaving home and they sat on a bench and enjoyed them before Carolyn brought out the bag of stale bread. Swans and ducks swam on the calm waters of the Pond, and Carolyn broke the bread into small pieces, handing it bit by bit to Danny so that he could throw it to them. Soon they were surrounded by ducks that had come off the pond to be nearer the source of the food. Danny could not conceal his delight as he fed the rest of the bread to them. They beat a hasty retreat when one of the swans showed rather too much interest and started pecking at their feet, and the two of them ran, laughing, back to the car.

Next, Marty drove the car the short distance to the Tisch Children's Zoo. Before entering the zoo, they were just in time to see the animal statues dance at the Delacorte Musical Clock. Carolyn missed most of the spectacle because she could not take her eyes off the absolute joy which was written all over Danny's face.

The entrance to the zoo was through the trunk of a make-believe tree from where they entered the Enchanted Forest which was filled with huge acorns, lily pads and a climbable spider's web. Danny let out a whoop of delight and ran from one thing to another, giggling all the time.

The attendant gave him a bowl of food to feed to the farm animals. He wandered amongst the sheep and goats, petting and giving them food, and then moved onto the cows. When he was asked if he would like to hold one of the rabbits, his happiness knew no bounds. He kissed the long, floppy-eared rabbit and cuddled it to his chest.

"Don't hold it quite so tightly, darling. He won't understand that you just want to love him, and he may be frightened," Carolyn reasoned.

When they came out of the zoo, Carolyn noticed an ice-cream van and walked Danny over to it. "You can have anything; what would you like?" she asked him.

"I don't know. What are you having?"

"Well," said Carolyn. "I fancy one of those big ice-cream cornets, with nuts on and a chocolate flake in. What would you say to that?"

Danny just nodded, his little face alight with pleasure. Carolyn ordered three cornets and, having paid for them, asked Danny to take one across to Marty who was sitting patiently in the car. When he returned to her side, she led him to a bench, where they sat in comfortable silence whilst they demolished their ice-creams.

"Did you have ice-creams when you were a kid?" Danny suddenly asked. "My Mom would never let me have ice-cream. I only ever had it once before."

Taking a tissue out of her handbag she wiped the remains of the ice-cream from around his mouth and nose. "Yes, my Mummy and Daddy both liked ice-cream too, so my brother and I often had some."

"Where are they now? Is that what you called your Momma and Poppa; Mummy and Daddy? I've never heard of a 'Mummy' before."

Carolyn nodded, sadly. "Yes that's right. That's what we call them in England. I suppose you could say a Mummy is an English Mom. They died, Danny, in an accident, many years ago. I still miss them though, because I loved them very much."

After giving it a great deal of thought, biting his bottom lip, he asked, "Both of them died? So you didn't have any family. What did you do?"

"I came to America when I was just twice your age. I came with my brother, and that's when we met your Poppa and his brother, and they became our family. Danny, tell me, if you had three wishes, what would they be?"

The boy sighed and put his head on one side. After giving it a great deal of thought, he replied, "I wish I never had to be afraid again; that I could belong to a family, and that every day could be like to-day."

"That's really not a lot to wish for, Danny. I hope it all comes true for you. You don't have to be afraid anymore, because no-one is going to hurt you ever again. If any time you're frightened or unhappy you must ask someone at the home to phone either me or your Daddy. Promise me you will."

The child smiled and nodded, his legs swinging backwards and forwards on the bench. They chatted together for some time, whilst Carolyn told some tales from her childhood. The little boy was agog to hear her stories and it was with great reluctance that, as the air was getting cooler, it was decided to return to the car.

As she dropped him back at the home, Carolyn took his face between her two hands. "I promise you, Danny, there will be more days like to-day. Your Daddy and I will come back to see you soon." She kissed him on the cheek and was touched when he turned his face to kiss her back.

When she arrived home it was to find Bob sitting in the lounge with his feet up on the coffee table, snoring gently, a newspaper open on the floor in front of him. He sat up with a start when she sat down next to him. "I was just readin' the paper, Darlin'. Have you been shopping?"

Carolyn laughed and cuddled up to him, burying her face in his neck. "Reading the paper, my arse. You were dead to the world when I came in. You've been working too hard. You're tired out. What you need is a couple of days off. Robbie...?"

"Yes, baby? I know that tone of voice of old. What've you been up to?"

"Please don't be cross with me, but I've been to see Danny again." Before her husband could get a word in, she continued. "We've had a lovely day. We went to Central Park and we fed the ducks, then went to the Children's Zoo, and we had ice-creams too, and I thought how nice it would be to have him stay here for a night or two and..."

Bob put a finger to her lips, "For goodness sake, Carolyn, take a breath. You're on one of your rambles. Why did you go to see Danny without telling me? I don't understand."

More seriously now, Carolyn looked into his troubled eyes. "Robbie, when have I ever not been able to read you like a book? Do you really think I don't know what you want here? But a child isn't like choosing a dog from the dog pound. You can't take him back if you don't get on or he doesn't fit in with your life. Before we even consider taking him on permanently, we need to make sure we're doing the right thing, not just for us but for him too. I know if it weren't for me you wouldn't hesitate to bring him home. I just felt I should get to know him and weigh up all the pros and cons."

"How did I ever get so lucky? You never cease to amaze and remind me why I love you so very much."

"So I thought," Carolyn continued, "that we could arrange for him to come here next weekend. We could go out somewhere special and perhaps ask Cathy and John to bring Bradley so he would have company. He could stay a night or two. It would give us chance to really get to know him and for him to get to know us."

Once Bob had agreed and arrangements had been made with John and his family, Carolyn wasted no time in ringing the home to ask the Supervisor to tell Danny that his Poppa and Carolyn would see him on the Friday morning.

Chapter thirty

Jeff continued to phone the hospital every day to leave messages for Cindy, so was pleased when he was told at the end of the second week that she had been discharged and had gone home. Unsure what reception he would have if he visited her, he dialled the telephone number of her apartment and held his breath whilst waiting for her to reply.

The answering machine clicked on and he was just starting to leave a message when she picked up the phone. "Hello, Jeff. How are you?"

"Hello, my love. More's to the point, how are you? Are you feelin' better now? Can I come and see you? Cindy, there's so much I want to say to you. Please, don't just shut me out of your life like this. I know I was a complete bastard, and if I could turn the clock back, things would be different, I promise you. I've missed you so much."

Cindy closed her eyes and took a deep breath. *Time to be strong, Cindy. Don't give in. He has to think I'm not interested.* Yes, I'm much better, thank you, Jeff. I just need to rest for a while and get my strength back. I have everything I need right now. Joe did some shopping for me so the fridge is quite full."

It took all his willpower for Jeff not to question Joe's place in her life, but he bit his tongue and said, "Well if you feel like some company or need anything, I'm your man. I just want to see you, Cindy; talk to you. I promise not to put any pressure on you, but this situation is just driving me mad."

"I'll phone you in a couple of days, Jeff. I'm not very good company at present. I'll be in touch. Thanks for calling. Bye now." Then the phone went dead.

He wandered into the kitchen and poured himself a mug of coffee before walking down into the lounge, where Carolyn was sitting at her laptop. "You busy?" he questioned.

"Never too busy for you, chuck. What's up?" Carolyn asked, looking up from the screen.

"I don't think Cindy's gonna forgive me, Mom. I think she's got someone else. Someone she was in love with years ago has turned up and they're gettin' cosy again. I've handled this whole thing really badly and I don't know how to make it up to her. I want us to be together. I just can't stop thinking about her. What shall I do?"

Carolyn stood up and put her arms around him. "Oh, you have got it bad, haven't you? Well, you know what they say, Jeff. 'Faint heart never won fair maid'. If you really love her, just keep telling her that. Don't give up, dear."

Carolyn filled Jeff in on her plans for the weekend with Danny. "You'll be able to meet your nephew. You can't have a long face when he comes to stay. He's had enough misery in his little life."

After Jeff had gone through to the Shop, Carolyn dialled Cindy's number. Once again the answering machine clicked in, but as soon as she heard her friend's voice Cindy lifted the phone and answered. "Carolyn, I'm here. Oh, it's lovely to hear from you. Thank you so much for the cards and the lovely flowers. Will you come to see me?"

"Oh, Cindy, of course I will. I'd have come before, but I didn't know whether you would want me to. I don't know what you two have fallen out about and I really don't want to know, but I gather Jeff has been his usual sensitive self and upset you. That mustn't stop us being friends. Can I come over to-day? I've so much to tell you. By the way, I swear that whatever we talk about will not be repeated."

A time was arranged and it wasn't long before the two friends were sitting together in Cindy's apartment, chatting like old times. If Carolyn hadn't been brought up to date with the mugging and the head injury, she would never have been able to tell there had been anything wrong with Cindy. "Oh, thank goodness, you look so well. I was expecting to see you pale and skinny and here you are looking the picture of health. I'm so glad." Carolyn couldn't wait to tell Cindy about Danny and how he had appeared in their lives.

Cindy hung on her every word, starved of news of this group of people who she had grown to be so fond of. "He sounds a lovely little boy, but I can only imagine how you felt when you first heard about him. What a shock. Where are you taking him on Friday?"

"The six of us are going ice-skating at the Rockefeller Centre. What a hoot that's going to be. There's only Bradley and Cathy who've ever skated before, so the rest of us are going to spend most of the time on our bums. It should be a good laugh though. We tried to persuade Jeff to come with us, but he's having none of it."

At the mention of his name, Cindy sighed. "How is he, Carolyn? For God's sake don't tell him, but I miss him terribly. I just don't know whether I can ever forgive him for the way he upset me. I won't burden you with my whole story, but I wanted to be honest with him and he was so judgemental. I don't know what I expected, but it wasn't that. I cried for days and decided I never wanted to see him again. Then all this happened. Did Jeff tell you I'd met up again with my ex brother-in-law?"

Carolyn nodded. "Well, he said something about an old love. He didn't go into details. He's very jealous and upset, Cindy. I have to tell you, this is the first time I have ever seen Jeff in such a state. But...I promised you there would be no pressure. Whatever you decide, it's up to you. I just hate two people I care about being miserable. Are you going to get back with this man?"

Cindy would have loved to have told Carolyn about the baby, but didn't feel it was fair to burden her with a secret which might cause problems between her and Jeff. She needed to keep that to herself, for now. "No, Carolyn, Joe and I are history, but I don't want Jeff to know that. This may sound hard, but I want him to sweat. He needs to realise just how much he's hurt me. Until then, there is no way we could have a future together. I promise you I'll get in touch with him soon. I'll talk to him and see what he has to say. I love him, Caro, but there is something else I have to tell him. His reaction to that will be the deciding factor. I trust you, Carolyn."

"You have my word, Cindy. I won't even tell him I've been to see you. Then he won't start trying to get information out of me." Carolyn kissed her friend and promised to let her know how Danny's weekend went.

※

Carolyn could hardly sleep on Thursday night with the anticipation of the coming weekend. She woke up to the sun streaming through the windows and a clear blue sky. She turned and shook Bob awake, kissing both his eyes and then the tip of nose as he came too, muttering under his breath. Oh baby, that's a nice wakenin'; come here."

Giggling, Carolyn sat up and swung her legs over the side of the bed. "Not this morning, sexy drawers. There's no time for that. I want to make sure everything's ready in the guest room and we have to have our breakfast. We're due to leave to pick Danny up in an hour."

Bob was awake now. "What you gotta check? You've moved things round that room a dozen times already. He's only stayin' two nights. Now we agreed, baby. We have to see how this goes before we start jumpin' the gun."

※

The Ice Rink at the Rockefeller Centre was packed with laughing, happy children and their families when they arrived, bumping into Cathy, John and Bradley at the arranged meeting place, outside the Rock Centre Cafe. After introducing Danny to everyone, they sorted out their ice-skates and staggered onto the ice.

Bradley showed off a little, being the only one at first who could stay on his feet. "Come on, Danny," he shouted over the noise and the laughter. "Grab hold of my hand. You'll be okay."

A smiling, happy Danny took the taller boy's hand and soon the two of them were skating round the rink, slowly to start with, and then faster, much to Carolyn's alarm. "Not so fast, you two," she shouted, stepping forward and immediately collapsing in a heap on the ice. "Oh, flippin' 'eck, I'll never get the hang of this," she laughed as she tried unsuccessfully to regain her balance.

The two boys soon appeared, finishing their lap of the rink. Danny was now shouting with glee, "Look at me! Look at me, I'm skating."

Bradley felt quite important, as he smiled at the group. "Come on, Uncle Bob. We'll take you round now. You hold one hand, Danny, and I'll hold the other."

A very apprehensive Bob did as he was told and the two boys skated him away, to the delight of onlookers who, recognising John and Bob, watched their antics closely. John decided he was going to beat a retreat, whilst the going was good and took hold of the barrier as if it was a life-line. "Cathy, you said you'd been before. I thought you could skate. You two girls go and enjoy yourselves. I'm just going to stay here and watch."

By now, Cathy and Carolyn were laughing hysterically and holding on to each other. They could see Bradley and Danny trying to raise Bob to his feet the other side of the rink. Cathy nodded, the tears of laughter streaming down her cheeks. "I have been before, Darling, but I was as bad then as I am now. I don't know about you, Caro, but I think John's got the best idea.

They managed to move around the rink, holding onto the bar, until they reached the huge gold leaf statue of Prometheus, where the water cascaded down steps around him. "I don't know about you, but the sound of that water is doing something to me with all the laughing. I'm going to have to get these skates off and find a loo," Carolyn spluttered.

It wasn't long before Bob and the boys joined them, and they stood for a while on the Esplanade to watch the skaters on the ice. "Now, we've had a meeting and we've decided what we'd like to do for lunch is go to McDonald's," Bob stated. "Bradley wants to introduce Danny to a 'Happy Meal'."

The two boys seemed to be getting on well; their heads together, seemingly sharing confidences, as they strolled along together. Cathy shouted after Bradley, "Don't go away now and get lost; that's my good little boy."

Bradley frowned and shouted back to her, "Mom, I'm not a little boy. I'm nearly ten."

Danny was very quiet for a while and then said to Bradley, "You're so lucky having a Mom that loves you so much. I wish I was someone's little boy." He told the other boy, in a whisper, how he used to lie in bed and imagine this lovely lady who would put her arms round him and hug him and tell him everything would be alright. She would smell nice and he would cuddle into her. He said his Mom had never hugged him.

The trip to McDonalds was another success. Once again, the men were recognised, but were pleased to pose for numerous photographs and sign autographs. They all chose their meals and sat with other families enjoying the occasion with their children.

Before putting him to bed that night, Bob and Carolyn sat either side of him on the comfortable sofa and let him watch some children's television. After the excitement of the day however, it wasn't long before Danny was fast asleep. Bob picked him up gently and carried him through to bed where he tucked him in, leaving a small light on in case he awoke and was afraid during the night.

Carolyn was up early the following morning, so after showering and dressing she tip-toed into the guest room. She was amazed to find Danny, fully dressed; albeit with his T-shirt on back to front, sitting upright on the side of the bed, which he had already made.

"Darling, you didn't have to get up and dressed by yourself, but what a good boy you are. Have you had a wash and brushed your teeth?"

Danny nodded. "Yes I have. I've always got myself ready and made my own bed. I usually got my breakfast too, but I didn't know how to do breakfast here. Mrs. Partington said if I wasn't a lot of trouble, you might let me come again."

Carolyn had to steady her bottom lip, which was quivering. "Well, of course you'll be able to come again, sweetheart. We're having a lovely time, and you're no trouble at all."

She led the child through to the kitchen, where John and Bradley were sitting with the other two men. Carolyn introduced him to Jeff, who made a funny face and was immediately accepted as a new friend. Bess was grilling smoked bacon, and the aroma was unbelievable to a small boy in a strange world. It seemed that one of the children at the hospice was very poorly, so Cathy had to spend her day there.

"Oh, Bess, that smells wonderful. Is it bacon butties all round then?" There were cries of agreement, and mutters of appreciation as the sandwiches were placed on the table in front of them. "Right then, what have you five men got planned for to-day?"

The possibility of going to a game had already been discussed, so Danny was brought into the conversation and asked if he would like to go. Jeff's suggestion was to go and see the New York Knicks who were playing basketball in a home game at Madison Square Gardens. "Tickets are hard to come by, but that won't be a problem. I have a contact who will make sure we get in."

Danny was wide eyed at the prospect of this exciting new outing. "I've never been to a basketball game. I don't know what's supposed to happen."

John smiled kindly at him, "I don't know either, Danny. But I tell you what; I bet Bradley, Daddy and Uncle Jeff will be able to explain the rules to both of us."

Carolyn saw them all off, then went through to the office to sit with Pam for a while. Because it was a Saturday, Penny and Tony had the day off, but Pam had come in to catch up with some paperwork. "I wondered whether you needed any help, Pam. I'm at a loose end for a couple of hours." Carolyn said.

"Oh, bother the paperwork," Pam laughed. "I want to hear all about Danny and how the day went yesterday."

The following morning, as arranged with Mrs. Partington, Bob and Carolyn went with Danny back to the home. Bob hugged him and ruffled his curls. "We'll see you again soon, son. I promise."

As Carolyn held out her arms, the boy put his hands around her waist and held on tightly. He put his head back and looked into her face. "Thank you for taking me out. It was lovely. I wish I was your little boy." She kissed his forehead, turned and walked away before he could see the tears streaming down her face.

Chapter thirty one

The House seemed very quiet over the next week. Carolyn and Bob were very subdued and Jeff seemed to wander around the apartment like a lost soul. Carolyn decided she had kept quiet long enough and as they were cuddling up together in bed one night she broached the subject of Danny. "My Darling, this isn't going to go away. We have to talk about it. What are we going to do about him? Please be honest with me, Robbie. What do you want us to do?"

Bob held her closely, stroking her hair and whispered, "I guess I want to bring him home, but I'm afraid."

"Afraid, darling? Why would you be afraid?"

Bob sighed and lay back on the bed; his eyes staring at the ceiling as though he were trying to see into the future. "Carolyn, if we bring Danny home, things will never be the same again. He'll be a huge part of our lives and we'll have to consider him in everything we do. We'll have to find him a school and he'll have to be taken and brought home each day. We can employ someone to help us with his care, but ultimately we will be his family and be responsible for him. I'm so used to having you to myself my darling. Would this make any difference to us?"

Carolyn turned on her side, resting her cheek on her hand. "Robbie, I suppose the fact that he is such an adorable child has to give the decision some sway. Perhaps if he was an obnoxious little bugger with spots and halitosis we wouldn't have to think twice about it, but he isn't. He's an unhappy little boy who just wants to be loved and I think we can do that. We have such a special relationship, Robbie. You and I have so much love for each other; surely we can spare some for Danny. I honestly think that far from it making our lives difficult, things could only be better."

The discussion continued as they were sitting having breakfast. Jeff ambled in, still dressed in his bathrobe and poured himself a cup of coffee. The telephone rang and he ran down the steps to answer it, calling up to Bob. "It's that Mrs. Partington from Social Services. Needs to speak to you."

Bob took the call and then came back up to the kitchen area, his face troubled. "Well, baby, it looks as though the decision's been taken out of our hands. Danny's been playing up since we had him to stay last week. Mrs. P. says he's been disruptive and difficult and now, apparently, he's stolen some money. They caught some older boys stealing so they searched all the lockers and found a twenty dollar note in his drawer. He won't explain how he got it, so he's being punished. They've asked the Community Officer at the local precinct to give the boys a talking to, and they've taken them down there. She suggests that unless we want to take a more active role in his upbringing, it would be better if we don't take him out again."

"Right!" Carolyn said, jumping up and swigging her coffee back. "Get your coat."

"Where we goin'?" Bob questioned; his mouth full of toast.

"That poor little boy, Robbie. He must be frightened to death being taken to a police station. I don't care what Mrs. Partington says; we have to go and talk to him. He'll tell me the truth. I don't believe he would steal money. Come on."

When they arrived at the Precinct, they were shown in to the Community Officer's room, where two boys of about eleven were sitting with Danny who looked small, slight and extremely miserable alongside the older, bigger children. Mr. Barnes, the Officer, was standing in front of his desk, leaning back with his arms crossed, looking very stern. Mrs. Partington and the Superintendent of the children's home were also in the room and introduced Bob and Carolyn when they entered.

As soon as he saw Bob and Carolyn, Danny jumped off his chair and ran to them. The tears streamed down his face as he gabbled, "I swear I didn't take any money. I didn't; I didn't. The money was from Uncle John. He gave it to me, honest. I didn't steal it. You have to believe me. They said I can't see you anymore, because I've been a bad boy, but I haven't."

Carolyn put her arms around the child and hugged him. "Stop looking so worried and frightened, Danny. Of course we believe you. I promise you, everything's going to be alright." She turned to the Community Officer, "He's my little boy. He wouldn't lie." The look on Danny's face was worth a million pounds. His smile lit up the room, and the tears stopped like magic."

Carolyn stared at Bob and raised her eyebrows, willing him to understand and take over the situation. Bob nodded and turned to Mrs. Partington. "You said we should stay away unless we wished to take a more active part in Danny's life. Well, we've decided we do. I don't know what the legal implications are; we'll have our legal people look into it; but we'd like to take Danny home with us now."

Danny was watching this discourse, his eyes agog, and when he heard his father say they were taking him home he gasped loudly. "For another night? I can come and stay again for another night?"

Bob knelt down, putting one arm around Carolyn and the other around Danny. "Son, how would you like to come and live with us, forever?

Danny couldn't speak. He just nodded and smiled at first Bob then Carolyn. It was agreed that he could stay with them whilst all the papers were drawn up, but in view of Bob being Danny's biological father Mrs. Partington did not foresee any problems.

The three sat in the car, Danny in the middle, smiling up at them with wide eyes. "You said I was your little boy."

Carolyn swallowed and nodded. "You told me you'd like to be my little boy, and you are. Do you remember your three wishes, Danny? Well, you need never be afraid ever again, because you belong with us now, and we are going to have such lovely times together. So you see, wishes can come true."

"What shall I call you?" he asked innocently.

"What do you want to call me? Poppa?" Bob asked gently.

"No, I'll call you Daddy," the child said.

"And Carolyn? Do you want to call her Mom?"

Danny looked very serious and shook his head vehemently. "No, not Mom."

Carolyn looked at Bob and put her arm around the boy's shoulders. "That's alright, Danny. You can call me Auntie Carolyn if you like. I don't mind. You want to remember your Mom and that's only right."

Danny shook his head again, and looked up at Carolyn. "No, you don't understand. My mom wasn't always nice and she frightened me sometimes. You're lovely and you make me feel safe and you smell nice. Can I call you "Mummy", because that's what you called your mummy in England?"

"Oh, Danny," Carolyn smiled through her tears. "I should like that very much indeed. I would love to be your Mummy."

It was a happy little trio who arrived home again at the House. "Home Sweet Home," Carolyn trilled as she put the kettle on for a cup of tea and poured some juice for Danny. Will orange juice do for now, sweetheart? We'll do a shop tomorrow and get all the things you like. Daddy's going to talk to Uncle John and see whether you can go to school with Bradley and we're going to do your room up and put posters on the walls and make it wonderful for you."

Bob put his head back and roared with laughter. "Mummy's rambling, Danny. That's what she does when she's excited. You and I will have to keep her in order, won't we?"

Jeff came in from the studio where he had been tinkering with a new tune which had been running through his head for a while. He was hoping Bob would pen some lyrics to it and then they would ask John to set the whole thing down on paper. It was a sad, haunting tune which mirrored his feelings at present. He had never felt so lost or miserable before over any of his previous encounters with women. He had come to realise that Cindy was the love of his life and he feared he had lost her through his stupid and selfish reaction to her story.

He stopped whistling the melody when he saw the smiling group sitting around the kitchen table. "Hi, little buddy," he said with surprise. "I didn't think we were expecting your company to-day."

"Uncle Jeff. Danny is going to be living with us from now on, and we hope you're okay with the idea," Carolyn said, in a manner which intimated, *"Because it's tough if you're not!"*

Jeff smiled with pleasure and ruffled Danny's curls. "Well, about time too. You're home with your family, where you belong, and I for one am delighted about that. Welcome, Danny."

Bob could see the boy's eyes were drooping and suggested he have an early night. "After all the trauma and excitement of the day, son, you must be bushed. Let us put you to bed and we can talk about things to-morrow." So saying, he lifted Danny in his arms and carried him through to the bedroom. Carolyn helped undress him and tuck him into bed. He was fast asleep before his head touched the pillow. They both kissed the sleeping child and tiptoed from the room.

By the time breakfast was served the next day, arrangements were in place for Danny to be enrolled at Bradley's private school, the following week. He would be assessed as to his ability before being placed in a suitable class. Whenever possible, Carolyn or Bob would accompany him in the car to school and collect him in the afternoon. At other times Bess' niece would be drafted in to help. The car would also transport Bradley, so Cathy and John would take turns on the school run.

When Carolyn poked her head round the bedroom door in the morning, she was surprised to find Danny still fast asleep. The little boy had been totally exhausted by the events of the day before. She watched him for a few minutes before bending down and kissing him. "Danny, sweetheart; it's time to get up now. Come and have some breakfast."

He stretched and yawned before muttering, "Okay, I'm just waking my eyes up." Then as he roused himself from sleep, he sat up wide-eyed and shouted, "Do I really live here now, Mummy?"

Carolyn laughed at the wonder on the child's face. "Yes, Danny, you do. Up you get and we'll get you washed and dressed so you can have some breakfast, then you can come through to the Shop and meet some of Mummy and Daddy's friends."

She sighed happily as the little boy jumped out of bed and ran into the bathroom. *Who would have ever dreamed it? I have a seven year old son,* she thought, hugging herself with delight.

ઠે∞ટી'ઝ∞ઈ

Chapter thirty two

Although still very quiet, Danny became a welcome fixture at the House, greeting all-comers with a beaming smile of welcome. Carolyn couldn't believe that a seven year old boy could be so good and commented on this to Cathy.

"Oh, don't get too complacent, Carolyn. He's frightened to put a foot wrong at present, but once he gets his feet under the table you'll have a hard time keeping up with that child. He wants to please you, and that's lovely. Make the most of it, sweetie, because if he's anything like Bradley he'll soon know how to pull your strings."

Danny and Jeff had become close friends in a very short time. The boy was so much like the child he had befriended all those years ago that Jeff quickly grew very fond of him and the two of them chatted and laughed together. Jeff would tell him stories of his and Bob's antics when they were children in the orphanage and Danny would sit with wide eyes taking it all in and giggling at some of the tales.

Jeff phoned Cindy every day and had nearly emptied the florist having flowers delivered to her, but she still made excuses not to see him. He had grown very despondent, wishing above all else that he could turn the clock back and make things alright between them. He missed her more than he could have thought possible and couldn't get her sweet face out of his mind.

It was Danny who stirred him into action one afternoon. He had finished school at lunchtime and, arriving home, threw himself next to Jeff on the sofa and excitedly showed him the drawing he had completed that morning. There's me in between Mummy and Daddy and that's Uncle John, Auntie Cathy and Bradley. That's you there."

He had drawn the third man on his own, in the middle of the group. He looked a sad, lonely figure and Jeff sighed. "Your old Uncle Jeff doesn't look very happy, Danny. Is that how you see me?"

The boy nodded and patted Jeff's face. "Yes you look very sad all the time. I was sad and I wished and wished. Then one day my wishes came true. If you wish hard enough, perhaps your wish will come true and then you wouldn't be sad anymore."

Jeff smiled at the innocence of the child. "Real life isn't always like that though, Danny. How would you suggest I make my wish come true?"

"You have to tell someone what you want. Otherwise they'll never know and won't be able to do anything. That's what I did. I told Mummy and she made everything alright."

"You're right, sunshine. I've waited long enough. I'm gonna take your advice and do exactly that. I'll go right now. Thank you, Danny." The startled child was surprised when Jeff picked him up from the sofa and swung him up in the air before hugging him and placing him back on the seat.

※

Cindy opened the door to Jeff wearing pyjamas, with a teddy-bear embroidered on the front. Her raven black hair was tied up in a ponytail and her face was completely devoid of make-up. "Oh boy, you could have given a girl some notice so she could glam up a little before you land on her doorstep," she said pulling a face.

"Why would you want to do that, when you look so adorable as you are? You'd look amazing wearing a bin bag, never mind those very fetching jammies. Are you gonna let me in?" Jeff asked, dreading that she would ask him to leave.

Cindy stepped back and signalled for him to enter the apartment. There were flowers everywhere and the scent was overpowering. Cindy nodded when she saw his expression. "Yes, Jeff. If you send me any more flowers I'll have to move out of this apartment to make room for them. They're beautiful, but I think enough is enough."

He laughed, despite himself. "I didn't know what else to do, darlin'. Cindy, I've been so miserable. I've missed you more than you'll ever know. I think of you all the time and if I could only turn the clock back, things would be so different. I'm so, so sorry for the way I behaved that night. You were right to be angry with me, because I had no reason whatsoever to judge you over something that happened all those years ago. Cindy, I love you very much and all I want is for us to be together. Please say you'll give me another chance."

Cindy held her breath for a second and then whispered, "You hurt me so much, Jeff. I wanted to be honest with you and you threw it back in my face."

Jeff nodded. "I know, baby, and I regret it more than I can ever say. I acted as though I've been a saint all my life and I haven't. I need to be honest with you too. There was a time when I was snorting cocaine and drinking myself silly every night. I've bedded more woman than I can remember, and ..."

At this point, Cindy put her hand on his lips to stop him talking. "Jeff, none of that matters to me; so long as it's all in the past.

"Just one more thing then, baby. I want you to know that I've told many women that I loved them, but I know now that I was never really in love with anyone until you. You are the love of my life. Will you marry me, Cindy?"

Cindy swallowed hard and took a step back. "Ask me again, if you still want to, after I tell you my last secret, Jeff. There was a reason why I had to tell you about my past. I needed you to know everything about me before..."

"Before what, Darlin'?"

"Jeff, I'm going to have a baby," she whispered breathlessly, biting her lip. When she looked up into his eyes, she was astonished to see his fill with tears and overflow, rolling down his cheeks.

"Are you telling me I'm gonna be a father?" he asked hoarsely. "When?"

"I'm around sixteen weeks, so in another five months, I guess." Cindy answered. "I just wasn't sure how you'd feel about it."

Nothing had prepared her for Jeff's next move. Sinking to his knees he put his hands on either side of her hips and held his face to her abdomen. For the first time he noticed the slightly rounded shape of her belly, and kissed it gently and reverently. "Hello you in there," he said. "It's your Daddy here. I just can't wait to meet you. I've been waiting for you for a very long time."

Cindy bent and wrapped her arms around his shoulders, kissing the top of his head. He stood up and held her close to his chest; squeezing her as if he would never let her go. "Cindy, I think this has got to be the happiest day of my life. Make it perfect by saying you'll marry me. This is so wonderful."

"Yes, please," was all she could say as his lips came down on hers and he kissed her as if she was the most precious, treasured thing in his life. He lifted her and sat her down on his knee, so he could hold and cuddle her.

"You know, my darling. Our backgrounds aren't so different. All both of us have ever really wanted was love and a family. When you told me about your childhood, it made me remember things about my own. Carolyn came with Bob and me to the orphanage years ago and we were able to find out something of our roots. I was envious at the time that Bob traced his parents, and so many years later I had an agency try to trace my background. I knew my mother's name was Pauline Simmonds, and that she'd died in 1975 but that was all. You should never dig things up if you're not prepared for what you find. My mother was a prostitute, and probably never even knew who fathered me. I was taken into care when I was three years old because of cruelty and neglect, just like you and your sisters. Tell me how anyone could be cruel to a three year old child. I don't remember anything about that, but I was in foster homes until I was eight and I do know that was an unhappy time for me. Somewhere in the deep recesses of my mind, I can remember being bullied and beaten and shut in the dark. Do you know, even to this day I hate being in confined spaces in the dark. I was in an elevator once and the lights went off. I had a panic attack and nearly passed out. Believe it or not, those later years at the orphanage, when I met Bob, were utopia after what went on before."

Cindy nestled against him, relaxed and happy at their closeness. "My poor baby. You're right; our childhood was similar. I suppose all our lives we've just craved to be part of a loving family. You found yours with Bob and then the Davidsons. Now we'll have our own family too. I love you, Jeff Simmonds, and I am going to be such a good wife and mother. Our child will never know cruelty because we will love and cherish him or her and they will never experience the dreadful lives we had."

"Let's go away together for a holiday, Cindy. Somewhere we can be alone and make plans. We've no work for the next couple of weeks, so I can be spared."

Cindy smiled, "I'd really like that, Jeff. What did you have in mind? We should try to go somewhere you won't be recognised too easily, or we won't exactly be on our own."

"Mmm, let me think," Jeff murmured. If I don't shave for a couple of days I'd have quite a growth of beard which would be a bit of a disguise, and I could wear shades and a baseball cap. We could take one of the cars and drive ourselves. Just go where the feeling takes us. D'ya know, I've always wanted to drive up the Hudson Valley. I believe it's beautiful this time of the year. What d'ya say?"

"I say, yes; let's do it. I'd really like that. When can we go?"

Jeff took Cindy's face in his hands and said, with a serious expression. "What would you say if I suggested we pick up a marriage license before left? We'd need one to get married and we may just decide to do the deed while we're away. I'll make sure the clerk realises that if word gets out, we'll know it was from there and we'll sue 'em." He pulled a "gangster" face as he said this, and they both laughed. "I'll tell the family we're goin' to be away a couple of weeks. They'll understand and they'll just be pleased we've sorted things out between us. I can't wait for you to meet Danny. He's such a character, and so like Bob. That little guy has suffered too in his short life, Cindy."

"I can't wait to meet him too. I'll need to buy a few new things and pack, then how about I meet you somewhere and we go to City Hall together. I'll phone up and make an appointment. Perhaps I could come back with you to see Carolyn and Bob and meet Danny, then, and we can tell them together that we've made up."

Jeff nodded and held her even closer to his heart, sighing. "Yes, and we'll do all of that first thing in the morning; but first we're going to phone for a pizza then have an early night. What I want to do right now is hold on to the two of you forever. I'm gonna come shopping with you, then I can pack whilst you're chatting to Caro. Darlin', I just can't bear to be apart from you right now."

❦

Next day their plans were put into action. With the marriage licence safely in his pocket, and giggling like a pair of naughty schoolchildren, the two of them arrived at the House in time to find Carolyn sitting at the table with Danny; her face and hands covered in paint. She jumped up with pleasure when she saw Cindy with Jeff and went to hug her. Realising in time that this was not such a good idea she spluttered with laughter. "Oh, Cindy, how lovely to see you. Just give me two minutes to wash my hands and I'll be right with you. We've been painting."

Jeff bent double with amusement. "Oh Mom, we'd never have guessed. You might like to wash your face whilst you're at it. Hiya dude. How's my boy?" he said turning to Danny. "This is Cindy, Danny. I thought you should know that I took your advice, and you were right. Sometimes, when you tell someone what your wish is, it really does come true."

Danny solemnly shook hands with Cindy, while he weighed her up from head to toe. "Hello. You're pretty. Are you the reason Uncle Jeff's been so sad?"

Before she could answer, Jeff put his arm around Cindy's shoulder and said, "To be absolutely honest, Danny; that was my fault, but it's okay now, and it's all thanks to you."

Danny gave them both a beaming smile and showed them his latest paintings. When Carolyn re-emerged they explained to her that they were going away for a vacation together, and Jeff disappeared into his bedroom to pack a bag. Bob and John were called in from the Shop and were delighted to see how happy the pair was together. They had decided to tell the family about the baby, so there was jubilation from the group at the news and a huge fuss was made of Cindy, which made her weep with pleasure.

Carolyn insisted that they sat down for a meal with them before setting off on their journey. Bess had prepared enough for all so it was served up and the six of them sat around the table, chatting happily together.

As Danny's plate of beef, carrots and potatoes was put in front of him, he pulled a face. "Mummy, what's for dessert?" he asked.

Carolyn winked at Cindy before replying. "Its ice-cream, Danny. But you can't have any until you've eaten your dinner, and that includes those carrots."

"Oh, alright," he answered. "I'd better eat the carrots first then, so I won't have to think about them. How much meat do I have to eat, before I can have my ice-cream?"

Despite trying hard to stay serious, there was hilarity around the table. John screeched at Danny's comments whilst Jeff nearly choked and had to be patted hard on the back by a laughing Bob.

"Oh good heavens," John spluttered. "Let me tell you; that child has been on this earth before."

Eventually Cindy and Jeff left to return to Cindy's apartment and collect her bags. They had decided to buy a black four-wheel drive, with darkened windows, for their journey. It was being delivered that afternoon to Cindy's address so could not be traced back to The Honeys. All arrangements were now in place for their trip.

Chapter thirty three

The two excited lovers were ready to hit the road at around 4 p.m. Cindy mocked Jeff on the amount of luggage he was taking with him for a drive upstate. "Goodness, how many cases are you taking?" she laughed as yet another fancy suitcase was deposited in the back of the car.

"Well, baby, you just never know what you may need." Jeff giggled, with a mysterious expression on his face.

In the excitement of at last being on their way, Cindy did not at first take heed of the direction they were taking, but after a while she noticed that instead of following the course of the Hudson River up the Henry Hudson Parkway, they were in fact crossing the Brooklyn Bridge. "Jeff, aren't we going the wrong way?" she asked with puzzlement.

"This is where it all started, you know; on the Brooklyn Bridge. This was where Bob and I met John and Carolyn," he replied.

"Yes, I know, but this isn't the way to the Hudson Valley, Jeff."

He didn't reply, but patted the side of his nose with his finger and continued to drive. Then they were on the Expressway and soon in front of them was the John F. Kennedy Airport. He drove around to a gate which was magically opened for them and soon they were on the tarmac driving towards a small plane.

"Behold, Cinderella, your carriage awaits," Jeff laughed, helping her out of the car. Harry appeared from no-where and began loading their luggage onto the plane. "I took the liberty of making one or two arrangements whilst we were at the House. I hope you won't be cross with me, but we're not going to the Hudson Valley. We're goin' somewhere wonderful with white sand and blue sea. We are going to Hawaii. I did it all on the Internet."

He looked so pleased with himself that all Cindy could do was put her arms around his neck and hug him. "But, Jeff, I haven't bought anything suitable for the beach."

"All that luggage, baby? Half of it's yours. I had a personal shopper sort it out whilst you were trying things on this morning. Gee, it's been hard not to say anything. I've been hugging this to myself and longing to tell you."

The private plane took off, carrying its happy cargo. There was champagne in an ice-bucket, a jug of orange juice and an assortment of sandwiches laid out for their enjoyment.

Cindy put her head back and closed her eyes in ecstasy. "Hawaii! Oh, darling, I've always dreamed of going somewhere like that. I can't believe you arranged it all without me knowing."

Jeff looked smug as he poured Cindy a glass of orange juice and himself another glass of champagne. "There's more. We are getting married in two day's time. It's all arranged. However, you may not be so happy when I tell you the other bit of news. I know I've got a big mouth, but I'm certain we'll be having company. I just sort of mentioned it to Carolyn," he said grimacing.

Cindy's heart was so full, she could hardly speak. "Oh, that will make everything perfect. Do you really think they'll come?"

Jeff nodded. "I do, yes. I don't know whether Cathy will be able to get away, but I'm sure the others will. You really don't mind?"

"I couldn't be happier," was Cindy's reply. "It's only right that our family should be with us."

❦

On landing at Oahu Airport a white limousine was waiting to transport them to their hotel. Jeff threw open the French windows, which opened onto a large balcony overlooking the sea. Palm trees decorated a beach of white sand; which, catching the sun seemed to shine like fragments of diamonds, whilst the turquoise ocean gently lapped against the shore. Jeff put both his arms around her shoulders and held her whilst they gazed at the beautiful view. "Cindy, I'm so happy I have to keep pinching myself. To think I nearly lost you, baby. I am the luckiest guy in the world.

Cindy sighed and turned in his arms. "Jeff, we are going to be so happy. Ooooh!" she murmured, moving away to put her hands on her stomach."

Jeff was all concern. "What's wrong, darlin'? Are you in pain?"

"No, I felt the baby move. Wow! It just felt like a butterfly in my tummy. I was told this would happen, but I wasn't expecting if for another week or so. It's called quickening." Her face was a picture of wonderment and she laughed as Jeff once again knelt and buried his face in her belly.

"Hey, you in there. Hi, its Daddy here. Are you enjoying all this too? We love you, little one." He kissed the bump, before standing up and planting a long lingering kiss on Cindy's lips. "Right, Mommy, how's about us the three of us having a little stroll along that wonderful beach and dipping our toes in the water."

The next day was spent swimming in the ocean and relaxing under the colourful umbrellas on huge sun-loungers. They dressed to go downstairs for dinner and were just about to cross the foyer when a whirlwind almost knocked Jeff to the floor. He picked up a giggling Danny and lifted him high into the air.

"What on earth are you doing here? You're the last person I expected to see," he said in mock surprise.

"We came on a little plane, and we didn't have to walk on hot coals either. Daddy said he would do if he had to, so he could be here with you."

"Gosh, so Daddy and Mummy are here too?" he said over the child's shoulder, winking at Bob and Carolyn who had joined them.

"Yes, and Uncle John, Auntie Cathy and Bradley too," Danny got out in a rush. We're going to surprise you to-morrow when you get married."

The look on Carolyn's face was hysterical. "Well that was the general idea, before me-laddo decided to announce our presence."

The four adults greeted each other with great affection and allowed Danny to lead them through to the terrace, where John and Cathy were showing an excited Bradley the marvellous view.

※

The sunshine, streaming through the windows, woke Cindy and Jeff up from a deep, dreamless sleep. She turned around in his arms, blowing gently on his nose and laughing as he twitched and then scratched it before opening his eyes with difficulty. "My goodness that was some party we had last night. I feel an early night would have been more appropriate. Thank goodness I didn't have too much to drink; else I'd be nursing an almighty hangover to-day." He yawned loudly, then sprang out of bed and ran to the window. "Baby, it's our wedding day. I hope you're not superstitious, because we're breaking all the rules here. I just couldn't bear the thought of being away from you last night."

Cindy sat up and hugged her knees to her chest. "I reckon we both did all the traditional things last time we were married, and look where that got us. I am so happy, Jeff."

A knock on their door heralded Carolyn and Cathy who bustled in like a pair of mother hens, oblivious to the fact that Jeff was standing in front of the window, stark naked. "We've arranged for a beautician to come and do our hair and make-up, so get yourself into the shower, Cindy, and grab everything you need. Come on, you're coming with us. As for you, Jeff Simmonds, get some clothes on before you get yourself locked up," a laughing Carolyn blustered.

An astonished Jeff, ran to grab a robe which he hastily donned. "Okay, bossy-boots. If you will come into someone's room unannounced you have to expect to see the occasional naked man.

※※※

By noon they were all dressed in their best and they gathered in a small function suite to await the transport. They were to be transported by helicopters to a private beach, where everything was in readiness for the wedding.

Cindy had chosen a cream and lemon organza dress, which was cut in such a way as to hide her growing baby bump. The diaphanous material swayed and moved as she walked, and the colour made her skin look translucent in the light from the window. It had shoestring straps and was ankle length. In her hair, which she left down, she wore a small crystal coronet. Jeff had never seen her look more lovely. Carolyn wore a long silk dress in pale blue with a halter neck, whilst Cathy had decided on a similar gown in baby pink. The pastel shades complimented Cindy's outfit perfectly.

The three men were all dressed in white tropical suits with fancy red waistcoats and red bow-ties, which the Wedding Co-ordinator had miraculously ordered the night before and been able to produce in time. Even Bradley and Danny's outfits matched with their white trousers, short sleeved shirts, waistcoats and bow-ties.

"Oh, my God, don't we all look grand!" Carolyn cried with pleasure, seeing all the people she loved so much, looking wonderful in their wedding finery.

At last they were led up to the helicopter pad, where two luxury helicopters were sitting waiting for them. Each one was fitted out with six white leather seats. Danny couldn't contain his excitement as they took off and flew the short journey to their destination. "I believe I can fly. I believe I can touch the sky..." he sang at the top of his voice, whilst staring out of the window. His parents and Jeff and Cindy, who were in the same helicopter, were so astonished by this outburst, that all they could do was laugh at the joyous face on the little boy, who was so thrilled by this new experience.

They landed on the secluded beach, where they found a garden oasis surrounded by palm trees. The area was decorated with tropical flowers and a flower covered arch. Hawaiian maidens greeted them and put a floral lei around each of their necks. The three girls kicked off their shoes to make it easier to walk in the sand. Seeing this, a laughing Danny and Bradley immediately sat down and removed their own footwear.

"Come on, Daddy. You too, Uncle Jeff and Uncle John. We're all taking our shoes off," a laughing Danny shouted at the top of his voice.

A minister in a white robe was waiting for them and conducted the service to the sound of the waves lapping against the shore, whilst Hawaiian music was played discreetly in the background. As the beautiful words, spoken by the minister, came to an end, and he said "I now pronounce you man and wife," two white doves were released into the sky, amid gasps from the watching group. A photographer took numerous pictures of the ceremony and promised these would be sent on to the newly-weds.

Champagne was produced and the new husband and wife were toasted, before they were waved off in one of the helicopters. Then the rest of the party followed to return to the hotel.

A wedding breakfast had been laid on for them, together with a three-tiered wedding cake. Bob gave a short speech, toasting the bride and groom. "Jeff, bro. If you have half the happiness with Cindy that I found with Carolyn, then you are a very lucky man. We all welcome you, Cindy, into this family. We already think of you as one of us. Good health and happiness to you both."

Jeff was on cloud nine, in his euphoria following the beautiful wedding. "Mom, Bob, just one thing. Cindy and I have been discussing it and we wondered if you'd mind us still living at the House until we can sort our own place out. This has all been arranged so quickly that we haven't had the opportunity to think of it until now. Once the press get wind of this, it won't be a good idea to live at Cindy's place."

"Of course you can, numpty. It's your home." Carolyn said. "Talking of which, please can we have a little party for Pam, Harry and the rest of the gang when we get back. They'll all be feeling a bit left out and it would be nice to do something special for them."

Jeff raised his eyebrows to Cindy, who nodded. "I think that would be lovely, Carolyn. I know how close they all are to you and I want them to accept me."

"You know," John suggested, "Now our family is growing, we really ought to think about buying a villa somewhere smart. A place we could go for holidays and take the children when we want to get away from the city. We could buy one between us and go together or separately, whenever we wanted. Somewhere with lots of rooms, marble floors, and a swimming pool; surrounded by high white walls, with electronic gates. Mmmm!" His eyes were closed as if he could visualise the very place in his mind.

No-one objected to the idea. Indeed, it became the main topic of conversation for the rest of the day with suggestions coming from all quarters as to where the "villa" should be. Eventually the two young boys were packed off to bed, whilst the adults continued their happy chatter into the early hours.

Bob, John and their families stayed on the island for another couple of days before returning to New York, leaving Cindy and Jeff to continue their honeymoon. After they were waved off by the lovers, Cindy turned in Jeff's arms and nestled under his chin.

"This has been the most wonderful time of my life, Jeff. What could have been better? A wedding in paradise with our whole family around us. I'm afraid to wake up and find it's all been a dream."

"Cindy, my love. Certainly my family are now your family, and I couldn't be more pleased about that. However, you have two sisters somewhere out there. Don't you feel the time has come to try and find them? I'll help you if you like. We could put a trace on them and make sure they know where we are if they want to contact us. Put the ball in their court so to speak. After all, they're older now and able to make their own decisions."

Cindy nodded. "Yes I'd like that, Jeff. I think of them often and wonder what they look like; if they ever think of me, and if they need anything."

"Okay." Jeff said. As soon as we get back home, I'll put the wheels in motion."

༺✧༻

Chapter thirty four

It took a few weeks for news of the wedding to appear in the press. One of the tabloids devoted a two page spread to The Honeys, relating their meteoric rise to fame. It listed part of their past lives and marriages and how their career had appeared to falter then rise like a phoenix from the ashes. There were older photographs taken at Annie's funeral and one of Bob being wheeled out of the hospital after the shooting.

Somehow they had managed to obtain a couple of photographs from the wedding in Hawaii. One of the wedding photographs was of the whole family with the two children; all of them looking relaxed and totally happy. Another had obviously been obtained from a fan who had snapped Bob and John with the children in McDonalds. The writer had evidently managed to delve into Danny's background and concluded his story by saying that the child was now a much loved member of the family. The article was very uplifting, dwelling on the group's popularity and also their approachability with fans. Everyone was pleased with the way the story had been handled. It was a very complimentary article and was written with sensitivity.

֍

They would not have been quite so pleased, however, if they could have seen the expression on the face of a woman, sitting in her apartment, reading the article. "Bastards; bastards; bastards," she muttered. "Look how smug they are. They ruined my life. That nigger's whore should be made to pay."

The past few years had not been kind to Nicole Simmonds. The publicity following the break-up of her marriage to Jeff and the notoriety that accompanied the court case had made her into a pariah in the eyes of the public. She had started taking drugs to numb the anger she felt at the way she imagined she had been treated. Nicole could see no blame attached to herself for her change in lifestyle, blaming only Carolyn and The Honeys for every bad moment she had suffered since. Because of her addictive personality, the drug habit had quickly got out of hand and the more addicted she became, the more she hated Carolyn.

Gone were the long blond hair extensions and expensive wardrobe. In their place was a severe short hairstyle framing her bloated face. She had lost weight, losing her curves, and wore scruffy, loose clothing. Fortunately, some of the large settlement she had received from Jeff still funded her habit and paid her rent. It was only this money that kept her from ending in the gutter and selling herself to buy drugs.

Nicole read the article through again, almost spitting at her fury over the comments made. "So you got married again, you weak, conceited prick," she muttered. "I hear she's pregnant, the mousy twit. At least I didn't have to get knocked up to get you to marry me. And as for you, nigger... Even finding a love child didn't make that whore leave you. That's so typical of her; accepting him as her own. Just look at all of you, smiling and patting yourselves on the back. Well, don't you count your chickens, because Nicole hasn't finished with you yet."

※

A party had been arranged for the family, staff and other close friends, to celebrate Cindy and Jeff's wedding. Now the news had drifted out and was in the public domain, there wasn't the same need for secrecy, so a catering firm was employed to prepare a sumptuous feast at the House.

On the morning of the event, the caterers came in to set up their equipment and to decorate the apartment with streamers and balloons filled with halogen, which were weighted down and floated up in the air on silver ribbons. Fresh flowers were placed around the party room in crystal vases, their scent filling the air with lovely perfume.

Bradley and Danny were to finish school at lunchtime, and Carolyn bustled around checking up that all the arrangements were to her satisfaction before leaving to pick up the two youngsters.

"Ta ta, Cindy, love," she shouted, giving her sister-in-law a wave as she left the House. Popping her head around the door of the studio she tip-toed in, planting a kiss on her husband's lips and smiling gleefully at the other two men, who were going through some music with one of their new signings. "I'll only be an hour and when I come back I want to see you all back in there, resting before to-night. See ya!"

They all nodded affectionately at her as she left the studio and, accompanied by Pete, took the elevator down to the underground car-park.

※

When the men drifted through to the apartment, later in the afternoon, Carolyn still had not returned. Cindy was just replacing the phone as they walked through the door, her face a picture of concern. "That was the school. Bradley and Danny are still waiting to be picked up. The school clerk said they'd been expecting someone ages ago. Whatever can have happened to Carolyn?"

They tried to raise the car phone, without success. It was ringing, but no-one answered. Next they rang both Carolyn and Pete's cell-phones. Pete's rang, but Carolyn's appeared to be turned off.

"There's absolutely no way she would leave those boys standing waiting for her. Something's happened," Bob fretted.

Jeff nodded, "God, I hope they've not been in an accident. Perhaps the car's broken down. I'll go through and see if Harry's heard anything."

However, Harry had no news for them and as the time passed it became clear that something untoward had indeed occurred. The police were alerted and Bill was despatched, with Cindy, to collect the two boys. An APB was put out with a description of the car and all they could do then was sit and wait for news.

A short time later, two detectives arrived to report that the car had been found, abandoned, on the other side of town. Pete had been pistol-whipped and left unconscious. He had been taken to hospital, but his life did not appear to be in danger. There was no sign of Carolyn. Harry hurried to the hospital to make sure Pete was alright and to try and find out what had happened.

By now, Bob was distraught, pacing up and down like a wounded lion, his hands to his head. "What can have happened? She must have been abducted. What if they hurt her?"

The more senior of the two detectives tried to be positive about the situation. "We have to set up some phone equipment in here. No doubt you'll be receiving a ransom demand. We need to be ready so that we can trace any phone calls. Whoever has got her will be too interested in how much money they can get out off you to want to harm her. You can rest assured about that. In the meantime, I'm sorry, but I think you are going to have to cancel your party."

John phoned Cathy at the hospice and told her to come to the House immediately. It was felt that safety was in unity and that they should all be in the same place. Meanwhile, Pam made all the necessary arrangements to cancel the party and an incident room was set up in the apartment. Harry phoned from the hospital to say that Pete was still unconscious, but not in any danger. However, they had not been able to establish how the car had ended up on the wrong side of town.

&&&

Carolyn opened her eyes slowly and moaned as the pain in her head took over, making her feel woozy and disorientated. She tried to take stock of her surroundings. She was lying on a single bed, the cover ripped and dirty. The walls of the room were covered in mould and the paper was peeling off. Judging by the shape of the ceiling, she was in some sort of an attic, as the only window was a skylight, high on the wall, above a wardrobe. *Where am I? How did I get here? Get a grip girl. Oh, my head hurts.* She sat up, willing her brain to work, so she could remember what had happened.

Slowly, things started to come back to her. She and Pete had been in the car going to pick up the children. *Pete! Something had happened to Pete. Oh God! Danny and Bradley would be waiting for her.* Realisation hit her like a sledgehammer. Pete was just about to reverse from the parking space when two masked men had climbed into the car. The one in the front had forced Pete to keep driving by threatening to shoot Carolyn if he refused. "Just keep driving, or this woman gets it," the man in the back seat shouted, shoving the butt of his revolver into Carolyn's ribs.

Pete's troubled eyes met Carolyn's in the mirror. "Just do as he says, Pete. I'm okay." Carolyn said bravely, holding her head high.

They had driven in silence for some time before Pete was ordered to stop in a quiet side street. The man in the back of the car with Carolyn used the butt of his revolver to hit Pete twice across his temple, knocking him unconscious.

"What have you done, you gobshites?" she shouted. "That man has a family. Please don't hurt him."

She was dragged out of the car and pushed along the road. Another vehicle was waiting there and she found herself forced into the back seat, so violently that she shouted with the pain. Terrified, but determined not to show her fear, she held her breath, whilst the car drove through unknown streets. Eventually, the vehicle came to a halt and she just had time to take in the sleazy neighbourhood and run-down buildings, before she was shoved up the steps into one of the houses. *Surely this is hell!* She thought to herself as she saw the state of the House she was in. It was like something from her worst nightmares. The smell alone was enough to turn her stomach. A mixture of alcohol and urine greeted her sensitive nose and made her want to retch. She just had time to take in the kitchen with a sink full of dirty dishes and food wrappings, then she was pushed up the stairs into a room which could only have come out of a Dickens novel. It was so sparse and filthy that she had to swallow hard to prevent the bile rising in her throat. Without warning, one of the thugs covered her mouth from behind with a pad of cotton wool and she felt herself sinking into oblivion.

Now she was fully awake and the horror of her situation was almost too much to bear. *Oh Robbie, where are you? I don't know what's happening. Robbie, I need you. I'm so frightened,* she thought as she tried to make sense of the events of the day.

Suddenly the door was thrown open and a woman walked in. An unattractive woman with short, lank hair, and a foul, harsh expression on her face. It took a few moments for Carolyn to register who this person was, until something in her demeanour reminded her of someone. "Nicole," she gasped. "Nicole, why are you doing this to me?"

"Because you owe me, bitch," the woman snarled. "I want you to suffer, like you've made me suffer. By the time your loving family find you, they'll have nightmares for the rest of their lives, remembering what you went through before you died. And you are going to die, whore. It's not gonna be pretty, and they'll be left without any doubt about what happened to you. The thought of that has kept me going, and I'm gonna relish every minute of it." She turned and left the room, but before the door slammed, Carolyn heard her shout "Have your fun with the whore. Rough her up a bit and enjoy yourselves. I don't care what you do. I'll be back later when it's time to finish her off."

The sound of her feet, thumping down the stairs, reverberated in Carolyn's head as she took in what Nicole had said to her.

※

As the daylight started to fade, the mood in the House turned to despair. There was still no contact from the kidnappers, and although Pete had regained consciousness he had been unable to give any helpful information. Bob couldn't sit down, but spent most of the time staring out of the window at the Manhattan skyline. *Oh my dearest love, where are you?*

He came back to earth with a bump as one of the detectives was speaking to the group sitting around the apartment. "This just isn't following the usual pattern. I would have expected a ransom demand by now. Is there any possibility that this could be something different? Do you have any enemies? Anyone who bears you a grudge?"

Jeff sprang to his feet, putting his hands to his mouth and breathing out loudly. "Dear God, you don't think it's anything to do with Nicole and Stella? Surely they wouldn't dare do something like this."

The detectives were quickly told details of the women's past involvement and their ultimate prosecution. Patrol cars were immediately despatched to the last known addresses, whilst the family again waited for news. When word came back that the two women were no longer at these addresses, Bob could stand the tension no longer.

He wandered through to the security room, where Harry, Marty and Bill were deep in discussion. The chatter stopped when they saw Bob at the door.

"What are you guys whispering about? Anything I should know?" Bob asked.

Harry nodded and gestured for Bob to take a seat. "Two things we've been able to glean. We've been puttin' out feelers amongst some of our old informants. Someone; a woman we've been told; has been recruiting muscle. Three heavies have been taken on for a job. Also, word has it around the circuit, that the Rottweiler, sorry Stella Baldwin, has married and is living over in Tribeca. We were thinking of paying her a visit. The cops won't have her new address and we'd kinda like to have a chat to her ourselves. Wanna come along?"

"Oh yeah! Anything rather than sit around here waiting. I'll just tell them in there that we're gonna drive around for a while."

❧

There was no problem being admitted to Stella's apartment. Leaving Marty and Bill in the car, Bob gave his name to the doorman. Once this had been relayed, Bob and Harry were shown to the elevator without delay. Stella met them at the door and ushered them inside.

"Well, this is a surprise, Bob. You are the last person I expected to come visiting. To what do I owe the pleasure?" Stella asked, with raised eyebrows.

"I believe you're married now, Stella," Bob commented, taking in the luxurious surroundings, and obviously expensive furniture in the apartment."

"Yes I am, and whatever you may be thinking, it was very much a love match. I never expected to meet anyone and be so happy, but it seems there really is someone out there for everyone. Now, tell me what I can do for you. I have a very uneasy conscience about the things I did to you. I realise now how much I hurt you, and I'm truly sorry."

This was so unexpected, and obviously sincere, that Bob spared no time in telling Stella the details of Carolyn's abduction. "So please, Stella, if you know anything; anything at all, please tell me."

"I swear to you, Bob, that is has nothing to do with me. Even in the old days, when I was another person, I would never have stooped to this level. However, you shouldn't rule Nicole out. She was so full of hate the last time I bumped into her. She blames all of you for everything bad that has ever happened to her. Did you know she's an addict?"

Bob shook his head, "No, I didn't. The police have tried to find her, but they can't trace her whereabouts. Have you any idea where she's living?"

Stella stood up and walked over to a bureau. Opening a drawer, she took out a slip of paper and handed it to Bob. "She gave me this when I met her about two months ago. I'm not saying she's still there, but it's somewhere to start. I really hope you find your Carolyn safe, Bob. Since Frank and I got together, I can appreciate the feelings you have for each other.

Bob and Harry went back to the street and climbed into the car, discussing their next move with Bill and Marty. They decided it wouldn't be a good idea to knock on the door and openly confront Nicole, but they would first make discreet enquiries, to make sure she was still in residence, and then take it from there.

"Bob, I want you to go home now, and leave this to us." Harry said firmly. As Bob started to argue, Harry interrupted. "Please, let's just do what you pay us for. You are too well known, so you'd be too conspicuous. You don't wanna put the whole operation in jeopardy do you? I promise you, if we find where she is we'll phone you immediately. You have my word. You know how much I care for that girl, Bob. I'll do everything in my power to bring her home."

Despite feeling wholly inadequate and fretting over the safety of his beloved girl, Bob saw the logic in Harry's words and so hailed a cab to take him back to the House.

ॐ✿✿✿

Chapter thirty five

After Nicole's departure, Carolyn sat on the bed with her forehead resting on her raised knees, dreading the sound of footsteps on the stairs. At the slightest noise she held her breath. She heard muffled voices downstairs, and a loud raucous laugh, then the heavy tread of a man climbing the steps. She jumped off the bed and stood with her back to the wall, her eyes circling the room in terror looking for a way of escape. There was none. She heard a bolt being slid back and then the door was thrown open by a grinning man of medium height and build with receding hair. The skin on his face was pock-marked and greasy and he had a nose like an eagle's beak. He was obviously drunk.

"Looks like I won the toss, pretty lady. Now you be nice to old Vinnie and there won't be no need for you to be hurt," he slurred as his arms went around her and he leant forward, his fetid breath making her want to retch.

Carolyn put her hands out to push him away. "Please, please don't. Look, whatever that woman's paying you, my husband will give you double; no treble the amount if you take me home."

"Perhaps later, sugar; but first Vinnie wants a kiss," he muttered, pulling her towards him, none too gently.

"Nooo!" Carolyn screeched as her hands came up to rake the skin on both sides of his face.

"You fuckin' bitch. Look what you've done to my face," he yelled, first slapping her across the mouth, then thumping her face with his fist. "If you want it rough, that's how your gettin' it," he shouted, grabbing her by the arm and punching her again, this time in the ribs. He took hold of the front of her blouse and ripped it, before undoing his trousers and letting them drop to the floor, leaving no doubt of his intentions as his erect penis bobbed into view. As he went to pull off her jeans, Carolyn moved quickly and, in the time honoured tradition, brought her knee up hard between his legs, causing him to scream with pain.

"That should deflate your ardour, you wanker," she laughed mirthlessly, as with great difficulty, he pulled his trousers back up and backed out of the room, hobbling.

"Round one," Carolyn muttered, wetting her index finger and raising it. When she heard the bolt pushed back into place, the bravado didn't last long. She realised that she had bought herself only a small amount of time. *"Beaky" will probably be back when he's recovered his composure, and this time he won't be alone. Thank God he'd been drinking, and his reactions were slow.* She quickly took stock of her injuries. Her face was bleeding; the sight in one eye was blurred and her side was on fire, where she had been thumped in the ribs. Her upper arms were smarting and sore from being gripped. She realised she would soon be covered in bruises.

She sat for a moment on the edge of the bed trying to form some sort of plan in her mind. Again her eyes roved the room, looking for something with which to defend herself. She looked up to the skylight above the wardrobe. "I've got to try," she muttered. Standing on the bed, she first climbed onto the bedside table and from there onto a chest of drawers. Letting herself fall forward, she was able to balance one foot on the door handle of the wardrobe and then to haul herself on top of it, first with one knee and then the other. She rested for a moment to get her breath before kneeling up and then hauling herself to her feet. The latch on the skylight was at the bottom and she pounced on it, trying to lift it so she could open the window. Again and again she attempted to lift the latch, but it was rusty and obviously hadn't been opened for many years. She banged on the window with frustration, whilst the tears ran down her face. She stood on her toes trying to see out in the possibility that she might attract the attention of a passer-by, but the effort caused her to lose her balance. She toppled off the wardrobe, the bed breaking the worst of her fall, before landing with a thump on the floor and banging her head on the chest of drawers on the way down.

"Ouch! Oh God, all that effort and nothing to show for it," she muttered sitting up and flexing her arms and legs, sure that she had broken something in her fall. Winded, she had to wait for a few minutes before she could raise herself to her feet and sit back on the filthy bed. Every bone in her body ached. Standing up again with difficulty, she opened the wardrobe but found it empty, except for one or two coat hangers. One of these was of the big old-fashioned wooden variety. *A weapon?* She thought, turning it one way and then the other in her hand. *Certainly better than nothing. Better try to conserve my strength for a fight, because, Beaky and pals, you're going to find that Carolyn Davidson Maples is no pushover.*

❧

Bob whispered to John and Jeff, the details of where he had been for the past couple of hours. It had been decided to send Cindy, Cathy with the boys back to John and Cathy's apartment as Danny had become increasingly upset by the atmosphere and kept asking for his mummy. They had been accompanied by two female police officers who were to stay with them.

Back at the House, one of the detectives, Barnes, approached the three men. "We're mystified by this abduction. I'm sorry if this sounds insensitive, but we're going to have to ask you some questions. Now, we've just heard that this isn't the first time the young lady's gone missing. If my information is correct, she disappeared about nine years ago in 1998 and didn't surface again until 2003. Is it possible she just decided to go off again?'

All three were furious at this question and John was the first to speak. "Absolutely not, detective. My sister was going through an unhappy time back in those days. Now, she has never been happier. Besides, how do you account for our man being injured? Are you saying she did that too, because Carolyn wouldn't do something like that."

Detective Barnes held his hands up to stop John. "Okay, okay! I just had to ask. I'm afraid I'm going to have to ask a few more questions you may not like, but believe me, if I had a dollar for every time a missing person had been harmed by their own family, I'd be a rich man now."

"What are you sayin'?" Bob stormed. "You think one of us has done something to her? For Christ's sake, man. Can't you just get out there and find my wife. She could be lying hurt somewhere."

"I said you weren't going to like it and you won't like me asking whether your marriage is a happy one. I'm going to ask you though, and I want a straight answer."

Bob let out a sob of frustration and nodded at the detective. "Very happy," was all he could manage to say.

John intervened, putting his hand on Bob's arm. "Detective Barnes, Bob and my sister are the most happily married couple I know. They are totally devoted to each other. Ask just about anyone who knows them and they'll tell you the same thing. He would lay down his life to protect her. Does that answer your question?"

"You really are barkin' up the wrong tree here, dude," Jeff added, concerned about the way the interrogation was going. "Have you traced my ex-wife yet? I bet you any money she's at the bottom of this somewhere."

༺༻

A limousine with blackened windows was parked on the opposite side of the street from the address Stella had given to Bob. The doorman to the block of apartments had been questioned by Bill and had been able to tell him that a Mrs. Simmonds lived in apartment eleven and was at home at present, having recently returned. A large bank note had ensured that the man would not alert her to their scrutiny, should she re-appear.

After patiently sitting for a couple of hours, a woman came out of the building and starting walking along the street. After a glance she was ignored by the watchers in the car. They were waiting for a young glamorous model with long blond hair, not a skinny older woman with short hair and no make-up. When she was almost out of sight, the doorman hurried across the road and knocked on the car window.

"You asked about Mrs. Simmonds. That was her; you just missed her," he said pointing in the direction the woman had walked. "She's let herself go lately. Used to be quite a looker."

Marty leapt out of the car and ran after the rapidly disappearing woman, leaving Harry to thank the doorman whilst Bill turned the car around so they could follow at a distance. Nicole stopped at a delicatessen and came out with a full bag. Marty gesticulated to the car and pointed to the deli, before continuing to follow his prey. Harry was able to determine that four packets of sandwiches and four cans had been purchased. He held up four fingers as Marty glanced over his shoulder.

Nicole hailed a cab and as she jumped in Marty leapt into the following car. Keeping the cab in sight, they followed. "Right, we know wherever she's goin' there are four people, unless one of those sandwiches is for herself. If it was her out recruiting, we also know she has three heavies, which means..." Harry said with raised eyebrows.

"That she's feeding somebody else," Marty finished for him.

The cab stopped outside a house in a run-down neighbourhood. The following car stopped at the end of the street and Bill turned off the engine. They watched as the woman paid the driver and walked into the House.

"I need to see if there's another way into that house," Marty uttered, getting out of the car. I'm keeping my cell phone on vibrate. If you have any news let me know, and I'll do the same, as soon as I know what's goin' on in there.

Marty moved stealthily down the narrow passageway at the side of the House and hauled himself over a wall. He found himself in a dirty back yard, strewn with litter. Cautiously, he moved along until he was able to peer in through a window. The woman was standing with her back to him and he could make out three men, wearing gun holsters, sitting around a table, where they had obviously been playing cards. He strained to try to hear what she was saying, but it was impossible. He watched as she threw the bag of food onto the table, sending cards and money flying. She was obviously very angry about something. Her face was a picture of fury as she turned and pointed up at the ceiling. Part of his special forces training had been learning the ability to read body language. This woman was obviously very unhappy about the way her cohorts were dealing with the situation. She leant forward until her face was close to one of the men and raised her fist at him. He firmly took hold of her wrist, and shouted back at her, obviously displeased by her attitude. The man took a packet of sandwiches from the bag, together with one of the cans and handed them to the youngest of the three men, who nodded and left the room.

Marty quickly took stock of the rest of the building. An upstairs window was slightly ajar. Climbing onto the roof of a lean-to, Marty was able to scramble along a ledge until he was below the window. It was an easy matter to loosen the catch and by hauling himself up he was able to slide through into the room. He quietly walked across to the door and opened it a fraction. Outside was a landing with stairs to the downstairs accommodation and a further flight leading up. His ears pricked up when he heard a man's voice upstairs.

"No not this time lady. Eat these. We wouldn't want you to starve now, would we? I don't know what you ever did to that witch downstairs, but she doesn't like you much. She sure ain't pleased that we've taken our time, though by the look of you, Vinnie's used his fists some. Well, I reckon you don't have much time left, so make the most of it."

"Oh, just piss off, you load of shite," came the reply.

Marty put his head back and squeezed his eyes shut. It took all his self control not to laugh with relief. *She's alive, and by God she hasn't lost her spirit.* He bobbed back inside the room and sent a text to Harry.

I've found her. In attic. Three armed men plus woman downstairs. Send for backup. Give me time to secure her safety. May need ambulance.

Harry was ecstatic and lost no time in relaying the information to Bob by cell phone. He knew once Marty made a move speed would be imperative and it would take time for the police to reach the address.

❧❧

Bob listened to what Harry was saying, holding his breath and gesturing to John and Jeff. As he disconnected the phone he turned to them, "She's alive. They've found her."

Detective Barnes and his partner rushed over to the group. "Did I hear right? Who's found her? Where is she?"

Bob told them everything he knew and patrol cars with an ambulance were despatched to the address, with the instruction not to use their sirens to alert the occupants. The two detectives started to take their leave, but Bob was adamant that he needed to accompany them, and after much argument all three of the men went with the policemen.

॰॰॰॰॰

Chapter thirty six

When the young thug had brought the food and drink into Carolyn, she had been ready for a fight. The wooden coat hanger was tucked down the covers at her side, ready at a moment's notice to be pulled out to defend herself. When the man left without confrontation she let out a sigh of relief and allowed her aching body to relax a little. She was a seething mass of pain from all her cuts and bruises, worse since the fall. Her head hurt badly and she could hardly see out of her right eye.

She closed her eyes, seeing her darling Robbie's face; his eyes full of love for her. "Oh, Robbie, I need you so much," she sobbed quietly. "I'm afraid I haven't much fight left in me and I'm very scared. I don't know how you're going to cope with all this. It's going to be so hard for you. Look after our lovely little boy, Robbie. He'll need you more than ever." *They say your life flashes in front of your eyes before you die,* she thought, as images from the past came to her mind. Robbie, the first time she had seen him on the bridge. The piggy-back in the snow from the subway, and The Honey's first ever concert. She saw his face as he hurried towards her in the airport, the day he had come for her; the look in his eyes when at last he told her he loved her. She wrapped her arms around her shoulders and imagined it was him, holding her and making her feel safe. Danny's face too came into her mind and she thought of some of the lovely, funny things he had said and done during his short time in their lives. How she loved that child. Her dear brother and Jeff. What a blessing they'd all been. *Look after each other, my darlings.*

She came back to earth with a jolt as she heard footsteps creeping up the stairs. Her hand went to her makeshift weapon and she sat rigid on the side of the bed. Her heart was beating so fast she could hardly breathe as she tried to focus, through swollen eyes, on the door. She heard the bolt pulled back and the door opened slowly. A man stood there with his finger to his lips. A man in black trousers and a black leather jacket with a wonderful; wonderful, familiar face.

"Marty!" she whispered with joy, as the tears streamed down her face. "What kept you?"

He quietly shut the door behind him and crossed over to the bed, where he sat and took both her hands in his. "You okay?" he asked gently. "Who did that to you?"

"I'm fine now. It was the pretty one with the big hooter. Marty, would you give us a little hug please," she replied, laying her head on his shoulder.

Marty had not had many successful relationships in his life. So much of his time had been spent away from home on missions with Counter Terrorism and then with the Special Forces unit. He had never had chance for a long term love affair or a steady girlfriend. Since working for The Honeys, he had become very fond of the whole family, but his love and respect for this woman knew no bounds. He put his arms around her and held her against his chest, knowing in his heart that this would be the first and only time he would ever have the chance to do so.

"We're not out of the wood yet," he muttered into her hair. "I want you to be very brave. You're to keep close to me at all times and do exactly what I tell you. You have to trust me, okay?"

Carolyn looked up at him and nodded. "Yes, I trust you, Marty. I promise I'll do everything you say." As footsteps resounded again on the stairs, her voice started to panic, "Oh God, someone's coming."

Marty put his finger to his lips and dived to the back of the door so he would be hidden when it was flung open.

Obviously not registering that the bolt had been pulled back, Vinnie stood there, a strap in his hand. "You won't get a chance to do the same thing again to me, lady. We've bin told to rough you up. I'm gonna teach you a lesson." His arm raised ready to bring the strap down on Carolyn. He laughed as he said, "This is gonna hurt; a lot I hope." He paused as he heard shouting from downstairs.

"The cops are outside at the front. Bring her down here, we gotta get out. They mightn't be watching the back," a voice yelled.

As he turned, his expression was one of shock when he saw the black figure standing there, a gun pointed at his knee. "My turn to take the class. Lesson number one. You never hurt a lady like that. Now, this is gonna hurt; a lot I hope." Marty snarled as he fired.

Vinnie yelped in pain and fell to the floor, rolling from side to side and holding his knee. Marty took hold of Carolyn's hand and pulled her towards the door. "We're going down those stairs, and you're to keep close behind me all the way" She nodded and obeyed without question.

Nicole's voice was heard from somewhere at the back of the house, shouting. "I want that whore killed. There's a bonus for the man who pulls it off."

Carolyn and Marty had just reached the hall when a big man wielding a Magnum appeared around the corner. Aiming the gun at Carolyn's chest, he pulled the trigger. Marty threw himself in front of her, taking the force of the blast. Holding his abdomen he sank to the floor. Carolyn screamed and dropped to her knees just as the front door crashed open and a policeman in a bullet-proof vest shot the assailant in the middle of his forehead.

"Marty! Oh God, Marty," Carolyn cried. "Someone help him, please."

Marty was unconscious and there was an enormous amount of blood oozing from the wound in his gut. His skin had taken on a translucent sheen and he seemed to have stopped breathing. Two paramedics rushed through the open door and one of them gently lifted Carolyn out of the way so they could assess the man's condition.

"It was meant for me," she kept repeating. "That bullet was meant for me."

"He's crashed," one paramedic shouted, as he started CPR, whilst the other took the defibrillator out of his pack. "Clear," he shouted as the paddles were applied to Marty's chest. Three times they were used, until with a bleep, his heart was started again. "We have sinus rhythm; he's back. We need to get him to hospital right now."

Carolyn was sitting on the stairs, holding her breath whilst watching their administrations and she let out a sigh of relief. "Oh, thank you God," was all she could say.

The man the police had shot had by now been covered up with a rug, and she watched as the younger of the thugs was escorted out of the House in handcuffs. "There's another one upstairs, in the attic," she told them. "He won't be running anywhere for a while. There was a woman here too. This was all her doing."

One of the policeman, sat down on the stair next to her. "We've found the guy in the attic, ma'am; no sign of any woman though. We'll need you to make a statement later, but right now you have to go to hospital and get yourself seen to. Your man, here, will be well taken care of."

※

The people waiting outside in the street where horrified when they heard the gunshots and the woman's scream. Bob had to be physically restrained from running into the House, especially when one of the policemen shouted from the door for a medic. When, after what seemed like a lifetime later, a stretcher was carried out, Bob pushed everyone away and ran towards the ambulance.

"Oh God, please let her be alright," he muttered as he approached the stretcher. All he could see was blood, and then he registered that it wasn't his wife. When he saw it was Marty lying there, although hating to see the man so hurt he was relieved that it wasn't Carolyn. However, his next thought was that perhaps she was dead and lying in that house still and cold. He turned and walked towards the door of the house like a zombie, terrified what he would find. Then he saw her; wrapped in a blanket, a paramedic with his arm around her helping her to walk.

She looked up and saw him. All her pent up emotions and brave facade disappeared as her face crumpled and she started to sob. He opened his arms and she almost fell into them, clinging onto him and all the while crying as though her heart would break.

"Robbie! Oh Robbie, I thought I'd never see you again. Robbie, Marty saved my life. That man tried to shoot me and Marty jumped in front of me. He looks so ill.

Bob couldn't speak at first. The tears streamed down his own face as he took in the sight of his beautiful girl, her face swollen and bloody; her eye black and almost closed. She flinched as he squeezed her to him, holding her as though he would never let her go.

"I think I may have a couple of broken ribs," she muttered, nestling further into his neck and looking up into his face. His dear, dear, face.

"I thought I'd lost you, baby. If I had, I just don't know how I could've carried on. Thank God, you're safe," he murmured, raining kisses gently on her battered face.

"Danny and Bradley, are they alright? Did someone pick them up? Carolyn asked suddenly.

Bob smiled, despite himself. "Trust you. Yes, darlin' they're both fine and safe with Cathy and Cindy.

John and Jeff were allowed through to see her, with Harry and Bill. They watched as Marty was lifted into the ambulance, accompanied by Harry who insisted he go with him. Meanwhile, Bob climbed in after Carolyn in the second ambulance.

No-one took any notice of the woman standing with the other onlookers, her face like thunder as she watched Carolyn and Bob in each others' arms.

⁕

Carolyn was given VIP treatment at the hospital and ushered through to a private room. Meanwhile, after examination, Marty was rushed down to the operating theatre for the bullet to be removed from his abdomen. They were told that he was in a critical condition and no promises could be made at this stage as to whether he would recover.

"I want no expense spared," John told the administrator at the hospital. "He's to have a private room and any necessary treatment. All expenses will be met by our company."

Whilst they waited for some news about Carolyn and their friend, they called in to see Pete, who had been kept in for a few days suffering with concussion, following his head injury. He was full of apologies for what he felt was his failure to keep Carolyn safe. Everyone was relieved that he seemed to have made a good recovery and assured him that he could have done no more in the circumstances.

"We know now what those bastards were capable of. They would have had no hesitation in shooting you if you'd offered any resistance whatsoever. How would we have broken that news to your family?" Harry said wisely.

Carolyn's facial injuries were mostly superficial, but the doctors were concerned about the possibility of any internal injuries from the fall. She had two broken ribs from the punching she had received and a nasty lump on her head. She was given blood tests and a very thorough examination before the family were allowed in to see her. The nurses tried to restrict the number of visitors, but Carolyn was adamant that she wanted to see everyone before she would agree to rest. Their dear faces were the best medicine she could have had.

Danny had been fretful about the whole situation and the secrecy. His intuition had told him something was dreadfully wrong and once he was told his Mummy wasn't very well and was in hospital he wouldn't rest until Cindy agreed to take him. After contacting Bob she sat Danny down and tried to explain that Mummy had been in a little accident and hurt herself. Bob was at first concerned that Danny would be frightened when he saw his Mummy's face so swollen and black, but he insisted that he needed to see her, so he could make her better.

When he was brought into the ward, the little boy climbed onto the bed and took her face between his small hands, kissing every scratch and every bruise gently and reverently. "I'm making you better, like you do me when I fall over," he said in between wet kisses.

Eventually, all the visitors were asked to leave so the patient could get some sleep. Bob was the last to leave and looked into her eyes for a moment before saying, "Darlin' you do know you're safe now. I've been watching you and you flinch every time the door opens. There's gonna be someone outside that door at all times. Not just one of our guys but a cop too."

"Did they get everyone, Robbie? Have they arrested Nicole?" Carolyn asked, then seeing his face, "No, I can see they haven't. I'll never have a moment's peace until I know she's behind bars. It's not just for me. There's you, Danny; John and Jeff and their families. Robbie, I think she's insane. She won't stop until she gets what she thinks is her revenge."

Bob stroked the hair from her eyes and kissed her forehead. "She can try, but we'll be vigilant.

I promise you are safe," he said again as her eyes darted once more to the door. As he took his leave he smiled over his shoulder at her and she blew a kiss to him.

Two minutes later he was back. The smile had left her face and she looked a picture of abject misery sitting up in the bed. He said nothing, just kicked his shoes off and climbed on the bed next to her. "It'll be a squeeze, baby, but it won't be the first time, will it?" he said as he wrapped his arms around her and they lay down together.

❦

Chapter thirty seven

After a good night's sleep in the safest place in the world, her husband's arms, Carolyn awoke feeling refreshed and far more positive. They were both given coffee and breakfast before she persuaded Bob that she was fine and he should go and check on Marty's condition. Detective Barnes poked his head around the door before he left, to appraise them of the situation.

"I thought you would like to know the present position," he volunteered. One of your abductors, a young thug named Aaron Dukes, has been arrested and charged. You may be needed to formally identify him. A second man was shot dead at the scene, and the third has needed surgery but will be formally charged to-day. We have a small problem there, in that he is complaining that he was shot by your man without just cause. If he survives his injury, we may have to charge Mr. Brewer with illegally discharging his weapon, unless it can be proved it was in self defence. Can you remember exactly what happened?

Careful, Carolyn, this is important. Choose your words carefully. "But of course it was self-defence," Carolyn lied. "Beaky came through the door wielding a strap, but when he turned and saw Marty, he dropped the strap and his hand went straight to his holster, like so," she demonstrated, reaching under her arm. "Marty was protecting me. He could have shot to kill, but he didn't. He shot low on purpose."

The detective nodded, "That's what we thought happened, but his gun never left the holster so we had to check. You'll swear to that in a court of law if necessary?"

"Of course I will," Carolyn agreed.

"Oh, one other thing," Detective Barnes said. "A body was found in the water below Brooklyn Bridge this morning. It's almost definitely Nicole Simmonds. Her blood showed a very high drug level. Judging by the fresh needle marks, we reckon she must have been high as a kite. A witness says he saw a woman staggering along the walkway and climbing onto the rails. We may never know whether she jumped or fell, but fact is, she's dead."

After he had left the room, Carolyn and Bob were quiet for a few moments, before he broke the silence. "Well, I can't feel any sympathy whatsoever for that woman. All I can feel is relief. It's over, Darlin'! It's really over."

Carolyn closed her eyes and let out a big sigh. "She was ill, Robbie. Mad as a hatter she was. But yes, you're right, we're free at last. Robbie, I lied about Marty shooting in self-defence. He asked me who had beaten me up and I said the one with the big hooter, and then when he came in he shot him. That detective mustn't know. Marty saved my life. Can we go and see him."

"We sure owe that man. You did the right thing, baby." Bob acquired a wheel chair from one of the nurses and they went up in the elevator to the next floor.

Harry was sitting on a chair in the corridor, outside Marty's room. He jumped to his feet when he saw Bob and Carolyn. "He's still not out of the woods, but he's conscious. It's certainly looking hopeful now. The doc says if there's no infection he should be okay. They're just checkin' on him now."

When the doctor came out of the ward, he repeated what Harry had already told them, but said they could visit for a short while. Carolyn was concerned to see him prostrate in bed, with wires and tubes everywhere, looking very weak and ill, but conscious. Bob tried to thank him for what he had done, but Marty was his usual inscrutable self, acting as though the whole thing had just been another day's work.

They quickly told him of Carolyn's statement to the police and, for the first time, his face broke into a smile. "That was a very satisfactory moment, though," he whispered, his voice hoarse. "I enjoyed seeing that piece of shit rolling round the floor like that. He got what he deserved."

Carolyn leant over and kissed him on the cheek, before Bob pushed her back to her own ward. "Oh I'm so relieved, Robbie. I really feel he'll be alright now. What he did was so brave," she said as he helped her back into bed.

"We need to get you home, where I can keep a proper eye on you," Bob said. "I'm goin' to try and find a doctor, or someone who can tell me what the delay is."

He came back a little later having had no success with his mission. "I can't understand what's goin' on. They seemed quite happy with you yesterday. Now they're sayin' they're waiting for some results to come back before they can tell us anythin'.

Just then, a doctor entered with a file and smiled at both of them before pulling a chair up to the bed. "Hello, I'm Doctor Wendy Caruthers," she said holding her hand out. "I have the results of your tests here. You have been through the mill, Mrs. Maples," she said patting Carolyn's hand. You must be a very strong young lady to have come through such an ordeal so well. I'm pleased to be able to tell you that your baby doesn't appear to have been harmed. Everything seems to be fine in that department. It really is a miracle, especially after the fall. You must be so relieved. I'm going to have to insist, however, that you stay in with us for a few days total rest."

At the doctor's words, Carolyn's fingers came up to her mouth as she breathed in sharply and looked at Bob with wide eyes. He seemed to be struck dumb by the news. "Doctor, did you just say I was having a baby?"

"You mean you didn't know?" Doctor Caruthers asked, looking from one to the other of them. "My dear, I would say you are at least twelve weeks pregnant. Haven't you missed a period, or had sore breasts."

Carolyn shook her head in disbelief. "No, I haven't; although the last two have been very light. I've just been so very busy, what with

Danny and then the wedding. Oh Robbie!" she said, looking at Bob again, her face full of joy, "We're having a baby."

Bob took her in his arms, his face a picture of mixed emotions. "Doctor, do you know we lost a baby some time back. Is my wife in any danger, carrying this one?"

Doctor Caruthers shook her head. "I'm pleased to say, everything looks normal, and let me tell you, after the ordeal that little person has been through and survived, I'd say he or she is determined to be born safely. I'll leave you two to take in the news."

After the doctor had left the ward, the sound started low in Carolyn's chest and then erupted into a giggle. It was so infectious that Bob started to laugh too and they hugged each other and the giggling continued, until they both had to stop for breath.

The first person they told the good news to was Danny when he was brought to the hospital the next morning. At first he was very quiet, rolling the idea around in his mind. "Does that mean I won't be your little boy anymore?" he asked, tearfully.

"Oh no, Danny," Carolyn said, wrapping her arms around him. You'll always be our little boy. Even when you're a big man like Daddy; I'll still say you are my little boy. You'll be the big brother and you'll be able to look after the new baby."

"Can I talk to it, like Uncle Jeff talks to his baby?" the child asked.

Carolyn nodded and was astonished when Danny put his face to her abdomen. "Hey you in there," he shouted. "This is your big brother here. Just to let you know I'll be waiting for you when you come out." He looked up at his parents, his little face wreathed in smiles, before asking, "How does it get out?"

EPILOGUE
2008

Eve and Benjamin Maples came into the world on a sunny and warm July morning. Their exhausted mother had spent the long labour alternatively cursing her husband and telling him how much she loved him. "There'd never be any babies in the world if men had to have them. You get all the pleasure and none of the bloody pain," she screamed as she pushed to deliver the second twin. Bob, who had endured every pain with her and whose hand was almost bleeding where his wife's nails had dug into the skin, was almost fainting with relief once Eve, the second baby, was safely delivered.

"Oh Robbie, they're so beautiful," Carolyn sighed. They were indeed beautiful. Two golden-skinned babies with their Daddy's deep brown eyes, fringed with black lashes.

This was not the first birth in the family. Cindy and Jeff's daughter, Emma Carolyn, had been born two months earlier. Amongst her first visitors had been Cindy's two sisters, Muriel and Hope, who Jeff had been successful in contacting. They were overjoyed at the reunion with Cindy who they had never forgotten.

Harry's status had been elevated to that of courtesy-Granddad to Danny, Bradley and Emma, and he had been eagerly awaiting the arrival of his two new charges. He would always be special to the family and was included in all their functions and get-togethers.

Cathy and John's wedding had been arranged for September. They had waited for Cindy and Carolyn to give birth so that both of them could be Cathy's attendants on her special day. Bradley was to give Cathy away, and Danny was to act as a page-boy, much to his chagrin. "I'll look a sissy in those velvet trousers," he announced. "Can't I wear a proper suit like all of you?" All the staff had been invited and Pam, together with Penny and Tony, had taken over the organisation of the event.

Marty Brewer had made a full recovery and was back at work. His loyalty and bravery would never be forgotten by those he had served so well.

❦❦

ABOUT THE AUTHOR

Lynne was born in Birkenhead, Wirral and spent a large part of her adulthood in Wallasey. Most of her working life was spent with Wirral Borough Council until she took early retirement in 1998. She now lives in the village of Llanfechain, Powys in the beautiful Tanat Valley, with her partner, David, three dogs, three cats and four sheep. She is very involved with village life and is a Secretary of the local Show as well as running the Dog Show each August Bank Holiday. Lynne spends a great deal of her leisure time at Trearddur Bay on the Isle of Anglesey.

Since retiring she has devoted a great deal of time to writing and is a member of an internet authors' group.

INTERNATIONAL PRAISE FOR BROOKLYN BRIDGE

Just a few of the many comments received from around the globe.

Your themes of love, friendship, acceptance and what true family means are so relevant and meaningful. This is the kind of writing which helps to restore faith in humanity and I think you have done humanity a huge service by writing it!
Zan, Barbados.

I absolutely adore sagas and yours makes me want to come back and keep on reading. Thank you for sharing this lovely story.
Carla, Gibralter

What a saga - LOVED IT! I have enjoyed every twist and turn in this book.
Bev, The Wirral.

A first-rate romance novel; wonderful descriptions, characters, and setting.
Kevin Wong, Halifax, Nova Scotia, Canada

What a story teller you are. - laughing one minute and nearly crying the next.
Lynn. Yorkshire

*If your book is made into a TV series, I am sure
millions around the world
will tune in to watch it.*
Neelu, Dubai

*This is a beautiful tale you have woven here.
You have written the proverbial
tear-jerker feel-good story.*
Michael, Toronto, Canada

*Romantic, dramatic, intimate, imaginative.
An addictive read.
A story I would recommend to anyone.*
Freddie, Dusseldorf, Germany

*Love is love regardless of the package it is
wrapped in and music can truly be
the unifying vibration of the universe.*
Miles, Indianna, USA

*It was very satisfying that these individuals with
shared values should come together.
This is wonderfully written,
easy to read, and captivating.*
Richard, California, USA

༄༅༄༅

Brooklyn Bridge has its own page on Facebook.
If you enjoyed the story, why not join.

Lightning Source UK Ltd.
Milton Keynes UK
27 June 2010

156167UK00001B/1/P